A Time to Mend

A Time to Mend

Safe Harbors Book One

SALLY JOHN WITH GARY SMALLEY

THOMAS NELSON
Since 1798

NASHVILLE   DALLAS   MEXICO CITY   RIO DE JANEIRO   BEIJING

Published in Nashville, Tennessee, by Thomas Nelson. Thomas Nelson is a registered trademark of Thomas Nelson, Inc.

Thomas Nelson, Inc., titles may be purchased in bulk for educational, business, fund-raising, or sales promotional use. For information, please e-mail SpecialMarkets@ThomasNelson.com.

Scripture quotations are taken from THE NEW ENGLISH BIBLE © 1961, 1970 by the Delegates of the Oxford University Press and Syndics of Cambridge University Press. Reprinted by permission. HOLY BIBLE: NEW INTERNATIONAL VERSION®. Copyright © 1973, 1978, 1984 by International Bible Society. Used by permission of Zondervan. All rights reserved.

Publisher's Note: This novel is a work of fiction. Names, characters, places, and incidents are either products of the author's imagination or used fictitiously. All characters are fictional, and any similarity to people living or dead is purely coincidental.

Page Design by Mandi Cofer.

Library of Congress Cataloging-in-Publication Data

John, Sally, 1951–
   A time to mend / Sally John, with Gary Smalley.
     p. cm. — (Safe harbors ; Bk. 1)
   ISBN 978-0-8499-1889-6
   I. Smalley, Gary. II. Title.
PS3560.O323T56 2008
813'.54—dc22

                                                   2007044358

For Tim

He has committed to us the message of reconciliation.

—2 Corinthians 5:19 NIV

The Beaumont family

Ben and Indio—Max's parents. Their grandchildren call them Papa and Nana. Their home, the Hacienda Hideaway, is a retreat center located in the hills above San Diego, California.

Max—Married to Claire. Founder and owner of Beaumont Staffing, a nationwide staffing firm.

Claire—Married to Max. Volunteer for community organizations and violinist.

Max and Claire's four grown children

Erik—News anchor for a local San Diego television station.

Jenna—High school English teacher. Married to Kevin Mason.

Danny—Lexi's twin. Software guru and surfer.

Lexi (Alexis)—Danny's twin. Gardener. Artist.

Others

Kevin Mason—Jenna's husband. Teacher, coach, and Marine.

Tandy Abbott—Claire's friend.

Neva and Phil—Max's employees and friends.

One

Huddled on the sofa in the dimly lit living room, Claire Beaumont gazed through the bay window. Car headlamps swept across a stand of eucalyptus trees. The automatic garage door rattled up. A long moment passed. The door rattled back down.

Its rumble vibrated through her. She clutched a throw pillow tightly at her waist.

The door between the garage and laundry room opened and shut. Her husband's footsteps clicked against the ceramic-tiled floors, across the kitchen.

Claire moaned. There was still time. She could scurry off to bed, feign sleep, forgive and forget. Carry on.

His footfalls clacked into the foyer and passed the front door. Then they went silent, muffled by the hallway carpet.

Claire's breath caught, squashed under the unbearable weight produced by the thought of carrying on.

Max appeared at the wide entrance to the living room and halted. "Claire! You're still awake?"

It was now or never. "I quit," she whispered, more to herself than to the man across the room.

"It's 2:00 a.m., hon."

As if she didn't know what time it was. Her heart slammed against her ribs and thrust the words upward again, more loudly this time. "I quit."

"It sounds like I've walked into the middle of a conversation here." With a distinct air of weariness, Max draped his sport coat and tie over the back of the nearest chair and then plopped onto it. "Okay. What do you quit?"

"I quit . . ." She froze. Normally she would not have waited up for him. Normally she would not have confronted him while the anger still boiled. No, normally she would not even have admitted she was angry.

Nothing about the night, though, resembled *normally.*

The grandfather clock struck two fifteen.

She'd had hours to figure out what she was quitting. Or had it been years?

"Look, Claire." His patient tone exuded sympathy. "I imagine you're upset because I missed the birthday dinner the kids had for you. Even though I'm taking you to San Francisco on Saturday, *on* your birthday, tonight was important. When you think about it, those four hardly ever get together anymore. They only did it for you. So it was your special time with them. You really didn't want me here."

"Don't tell me what I didn't want." Ignoring the pathetic warble in her voice, she pressed on. "You always do that. You always think you know what I want or how I feel."

"I'm lost here. What are you talking about? I missed one lousy dinner."

She shoved the throw pillow against the cushion and unfolded her legs. "It's not that you missed one lousy dinner." Her voice steadied. "It's that you've missed thirty years of dinners and events. I can't live like this anymore. All of a sudden, I'm tired."

"Hon, we're both tired. We'll talk tomorrow."

"No, Max. I mean I'm *tired.* I'm tired of the whole charade."

"How about we take a vacation? We'll do the cruise thing again. You enjoyed that. September might work—"

"No." She shook her head vehemently. "I'm tired of pretending everything is fine. I'm tired, really, of letting you off the hook. I quit. Tonight was the last straw."

"'The last straw'? What in the world does that mean?"

"I don't know." She stood on unsteady legs. "I just don't know. But I can't talk any more right now. I'll sleep in the guest room."

She sidestepped the coffee table and breezed past him, heading toward the hall.

"Claire, honey, come on." He used his husky voice—the one with the unmistakably masculine timbre, the one that always assured her things would be all right.

She didn't break stride.

Shaking from head to toe, Claire spread an extra blanket over the bed and climbed in. She was wearing flannel pajamas in the middle of July in Southern California, and she couldn't get warm.

Her thoughts whirled as she stared into the dark with wide-open eyes. She'd never slept in the guest room before. She probably wouldn't literally sleep in it tonight either.

Dear God, what just happened?

No. She couldn't go there. Not yet. She'd wait until the sheer emotion of it dissipated. She'd wait for rational thought to return.

Her heartbeat thundered in her ears.

Help me, Lord!

A picture of the evening came to mind—the evening Max had missed. Their grown children and one son-in-law had treated her to a surprise birthday dinner. Erik, Daniel, Alexis, Jenna, and Kevin cooked and danced like five wild chefs in her kitchen. They made her laugh. They made her feel like a queen.

But in the end the scullery maid won out.

Claire rolled onto her side, curled herself up into a tight ball, and prayed for the night to end.

Two

Hunkered down outside on the patio flagstones, the area lit by spotlights, Max fiddled with his grill and swore under his breath. Things were gummed up. He rose, thumped the lid with his knuckles, raked his fingers through his hair, and swore again.

The kids had used it tonight. Specifically, Erik had used it. Or, rather, dismantled it. Their thirty-year-old son never could be trusted with anything mechanical.

Had Claire been so ticked off she refused to keep one eye on his prized possession? It wasn't like her to ignore such things. And what was all that nonsense about quitting and pretending? Pretending what? And waltzing off to the guest room! That was a first.

He shook his head and walked across the patio. Long strides carried him toward the pool. He rounded it once, twice, and kept on going for a third.

Sure, she had a right to be upset. It was her birthday dinner with the kids, a rare occasion in recent years. He should have been there. But his workday had been scheduled long before they decided to surprise their mom. When business involved other people, his day was not his own. Besides, he and Claire would celebrate her real birthday in San Francisco on Saturday the seventeenth. Just that morning she had mentioned how she was looking forward to it.

To have the kids show up unannounced and fix dinner must have meant the world to her, though. Naturally, she had wanted him to share in the special event. That made sense. What he couldn't wrap his mind around was her overreaction to his inability to get there in time. The circumstances were so far beyond his control.

Claire's overreactions were few and far between. She understood the agency—the one they'd founded together almost thirty-three years ago—often had to be prioritized. It was the nature of the beast. She accepted his late arrivals to family functions with more grace than he deserved. At times she fussed, of course, often with a sarcasm that made him laugh. He always did his best to make up for it with gifts and special family trips. It wasn't as if he was a totally absent husband and father.

So what was with tonight? Man, tonight wasn't even close to being his fault! The jet had been out of commission!

He'd arrived home to find her not fussing but sitting there, coiled on the couch like a silent jaguar waiting to pounce. And here he'd spent most of the evening waiting in the private lounge at the Sacramento airport, thinking his backside was covered.

Should he go into the guest room and wake her? And do what? Apologize for the kids making plans without consulting him first?

He didn't think so. If Claire wanted her space tonight, that was just fine with him.

Three

Claire watched the first rays of sunlight paint the distant rolling hills. She sat in the gazebo at the end of a stone path in their backyard. It was located in the farthest corner from the house—as far as she could remove herself from Max without getting in the car and driving somewhere.

Wrapped in a terry-cloth robe, bare feet propped on another cushioned wicker chair, she listened to morning birdsong and drained an entire carafe of coffee. She waited for the sun's warm glow to invade the shadowy canyon that lay at the base of those hills.

She waited, too, she imagined, for a warm glow to seep into her own dark heart.

"Morning." Max's voice startled her, and she turned. He kissed the top of her head and pulled a chair from the table. "Mind?"

Well, she did. Sort of. At the sound of his voice, her stomach lurched, as if she'd eaten an entire quart of Choco-Cherry Chunk ice cream all by herself.

Rather than wait for a reply, he sat, coffee mug in hand. "The grill's broken." Gazing toward the sun, he sipped from the cup.

Claire stared at him, replaying his comment a few times. *"The grill's broken . . . The grill's broken."*

Okay. So that's where they were. Last night hadn't happened. She could chalk it all up to just another "Max snafu"—a phrase their daughter Jenna had coined as an adolescent when she learned "snafu" was an acronym for "situation normal, all fouled up." Max's late arrivals and absences were a normal part of the Beaumont household. The confusion they created had become the stuff of family lore. Someday they would all laugh about Max sitting in the Sacramento airport while the kids cooked a birthday dinner for her.

Which shifted the whole point of the fun evening onto him. It made her the butt of the joke.

The ache in her stomach burned now. It rose up into her throat.

Last night had happened. Chalking it up to a "Max snafu" wouldn't cut it this time.

"'The grill is broken'?"

He looked at her. "Yeah, it is."

"Oh, I believe you. I just can't believe those were the first words out of your mouth."

With a slight shrug, he drank from the cup and turned his head again.

His mind was elsewhere. Though he easily functioned on four hours of sleep, he wasn't at his best before coffee. The puffiness around his eyes told her he had not slept well. His short, thick, black hair was damp. His face, with its fifty-five-year-old creases and dimple smack-dab in the center of the chin, was smooth shaven. Dressed for the office, he wore a white polo shirt and beige linen slacks. His matching jacket would be hung neatly on the back of a kitchen chair.

She should wait, catch him at a better time.

But she always did that. She always held back, measured her words, pretended everything was fine.

The burning sensation engulfed her now. She heard her own breathing, the shallow gasps. Her thoughts raced, and she could no longer contain them.

"We have to talk about last night."

He turned to her, squinting as if he hadn't heard her correctly.

"Yes. Right now. I've finished off a whole pot of coffee here trying to figure out what happened. Then you sit down and right off the bat talk about the grill. Next you're going to stand up and say you've got a seven-thirty meeting."

"Well, actually—"

"Max!"

"It's at eight o'clock."

"Which gives us—what? Ten whole minutes to figure out our future?"

"Wait, hold on there. This sounds like a little caffeine overload to me."

"I slept in the guest room."

"That's okay, Claire. You were clearly upset, and you had your reasons. No problem. Today's a new day. Let's just move on."

"I can't. I can't shove this one under the rug."

"There's nothing to shove under the rug. This is our life. It always has been."

As his voice gathered enthusiastic steam, Claire anticipated his monologue. She could have delivered it herself verbatim.

"I have a company to run, and sometimes, yes, it interferes with our private life. When you and I started the business, we knew it would have to come first. But we agreed to prevail, right? We would stay strong, because it's such an important work. Every year thousands and thousands of people find jobs because of Beaumont Staffing. We impact society for the good. We make a difference in the world."

"That commercial's getting a little stale, don't you think?"

His jaw fell.

"The point is right here and right now." A mirthless chuckle erupted from her throat, an uncontrollable noise of disbelief that frightened her. Words flew off her tongue. "You sat down and talked about the grill. Good grief, I'm playing second fiddle to a grill! And now I know exactly what happened last night. When I said I'm tired of the charade, I meant I won't play second fiddle to the company. Yes, we agreed ages ago that it would interfere with our private lives, and we would prevail. But, Max, we have prevailed. We've made it to the point where the business doesn't need to interfere anymore. It's no longer fighting for its life. And neither is it tripling in size. It doesn't need your attention day and night."

"I missed dinner because the plane broke down."

"You're changing the subject, but all right, let's go there. You didn't miss dinner. You missed Lexi all excited about her workday. She never gets excited about anything. You missed Danny's questions about his own company. He sounds like he's drowning in it. He needs your expertise."

"I'll call the twins later. Catch up."

"You missed Erik referring to you as The Putz. Capital letters."

He took a leisurely sip of coffee before replying but didn't look at her. "I'm sure he had a few beers under his belt."

"Nobody disagreed with him, and they weren't drinking."

He shrugged. "I suppose there's a Jenna story too?"

Claire pressed her lips together.

Max sighed and set his mug on the table. "I suppose she has major news, like she's pregnant or something."

"No. She just . . . She just reminded me of myself." Claire's voice sank, and she closed her eyes. Her older daughter's behavior cut her to the quick. It was subtle, something she'd noticed before but had always chosen to ignore. Until now.

"How's that?"

Claire looked at him. "She worships the ground Kevin walks on."

"That's pure nonsense. Jenna's the most stubbornly independent of them all."

"Except when Kevin says, 'Jump.' He makes subtle, sarcastic comments about her, about her teaching or whatever, and she smiles through it all. 'How high, Kev?'"

"That's harmless."

"Well, thirty-two and a half years of asking how high isn't harmless."

His brow wrinkled.

"I've worshipped the ground you walk on, taking second place for the sake of the business. I thought I was supposed to. But now . . ." She paused. "It's over. That's what I quit. Max, I want to play first fiddle."

He inhaled deeply and exhaled, his shoulders rising and falling. "You are first. I admit the company consumes much of my time and attention. But, Claire, you are my real priority."

"Then prove it. Call in sick today."

"That's hardly a fair request, and you know it." He stood, nearly overturning his chair in the process. "For crying out loud, we're flying to San Francisco for your birthday tomorrow. We'll have two full days together to discuss anything you want. All right?"

A pang ripped through her chest, so sharp she thought her heart had literally snapped shut right then and there. It wasn't his red face or low, angry tone that delivered the blow. It was his blatant disregard for her in choosing to go to work.

She shook her head. "Sorry, Max. I'm fresh out of days to wait for you."

"I really have to get to this meeting."

She waved her hand, shooing him off like the deaf fruit fly he was impersonating.

He turned on his heel and hurried down the gazebo's two steps. No kiss, no good-bye, no apology, no indication when he'd be home.

So much for being straightforward about her feelings. Evidently he didn't believe her declaration that she was out of days.

Evidently she didn't believe it either. Evidently she didn't believe a thing she had said.

Because, of course, she would go to San Francisco with him. She would rave about whatever pricey gift he gave her and pretend last night was no big deal. Life would go on. Like always.

An image of Jenna came to mind, smiling almost vapidly and in essence asking, *"How high, Kev?"*

It was way past time her daughter saw a wife who kept both feet firmly planted on the ground, no matter the consequences.

"Max!" Claire shoved back her chair and rose, whirling around and shouting across the spacious yard. "Max!"

He stopped, halfway through the sliding glass door, and turned.

"If you go, I won't be here when you come home."

"Suit yourself!" Even from her distance, she heard the rattle of the door's glass as he banged it shut.

And that was that.

Almost in disbelief at how quickly it had happened, Claire slumped back onto the chair and wrapped her arms around her torso, shivering in the sun as her face contorted with tears. Despite everything, she had hoped for a different response. For Max to fight—to attach some worth to their relationship, to acknowledge her. It was only fair. She had given him all of herself—her hopes, her dreams, her identity—allowing him to mold her into his perfect companion until she'd lost her own identity.

And that's what this was all truly about. She couldn't remain the person he had created. And he didn't have room for anything different.

Four

An hour behind his usual arrival time, Max entered the front glass double doors of Beaumont Staffing.

Thirty minutes and light-years from the community where he lived, his office was located in a busy strip mall near intersecting freeways. It had a private rear entrance with reserved parking spaces, but Max preferred using the large public lot and front door.

It was his favorite time of the day.

He paused just inside the door and waited for the full impact of the scene before him to settle in.

"That commercial's getting a little stale, don't you think?"

Yeah, all right. He could be a jerk, but that snide remark was totally out of line. A low blow and undeserved. What was up with her? Maybe he could blame hormones. Wasn't she in menopause or something?

"Excuse me." A young woman stood before him, a glassy-eyed child on one hip, a large diaper bag on the other, an uninhibited expression of fury on her plain, narrow face. The girl was ticked.

"Sorry." He stepped aside and opened the door for her.

She started through it without a glance or thank-you.

"Ma'am," he said. "Ma'am!"

She turned.

"The checks will be ready by ten o'clock." It was Friday, payday. A steady stream of people would flow through the office to pick up

12

checks. Some, like her, would have children in tow and wear an obvious look of dire need. He figured she'd been told her check wasn't available yet.

"I know, but I'm here now. They told me I'd get paid *today*."

"You will. Just later."

"I got a life for later," she muttered and continued through the door he still held open. "Can't spend the whole freaking day riding buses around the county."

Max dug into his jacket pocket and quickly pulled a hundred-dollar bill from his wallet. "Hang on a sec." A quick step and he was beside her, shoving the money into the front pouch of the diaper bag.

She twisted around. "What are you doing?"

"Just giving you a little something to help tide you over."

"Huh?" She began digging in the pocket.

He smiled and went back inside to where the lobby overflowed with people. All ages, sizes, shapes, and cultures. All in search of temporary work. Some stood at the counter, which was centered along the back wall. Others sat in the glassed-in waiting areas—one on his right, one on his left—filling out applications or watching morning news programs on the wall-mounted televisions while waiting to be interviewed.

Behind the counter were three fresh-faced, perky, bilingual women —his first line of customer service. They answered phones and fielded the one thousand job seekers who walked through the door every month. In the back offices were twenty more staff members, whose task it was to find them temporary jobs.

"Hey, Max!" one of the receptionists called over the hubbub. "Phil's on his way over."

"Thanks." He gave her a wave and headed down the hallway toward his office.

He could feel his smile. Yes, it was his favorite time of the day.

The impact of this shot through him now. Sometimes it hit him like a jolt of energy, a caffeine buzz after a triple espresso. Other times it was a slow-spreading warmth, like the glow of contentment after a few sips of good scotch.

"That commercial's getting a little stale, don't you think?"

Today it wasn't quite buzz, wasn't quite glow. More like a brain cramp.

Five

Claire's finger shook so badly she couldn't press the phone's On button. She set the cordless receiver on the kitchen counter and balled her hands into fists.

All thoughts of safety and security had fled her home. Expressing her innermost feelings to Max and getting no response in return proved what she feared: all his years of relating to the world through the eyes of a businessman had deadened something inside of him. He couldn't respond with his heart. Could he feel anything anymore?

Good negotiator that he was, he would smooth things over between them by helping her see things his way. He would convince her she was wrong. To emphasize his point, he would give her jewelry. Probably flowers too.

That was how it worked whenever she hinted at going negative on him, whenever she mustered enough courage to quit pretending.

A casserole dish filled with sudsy water caught her gaze. Two pots also in need of scrubbing sat nearby on the stovetop. Not bad considering that last night the kids had used almost every dish and utensil she owned.

She pictured them there, all five, dressed in white chef jackets and tall hats, bebopping to rock-and-roll music blasting from the radio as they unloaded grocery bag after grocery bag. They'd brought all her favorite foods and even a bakery cake topped with purple-frosting roses arranged in the shape of "53."

"For you, Mom." Erik, her eldest at thirty, grinned. "A birthday extravaganza. Six courses!"

"Seven." Jenna corrected. "Remember, the sorbet to cleanse the palate counts as one."

Lexi added, "We will totally clean up."

Well, Claire didn't buy that promise, but she did count on Danny's guarantee, underscored by son-in-law Kevin's solemn nod: "Dad's on his way."

She remembered the moment the phone had rung.

She remembered answering it gaily, expecting to hear her best friend's voice. Naturally, Tandy had been the children's accomplice, the one who'd made dinner plans with Claire, ensuring she'd be home at six on Thursday night. But instead of Tandy, the kids had appeared with groceries and promises that Dad was on his way.

"Claire!" It was her husband. His energetic voice rose above the chefs' clamor. "Surprise!"

Wham. Emotional whiplash.

"Dad's on his way," they'd said. Such empty words. Only a fool would believe them.

The laughter in her throat died a quick death. With a too-familiar sense of resignation, she sat on a counter stool and closed her eyes to shut out the swirl of activity before her.

The thing was, it was so typical. So nauseatingly typical. Why had she assumed for even a split second that tonight would be different?

"Claire? Are you there?"

"Mm-hmm." Her fingers ached. She loosened her grip on the phone and noticed the ache in her stomach. There wasn't a thing to be done except endure the discomfort. It always went away . . . after a time.

"Oh, man!" he cried.

She visualized Max slapping his forehead in that dramatic way some people thought winsome.

"Did I call too early?"

"Too early?" She shifted on the stool. "Too early for what?"

"The surprise. But I hear music. Oh, please, please tell me the kids are there already."

"The kids?"

"Claire! Give me a break!"

Her pleasure in making him squirm really was twisted. "They're here."

"Whew. Were you surprised?"

"Astonished."

She felt a hand on her arm and opened her eyes. Jenna was leaning across the counter toward her.

"Is it Dad?"

She nodded.

"Dad!" Jenna bellowed in the articulate teacher voice she'd acquired about the time she turned three. "Get your derriere home *tout de suite* or you'll be sorry!"

Max laughed.

Claire said, "He's laughing."

Jenna flipped her long, black hair over her shoulder. "I'm serious, Maxwell!" she barked. "Kevin and Erik are lighting the grill even as we speak. Your grill. Your precious, brand-new, top-of-the-line grill. Need I say more?"

"My grill?" The panic in Max's tone was not total fabrication. He adored his covered-patio kitchenette with its built-in gas grill, ceramic-tiled workspace, and surrounding low brick wall. "Not my grill."

Claire gave Jenna a thumbs-up and got a smirk in reply as her daughter sashayed away.

"Aw, Claire," he said.

That was when the full impact hit. Her insides felt like a rug being shaken. Up. Snap. Down. Up. Snap. Down. Max. Was not. Coming.

"I can't make it in time. There's no way."

A whooshing sensation filled her ears, and the kitchen hullabaloo dimmed. Max's litany became unintelligible. She heard bits and pieces. "Sacramento . . . jet repairs . . . three hours minimum . . ."

As he talked, she swiveled on the stool and faced the adjoining family room. Large sliding doors and wide bay windows filled most of two walls, giving a clear view of the backyard. Shadows already touched the swimming pool. Nearby, thick groves of eucalyptus trees filtered rays from the sun, while lush flowers bloomed in terra-cotta pots scattered about the yard. Coastal dampness thickened the scents of jasmine and citrus. The peaceful scene calmed her.

"I'm sorry, Claire." He always was. And he did mean it sincerely.

"I know."

"At least it's not really your birthday, right? We'll be celebrating in San Francisco on the real day. Hey, do you mind keeping an eye on my grill? You know how Erik and Kevin are."

The music volume jumped to eardrum-shattering level. The Stones and her kids screamed they could "get no satisfaction," drowning out Max's voice. Claire turned back around toward the kitchen and watched as the five revelers danced wildly about, waving wooden spoons, beckoning her to join them.

Max was wrong. No matter the date, it was her birthday, with or without him.

"Gotta go, Max!" she shouted into the phone. "Bye!"

She hit the Off button, picked up a wooden spoon they'd set out for her, and discoed her way into the kitchen . . .

Now Claire blinked away the memory. It had solidified something in her. A resolve.

She picked up the phone and pressed the number with a steady finger.

"Hello?"

"Tandy, I need a place to stay."

Six

I mean, since when do my kids cook?" Max groused. "If I'd known they were going to use my grill, I would've canceled the trip to Sacramento yesterday."

Seated on the other side of his desk, Neva Martínez-Rhodes crossed her legs and smacked her gum. "Claire really should nail your carcass over the fireplace."

Next to her, Phil Singleton shook his head. "Nah. He's just being overly dramatic. Aren't you, Max? You're not really saying you'd cancel for the grill, but you wouldn't cancel for Claire's birthday dinner."

"I didn't know it was her birthday dinner in time to cancel! And it wasn't her official birthday dinner. That happens tomorrow. In San Francisco. With me."

Neva swung her crossed leg back and forth, her jaws working at the piece of gum, and studied him. The petite Hispanic woman resembled a meteor in everything she did. Compared to her, Max saw himself as a lethargic slug. Which was probably why she'd been his right-hand person forever and a day. He trusted her capabilities and usually her opinion.

"Nail my carcass?"

"That's what I said." She nodded. "Did she?"

"Almost."

"Good for her."

Neva had gone with him the previous day to visit the office in Sacramento. She overheard his conversation with Claire when he explained the company jet needed repairs and he wouldn't be home on time. She understood his wife's disappointment.

Phil cleared his throat. "Max, you look like something a dog would be proud to drag inside and lay at his owner's feet. Care to elaborate?"

Max studied the two employees who also happened to be his closest friends.

Neva had been his director of operations since he created the position, less than two years after opening the doors of Beaumont Staffing. At that time he and Claire were almost bonkers trying to run things themselves. His niche was networking with clients; Claire's was playing her violin with the symphony. Nobody was managing the office until Neva stepped in. Hardly out of her teens, she'd been bilingual, extroverted, and eager to work for a pittance.

Phil was tall and blond with Nordic features. He'd joined the team a dozen years ago, when technology sprouted wings, and Max realized he was Gulliver, tied fast to the ground with other concerns. Phil led Beaumont Staffing into the twenty-first century and now, as director of technology, oversaw the selling and servicing of software. He was also one heck of a tennis partner.

They weren't just being polite. They wanted to know what was going on with him and Claire.

Max gave them the highlights. He omitted Claire's derogatory jibe about the stale commercial—after all, they were an integral part of the agency—and ended with that nonsense about not being there when he got home.

Neva and Phil exchanged a glance and then resumed staring at him.

"What?" He shrugged. "We're having a spat."

Neither of them replied. He stared them down.

At last Neva said, "Yeah, right. Max, for your information, you left 'spat' behind about the time you went off to separate bedrooms."

Phil added, "Most definitely by the time she announced the ultimatum about not being there when you got back."

Max shook his head. "She won't literally leave, no matter how serious the *spat* is. Walking out has never been an option for us. Period."

But a memory snagged his attention. No, not so much a memory as an impression. A gut-wrenching impression of his body being ripped apart.

Walking out had been an option . . . once.

But that was—what? Thirty-one, thirty-two years ago. And there had been a reason then. Claire had done the unthinkable—

He vaulted over that thought and landed in another place.

He was back at the beginning, and he remembered it as if it were yesterday. He'd been in college, studying in the library. October. Ten o'clock at night. His last year. A stranger walked past his table. Their eyes met. He smiled. She smiled. Her name was Claire Lambert.

Hokey as it sounded, he'd been smitten. Totally, head-over-heels, dizzily so.

He still was. Always had been.

What had happened? Claire wouldn't . . .

Max glanced at Neva. Her brows raised a fraction of an inch. She knew their history. Not the details, but she'd been there when things happened, close enough to catch the drift that walking out had at one point been a very real option.

She uncrossed her legs. "So maybe turning fifty-three is throwing her for a loop. It happens." She shrugged. "One of life's mysteries. You'll work it out over the weekend."

Phil tapped a pen on his knee. "I don't know, bud. You'd better get the earrings to go with that diamond necklace."

Max smiled. "I called the jeweler first thing."

Phil chuckled. Neva lowered her gaze to the notebook on her lap.

They knew he'd chosen a special necklace for Claire's birthday gift and debated about including the earrings. The price of the necklace alone wasn't exactly understated. Its style was, though. Its style was pure Claire.

He glanced at the five by seven of her on his desk. She had those classic high cheekbones and chin-length, light-brown hair. The recently added bifocals with rectangular lenses framed in lavender gave her a certain dignity. She always wore tailored clothes, always radiated serenity.

Until this morning.

"That commercial's getting a little stale, don't you think?"

"If you go, I won't be here when you get home."

Max massaged a tight knot at the back of his neck.

Seven

Jenna Beaumont Mason closed up her cell phone and slid it inside the zippered pouch of the beach bag that lay beside her on the blanket. Why wasn't her mom answering or calling her back?

A movement at the ocean's edge caught her attention. She straightened her Gucci sunglasses and leaned back on her elbows to enjoy the delicious view of her husband as he strode from the water and through the sand.

On second thought, he didn't stride. He swaggered. Kevin Dean Mason was indeed a hottie. Six feet even. Shoulders from here to Timbuktu. Brick-house solid all the way down to his toes. Flaxen-shaded hair, buzzed short, like during his stint in the Marines. Eyes the color of a night sky when the first stars winked on. His bronzed skin glistened with water.

"Hey." He grinned, a meandering lift of first one corner of his wide mouth, then the other, until finally the lips parted.

"Hey, yourself."

He sat on the blanket, his damp leg brushing against hers.

"Yow!" She jerked upright. "You're freezing!"

"Sorry, babe."

He scooted away, and she scooted nearer. "Oh, that's okay. I mean, it's not like I didn't have goose bumps already. You are one fine-looking dude."

Laughing, he slid on his sunglasses and propped his elbows on his bent knees. "And you are one hot chick, which is the only reason I left those perfect waves."

"We're hopeless."

She leaned over and kissed the tattoo on his upper arm. Years ago tats had been a definite turnoff—in her top ten of "Yuck Factors in Guys." That was before Kevin walked into her life three years ago. And now there she was, kissing a *Semper fi* banner under an eagle perched on her husband's bicep. She accepted it as part of his past, kind of like her boxed Madame Alexander dolls that took up an entire closet shelf.

He nuzzled her cheek. "Want to go out for dinner and a movie tonight?"

"Hmm. Is the good-looking dude asking the hot chick out on a date?"

"Most definitely. It's time to celebrate."

"What are we celebrating?"

"School's out, and football practice doesn't start for two weeks. I feel like a kid who has nothing to do but play with his best buddy."

She leaned against him. "Oh, Kevin. Our life is beginning to resemble a fairy tale, isn't it?"

"I don't remember any fairy tales with plain old high school teachers in them."

"So we'll write our own script." She thought about how he was finished with the military, teacher certification classes, and *assistant* coaching. He was head football coach now and taught PE in the same building where she taught English. "We get to flirt between classes and spend half the summer lounging at the beach. Last but not least, we have no big outstanding debts. How fabulous is that?"

"Hmm. Did you say no big outstanding debts? Then why is it we taught summer school?"

She smiled. "Well, in this fairy tale there's no rich prince or princess, so we take on extra jobs. But that's okay, because we have something far better than money and eons of idle time: we're committed to helping teenagers."

"Which means we're fruitcakes. Now how fabulous is that?" His laughter was infectious.

"Hey," he said, "your shoulders are turning pink. I'll put some more sunscreen on them."

"Thanks." She lay down on her stomach.

"Who was on the phone?"

"Phone?"

"I saw you on your cell." His hand glided over her back, the lotion cool against her warm skin.

"I was calling Mom."

"Again?"

"Yeah, she's still not answering."

"You know she had a good time last night."

"Definitely. I haven't seen her laugh that much in ages. I guess I just wanted to relive it with her." She didn't try to explain further. Kevin was clueless when it came to mother-daughter emotional connections. "We did a good job on this one, didn't we? Those chef outfits Erik got were so great."

"Yeah. He seems to know everybody in San Diego County."

"Or else they know him."

"Guess that comes from being a hotshot TV news anchor." He rubbed the lotion over her shoulders. "Your mom wasn't laughing while she was talking to your dad."

"The Putz."

"I've been thinking. Maybe we shouldn't be so quick to call him that."

"Kevin, he didn't come for her surprise party. That's like the rudest thing I've ever seen him do. Or not do."

"But he had good reason."

She whiffed her disdain. "Good excuse, you mean."

"The plane broke."

"The dog ate my homework."

"Not the same thing. You know, I really respect your dad. He's got a job to do, and he does it. He's totally focused. He would have made an excellent Marine."

Jenna rolled onto her back to scowl at him. "His priorities are all mucked up. They always have been."

Kevin shrugged. "Four kids. A huge house. His own business. A man's gotta do what a man's gotta do."

"Four grown-up kids who don't need his money, and a house that's all but paid for. And he's got a gazillion assistants. He doesn't have to do it anymore."

"But it's his life. His passion."

She stuck out her tongue.

"Did I mention he also has one extremely spoiled princess of a daughter, who still likes her big birthday and Christmas checks that could pay almost a year's rent on our apartment? And her name is not Alexis."

"I may change my mind about that date."

He chuckled.

A tinny version of "We Are Family" rang out from her beach bag. "It's Mom."

Kevin groaned and lay down on his back.

"I have to talk to her." Jenna pulled out her cell. "Mom. Hi!"

"Hi, honey. Did you need something? You called four times."

She'd been eager to hear her mom's reaction to the surprise dinner. "I was just wondering how you were after your big night."

"Oh, uh, fine. It was a . . . a fun evening. You guys really outdid yourselves. Thank you again, hon."

"Are you okay? You sound funny."

"I'm fine."

"What are you doing?"

"Not much. What are you doing?"

"Kevin and I are at the beach. Del Mar. It's so great to be off school together. No papers to grade. No lesson plans to write. No place we have to go."

"That's nice."

"You must be packing for San Francisco?" Jenna waited through a silence long enough to prompt her to say, "Mom? Are you still there?"

"Mm-hmm." Her mother's voice sounded like a choke.

"Mom! What's wrong?"

"I'm sorry." Jenna listened as her mother inhaled loudly and her voice went up an octave. "It's really not a big deal. I thought I could talk and explain."

"Explain what?"

At the sound of Jenna's panicked tone, Kevin sat up and touched her leg. She shrugged at his puzzled expression.

"Mom?"

There was a loud exhale. "I packed, but I'm not going to San Francisco. I'm going to Tandy's."

"Huh?"

"I—I'll explain later, okay?" Tears filled her mom's voice. "Don't worry, hon. I just want a little space for a couple days. I'll call you soon. Bye."

The line went dead.

Jenna stared at the phone. A wave of disbelief gushed through her, quickly overswept by one of dread. Her mother had packed her bags to go to a friend's house less than an hour away?

Now anger steamrolled its way through her. Leave it to her dad to barge in and tear apart a perfectly good fairy tale. What a putz.

Eight

I shouldn't have told her, Tandy." Claire strode alongside her friend. "It was way too much information for Jenna."

"What's done is done." The redhead pumped her elbows and blew out a breath. "Let's pick up the speed a bit, shall we? There's a reason they call this power walking. You're going to feel the power, Claire. You're going to feel the burn. It's going to tell you that Claire Beaumont is a *woman*! A woman who knows her own mind and isn't afraid to speak it! Ooh-rah!"

Claire's legs were longer than Tandy's, but she had never been able to keep pace with her. They'd met ages ago, when Erik and Jenna were in elementary school with Tandy's son and daughter. Since then they'd powered through thousands of miles together.

"I appreciate the pep talk." Claire spoke between huffs as they zipped along block after block, past one identical condominium building after another, the same six palm trees in front of each.

"Pep talk, schmep talk. It's the truth."

"Jenna will tell the others."

"So? Somebody's got to. No reason for you to blubber through three more phone calls with your kids."

"But they don't really need to know. There really isn't anything to know at this point. I mean, Max and I had an argument. Granted, that's not a common occurrence, but, really. What's the big deal? I packed and—" She stopped midsentence. "I didn't really move out, did I?"

"The sooner you admit it, the sooner you can deal with it."

"But I'm a Christian. Christian wives don't move out."

"What am I, chopped liver?"

"It was different for you. Trevor was cheating on you and refused to end it and was mean to you."

"Maybe—in another sense—Max is cheating on you."

Claire shook her head. "No. He's not. And I don't think I've literally moved out. Physically, yes, for now. I just want some space."

"Anyway, sweetie, don't worry about tomorrow. Take it one day at a time. Trust me. You will get through this."

She glanced sideways at her old friend. Tandy echoed the exact words Claire had preached to her on more than one occasion. The first was seven years ago, the night Tandy had kicked her husband out of the house. Another time was right after she'd signed the divorce papers. Then there was the day they'd locked up her house and followed the moving van to her new home, a condo forty minutes away. And her daughter's wedding, when Tandy was forced to share every special moment with her ex-husband's new wife.

"Hey." Tandy reached over and lightly punched her shoulder. "Max may be a putz, but he's no Trevor the Toad. Okay? He's no babe magnet. He has no Big-Hair Bimbo from Bishop waiting in the wings."

Claire nodded. Max would never expect her to pose for a family photo with *his* second wife. Would he?

She raised her elbows higher and tried to pump away all such crazy notions. It didn't work. Something inside her vibrated with a sense of dread she hadn't felt in a long time. True, Max was not a babe magnet. But he was winsome. He was personable to a fault. He hugged freely and frequently. People liked him. Women adored him. Why wouldn't he have someone waiting in the wings?

With the intensity of an eighteen-wheeler rumbling over her entire body, the sense of dread gave way to the full-on assault of an old fear.

That woman in the wings would be Neva.

Nine

In their apartment's living room, Jenna stretched on her tiptoes, grasped Kevin's face between her hands, and kissed the pout on his mouth.

"Kev, this will only take a few minutes. Come on, give me a smile, big guy."

He kept his hands propped on his waist and those fabulous lips of his angled off center.

She grinned. "You're kind of cute when you're miffed."

At last he relaxed and put his arms around her waist. "I'm not miffed." He kissed the tip of her nose. "It's just time to go. While you were getting ready, I made reservations."

"You did? For where?"

"I'm not telling." He winked. "But egg rolls and downtown are involved."

"At Horton Plaza? You don't like that place!"

"You do, though. I thought it might cheer you up."

"Oh, Kevin, it sounds perfect. Thank you."

"You're welcome, but we gotta go—like, now, or we won't get to the movie in time."

"Okay, okay. I just need five minutes. Ten, max. I have to call Erik and the twins."

"Call them from the car."

"I can't." She shook her head. "Kevin, Mom just left Dad! It's not a car conversation."

"Hey." His voice a whisper, he lowered his face toward hers. "Pretty lady."

All concerns drained from her on the spot. It was his magic—his nearness, his navy blue eyes zeroing in on her, the way he uttered his pet name for her. Like a magnetic field, they pulled her up and out from anxiety.

She smiled softly. "My true north speaks."

"Yeah." He rested his forehead against hers. "Listen. I love your folks. They're the greatest. I've never known such support outside of the military. But, Jen. This junk happens. It's called life. You just gotta keep on truckin'." He leaned back with a grin. "And let me cheer you up."

"Okay."

"Okay."

"But the thing is—"

He groaned his exasperation, rolling his eyes.

"Let me finish. The thing is, it's my family." She tapped his bicep. "It's like your *semper fee* thing."

"*Semper fi.* Long *i.*"

"I knew that." *Stupid Marines.* "It means 'always faithful.' Same for the Beaumonts. I wouldn't exactly be a loyal sister if I kept them in the dark about this, would I? It'd be like leaving them behind."

Kevin growled and hugged her tightly. "You are goofy, Jenna Mason."

"But you love me."

"I love you. I'm crazy about you. Or maybe I'm just plain crazy."

She nestled against him. Poor guy. He hadn't grown up in a close-knit family. His divorced parents lived in Indiana, and he only had one sibling—a sister, much older—who lived in New Jersey. Even though they didn't see much of each other anymore, Jenna still had good memories of her childhood with her siblings—the kind Kevin didn't have, the kind that kept them tight through the tough times.

Eventually he would come to understand what family ties meant.

Jenna broke the news to Erik first.

"It's about time," he said.

"Huh?"

"Mom's put up with Dad long enough."

"Well, I agree he can be disrespectful, not showing up on time for things."

"Or even at all. Beginning twenty years ago, with my ball games and your music recitals."

"But it's not like he has a girlfriend or beats Mom or doesn't pay bills. You don't think he has a girlfriend, do you?"

"When would he have time for one?"

"Yeah. Gosh! They've been married for thirty-two years! Thirty-three next month! They must love each other. Nobody stays married for that long."

"Convenience, Jen. I remember helping Brett Abbott move his mom into the condo." He referred to his childhood friend, Tandy's son. "And then his sister's wedding fiasco. What a mess. Mom was right there with Tandy through the whole thing. I'm sure she'd just as soon pretend everything was hunky-dory with her and Dad rather than go that route."

"She can be an ostrich."

"Exactly. I have to get to work. Thanks for calling. I guess."

"I thought you should know."

"I'll call Mom."

"Oh, Erik, it's her birthday tomorrow, and they were going to San Francisco! After all this, do you think Dad will even remember?"

"Who knows? Who cares? Listen, Jen, this junk happens. Okay? You gotta let it go. Tell Kevin hi."

And that was the end of her conversation with her big brother, her closest friend for most of her life. At least until they'd grown up and he started parroting her husband.

Guys.

She looked at the phone, hesitating to punch in the number. Her younger brother, Danny, could be squirrelly when it came to their dad. He'd say "putz" in one breath and "hero" in the next.

Did she want to bother?

Kevin was waiting. She'd save Danny for later.

What about Lexi?

Jenna blew out her frustration. Lexi had been born aloof. The two sisters hadn't connected on an intensely deep level since Jenna was in third grade and Lexi in first. That was the year Danny was sick a lot and some bully attached himself like a fungus to Lexi until Jenna punched the kid during recess, breaking his nose.

Lexi was still aloof, except when it came to Danny or Nana and Papa.

Bingo. Forget both twins. Jenna hit the speed-dial number for Indio and Ben Beaumont.

Ten

Before she'd finished saying, "Hacienda Hideaway," Indio Beaumont heard a familiar yammer through the telephone.

"Nana!"

That would be Jenna, her effusive granddaughter. Indio intuitively turned off the stovetop burner and made a beeline for her favorite chair in the corner of the kitchen, next to the fireplace.

"Jenna. What's wrong?" She settled into the overstuffed rocker, planted her cowboy-booted toes against a small footstool, and set the chair in motion.

"Oh, Nana! You'll never believe what happened! Dad missed Mom's surprise dinner last night. Not that you wouldn't believe *that* part. You probably wouldn't believe it if I said he *did* show up."

The girl had inherited all of Max's dramatic tendencies. Indio knew it was best to just let her emote without interruption until she got to her point. She still hadn't figured out how the girl taught English lit.

After skittering down a myriad of rabbit trails, Jenna paused and drew in a breath. "Mom left Dad. She moved in with Tandy!"

Indio stopped rocking.

"And that's all I really know except this is so awful. They've always been the picture-perfect couple."

Dear God. "What exactly did she say?"

"That she needed some space. Why would she need *space*? My gosh, she's fifty-three years old. She sounds like one of my sixteen-year-old students."

"Jenna, what else did she say?"

"Oh, I don't know. Not to worry. Stuff like that."

"So we leave things at 'stuff like that.' We won't worry."

"But she's never done anything like this before!"

And only the Lord could say why not. Indio rubbed her forehead. "I know. This isn't like your mom at all. Oh my. But . . ."

"But what?"

"But . . ." Indio had no words to give her upset granddaughter. The truth was, she felt as though she'd had the wind knocked from her. Max and Claire, separated? There remained only one thing to say. "But, well, God is good. Hallelujah."

"Nana, please!"

"Can't help it, dear." Her habit of praising God annoyed most people. In particular, it drove her four grandchildren up the wall. No matter. If they were listening, she simply explained it to them again. "Jenna, you know I say those things to remind myself God is right here with me, and He's waiting for me to say, 'Help.'"

Jenna moaned. "I don't have your faith."

"I think you do, dear, but you haven't exercised it as much as I have. I'm going to pray now, okay?"

"Okay." Jenna's voice was barely audible. "It's probably why I called."

"Okay." On the heels of another 'Hallelujah,' the prayer took flight. "Holy Father, we need Your help. Thank You that You are with Max and Claire right now. Please heal the wounds between them. Bring them to reconciliation. Please comfort my grandchildren. In Your precious Son's name, I ask this."

"Amen." Jenna sighed. "I'm sorry I fussed at you. I just don't get why you say God is good when things are so awful."

"It takes practice." Indio laid a hand on her chest. There was a tightness inside, as if a clothespin had clipped itself onto her lungs. "It takes years and years of choosing to recognize that God is God. He alone deserves praise and glory, no matter how awful things look."

"How can you be so sure He'll answer?"

"Because He has answered, time and again. Now you'll probably start to worry later tonight. Simply say, 'Help.' He doesn't want you being anxious."

"Okay, okay." Jenna's tone indicated the subject was closed. "Speaking of grandchildren, I told Erik but not Danny or Lexi. They should know, too, don't you think? As soon as possible?"

Indio waited for her to continue. If she'd learned one thing as a nurse for thirty years in the rest home, it was to refrain from assuming another's burdens. One resident alone bore far too many heartbreaking situations for a caregiver to involve herself with.

But Maxwell was her son. Claire was her daughter-in-law and a friend. Their situation was not Jenna's burden alone to carry.

"I'll call the twins."

"Thank you, Nana."

"You're welcome. Put this out of your mind, and don't feel guilty."

A few moments later they said good-bye, Jenna obviously calmer than when she'd called, Indio struggling for breath.

Hand on her chest, pressing at her lungs, she sat there. What was that feeling?

Guilt. That old reminder of how she had wounded her son in ways only a mother could. Unwittingly and out of her own immaturity, yes, but still, she was at fault.

She'd borne two sons: BJ, the perfect prince, and Max, the troublemaker. They seemed to come out of the womb already labeled. She never realized until it was too late how blatantly she'd communicated to Max that he was just a loser, a pain in the neck, a grave disappointment.

Tears of shame burned her eyes. *Lord, help!*

Indio swiveled the big rocker toward the wall. Only about six feet in width, it ran from a corner to a doorway's edge. Of the countless walls in the age-old hacienda, though, it was the most important to her. Floor to ceiling, it held her collection of what she called "Jesus reminders."

Fifty-nine at last count, the reminders included a variety of crosses and crucifixes—all styles, sizes, and materials, from large to tiny, simple, squared-off polished oak to intricately twisted wrought iron, Mexican to Celtic. Interspersed were framed paintings and drawings of Jesus, from the early Italian rendition of a chubby babe on His mother's lap to a sketch downloaded from the Internet. That one depicted Jesus laughing, His grin so infectious she could almost hear His guffaw.

But that one was not for tonight.

She eyed the display one piece at a time. Two were left over from the original chapel, which had been a small room off the kitchen. A hundred and fifty years old, they were tiny and carved from wood. Most of the other pieces had been gifts, treasures from her family as well as from guests who stayed at the Hacienda Hideaway. Everyone saw how Indio drew strength from the Crucified One.

At last she settled upon a crucifix made of rough-hewn pine. Though no taller than eight inches, its carved details left little to the imagination. There were the thorns on His forehead . . . the spikes in His hands and feet . . . the speared hole in His side . . . the trace of a loincloth that gave the sense it was not part of the real-life version. The body drooped. The wounds bled.

"Lord, haven't we dealt with this already? Haven't I already received Your forgiveness? Please, please remind me that I do not have to feel guilty either."

A peace slowly enveloped her. Her breathing grew regular. She was forgiven.

Thanks to her, Max had grown up believing himself unforgivable. He made all the wrong choices a kid could make. His grades were the worst, his friends punks, his young body poisoned with legal and illegal drugs.

Yet he pulled himself out from the pit by working hard and starting his own business. He married Claire, the best influence that had ever touched his life.

And despite all that, things were not right with her son.

Eleven

Like clockwork the three of them called, one after another.

Claire fielded questions from her offspring while cooling down from her power walk. She sat in the early evening shadows on Tandy's small patio, water bottle in one hand, cell phone in the other.

Erik called first. He was a local newscaster with the looks, charm, and honeyed baritone voice that could easily woo a national network.

"Bravo, Mom."

"Erik, don't take sides."

"He's a putz."

"He . . . We've both let business take priority over everything else for far too long. Now we need to make some adjustments, that's all."

"Whatever. Can I do anything for you?"

"Just don't worry, all right? I'm okay."

"You're comfortable at Tandy's?"

"Yes."

"I mean, if you need a place to stay, you could call Jenna."

She chuckled with him.

"Just kidding, Mom. You're always welcome at my condo. I'll sleep on the couch. If I can find it. Bye."

Lexi was next.

"Mom?" Her voice always hovered slightly above a whisper. "Nana called and told me."

Claire shut her eyes. Of course Jenna would call their grand-mother. Who would in turn tell Max's dad . . .

"Are you okay, Mom?"

"I'm okay." The words grated, but she had to be *okay* for the kids' sake. "Don't be upset."

"Well, I am. How could this happen? You two have always been the model-perfect couple."

Claire sighed. Her twenty-six-year-old internalized the whole world. "Lexi, I'm upset with your dad. I'm at Tandy's, trying to figure out how to straighten things out with him. All right? No big deal." She winced. *No big deal. I moved out, that's all.*

"It's—I don't know what it is! It's not you."

"Sweetie, you can come over if you want."

Claire continued consoling until her phone beeped. She glanced at the ID screen. "Danny's calling. We'll talk later?"

"Yeah, okay. Bye, Mom."

"I love you."

"Yeah. Me too."

Claire cut the connection and opened the incoming call. "Hey, Danny."

"Hey, Mom."

"I know Nana called you. Yes, it's true, I'm at Tandy's. I'm cool-ing down." In more ways than one. "I'm fine. Erik, Jenna, and Lexi are fine too."

His laugh sounded forced. "I'm the last to know? I'm always last, every which way."

"Lexi was born last."

"Yeah. I made it six whole minutes before her. So how's Dad?"

"Uh, I don't know."

"You haven't talked?"

"Actually, he may come in last on this one."

"Good grief, Mom. You leave him and don't tell him?"

"I haven't left—" She sighed. Of her four children, Danny most easily disarmed her. He made her forget she was the parent who really should have all the answers.

"But you moved in with Tandy."

"For now. And I did tell him." She gave him an edited version of the morning conversation, carefully tap-dancing around certain details so as not to point the finger at his father. "I wanted to talk then, but he had a meeting to go to. The last thing I said was I wouldn't be there when he got home. So he knows."

"No way does he know, no matter how straight you think you said it. I can't believe it myself. This just isn't like you, Mom. You never bail out on anything."

"I'm not bailing. I'm . . . restringing the violin of our marriage. The notes have gone sour."

"Ha! And you just now noticed this? After all these years of playing—what? What would you call it? Bach's Mass in XYZ Minor? Beethoven's Symphony no. 6,071?"

"Danny! Just back off a little, will you? I can't explain it right now."

"Okay, okay. Chill. All I know is you always said divorce was not an option. That you wanted to do things the right way—"

"Divorce! I'm not talking divorce!"

"You left him."

Claire pressed the water bottle against her forehead. Everything was so black-and-white for Danny. "I need some space for a while. I'm not considering divorce. All right?"

"Sure. If you say so."

Silence hung between them for a long moment. Her heart hammered in her ears.

"Nana told me to stop leaping to the worst-case scenario. Mom, I'm not leaping. We're already dead center in the worst-case scenario."

"I'm sorry," she whispered.

"Do you know how totally *unreal* this whole scene is? You and Dad, separated? You just turned everybody's world upside down.

Yours, Dad's, mine, Lexi's and Jenna's, Erik's—well, maybe not Erik's. Who knows what that would take."

Claire doubled over.

"So you can't be fine, Mom. You can't even be anywhere near *okay.*"

"I am."

"Give me a break! If you're *fine,* then I guess you just don't give a rip that you turned our worlds upside down."

Oh, Daniel, don't do this to me! "Danny, I have to be *fine.* I've always had to be *fine.* It's what a mom does."

"You're in denial."

Indignation surged through her, and she straightened up in the chair. "Daniel, that's enough. Stop being such a bulldog."

He didn't reply.

Her shoulders sagged. "I'm sorry I've hurt you. I'm sorry I hurt your dad and everyone else. It just—it just can't be helped right now. I have to figure this out."

"Nana said she's praying for reconciliation."

"That's . . . appropriate. Are you okay now?"

"No. Are you?"

"Probably not." She sighed heavily. "I have to hang up now. Good-bye, Danny."

"Yeah. See ya."

A light breeze chilled her arms. Claire hugged herself.

Reconciliation.

A good word. A good goal.

She couldn't imagine what it would look like.

She wasn't even sure she wanted it.

Maybe she wasn't fine. Maybe she was contemplating divorce.

God, I followed all the rules! Why is this happening?

Zero hour approached. Any minute now, Max would arrive home and find the note she'd left for him.

Claire shivered in the corner of the sofa. Was it really less than twenty-four hours ago she'd sat in just the same way, waiting for Max to show up long after the surprise dinner?

Tonight, though, the sofa was floral and in Tandy's condo, and Claire had no idea if Max would come or even call. Tonight, somehow, was worse. So much hung on his response to her ultimatum. Her first-ever ultimatum.

And there was the aftermath of her conversations with the kids. Danny's relentlessness especially had shaken loose ugly things that wouldn't go away. She *wasn't* okay. She didn't have answers. She was becoming acquainted with anger. Rage. Fury, even. Her nerves tingled. She imagined them to be like power lines with electricity pulsating, waiting for a switch to be thrown.

She was certain of only one thing: there was no turning back now.

Twelve

Max stared at the small piece of linen stationery in his hand. The words, written in Claire's neat cursive, shimmied and bounced before his eyes.

He set the paper back down on the kitchen counter and placed the decorative frog figurine back on top where he'd found it—above the "Max," which was underscored with a wavy line.

Max.

He blinked and tried reading the note again.

I'm at Tandy's. Overnight. I need space. Maybe I'll stay longer. I don't know. I only know that something has to change between you and me. I'm sorry.

"She's at Tandy's? What has to change? I still don't get it." He spoke aloud to the empty kitchen, set the jeweler's gift bag next to the note, and pulled his cell from his pocket.

Claire answered on the second ring. "Hi, Max."

"I don't get it."

After a moment, she said, "You're referring to the note?"

"Right."

"Let's start with this: How does the note make you feel?"

"Claire, I'm not in the mood to play games—" He clamped his mouth shut. He might be slow on the draw with whatever female crisis she was going through, but he understood that a description of his long day or his two trips to the jeweler to pick up her birthday gifts because they hadn't been ready the first time was not what she wanted to hear.

"And I'm in no mood to skirt the issue. It's a simple question, Max. I need a response."

"All right. I feel confused."

"That's a mental condition. How . . . do . . . you . . . *feel*?" She slowly enunciated each word. "Happy, sad, angry, relieved?"

"I'm starting to get annoyed, because we're talking on the phone instead of packing for our trip."

"Annoyed. This is progress."

His head pounded. Add migraine to the list. But she'd probably call that a mental condition.

"You just read my note, which says, in essence, I have left you." Her voice jumped a few notches above its usual alto. "Your reaction to that information is to feel *annoyed* because the schedule changed. *Excuse* me?"

He didn't have to wonder how she felt. The wonder was over the fact that he couldn't remember her ever having displayed such blatant anger.

Okay, she had his attention.

"Claire, why aren't you here? I can't fathom what's going on."

"Fathom it, Max! I packed a bag, and I'm not coming home."

His feelings from that morning burst upon him, vicious in their intensity. Instantly he was reliving a moment from thirty-some years ago—the moment Claire had told him there was someone else. "I feel like I'm being ripped open and turned inside out. We promised we'd never do this."

Not even the sound of her breathing came through the phone.

"Is there someone else . . . ?" His lungs burned. They offered no more air for speech.

"No! No, Max." Her voice sank to a hushed tone. "I would not do that to you. It's nothing like that."

Air rushed into him again. "Then what is it? What do you want from me? I'll do anything."

"Oh, honestly, Max." She sounded near tears now. "I told you last night. I told you this morning. I told you in the note. Can't you comprehend a thing when it comes to our relationship?"

He slid onto a stool at the counter and rubbed the back of his head. Nausea gripped his throat. That probably didn't count for feelings either. That would be a stomach issue.

With effort, he recalled the morning conversation. "You said you don't want to play second fiddle to the grill."

"Yes."

His stomach churned. "Whew. Got one right."

"There's more."

He leaned forward until his forehead lay against the cool countertop. "Nor do you want to play second fiddle to the business."

"A-plus."

"Which means what?"

"I've been thinking all day, Max, and I can only come up with one answer. You won't like it."

"Claire, just spit it out."

"Sell."

"Sell?"

"Sell. The whole kit and caboodle."

He bolted upright, grunting his disbelief. "Sell Beaumont Staffing?"

"There is no other way around this. It all comes down to me or the company. You have to choose. I need you to choose, because I don't want to keep living in this gray twilight, wondering when you're going to show up for our life."

"But the agency is my life!"

She didn't reply.

"You know it is!"

"Yeah." Her voice went whispery soft. "It is your life. I think that's the whole point here."

"Claire, I can't choose between you and the company!" Lights flickered in his peripheral vision. He shut his eyes. "You're something totally different to me. You're my wife. There has to be another way—Where are my pills?"

She sighed. "You have a migraine. The pills are in our medicine cabinet. Get the ice pack out of the freezer."

He did as he was told.

"Are you all right?"

"Mm-hmm." He stumbled through the kitchen.

"Max, I can come home. Or—or call me if you don't sleep. If you need something. Okay? I'll come."

"Mmm." He closed his phone.

The world faded from view, along with all confusion about Claire's irrational behavior.

Thirteen

Claire, you cannot go home!" Tandy stood, arms propped against the sides of the living room doorway, blocking her exit.

"He's sick." She stood before her friend, shoulder bag in hand.

"He'll take his pill and sleep. There's nothing you can do for him."

"I can be there for him!"

"Like he was there for you last night."

"This is different. He's totally out of it." Why else would he dig up the past?

Then again, could it be an indicator? Was that the last time he'd actually felt anything—when she almost left him for someone else?

But that had all been dealt with long ago, forgiven and forgotten. Hadn't it?

She should go to him.

"Did you ever think he uses these migraines to control you?"

"Tandy! What an awful thing to say! He can't create them at will. He doesn't get them often."

"When does he get them?"

"When he . . . I don't know. When things are out of control. Business situations."

"Or like now. He can't control you, so he goes powerless." Tandy pointed to the couch. "Sit down, Claire. I'll be right back."

She didn't sit; she collapsed. Her bones liquefied. Her hands shook. She had held nothing back from Max. She had lost control. She had not skirted issues or pretended. Why, oh why had she ever started pretending all those years ago? She didn't even know how to be real with him.

Tandy returned and set a mug on the end table. "The green tea you requested. You okay?"

"I'm calming down. I can't believe I said all that to him. I've never been so mad."

"You have been, Claire. You've just never expressed it."

She stared at her friend.

"Right?"

Claire nodded. "Wives aren't supposed to be mad."

"What a bunch of drivel that is."

"I always figured he'd explode."

"And that would kill you?"

"Yes."

"Well, give yourself a pat on the back. You have lived to be mad another day." Tandy disappeared into the kitchen.

"I don't want a pat on the back," Claire called after her.

Tandy didn't reply.

"And I don't like being mad."

Claire rested her head back against the couch. She just wanted to be real, to be the real Claire Beaumont. Not that she knew her anymore. Ages ago she had. Before she met Max she was confident; she was focused on her dream to teach and play music. Then she met him, and somehow his love exposed what she didn't have: a family support system.

Almost at once she received from him a sense of safety and security, all the warm fuzzies she had never felt. She loved him like crazy. She wanted to be the best wife. She promised herself she would be. She promised Max she would be.

She shut her eyes.

What about that promise?

And what about that other one—the one Max had just referred to? Thirty-one years ago, when she almost walked out of their marriage, they'd promised never to take that route. They'd promised to make things work, no matter what.

Silly, naive, saucer-eyed kids.

Tandy came back with her own mug of tea and settled into the recliner. "He'll be fine without you tonight."

"I suppose," she murmured, still following a different train of thought. "Do you remember I told you he and I promised we'd never leave each other?"

"You're not talking about that pablum we all swore as part of our marriage vows."

Claire winced.

"Sorry. I really am working on my bitter attitude." Tandy made a wry face. "Seriously, yes, I remember. You promised sometime after you were married that you'd stay together forever. Let me guess. He brought it up just now on the phone, right?"

She nodded.

"You haven't *left* him, left him. You've just called a time-out. Okay?"

"I wonder."

"Give yourself a time-out. I ordered pizza. It should be here in twenty minutes."

"Pizza?" Claire grimaced.

"Hey, my house, my dinner menu."

"I thought you were supposed to be pampering me."

"I am. I'm pampering you with the empathetic coping mechanism otherwise known as gorging on junk food. You think I need pizza?" Tandy grabbed at her waist. "And I've got two bags of Mint Milanos waiting in the cupboard. One for each thigh."

Claire couldn't help but giggle.

"If you're a good girl, I'll let you have your own bag."

The chuckle dissolved into a sob. "Oh, Tandy! What would I do without you?"

"Eat both bags?" She laughed. "Now blow your nose and drink your tea. It's going to be a long night."

The orchestra played Beethoven's Fifth. Always a favorite of Claire's. Her bow leaped across the violin. Her fingers flew. *Allegro con brio!* Brisk! Lively! Spirited!

Ba, ba, ba, bummm.

Again.

And again.

Ba, ba, ba, bummm.

It was her phone ringing.

Claire opened her eyes and rolled over. A tidal wave of information greeted her along with sunlight peeking through venetian blinds: The mattress was lumpy. She was in Tandy's guest room. She was angry at Max. Not only had she admitted that to herself, but she had even told him she was angry. She'd eaten half a pizza and a fourth of a bag of Mint Milanos. She'd watched a horrible shoot-'em-up movie—under the circumstances, Tandy disallowed romantic feel-good comedies—until midnight. She'd tossed and turned for hours. The clock now read six fifty.

And it was her birthday.

Beethoven rang out again.

She grabbed the cell off the nightstand. Holding it at arm's length, she squinted at the ID. The incoming number belonged to her in-laws. She could have guessed. They were always the first.

"Hello."

"Happy birthday, Claire!" Indio and Ben's voices greeted in unison.

She couldn't help but smile. The couple would be huddled over the same phone, both in blue jeans and boots, ready for the day at their remote estate in the hills above the city. They lived in a sprawling old hacienda. Despite Ben's white hair and Indio's thick, salt-and-pepper braid, the two acted much younger than seventy-something. They both still rode horses and chopped wood. He was tall and rugged. Indio—named after the California city of her birth—joked about her own features, which carried none of her Irish father in them. She resembled her mother, a full-blooded Kumeyaay, with dark hair and eyes and a short, pudgy stature.

"Thank you."

"I'd better tend to the horses. You have a good day," Ben said. "Good-bye."

"Thanks, Ben. Bye."

"So," Indio said. "Jenna called yesterday."

Her voice always reminded Claire of a primitive wind instrument, such as a panpipe: low, breathy, haunting. It wove itself in and out of the melody of other family members' voices, all the while anchoring them.

"Claire, how are you?"

Tears welled. "I'm sorry."

"I know you are."

"I'm so sorry I've hurt you and Ben."

A long moment passed before Indio responded. "We love both of you." Her voice lost its strength.

"I got—I got to the point where I just couldn't go on."

"Go on with what?"

Claire cringed. Indio knew with what. It wasn't as if she hadn't noticed Max's behavior over the past thirty-some years.

"Indio, I don't want to vent to you."

"You never have."

She pressed fingertips to her eyes. No, she never had. She believed a properly submissive wife did not call the mother-in-law and gripe, especially not if that mother-in-law was as vocal about her faith as Indio was.

"Dear, I'm inviting you to vent. I really want to understand what happened."

Claire sighed to herself. After all the Christian rules she'd broken, one more couldn't matter. "I don't think I understand it myself. When he didn't show up for the dinner, something snapped inside of me. I clearly saw how I'm playing second fiddle—to the agency and every business relationship he has. I mean, I feel like a placeholder. I hold the house in place. I hold our social life in place. I hold the kids in place." *I hold his physical needs in place.* "Does any of this make any sense? Oh! Don't answer that. I am not going to drag you into it."

"Well, we are in it. That can't be helped."

Claire hugged her knees to her chest. Sugar-coating was not part of Indio's repertoire. "I've tried to be a good wife. I've tried my hardest to be the epitome of submissive. I thought I was doing things God's way. Or what I thought was His way. I'm not so sure about that anymore. I used to hear women complain about feeling like a doormat. I never did. I thought, *Wow, I must be on the right track.* Now I think if I did feel like a doormat, it might be better. At least that would mean I was noticeable. He could wipe his feet on me. I'm sorry. I'm sorry. Please forgive me."

"Oh, Claire. This is a two-way street. What you say does make sense. I know my son. I made mistakes with him. The tentacles go deep." The subject was Indio's soft spot, the only place in the musical score when her pitch went almost squeaky. "I'm sorry."

Claire knew about Indio's deep heartache. On paper, Max appeared to be a dutiful son. He gave lavishly to his parents when it came to material things. He never spoke a negative word about them. He celebrated Christmas and their anniversary with them. Yet on the everyday level, he went out of his way to avoid them. There were no drop-in visits or casual phone conversations or regular dinners.

Indio believed he still lived in the shadow of his older brother, BJ. She and Ben had placed that shadow squarely on his little-boy shoulders. BJ could do no wrong. Max did everything wrong.

As far as Claire could tell, Indio was correct. Max always heard those old voices of his parents. They continued to compare him to BJ, and he always came up short.

But, good grief, Max was a grown man.

"Indio, he's responsible for his choices. This one is not your fault."

Indio hummed out a breath, as if she were tuning the pipes. "Anyway." Her voice returned to normal. "This isn't about me. Let's get back to you. How are you?"

"Fi—" Claire stopped herself. Today she turned fifty-three. She was talking to a woman who had obviously loved her for more than thirty years. She had upset everybody's apple cart, from her husband's to her kids' to her in-laws' to her best friend's. Wasn't it time to get real?

"I was going to say fine. But I'm not fine. I'm angry, and I don't know how to be angry. I'm so upset because I've hurt my entire family. I'm at a loss as to what to do next. Oh!" A sudden, overwhelming sense of comfort burst upon Claire.

"What is it?"

"Oh!" She closed her eyes. "I just had this weird sensation. I feel all warm and cozy like . . . like—Oh my. Like when I was visiting Aunt Helen."

She hesitated. How could she describe what that childhood memory felt like? "She lived here in San Diego. I came one summer, all the way from North Carolina, without my parents or brothers. I distinctly remember snuggling with a stuffed lion in her feather bed, and I felt so incredibly . . ."

She stopped again, lost in the vivid recollection of her aunt's love. It had felt so new, so right, so incredibly— "*Safe*. That's what it was. I felt safe. I'd never felt safe before."

An awful truth struck her. Had she ever felt safe again?

"Claire." Indio paused. "Does Max scare you?"

"I—I don't know."

"But you're saying you feel safe now, away from home, away from him."

That was true. She wasn't in her own house. She wasn't with Max. Max was probably as angry with her as she with him. The future was a black hole. She shouldn't feel *safe*. But she did.

"Yes," she whispered. "That's what I feel."

Neither spoke for a few seconds.

At last Indio said, "Then perhaps you did the right thing. God will work it out for your good, for Max's good." She paused. "You know you're welcome to stay here anytime."

"I appreciate the offer, but no. I can't."

"All right. I suppose that's best. Will you keep us posted?"

"Yes."

"Maybe you could come for dinner." Indio's tone welcomed, but in a guarded way. "Happy birthday, dear."

"Thank you."

After the good-byes, Claire reached behind her and twisted open the venetian blinds. Sunlight poured into the small bedroom. Birds sang. Palm trees swept blue sky. The scent of arid summer heat drifted inside.

And she felt so . . . incredibly . . . safe.

Fourteen

Outdoors on the side porch, Indio ended her phone call with Claire and walked into the house. A few steps led her through the laundry-slash-mudroom and into the kitchen. Her private hiatus ended at that point.

Paquita Guevara stood at the island, filling a big basket with croissants. She was an ageless woman, built like a washing machine, with two long, black braids. She glanced up, concern obvious on her flat face. "How is Claire?"

"Actually . . ." Safe was how her daughter-in-law was, much as that flew in the face of reason. "She's all right."

Paquita shook her head. "So sad. But maybe for the best, hmm? Now they fix things."

Indio smiled and watched Paquita carry the basket through a doorway. It was time to serve breakfast to the guests.

Several years before, when she and Ben retired, they'd remodeled their home and turned it into a retreat center, the Hacienda Hideaway. The setting was perfect: a 150-year-old dwelling tucked away on acreage in the quiet hills above San Diego. Ben's great-great-grandfather had mined gold in the area and eventually bought the property and built the house. Beaumonts had grown up in it for generations.

Indio felt a timelessness in the old, red-tile roof and thick adobe walls. In spite of updating, the house was still the original U shape. A covered veranda hugged the interior of the U; a courtyard filled its center.

She had resisted excessive change in the kitchen. The island and appliances were new—necessary accommodations for guests—but she'd claimed the rest of the large room for personal use. The original stone fireplace and wood-plank flooring remained, along with her scruffy oak table. She added braid rugs, a couch, and her rocker. Over time she created her wall of "Jesus reminders."

At the side of the fireplace, a framed family photo hung behind the table. She stopped now in front of it, thinking about Max and Claire as she stared at the faces of her loved ones.

She and Ben weren't too keen on displaying family photos. Her husband likened it to scab picking: why keep exposing the wound? Pictures only reminded them of who wasn't there for the camera's click. Pictures only reminded them that thirty-four years ago their older son, BJ, had gone to Vietnam and never come home.

But Jenna had married, and photos were taken. And Indio adored her grandchildren. She treasured the sense they gave her of posterity, of life itself. Ben hadn't fussed at her decision to hang this one.

It was a toothy photo, everyone grinning from ear to ear.

Jenna glowed in her froufrou gown. Though her facial features were finer, and she was tall, she had—like Max and Indio—the black eyes and coarse, black hair of Indio's mother.

Kevin, her groom, was resplendent in Marine dress blues.

Erik's charm twinkled from greenish-brown eyes.

Danny, square shaped like Max, still looked boyish with curly brown hair.

Lexi, his fraternal twin, had Claire's light brown hair and was birdlike in build.

"Thinking of taking it down?"

At the sound of Ben's voice, Indio looked over her shoulder. Her husband lumbered across the room. At seventy-eight he still reminded her of Ben Cartwright on the old western television show *Bonanza*. Though his eyes weren't black, he had the identical silver mane and broad shoulders. Most often he wore a shirt with dolman sleeves, leather vest, and blue jeans. He towered over her.

"Now why would I think of taking it down?"

He raised bushy brows. His eyes, blue as the desert sky, did not twinkle. He placed an arm around her shoulders and hugged her. "Because Max's family just got a big ol' hole in it."

Fifteen

The ripple effect was going to unravel her.

Seated on the floor beside her open suitcase, Claire rummaged through clothes, unable to decide what to put on. Her earlier sense of comfort dwindled as she thought about the impact of her actions on others.

Max had a migraine.

Indio and Ben, the dearest of in-laws, were hurt.

Jenna was upset. Her distraught birthday call moments before had indicated she'd neared basket-case level.

Which would make Kevin unhappy. He would take sides.

Then Jenna would take sides. If she succumbed to that misrepresented submissive role so perfectly modeled by Claire, then her side would be the same as Kevin's.

Which would be Max's side, because now that Claire felt safe enough to admit it, Kevin had a chauvinistic streak as wide as a six-lane freeway.

She didn't want anybody taking sides!

Lexi was scared, Erik encouraging—although in a detrimental way—Danny too hung up on pat answers that would, in the end, let him down.

Tandy empathized to the unhealthy point of overeating and overdrinking. Then reversed her original opinion and concluded that Max was, after all, exactly like Trevor the Toad.

Was that supposed to help?

And what of Max's business associates? Neva and Phil—

"Claire?" There was a rap on the door.

"Come in, Tandy."

Her friend opened the door and gazed at the mess. "Whoa! I told you the closet is yours. And three drawers in the dresser."

"If I move in, then that means I've really and truly moved out."

"Aw, Claire," Tandy whispered. "It just means you'd rather not live in a chaotic environment even for a day or two."

"Oh, I don't know—Why are you whispering and shutting the door?"

Tandy leaned back against it and tucked a strand of hair behind her ear. "I thought it best to let you whine in private for a few moments. Gather your wits about you, as they say." Her smile faltered.

"No." Claire groaned.

"Yes, I'm afraid so."

"He's here?"

Tandy nodded. "With birthday gift and flowers in hand."

"I'm not even dressed yet. I'm not ready— Tandy, what do I do?"

"Take a deep breath. Get dressed." Her friend shrugged. "Smell the roses. Open the gift. And don't give in."

Melodic strains of Bach's Mass in B Minor trailed Claire down the hall. They emanated from the direction of Tandy's room. She'd promised to soak in the tub, out of earshot, with the CD volume on high.

Claire paused in the kitchen doorway and watched Max standing near the sink, coffee mug in hand, gazing out the window.

He was not a large man, but he somehow managed to fill the entire room. There had always been a presence about him. A solidity. It was one of the first things that attracted her to him.

He turned. Dark shadows ringed his eyes. "Hi." He gave her a tiny smile.

She almost melted. What was she doing? "Hi."

"Happy birthday."

"Thanks. How's your head?"

"It's all right."

"You didn't have to drive all the way over here."

"It's your birthday." He gestured toward the table. "Gift time. I thought I might still entice you to go to San Francisco. The plane's ready. A pilot is on standby."

She saw a dozen long-stemmed roses in a crystal vase. Red. Her favorite. A gold gift bag sat next to them. "Max, I'm not ready."

"For San Francisco?"

"For San Francisco. For gifts. For you. For us. For anything that resembles life as we know it."

"The status quo is so awful?"

She nodded. "It is so awful. I'm sorry."

"I'm whisking you off to your favorite city! That's so awful? I bought you diamonds! That's so awful? Claire, I don't understand this. We have a good life together. Yes, I admit, I'm a pain in the neck, that business preoccupies me at times, but—"

"At times?"

"All right, most of the time. But that's probably a good thing. You wouldn't want me around more than I already am."

"You're doing it again. Telling me what I wouldn't want."

"I'm just saying—"

"Max, I know what you're just saying. You're saying you like life the way it is. You like how we attend social-slash-business functions together. How I volunteer and keep us in the society columns. You like that I run our household. You like that I can entertain clients at the drop of a hat."

"What is so awful about any of that? You like being sociable. And you have your own life, your music, your friends."

She crossed her arms and frowned at the flowers. "Playing violin now and then with other wannabe musicians and dining out with

Tandy maybe twice a month is hardly what I'd call my own life." She snorted in frustration. "That's not the point."

"Then tell me what the point is so I know what I'm dealing with here!" His exasperated tone surpassed her own.

"I can't."

"Just try! Please."

"You never listen."

"Hey, you got my attention, all right? I am listening."

Welcome back to your real world, she berated herself. *Queen for a night with the kids. Safe and secure for half a morning while hiding out in Tandy's guest room.*

An image of a smiling Jenna flashed in her mind. *"How high, Kev?"*

How high, Max?

It was time to end it.

She pulled out a chair and sat, averting her eyes. "All right. Yes, on the surface, we have a good life. All our needs are met and then some. We have our health. We have friends. Our kids are gainfully employed." She paused. "But two nights ago those kids made me feel like a queen. You made me feel like a scullery maid."

"A scullery—That is totally ridiculous! A trip on a private jet and diamonds aren't queen treatment? Not like—what did you call it?— first fiddle? What is wrong with you?"

"Why does something have to be wrong with me?" She looked up at him. "I'm just describing how I feel. There's nothing right or wrong about how I feel."

"It's hormones, isn't it?"

"Oh, honestly, Max! We can't always reduce my feelings to that."

"But why now? Why all of a sudden is the status quo so wrong?"

"Because the status quo requires me to live a charade. To ignore what I'm really feeling, maintain an even keel, not rock anybody's boat. To bend to your every whim in order to keep you happy." She took a quick breath. "This morning when I woke up, I felt safe, all warm and cozy and secure. Then I saw you, and, *pfft.* It vanished like a puff of smoke."

He blinked a few times as if he'd been slapped in the face.

"Max, there is nothing you can *fix.* Just leave me alone."

She slid from the chair and rushed down the hall, back toward her safe room.

Sixteen

Jenna greeted her dad at the door with a long, hard hug. "Hi."

"Hi, yourself." He kissed her cheek. "Thanks for inviting me over."

"No problem. Come inside."

As he entered, Kevin shook his hand. "Hey, Max. How you doing?"

"I've been better." His attempt at a smile ended in a grimace.

Jenna studied her dad. Even if her mom hadn't told her, she would have seen the signs. He'd had a migraine the night before. The remnants were still there in the haggard droop of his shoulders, the darker-than-dark eyes, the tousled hair that normally didn't appear long enough to tousle.

"Sit, Dad." She pointed to the plate of dip and cut-up vegetables on the coffee table. "Munchies. Dinner will be ready in about half an hour. Want some iced tea?"

"Sure."

Kevin wiggled his wrist, as if pouring from a bottle.

She shook her head.

His brows went up.

She widened her eyes and shook her head again.

Still looking at her, Kevin said, "Max, you want a beer instead?"

"Sounds even better."

"When did you last take medication?" Jenna asked, glaring at Kevin.

Her father's hand waved in dismissal. "Don't worry, Mrs. Mason."

"Dad."

He leaned over and picked up a carrot stick. "Early this morning. Sevenish." He scooped dip onto the carrot. "I should thank my lucky stars I never had you for a teacher."

Kevin laughed as he strode toward the kitchen. "Some of the guys call her 'Ms. Bullhead Mason.'"

"Not to my face." Jenna tossed her head.

"I'm sure not." Her dad smiled. "You get that streak from your mom."

Jenna rolled her eyes. It was an old joke. Her mom didn't have one ounce of mulish tendencies.

"Dad, I talked to her."

"Mmm." He chewed his carrot.

"I told her you were coming over."

He nodded.

"She and Tandy and Lexi were going shopping today, then out for dinner."

He swallowed. "Good. She should have fun on her birthday." Kevin handed him a bottle. "Thanks, Kevin. Well, cheers." He held it up. "To your mom."

Kevin clanked his bottle against her dad's. "Cheers to Claire."

"Dad, we're not taking sides."

"I wouldn't want you to, hon. Your mom needs some space, and I need to give it to her. Along with a few diamonds, I guess."

"Diamonds?"

"She didn't mention my gift?"

Jenna shook her head. "She said you went over to Tandy's this morning."

"I put my gift on the table. It was unopened when I left."

"What was it?"

"Diamond necklace and earrings."

Jenna sighed. "I'm sure she loves them. You are a generous gift giver, Dad. Extravagant."

He shrugged. "I couldn't always be, you know. Not in the beginning. Couldn't afford more than one decent suit, let alone jewelry. Guess maybe I'm trying to make up for lost time." His eyes flicked in her direction. "She did mention something she wants that's beyond my means, though. Maybe that's why she's so bent out of shape."

"What does she want?"

"She wants me to sell the agency."

Jenna stared at him.

Kevin burst into laughter.

"What's so funny?" she said.

"It's so totally inconceivable! I mean, it's his life. Right, Max?"

He nodded. "I think the French call it *raison d'être*."

"Dad, give me a break. The agency is your reason for being?"

"Hon, you know the history. I was sixteen when I got my first temp job. The industry saved my life. Those first jobs and relationships got me out of bed in the mornings and in bed most nights instead of out bar hopping. Years later I started helping other guys find jobs—all those losers I'd hung out with in school. It was the biggest high I'd ever flown. Not much has changed since those days."

Jenna had no response. According to her grandmother, Max could easily have gone off the deep end if he hadn't stumbled onto this passion. And, Nana always added, met her mom, who'd been his right hand in the early days.

Why did he always forget that part of the story?

Kevin leaned forward and propped his elbows on his knees. "Did Claire give you any warning about what she was thinking?"

"No. It came totally out of the blue."

"Sounds like unnecessary roughness on the playing field."

"Dad, she gave you warnings."

Both men turned to her, puzzled expressions on their faces.

"Whenever you show up late to something, she gets real quiet. Like at our wedding rehearsal. She totally checked out after you got there. Kevin's mom thought she was sick. It happened at Nana and

Papa's anniversary dinner too. She usually buys a new outfit soon after. You know. Mall therapy."

The guys exchanged a shrug.

"That's a warning?" Kevin asked.

"It's subtle, yeah, but this kind of stuff builds up. You know?"

Her dad shook his head. "Not exactly. Our schedules often conflict. She's a busy woman. She understands. We've been like this since before you were born."

"Okay. What about yesterday? She told you to stay home or else she'd be gone. That was pretty straightforward, I think."

"Jen." Kevin's tone admonished. "We don't want to get in the middle of it."

She opened her mouth to retort but stopped herself. Somebody had to keep peace in their home. "You're right." She turned to her dad. "We're just here to offer support. You don't need our opinion."

"Thanks. Speaking of support, Kevin . . . There seems to be a problem with my grill."

Yeah. I meant to explain what happened with that."

Her dad smiled. "The new parts will be in next week. You can come over and help me put them on. So how exactly did you and Erik dismantle it?"

Jenna headed to the kitchen. Dinner with the girls would have been a lot more fun.

Seventeen

Sunday evening, Claire set two iced teas on the kitchen table next to the vase of roses and the still-unopened gift bag. She sat. "Tandy, I'll cook omelets for dinner."

"Nah. I'm used to ordering from a restaurant." Tandy stretched out, propping her feet on another chair. "There's every kind of food imaginable just two miles down the road. No muss, no fuss."

"I don't mind. You worked all day." Her friend was a real estate agent and had held two open houses that afternoon. "I napped all day."

"I'm supposed to be pampering you, remember?"

"You are."

They'd gone to the early service at Tandy's church. It was larger and noisier than Claire's, but it imparted a sense of peace. The sermon was about Jesus as the Lion of Judah, mighty protector of His people. She'd remembered again the stuffed lion from her childhood, the security she received from holding it close. She slept away the afternoon and woke up still feeling snuggled in a cloak of safety.

The phone rang, and Tandy groaned. "I can't remember why I decided to be a Realtor."

Claire rose, plucked the cordless off the counter, and handed it to her friend. "Because you're so good at it."

"Yeah, right." The phone rang again. "Which is why I still can't make ends meet without the Toad's monthly checks."

Claire opened the refrigerator and tried not to think about Max mailing her a monthly check so she could pay rent and buy food until she . . . Until she what? Taught private violin lessons? Big money to be made in that. Plenty enough for Southern California living. Maybe he would direct deposit for her. That would ease the humiliation somewhat, not having to handle a piece of paper he had handled.

Tandy answered the phone. "Hello. This is Tandy Abbott."

Claire bent over in front of the fridge and spotted eggs, green onions, cheese.

"Hi, Max."

Cool air brushed her face. Claire squinted at the fridge's bright light.

"Hold on." Tandy paused. *"Psst."*

Claire didn't move.

"He says he has to ask you about the gardener and cleaning lady."

"What's to ask?" she muttered to the egg carton. "They come. They go." Straightening, she shut the door, set the carton on the counter, and took the phone.

Tandy mouthed, "Be strong."

She nodded. "Hi."

"Hi. Just wondering if there's something I'm supposed to do for tomorrow. You know, household-wise."

"Nope." The cozy mantle of safety slid from her shoulders. Her arms prickled with goose bumps.

"Okay. Just thought I should ask."

"Mm-hmm."

"They know what to do?"

The mantle swished to the floor, soft folds piling about her feet.

"Claire?"

"Yes, they know what to do."

"All right. You ready to talk yet?"

"No."

"Should we call a counselor? Hon, I'll do anything. Oh . . . wait, hold on a sec. Phil, it's over there. Ask Neva— Sorry, Claire." His voice became muffled as if he was pressing the phone against his shirt.

Claire jerked the phone away from her ear and looked at it. *Unbelievable.* She hit the Off button.

"What?" Tandy asked.

"He told me to hold on."

"Cheeky."

"Yeah." Anger darted through her. "He was talking to Neva and Phil."

"Claire, don't let him get to you."

"Guess it's party time. Too bad they can't *grill.*"

"In all fairness, maybe he just needed to be with friends, like you with me."

"Phil, yes. But Neva?" Old, unfounded fears jumped into her imagination.

"Let it go, Claire."

"Tandy, the mind reader." She tightened her grip on the phone and clenched her other hand into a fist. "The woman has spent more of the past thirty years with him than I have!"

"It's the nature of the modern business world. Let me repeat, Max is not like Trevor."

"Oh! It doesn't really matter. If Neva wants him, she can have him."

"So you found eggs?"

The phone rang.

Claire set the phone on the counter and held up her hands as if warding off an attacker. "No way."

They listened to six more rings. Tandy's machine picked up.

Max's voice came through. "Claire, we got cut off." Silence. "Claire, I know you're there. Pick up, please."

She crossed her arms.

"This is ridiculous." He clipped his words, clearly frustrated. "I can't believe how you're behaving. Pick up the phone!"

Claire flinched. Max had never raised his voice to her like that, never said such awful words.

"All right." He lowered his voice, but the anger remained. "Be that way. I don't know how you expect us to work things out if you refuse to talk. But don't worry. I'll leave you alone from now on."

The machine went quiet. After a moment, its red light blinked on.

"I'll leave you alone . . ." It was the message Claire had wanted to hear.

Wasn't it?

Tandy handed her a paper towel. She felt, then, her cheeks, as wet as if she'd been standing in a downpour.

Eighteen

Max lost interest in alcohol before he turned twenty-one. As a teen he figured out it slowed him down too much. As a successful businessman, he could not afford to slow down.

Now, though, Claire was gone, and business success didn't seem to matter much. When his good friend Phil showed up with means to forget those most difficult of new developments, he made a conscious choice to slow down as much as possible. Life would hurt less.

"Philip." Max raised his glass toward his friend. "Have I mentioned what fortuitous foresight it was on your part to bring this magnanimous gift of rather excellent scotch?"

Phil laughed. "Only once or twice, bud."

Neva slid onto a chair across the round patio table from him. The pool shimmered behind her in the twilight. Her dark hair shone, a crown of curls. She wore a short skirt and sleeveless blouse.

"Nevie! My Dulcinea! Have I mentioned what a fine-looking woman you are?

"Max, you're really an ugly drunk."

"This is true." He enunciated each syllable with great care. If he could still do that, he wasn't too far gone, was he? "Which accounts for the reason I eschew such overindulgence. I need only one hand—nay, one finger—to number the time—since my wild and crazy adolescence—that this unhappy happystance, uh, unhappy happerstance, uh, that it has happened."

"You need some food. Dinner will be ready in a few minutes."

"Mmm, mmm, mmm. I can hardly wait. Neva's world-famous enchiladas."

"You won't like them so much after you've upchucked them."

Phil said, "It could ruin the delectable taste for life."

"Nah." Max shook his head. "Neva, have I mentioned what a fantastic cook you are? Our kitchen is strictly a la-bor-a-tory here. A place for Claire to conduct experiments. To delve into the intricacies of gourmet. Nothing quite so basic and satisfying as *enchiladas*." He savored the word, letting it roll off his tongue in true Español style. "Claire could learn a thing or two from you."

"Nope. We're not going there, mister."

"What? I can't insult her once in thirty years after what she's done?"

"I'm outta here, guys."

Max blinked a few times until Neva came back into focus. She was on her feet.

"You two can take care of each other."

"Aw, come on, Nevie. Don't you reject me too."

"Get a grip, Beaumont. Phil, I suggest you put him to bed, and stay put yourself until morning."

"Yes, please do, Philip." Max nodded solemnly. "We have a guest room, you know. The last person to sleep in it was my wife."

"Good-bye." Neva waved a hand and left.

"See you, my Dulcinea!"

Phil sat up straighter. "I hope she doesn't take the food with her."

"Who needs food? I need another drink. Where's the bottle? Uh-oh. She wouldn't take that, would she?"

"Nah. Would she? No. There it is. Good."

Max stared at the finger his friend pointed toward the booze and suddenly knew he'd had enough. "I've had my fill, Phil." He grunted. "My fill of John Barleycorn and of women. Did you know my mother rejected me?"

"Uh-oh. You're talking about your mother. Definite sign you need another drink."

"All the women in my life rejected me. Pammy in high school, junior year. DeeDee, college, second year. *Claire*. Out of the blue. After thirty-two years. Now Neva. Do you see a pattern going here?"

"Neva will be back. You sign her paycheck."

Max lifted his head and peered into Phil's face. "That's kind of low. Even in my excessively inebriated state, I can see you have a diseased attitude toward women."

"Yes, I do. Which explains why I am still a bachelor and always will be." Phil's chair scraped on the concrete. "Let's eat."

"Nope. I'm going to bed." Max staggered to his feet. "Make yourself at home."

"I don't think I have a choice. Neva rode with me. She had to take my car. And she probably hid your keys."

"She's a good woman."

"Yep. The best."

They meandered across the patio.

"Claire's a good woman too. I really do like gourmet."

Phil patted him on the back.

A few moments later Max flopped onto his bed, aware enough to realize he was still fully clothed and spinning in a fog that was, unfortunately, not quite thick enough to obliterate the image of Claire walking out of his life.

Nineteen

Late Sunday night, Claire climbed onto the lumpy mattress, Max's voice still playing in her head. *"I'll leave you alone."* It was the scariest thing she'd ever heard. Shivering, she pulled the covers tightly around her shoulders.

Maybe she should call him.

And say what?

I don't really want to live without you. I need you. Don't leave me. Come and make this work between us.

She shook her head. "No, Max, that's not it. I don't want to depend on you to save me any longer. God saved me. One time, anyway. I wonder if He would again? God, are You still listening?"

Her aunt Helen had talked about Jesus, about His love for the whole world, including His love for little Claire Marie Lambert. He had seemed real at Helen's house on the West Coast. At her parents' house on the East Coast, He did not exist.

Cancer took Helen at a young age. Claire was thirteen and had visited her only twice. Within weeks of graduating from high school, Claire headed to college in San Diego, far, far from home. She harbored great hopes that the spirit of Helen existed in the city where she had lived and died.

The first eighteen months were hazy, the details insignificant. She made new acquaintances. She went to class. She worked on campus, in an office.

Then she met Max.

She smiled now in the dark. "Remember, Max?" she whispered aloud as if he were there. "It was trite as all get-out, the way we fell in love at first sight. I can still feel the butterflies. I don't think I ate for weeks. You took me to that romantic hacienda where you grew up, and I met your parents. That was when I knew beyond a shadow of a doubt I wanted to marry you."

He didn't get along well with Ben and Indio, but Claire immediately liked them. "Family" and "Aunt Helen" were written all over their countenances. They were good, solid people she'd met within a year of BJ's disappearance. He had joined the Navy, become a pilot, and fought in Vietnam.

That was another bone of contention with Max. Although he buckled down in college—quite a feat considering he nearly failed high school—he still could not measure up. After all, his brother went off to war. His brother was a real hero.

After BJ was declared missing in action, there was no way on earth Max could ever be good enough. He competed with a ghost. Who could win at that?

Claire didn't understand much of that until later. What spoke to her, though, was Indio's unwavering trust in Christ. Even as she reeled from the news of BJ and endured months and then years of not knowing what happened to him, she proclaimed God's love for her.

In spite of Aunt Helen's and Indio's openness about their faith, Claire hadn't been interested until sometime after she and Max eloped. Their marriage and their business had both been on the verge of collapse. She had nowhere else to turn. Guilt and despair were eating her alive. She went to church and found relief in the music, in the friendly people—and in hearing that Jesus forgave her. By then she'd had major things that needed to be forgiven.

Eventually Max joined her at church. They even sought counseling with the pastor. He helped them see that love was a verb, that they needed to forgive each other, reorder their lives, and promise never to walk out.

Simple enough. They embraced Christian rules that weren't difficult to keep. They seldom missed church; they raised the children in it. They were kind and hospitable. They were generous with their money and material possessions.

The butterflies flittered away at some point, but she adored Max. Their dream to create a business to help people find jobs was coming true. Soon their first baby was on his way, another dream realized.

Things fell into place. Max was the head of their household. Claire was the epitome of a properly submissive wife.

And that was where it all went haywire.

How she had longed to be a good wife! She heard the key was in *submission*. So she listened to all the tapes and read all the books she could find on the subject and took copious notes. Her newfound knowledge could be lumped together under one title: "If Hubby Ain't Happy, It's Your Fault, Woman."

Wacky as that sounded, it suited her. She liked following orderly steps and keeping rules.

"You know what, Max? I see now that I got the title totally wrong. But you know I willingly embraced it. And I took full credit for every unhappy moment you ever had."

The absurdity of those words sank in. She yelped a loud laugh and smashed a pillow over her face to muffle the noise. "Good grief!" she squealed. "I need a shrink."

When the giggles finally subsided, she removed the pillow and sighed. "Or I need You, Lord. Are You still with me? Indio would say yes. Okay, so here's the thing: Max was only happy when he was working. Ergo, I let him work all he wanted. I took over more and more with the house and the kids. I tried not to whine or pout. Whenever he chose office over family, I let him off the hook. 'Fine. See you when you get here! No problemo!' A wife can't go around embedding hooks in her husband and then expect happy smiles from him, can she?"

She exhaled heavily. "There's more to it than that. While I was busy keeping him happy, my identity went away. It got all mixed up with his. I lost my own voice, my own opinion. I couldn't be real. I wore a mask, always pretending life was fine. I don't think that's the way it's supposed to be. Is it?"

She shut her eyes and willed her mind to stop spinning. He probably wasn't even there, let alone listening.

Claire awoke with a heart thud. On the bedside table, Beethoven rang out. Grabbing the cell phone, she glanced at the clock. It was four twenty-two.

The phone display lit up, and she saw her home number. Max was calling.

Anger flooded through her, an instantaneous bursting of a dam.

She punched the On button. "What?"

"Claire, I'm sorry."

"You said you wouldn't—"

"Claire, your dad called."

The hot flush of wrath intensified. Her dad. Typical. He hadn't thought to call on her birthday yesterday, wouldn't bother to remember to send a card or—

"It's your mom."

Her mom. Claire went still. There would be only one message about her mom.

"Honey, she's gone. I'm sorry."

Twenty

From her window seat in first class, Claire eyed the passenger beside her. Wrinkled and tanned, chunky jewels on fingers and wrists, effusing a thickly sweet fragrance, the woman displayed obscene wealth with a flourish.

She was on her third whiskey sour.

And they were only halfway to Chicago.

Claire unbuckled her seatbelt and whisked her handbag off the floor. "Excuse me." She shuffled around the woman, hit the aisle with a purposeful stride, and lurched to the back of the plane.

She was on her way to Fayetteville, North Carolina, to bury her mother. Literally bury her this time. The other time, many years ago, had been a figurative burial, a coming to terms with Alzheimer's.

"Ma'am."

Claire focused and saw she was at the tail end of the plane, alongside a galley.

A young flight attendant smiled. "That lavatory is available."

"Oh, I don't need— May I just stand here for a bit?"

"Sure. Are you all right?"

Claire nodded. Bald-faced lie.

Her mother was dead. Again. Still. For good this time.

Jenna and Lexi had offered to accompany her. They'd never known their grandmother, though. How could they? Claire hadn't known her.

At least the woman had the decency to die the day *after* Claire's birthday. Maybe that was supposed to cancel the horror she'd managed to thrust into every birthday Claire could remember from childhood.

From childhood? What about the horror of the other night? What about on her thirtieth? What about countless others since she'd married Max?

He had stepped in where her mother left off.

Claire shuddered.

Max was coming, but not *with* her. He would arrive Wednesday. He would come on the company jet as soon as he could. Certainly in time for the visitation, he said.

Typical Max snafu. He wasn't with her *here and now*.

But considering the unfinished business between them, did she even want him there?

Claire had driven home before dawn; Max greeted her with a hug. She didn't ask questions about the snores emanating from the guest room. Max simply said, "Phil." While she packed, he went about making all the arrangements for her: a limo to the airport, the flight, the hotel, a limo for in between. Neither mentioned the current situation.

Their marriage cruised into limbo.

"Ma'am, are you sure you're okay?" The flight attendant leaned toward her and whispered. "You're awfully flushed."

"I'm okay." She touched her face. It was hot and damp. Her breathing was labored. Her legs shook.

Another woman—not a flight attendant—appeared at her elbow. "Why don't you sit down here?"

"What?"

"You're welcome to sit here." She gestured at the last row, at three vacant seats.

"Oh."

The attendant touched her elbow. "I'll get you some water."

"Thank you." Claire turned and slid into the farthest seat. There was no window next to it.

"Please." The woman spoke again. "Take the aisle seat."

"No. Thank you. This is—this is . . . fine."

"That seat makes me claustrophobic."

"It's fine."

The attendant handed her a cup of water. "Here you go, ma'am. Let me know if I can get you anything else."

"Thanks."

"Remember to buckle your seatbelt while seated, please." She rushed off.

Claire's chin quivered. Water in one hand, handbag in the other, she felt helpless. She couldn't take any more. She really couldn't. A tear slid from the corner of her eye.

"Let me help." The woman lowered the tray for the seat between them, relieved her of the cup, and set it on the tray. "Now you can take care of the seatbelt. You know how they are about that." She smiled.

Claire stared at her. Her eyes were soft, a light blue. She wore a white blouse with tabs at the shoulders. She was a pilot. Maybe she thought Claire was a security problem. She should explain.

"My mother died yesterday."

"I'm sorry. Had she been ill?"

"My whole life. She was an alcoholic."

"I'm so sorry."

Claire hugged her purse tightly and turned away to cry in private.

The kicker was not her mother's life or death. It was that, in a very real sense, Claire had married her mother. Not that Max drank. In spite of Phil's snores and the half-empty bottle of scotch she'd spied in the kitchen, Max did not drink. No. Max worked.

And he would work no matter what. No matter that it had taken him out of her birthday celebration. No matter that it left her to travel alone back to the hell of her childhood. He would work until the day he died.

Why, God? Why, oh why did You do this to me? I kept all Your rules and then some. I bent over backwards to keep Max happy. He still chooses work and everyone else over me. Just like my mother. Just like my dad, who never had the time of day for me.

   Are You there, God? What is it You want from me?

   Claire unfastened the seatbelt. She slid off her shoes, pulled her knees up to her chest, and scrunched herself into a tight fetal ball, wishing with all her might that the plane would just fly her to the moon.

Twenty-one

The mere mention of Fayetteville, North Carolina, raised Max's hackles like nothing else could. Spending half a day in the city almost put him over the edge.

At least he hadn't punched anybody.

Not yet, anyway. He still had another twelve hours to go.

The main target of his animosity sat across the kitchen table from him. His name was George Lambert. Without a doubt, even at the age of eighty, he was the meanest son of a gun Max had ever met. He also happened to be Claire's dad.

"Max." She turned to him now, moving within the confines of his arm draped over the back of her chair. "What do you think?"

"Whatever you think is best, hon."

Max had no idea what they were talking about. He'd assigned himself specific jobs: take care of travel details, carry the luggage, remain by Claire's side throughout the ordeal, not punch his father-in-law, and agree to anything that would hurry along their departure.

The light touch of her hand on his knee brought him back into the present. He looked at her. "Hmm?"

"You're sure the extra weight is okay? It's ten or twelve boxes."

George set down his coffee cup. "Some are heavy." His *are* sounded like *er*. "Doodads, books, all kinds of junk. Lou never could throw a thing out."

Evidently George couldn't throw out a *thang* either. Except when it came to human beings, like a wife. He'd stuck Louise in a nursing home at the first sign of dementia fifteen years ago. And then boxed up all her stuff. Why would he bother to save her *thangs* when he couldn't hold on to her?

Max still had no idea how Claire had emerged from the likes of George, a bona fide jerk, and Louise, an alcoholic for most of her so-called sane life.

At the end of the table, Steve cleared his throat.

Steve was the number-two meanest son of a gun Max had ever met. He also happened to be Claire's younger brother. The youngest, Jim, had headed back to Alaska about thirty minutes after their mother's body was buried that afternoon. Jim was a sweet guy. Except for a few quick trips to San Diego, the funeral had been his first visit to the Lower 48 in decades.

Steve said, "The boxes are at my house. In the attic."

"Okay," Max said. "We'll pick them up in the morning, on the way to the airport."

"Won't be there in the morning."

"You or the boxes won't be there?"

Claire squeezed his knee. "What's a better time for you, Steve?"

"Now."

"All right." She looked at Max again. "So the extra weight won't be a problem? If it is, I'll sort through her things before we leave."

"It won't be a problem."

George said, "Plane's big enough, huh?"

"Yeah, it is." Max met his glare with one of his own.

The animosity was a two-way street. He'd always known that. Claire's dad had resented him since the day they'd met, probably before. It had nothing to do with Claire. She'd left her family right out of high school and hadn't looked back. It wasn't as though he'd stolen her away from them. He guessed it had more to do with machismo. A guy thing. Whose rock pile was bigger.

Claire stood. "Let's go, then."

Good idea, he thought and unclenched his fist.

That night, Claire huddled against Max in the Marriott bed.

When he'd climbed in beside her, she frowned as if in protest. He hesitated, and then she began to cry. Something broke between them.

He held her close. She hadn't cried yet, at least not in Max's presence. It was a sad type of crying, a whimpering.

He figured he'd whimper, too, given such losers for parents. His were a pain in the neck, but they couldn't hold a candle to the Lamberts. They were, hands down, a piece of work.

He kissed the top of her head. "I'm sorry you had such a terrible life."

She buried her face against his shoulder. After a time, he heard a deep sob wrench her body.

"Max, please don't leave me." Her voice was a hoarse whisper.

His response was immediate. Say what? Don't leave *her*? Was she kidding? Half the contents of her closet were at Tandy's. She left him a *note*, for goodness' sake, telling him she'd left him.

Exactly where did she get off saying not to leave her?

His anger simmered on a low burn. Sleep would be a long time in coming.

Twenty-two

"What happened to our weeks of fun in the sun?" Jenna pouted and crossed her arms.

"Jen." He stuffed his baseball glove into the gym bag on the bed. "It's only a couple games a week."

A friend of his had injured some body part, so Kevin was invited to take his place on a softball team for the remainder of the season. The league didn't play in their neighborhood. It was at least a half hour's drive to the field.

"Plus a tournament this weekend." He dug through his sock drawer. "Saturday and Sunday."

It was all news to Jenna. She'd just walked in the door after a trip to the hairdresser's and grocery store.

"But, Kevin, we have dinner plans!"

"So we'll eat late." He shoved socks into the bag and zipped it shut. Straightening, he looked at her. "I miss playing."

The little-boy expression on his face annoyed her. When a student displayed such innocence, warning bells went off in her head. It usually accompanied statements such as "I promise I'll turn it in tomorrow."

But Kevin wasn't a kid at school. He was her husband, and she loved him.

She untwined her arms, relaxed her pouting lips, and toned her voice back to normal. "I know you miss it. You haven't had a chance to play in forever. It's just that I was counting on these two weeks to be like a vacation, like we were out of town and nobody could reach us."

"We still have the days and most nights. You want to come watch?"

"Uh, gee, thanks. I always like to watch grass grow." She rolled her eyes.

"We're not talking the Padres." He winked. "You've never seen *me* play. Things start smoking when I'm out there on the field."

She laughed. "Nothing feeble about your ego, Mason."

He walked around the bed and wrapped her in a bear hug. "I'll take you out for pizza."

"No, thanks. Now that I think about it, this might be a good time to get together with Brie and some of the others." She disliked how her core group of friends seemed to be drifting apart post careers and marriages. "Maybe we can start a regular girls' night out again."

"Yeah. That sounds like fun for you."

"So, big guy, when are your games?"

"I put the schedule in the kitchen."

"Okay. I'll work on my schedule, and then I'll fix us an extra special dinner. There was a sale on porterhouse steaks."

"Mmm. Hey, thanks for understanding. I've heard some gruesome tales about wives and their apron strings."

She smiled. "You didn't seriously have doubts, did you?"

"Well, I did notice a little pout. It's been a rough week for you."

She rested against him. Her mom and dad were flying home from her grandmother's funeral, but Kevin wasn't referring to Louise Lambert's passing. Jenna had never known the woman. She'd only seen her a few times, and she was always, as her mom predicted, three sheets to the wind. Not a pretty picture. Claire never pressed the issue of that relationship. After all, the kids had Nana and Papa.

What Kevin meant by rough week was her parents. Jenna didn't know where things stood between them. Maybe they were figuring it all out over the Grand Canyon. What else could they do, stuck in a small plane together for hours on end?

He cleared his throat. "Did I mention it's a coed league?"

Jenna looked up at him. "Coed?"

"So if some gal drops out, I'll put you on the roster. Okay?" He smiled.

"Yeah, right."

He laughed.

A tug-of-war pulled on her emotions. It pulled at her mouth and arms and throat. She wanted to pout and whine and cross her arms.

No, she didn't. She was not jealous of other women—*athletic* women—playing on the same team with Kevin. She was secure in who she was. It didn't matter she'd been chosen last for every physical activity in her life, including in every PE class and neighborhood pickup game. Always, from preschool through college. It didn't matter that her one attempt at dance class ended with a broken arm when she was five. Nor did it matter that she couldn't throw a ball or swing a bat to save her life.

Nor did it matter that Kevin was well aware of all that.

"Kevin, you know you can be a real jerk?"

"I'm sorry. Bad timing for yanking your chain."

"Timing and subject matter."

"Forgive me?"

"Maybe."

He slid his hand through her hair and lowered his face to hers. "I love you. I love you just the way you are, uncoordinated and musically gifted."

She wrinkled her nose at him.

He kissed her then.

And he kept on kissing her until she forgot why it was she wanted to pout.

Late that night, Jenna awoke, fully alert. A sense of dread enveloped her.

She should have called her mom and asked about the funeral.

She hadn't because what she'd really be asking was where her mom planned to sleep that night. And Jenna wasn't exactly sure she wanted to know the answer to that question.

The clock on the dresser read two eighteen. Nighttime scents and insect noises came through the open window. Light from a streetlamp cast a yellow glow in their room.

And something wasn't right.

Beside her, Kevin sprawled on his stomach, his breathing deep and slow. When they'd first married, he never slept that way, dead to the world. In those early days he'd lie stiffly on his back, as if alert and ready for action even in his dreams.

Jenna rolled onto her side and laid a hand on his shoulder, needing to feel his strength.

As a little girl she had battled nighttime fears. Her mother and Nana encouraged her to pray through them. But, like other childish things, the uneasiness faded with time. She grew up.

So what was with tonight, all of a sudden? Nana would tell her to pray. She would tell her that God was in control.

Jenna searched her memory for the simple prayer she'd learned at her grandmother's knee. It didn't come.

God wasn't coming. Her mommy and daddy were separated, and God wasn't coming.

The sense of dread engulfed her like a heavy wool blanket, smothering her with horror.

Twenty-three

Indio aroused herself from a fitful sleep at 2:50 a.m. and gave up the notion that she could get a good night's rest.

She repositioned pillows and leaned back against them.

Ben stirred. In the bright moonlight that poured through the windows, she watched him roll from his back to his side toward her. "Need me?" he murmured.

"Yes," she whispered. *Thank You, Lord, for this man who is so in tune with me.*

"Ah." There was a grin in Ben's voice. "It's a bird night."

"Mm-hmm."

They listened for a few moments. It tickled them both to catch the odd sound of birds singing in the dead of night. They imagined that the dulcet notes were praises to the Creator.

"I should have called them, Ben." The clothespin snapped shut on her lungs again. She began to knead her chest bone.

"I recall you quit worrying about Max and Claire flying a long time ago."

"I wasn't concerned about them flying." When Max first bought the plane, Indio's faith had taken flight every time he flew in it. She bugged him, phoned after each leg of a trip, until he told her in no uncertain terms to stop. She could still hear him declaring in a sharp tone that he was not BJ, he was not a Navy pilot, he was not in Vietnam.

Indio sighed. "Maybe they reconciled on the trip."

Ben scooted up to a sitting position and put an arm around her shoulders.

She leaned into him. "It couldn't happen that fast, though, could it?"

"No, it couldn't."

"God could have made it happen that fast."

"Yes, He could."

"Oh, Ben."

"Shh." He rested his chin atop her head. "Remember our story. God had quite a few kinks to iron out along the way in our marriage. It was a long process. The same holds true for them."

"We could have taught them more diligently what we learned."

"Love, we showed them by how we relate to each other. Preaching at them would have fallen on deaf ears."

"It's just so obvious how backwards they've got it."

"Climbing up to your pulpit, are you?"

Indio ignored his remark. "They look to each other for happiness and security, like they've got the power to give that. Claire bottles things up instead of communicating with him. And he certainly is the world's worst at communicating when it comes to heart issues. Now they're reaping what they've sown, and it's destroying any shred of love they might still have for each other."

"Finished yet?"

"No. They are two selfish, selfish people."

"Who needs prayer."

I'm too mad to pray.

Now who wasn't communicating? "I don't really feel like it."

"You can be prickly, woman."

"Oooh! I just want to shake some sense into them."

He chuckled. "Listen. This is part of their journey. We can't take it for them."

She moaned against his shoulder. "Why do I lose it whenever it comes to Max? After all these years!"

"Because you keep taking back the sins God has forgiven. Yes, we screwed up parenting him. We put BJ on a pedestal and made Max feel unworthy by comparing him. But we have confessed all of it to Max and God. We've tried to make amends. We love on Max the best we know how. Indio, let it go."

"Max hasn't let it go."

"And is that your job to make him? You even think you can make him?"

"No." She wiped a tear on his cotton T-shirt.

"We can only pray for them."

"Go ahead."

"Guess we know why I woke up." He wrapped his other arm around her. "Dear Father, we come to You with praise and thanksgiving. We have anxieties about Max and Claire. We pray for their healing, for their reconciliation . . ."

He continued. After a time, Indio breathed easier. She fell asleep to the soothing rumble of her husband's voice.

Twenty-four

At 3:20 a.m., Claire shifted on the lumpy mattress and turned on the bedside lamp. She wondered if she would ever sleep again after what she had done.

Twenty-four hours ago she had been sound asleep in—of all places—a Fayetteville, North Carolina, hotel and in—this was the mind-boggler—Max's embrace.

Their morning conversation that followed had been subdued, centered around details of leaving the city.

As always, they were eager to put the city far behind them as quickly as possible. Unlike always, though, she could not shut off the childhood memories. During the cross-country flight home, they'd bombarded her. So strong was the attack, she broke a self-imposed cardinal rule set back in the days when her sole purpose in life was to keep him happy: she interrupted his work.

Maybe the fact that he had been there for her prompted her to move from the window to the aisle seat across from him. The jet could accommodate eight. Max had chosen to sit apart from her. He'd spread his work things on the seat beside his, opened up the laptop, and explained that he wanted to finish some things so he'd have less to do when they got home.

"I told you about feeling safe at Tandy's?"

He looked up from his laptop, a question on his face as if he hadn't heard her.

She repeated herself. "Remember I said I felt safe at Tandy's?"

His black eyes were onyx hard, his thin lips a straight line. Clearly he was in business mode.

"Max, I need to talk."

He exhaled as if he'd been holding his breath. "I thought you might use this time to rest."

"My mind won't stop. Do you remember? Being at Tandy's reminded me of being at Aunt Helen's and sleeping with my stuffed lion, all cuddled up in safety."

"You said when I showed up that feeling vanished like a puff of smoke."

She nodded. "Last night it was different. I—I felt all cuddled up in safety. Thank you."

He gave a half nod.

"Actually, I felt safe from the moment you walked into the funeral home."

The corners of his mouth dented inward.

She had imagined he might not show up at all for the visitation. But he'd come, and only fifteen minutes late. He marched in, a determined expression on his face—the one he always displayed in Fayetteville. It wordlessly announced, "Don't mess with me."

His black designer suit and teal rep tie stood out in sharp contrast to what others wore. Although shorter than her dad and brothers by several inches, his square frame and that presence he carried made him appear bigger and stronger. He had gone immediately to her side and hadn't left it until boarding his private jet.

She said, "It reminded me of when we first dated. I knew you could whup my dad with one hand tied behind your back."

The corners of his mouth slid a millimeter upward. "I didn't meet your family until after we eloped."

"But they still scared me long-distance. You made all the difference, almost the instant we met in the college library. My knight in shining armor. I remember the first time we spent the night together. I didn't miss my stuffed lion after that."

She wondered when she had begun to miss the lion again. She wondered if Max wondered.

He smiled. "Our first night together, I thought I'd died and gone to heaven."

"It's a good memory, then?"

He laughed.

She dug in her handbag for a tissue.

The pilot interrupted, coming back to tell them something, and the moment passed. Afterward, Max excused himself and returned to his laptop. She blew her nose and eventually napped.

One-sided as it was, the conversation with Max had felt good and right. Traces of security lingered even as they landed in San Diego. In the limousine she scooted next to him until their shoulders touched. Quiet was okay, as long as he was close by. Maybe they could go home and begin figuring out what had happened last week. Maybe her mother-in-law's reconciliation prayers were being answered.

He took her hand. "Claire, I have to stop at the office. My car's in the lot. I told the driver to take you on home. I should be there in, uh, an hour." He squeezed her hand and let it go.

She stiffened. His ballpark guesses on time never hit the mark, and he knew that. And he knew that she knew.

"Two hours, tops. You can get settled in. We can order pizza. Or I'll swing by Mille Fleurs, bring home something nice. I'll call you before I leave. We can decide then."

"Mm-hmm."

"You'll be fine, hon. I won't be long. I know how hard this trip was on you."

"Mm-hmm."

Ten silent minutes later, he kissed her on the cheek and got out at the office, attaché and overnight bag in hand.

Two minutes after that, alone in the back of the limo speeding toward home, Claire began to shiver. Fears swooped upon her, typ-

ical aftershocks from a visit to her hometown. She felt an overwhelming sense of insecurity and ugliness. She usually managed to swat such
thoughts away by reminding herself she was an intelligent, grown
woman with a family who loved her and important community work
to do.

But her defenses were down tonight, lowered because Max had
comforted her. He had made her feel safe and secure. He had shown
up at the funeral home, her knight.

Now he was gone. *Pfft.* Like the wind.

She should have told him she needed him to stay with her. One
or two or whatever hours from then would be too late.

But hadn't she already told him? Hadn't she already revealed her
heart to him in such an obvious way that even he could catch on?
Hadn't she given him all the credit for her feelings of safety and security? Last night she had begged him not to leave her. Why wouldn't
he care enough to skip the office for one evening?

Because his heart remained impenetrable. He couldn't feel a
thing. He thought all was fine again now that she'd cried on his
shoulder. He figured they'd carry on, slide back into the status quo.

Shortly before the exit to her house, she gave the driver Tandy's
address. He had to backtrack, get off the freeway and back on, take
another one that cut inland, meet heavy side-road traffic. She figured the extra cost was less than her funeral costs, which she surely
would incur if she drove herself.

The man carried her luggage and all those heavy boxes of her
mother's into Tandy's condo, stacking them neatly along the entry
wall. Her friend didn't even raise an eyebrow.

Claire reached Max on his cell at the office. "I'm at Tandy's."

"Oh, honey."

She closed her eyes. His term of endearment didn't touch the sore
part inside of her. "Thank you for being at the funeral and after. It—
it just isn't enough."

"I don't know how else to do it."

"And I don't know how else to say I can't keep it up."

"Keep what up? Our life? Blast it, Claire! I don't get it! Weren't we just fine on the plane?"

"We were fine on the plane, and then *you went back to work*. You left me, Max! You leave me every single time work takes precedence over us."

"That's quite a stretch, Claire. Another low blow. Worse than the stale commercial remark."

"I'm sorry."

"Yeah. Guess that's why you've moved out."

"I'm sorry." She pressed a fist to her stomach. "I don't think I have a choice. For now."

"For now. Well, do me a small favor and call when 'now' is over." Deep anger and hurt came through his tone.

Her stomach ached. "I'm sorry. I—I'll call." She didn't know how to end the conversation.

Max did. He hung up.

Twenty-five

Claire really didn't know why she was there.

Fingers gripped around the steering wheel, she gazed across the big parking lot. She had parked several rows away, out of sight of any casual observer, but the angle gave her a clear view of the Beaumont Staffing storefront.

Was she going inside or not?

It was a busy place, centered in the strip mall between a gift shop and a travel agency.

If she went inside, she would have to smile at the front desk women and ask if Max was available, and could they please page him if he wasn't in his office.

It galled her, how she had to ask permission to see her own husband. Millions of dollars in sales had made him inaccessible.

Someone emerged now from the building. A young woman. Attractive, with shoulder-length blonde hair. She grinned and glanced over her shoulder.

Max was on her heels.

They stood together on the sidewalk, conversing, laughing. Max touched her forearm.

Tandy said somebody was going to sue him someday. Claire doubted it. He was too endearing. Women loved him.

Max gave the stranger a quick, one-armed hug, and then he went back inside as she walked away.

The whole thing lasted only three minutes, but waves of fear and anger gushed through Claire.

No way was she going inside.

Unable to either get out of the car or drive away, Claire just sat and waited for the pain to subside. She hadn't always despised the business. Beaumont Staffing truly was a dream come true. Max's dream, first of all, but he welcomed her to join him in it.

Thirty-three years ago next month, she and Max had found the office space. Back then it had been small and unassuming. But it had grown up along with the palm trees around the lot. The entrance doors were now double ones and led into an expanded version of the original area. Plate-glass windows revealed a busy lobby. A large sign sat atop the walkway overhang. *Beaumont Staffing—The Door to Your Future.* Royal blue lettering and silver designs. Overall the effect was warm and welcoming.

Had they been crazy or what? They'd planned to save the world one person at a time by finding them employment. Caution never entered their minds. With wild abandonment, they signed a year's lease on this very office. She remembered the owner's bewilderment, how he shook his head as if he couldn't believe he had agreed to such generous terms.

It was all Max, of course. She knew firsthand the force of his personality. It was infectious. She hadn't been able to get enough of him. Eight months after the lunacy of love at first sight, she eloped with him, eager to be his wife and his business partner, forever and ever.

Tears burned, and she pressed her lips together to keep from crying. What had happened to them?

"Claire?"

Startled at the voice calling out her name, Claire turned toward the window and saw Neva, longtime employee at Beaumont Staffing. The woman moved in her direction, skirting several parked vehicles.

Claire's muscles tensed. Her tears vanished, and she arranged her expression into something more neutral: not quite friendly, not quite cold.

Steeling herself like that was an old, habitual response to Neva. There were obvious reasons for it. Neva was everything Claire was not: petite and cute and bilingual with an intriguing accent. And Max's business partner.

Neva reached the empty slot next to Claire's car and removed her sunglasses. "Hi. How are you?"

"Okay." Her smiled faltered. "You know."

"Yeah."

"How are you?"

"Concerned for you and Max." Neva's eyes glistened.

That was the other thing about Neva that bugged Claire. She could be so kind. It made it difficult to unabashedly dislike her.

"Thanks," she said.

"Are you coming inside?"

"I . . . Max and I . . ." She shrugged. Ten days had passed since they'd last talked. There were household details needing attention, new roles to be determined, boundaries to explore. No wonder she'd been sitting in the hot car for half an hour. She'd forgotten how to throw caution to the wind and embrace the unknown.

"Yeah," Neva said again, as if she totally understood Claire's dilemma. "Do you have time for coffee?" She nodded toward a Starbucks at one end of the mall.

Claire's muscles relaxed a little. She didn't mind delaying her encounter with Max, even if it meant hanging out with Neva. "Sure."

They sat at a corner table and sipped iced Americanos.

Claire asked, "Does Max still avoid this place?"

"You mean like the plague?" Neva chuckled. "No. He either had to give up espresso or his one-man boycott against the entire chain."

Claire's stomach tightened again. It was news to her. Max, the eternal supporter of "the little guy," such as he himself once was, refused to patronize the coffee chain store when she was with him.

Neva said, "You know how we'd send the newest staff person to get him coffee at that independent café down the road?"

She nodded.

"About eight months ago we hired Sarah. Have you met her?"

Claire hadn't, but she took a wild guess. "Long blonde hair?"

"Yeah. She's different." Neva's eyebrows rose. "Kind of flaky but endearing. Save the whales and all that. She reminds me of Lexi. Anyway, Sarah refused to waste gas driving when she could simply walk a few steps to the evil chain store. So she bought coffee here and put it in a thermos mug. Then she'd wait to give it to him, pretending it took her longer than it actually did. One day she forgot to wait long enough, and he caught on. He just laughed and quit the boycott that very day."

"Why?"

"Why what?"

"Why did he quit?"

Neva's smile faded. "He realized how silly he was being, I suppose."

"And he realized that because this Sarah called him on it."

"Well, we all supported her."

"Whatever." Claire heard the envy in her tone, but she wasn't about to pull back now. She was always playing second fiddle to the likes of Sarah and Neva. "You know what, Neva? I feel left out of Max's life. The office is his home; the staff is his family. It's always been that way."

"We're not. Not really."

"Give me a break. I mean, does this not register with you? A stranger named Sarah can call him on something and he flip-flops long-held, die-hard convictions. I finally call him on his marital priorities, but he doesn't laugh. He doesn't even consider changing one thing about his lifestyle."

"I don't know how you waited so long."

Claire blinked, taken aback.

"Really. My ex-husband couldn't even handle it for five years before he moved out." Abruptly, she lifted her coffee and directed all her attention to taking a drink.

Another wave of ambivalence rolled through Claire, a churning mix of fondness, respect, envy, and anger. The anger part rose to the top.

"Is there more to that analogy?" She snapped her words. "Like maybe the agency is your first priority too? That there was no reason for you to leave it in order to save your marriage?"

Neva looked up. "Claire, I didn't mean it that way. I was over thirty before I married. I should have known better. He didn't understand my lifestyle from the get-go or why I wasn't interested in having children. He didn't understand my passion for working with people. You and Max have a long history together."

"A long history of me playing second fiddle."

"It could look like that. If you think of Max as playing first fiddle, though, it explains why Beaumont Staffing is so great. You two work as a team. You've always given him the freedom to succeed."

"Right. That was my role—to let him go succeed outside the family. But while he was off being free and happy, our marriage got lost along the way."

Neva nodded. "It seems inevitable in this culture, doesn't it? Oh, Claire. You'll work it out. You and Max are special."

In the warmth of Neva's concern, Claire's anger melted. "You don't think I'm being unreasonable, then?"

"Let's just say I'm a woman who can empathize. I'm also his coworker." She winced. "And the consummate fence-sitter. It's the best way to urge clients and temps to get along."

Claire studied Neva's unlined face, its delicate features. In it she saw a femininity and an independent streak—qualities she herself did not possess.

"Neva, you probably wouldn't put up with a man who gave 99 percent of his attention to another woman."

"Max doesn't—"

"Yes, he does! The staff is made up mostly of women. Women who adore him because he's charming and attentive."

"Okay, okay. He is those things, but it's not like he's there because we're mostly women."

"The thing is, though, you are in his day-to-day life, and I'm not. Sarah can change his mind, but I can't. That just doesn't seem right somehow, does it?"

Neva opened her mouth to speak. Claire didn't give her the chance. "It's not about Max playing first fiddle! It's about you and his entire staff playing first fiddle instead of me. And now I'd better leave." She stood. "Before I make a complete fool of myself."

As if she hadn't already.

She hurried back out into the bright sunshine and the safe confines of her car, where no one could witness her meltdown.

Twenty-six

Max touched the leather passenger seat as he climbed into Claire's car. "Yow! Hot! Why don't you have the air on?" He saw the key in the ignition, reached over, and turned it.

Seated in the driver's seat, Claire tsked. "Sarah would disapprove."

"Sarah?"

"Your ecoflake." Claire's face gleamed with perspiration.

"What does Sarah have to do with us sitting in a hot car?"

"She didn't want to waste gas driving to some coffee shop down the road, so you changed your mind about Starbucks. I thought the same principle might apply here. We can endure a little heat to help save the planet."

"We're meeting in the car, Claire. If you came inside, it wouldn't be an issue."

She turned away and pressed the automatic buttons to close the windows. As they swished upward, he shut his door and flipped the fan on high.

Claire had phoned him from the parking lot and said she wanted to talk, but she didn't want to come into the office. After ten days of not hearing from her, he would have agreed to almost anything, unreasonable or not.

In an attempt to play things her way, he hadn't called her. Not because of any great self-discipline. Who needed to bother with discipline when anger served the same purpose? If she wanted space, he'd give her all the space in the world and then some. He had plenty to keep himself occupied.

But just that morning he'd whiffed one of Phil's mediocre serves on the tennis court and promptly thwacked his racket against the clay floor. His already overfilled schedule now included trips to the sporting goods store and the chiropractor.

The truth was, he missed her. Yes, he did. And he could be man enough to admit it.

"Sorry, Claire. I could say hello first and complain second."

She turned to face him, her eyes hidden behind dark sunglasses. Fine lines bunched up around her compressed lips. "Hello."

"How are you?"

"Okay."

"Reach any conclusions yet?"

"Max." She exhaled loudly. "You're pressing. I can't handle that."

He wiped a hand across his mouth, pushing back a smart retort.

"I just wanted to touch base," she said. "In person."

"Why?" He caught sight of wrinkles crimping around her lips again. How was it he kept saying the wrong thing? "Sorry. It doesn't matter why. I'm glad you came. I miss you, honey."

"Max, do you realize you call Neva 'hon' and 'honey'?"

"I don't—"

"You do. As well as most females. And you hug everybody."

"Yes, everybody. Men and women. I'm demonstrative that way. I admit it."

"Don't change the subject. I used to get so jealous. But then, you know what? I figured out you're not even aware of what you're doing."

"I'm not. No big deal."

"Right. No big deal. Except where does that leave me? Hugs and honeys mean diddly-squat from you."

He stared at her. "Why didn't you tell me?"

"Right. You would have told me I was being overly sensitive and to forget it."

He rubbed the back of his neck. Her accusation hit home. He would have said she was being overly sensitive. He told her that often enough because she *was* oversensitive about the most ridiculous things.

"Claire, we're getting nowhere fast here. This can't be what you came to talk about." Frustration was eating a hole in his gut.

"No." She bit her lip. "I came because I wanted to ask you in person to forgive me for putting you through this."

"Hon—Claire, of course I forgive you. But what are you going to do?"

She didn't answer right away. "I want to play my violin. I want to play seriously again. And I . . ."

"And you what?"

"Remember the stuffed lion? How I felt safe with it, and then I didn't need it anymore after we got together because you made me feel safe?"

"Yeah."

"I want to figure out why it was I stopped feeling safe with you."

He shook his head. "I don't get it."

"You don't have to, Max. I don't know if you can. Look at this." She held out her hand. "I'm shaking like a leaf because I'm actually telling you what I think and feel and I'm not pretending I don't hurt inside." She took a deep breath and released it. "I guess while I'm at it, I might as well tell you everything. I bought a stuffed lion at a toy store. His name is Judah."

The absurdity of her words smacked him like a two-by-four to the head. A stupid stuffed toy? Who did she think she was, to turn their world upside down? To think she could just quit her life and ask forgiveness? To blame him for her fears? To sleep with a stuffed animal instead of him?

He stopped weighing his words. "Well, if you're only sleeping with a stuffed animal, I guess that's fine. *Is* he the only one you're sleeping with?"

"I never— Honestly, Max!"

"Evidently I'm letting you down again, like I did thirty-two years ago." His voice rose. "I was just wondering, that's all."

"How dare you bring that up! That's got nothing to do with—"

"It doesn't? It's got everything to do with it. I'm not what you need me to be, so you're just going to quit."

"You never forgave me that, did you? And you won't forgive me this. And I wonder why my hands shake when I'm with you?"

"That's right. Blame it all on me. Just like the other time."

"Get out of my car!"

His hand was already pulling on the handle. "Gladly." He climbed out and slammed the door shut.

The window went down, and Claire leaned toward it. "Oh, by the way . . . happy anniversary."

He watched her drive off, the white luxury car gliding down the long row. Red brake lights lit up. The car turned right, left. It reached the exit, stopped momentarily, and cruised out onto the busy four-lane.

Anniversary?

A searing heat raced like wildfire through Max, consuming even the anger.

How had he forgotten?

Twenty-seven

Late afternoon sun rays scorched the hills above San Diego. Indio, kneeling in the Hacienda Hideaway's front yard, wiped her shirtsleeve over her sweaty brow. She grasped a squishy green tendril between her gloved hands and tried to wring the life right out of it.

Beside her, Lexi laughed. "Nana, pull like this." She swiftly yanked a three-foot section of the ice plant clear out of the dirt, roots and all.

"Child, I swear your scrawny arms don't have a muscle on them. How do you manage that so effortlessly?"

Lexi jerked another piece loose and plopped it on the growing pile behind her. "I guess you're just too old." She raised her chin and made eye contact from beneath a floppy straw hat. A smile tugged at her lips.

Indio leaned back on her heels and chuckled. "You think that lame challenge is going to help?"

"Of course it will." Lexi giggled. "It's so easy to get your hackles up."

Indio cherished the moment. The girl laughed too seldom, even prior to the mayhem her parents had stirred up.

"Nana, I want to cover this whole section with purple alyssum and rosemary."

Indio surveyed the landscape.

They owned more than three hundred acres, inherited from Ben's family. Sparse vegetation grew on the hilly, desertlike terrain.

Occasional oaks and eucalyptus provided areas of shade. There was a gravel drive and a parking area.

The pale greens and browns had always bothered Lexi. She'd been planting flowers on the place since she was five years old.

Indio turned to her now. "Lovely as new plants sound, why now? This ice plant is healthy and flowering and holding the terrace in place. And it's such a dry year. I don't like the thought of watering."

Her granddaughter jerked out another section with a violent twist of her body. "Sometimes you just have to *kill* off the old to make way for the new." Her tone was harsh. She muttered an expletive.

Indio stared at the back of Lexi's hat. The girl wasn't talking about flowers. "What's on your mind, child?"

Lexi remained quiet for a long moment. It was her way. Indio waited.

"Nana." Lexi paused. "Was Uncle BJ like Dad?"

Something between a sigh and a groan constricted Indio's throat. Being a grandmother, she thought—and not for the first time—was more difficult than being a mother. Not the "If Mama says no, ask Grandma" part. Spoiling was the easy part. It was the idea that all things being equal, she would die or become incapacitated long before she could pass on to Lexi everything she had learned from life.

Lexi glanced over a shoulder at her and then turned back to her work. "If you don't feel like talking about him . . ."

"No, it's all right. What are you thinking of? I've told you a lot about your uncle BJ through the years."

Lexi nodded, still bent over the ground. "Mostly just facts, though. He was taller than Dad and looked more like Papa. He got better grades than Dad. He was an all-star athlete. He never got in trouble when he was a kid. He was a Navy pilot. He's been MIA for a long . . . long time." Lexi paused, as did everyone at that point in BJ's history.

His was a never-ending story.

Lexi said, "And he would be fifty-seven this year."

"Yes. What is it you don't know yet?"

Lexi's hands stilled over the dirt. "Would he have been so hung up on making money that he would reject his family?"

Indio pulled off her gloves and crawled over to Lexi. "Oh, child. Come here." She enveloped her in a hug, knocking off the big hat.

Lexi cried softly against her shoulder.

"Your daddy hasn't rejected you, not deep inside his heart. He wouldn't do that. He just . . . he just got sidetracked along the way." She smoothed back Lexi's long, damp hair.

Dying plants lay in piles all about them. The earth lay bare, exposed to the sun's blistering heat. It looked the way life felt.

What a mess, Lord. What a mess.

She rocked her granddaughter and let her weep in silence.

Lexi didn't cry for long. Indio let her slide from her arms. With a wordless nod of thanks, she sniffed, jammed her hat back atop her head, and grabbed hold of another section of ice plant. Indio joined her.

Of the four grandchildren, Lexi disquieted Indio the most. There was something broken inside of her. Indio imagined the girl's struggle had begun in the womb, a space she'd had to share with her twin, Daniel. With his boundless energy and single-mindedness, the boy rivaled Winnie the Pooh's springy friend Tigger. He could easily have sucked the life right out of Lexi before birth. Not that he didn't adore his little sister, but he'd emerged fully clothed in confidence and ability. Lexi came out naked as a jaybird.

Indio didn't think that was it, though. Lexi worked diligently and forged ways around her dyslexia and shyness. She improved all the time, creating beauty in her art and her gardening. No, that wasn't it. Indio believed "it," the core issue, was the rejection she felt from her dad.

The old guilt reared its ugly head again.

Indio had become a mother at the age of eighteen. She was too young. It didn't matter that BJ was the ideal child. Within two years Max was born, and he wasn't the ideal anything except squeaky wheel. He got attention, all right, but not the nurturing sort he needed.

Lexi interrupted Indio's reverie with a gesture toward the road, a long stretch of dirt. It meandered like a question mark through trees and hills, a full ten-minute drive up from the main highway hidden from view.

She looked that direction and saw dust swirls in the distance. A car was coming.

"It's Mom," Lexi said.

Indio recognized the fancy white vehicle. She sat back on her haunches and waited.

"Today's their anniversary." Lexi's voice sank to a whisper.

Apparently Max and Claire were not celebrating together this year.

Indio sighed. She loved her daughter-in-law and considered her a friend. Claire was the best thing that could have happened to Max. Indio thanked God often for her impact on his life.

But now, on the very date she had welcomed Claire into the Beaumont family with open arms, Indio wanted nothing more than to tell the woman to turn that car around, take all the junk she'd stirred up, and head back on down the hill.

Twenty-eight

Claire, if you keep churning away like that, I won't have to buy any butter this week."

At the sound of Indio's critical tone, Claire squirmed. She hadn't moved a muscle, but her mother-in-law saw inside her as though she were some dissected bug under a microscope.

In self-defense, Claire sputtered an apology she didn't really mean. "Excuse me for coming tonight. I don't know why I did."

She should leave, but embarrassment glued her legs to the big wicker chair. She seldom sniped at her mother-in-law, even when Indio was at her most annoying.

Of course, Claire knew why she had come.

The scene before her was like sitting inside a hug. She and Indio had lingered in the dusky courtyard after dinner, drinking iced herbal tea. Water trickled down the fountain's tiers. Now and then a gentle breeze jiggled a distant wind chime, clunking bamboo in a soft, natural rhythm. Flowering bushes perfumed the night air.

Nearby, light poured out from the living room's open double doors. Inside, Lexi and Ben played their perpetual game of canasta. Samson, the big old golden retriever, would be nestled under the table, while Willow, the frisky cat, swished her fluffy yellow tail in his face, inviting him to run with her.

At last Indio broke the silence. "We both know why you came. It's why Lexi comes. The Hacienda Hideaway is a safe harbor for you."

"The dynamics seem a bit off tonight."

"Anger can do that, you know. Snuff the peace right out of a place in two seconds flat."

Guilt landed so heavily, it could have been the dog jumping onto her lap. She thought again how she used to believe wives should not be angry. She did not like feeling anger, but what she liked even less now was denying its existence.

"All right, yes. I am angry. He forgot what day it was. He forgot today is our anniversary."

"Did you expect him to remember it?"

"I had hoped so."

"In the middle of what's going on?"

Now Indio was defending Max!

"Actually, I thought because it *is* in the middle of this mess, he would remember more easily than ever. A person who cared would be extra sensitive to things like anniversaries. I thought he would feel upset. I thought if I went to see him, it would help. Silly me."

Indio didn't respond.

Good grief. Claire knew she'd always behaved as if it was her wifely duty to comfort Max and thereby keep him happy. Maybe, though, she'd gone to see him earlier that day more for her own sake. If he felt better, she would certainly feel better. But it had all backfired, and now she seethed with anger and embarrassment.

"Indio, am I responsible for his happiness?"

"No, you're not." The older woman sighed heavily. "I'm thinking about a speaker who was here once to lead a retreat. I'll never forget what he said. According to him, the human brain is wired with a craving for relationship, for meaningful connection with other humans. We need it like we need air to breathe. We get desperate if we don't have it."

"Well, any loving relationship Max and I ever had has gone down the tubes, and I am feeling desperate."

"What happened? Do you know?"

He left me. Over and over and over again, he left me. And now she had left in a desperate attempt to what? Fix things? Or end things?

Claire said, "I don't understand it. But, Indio, I am so sorry for hurting you."

"Can't be helped." Her mother-in-law grimaced and rubbed an area around her breastbone, her stubby fingers making circular motions.

"Are you all right?"

"Hmm. Just feel a little tightness in here."

"Have you felt it before?"

"Now and then. It's just plain old stress. You'd think I would have learned by now how to let it go."

"I'm sorry. I shouldn't have come. I'm sorry for—"

"Claire, stop apologizing. That won't make anything all right."

Indio's chastisement rained over her again like hot sparks from a bonfire. Claire flushed from the singeing. Sometimes she really did not like her mother-in-law.

Indio stood. "Well, I'm tired, so I will excuse myself. If you don't want to drive back into town, you know you're welcome to sleep in one of the guest rooms."

Claire swallowed one last apologetic lament. "Thanks. Good night, Indio."

The older woman walked away, her usual spry step slowed.

I'm sorry, God. I am so sorry.

Claire did not mean to remain in the courtyard. She wanted to leave, but the hot ash of Indio's words hung thick in the air, blinding her to an escape route.

Indio was angry. There'd been no welcome tone in her invitation to stay. She'd told her to stop apologizing.

But how else was she supposed to deal with the guilt? Go back to Max and pretend everything was hunky-dory?

Oh, God. What do You want from me?

Hey, Mom." Lexi slid onto the wicker chair vacated by Indio, the yellow cat draped in her arms.

The guilt crescendoed now. Claire's ears rang with it.

"Papa won at canasta," Lexi said. "Again. Surprise, surprise. I told him grandpas shouldn't be so competitive. He didn't agree."

With effort, Claire tuned in to her daughter and hung on to her words. Lexi hurt. She needed Claire to be her mom. No matter her age, she would always need that. Claire would not—she simply would not—repeat her own mother's behavior. Claire was a nurturer. She *was.*

Lexi was still speaking. "He is so way ahead in points, it's not even funny. I swear, he hasn't let me win since I turned twenty-five."

Claire cleared her throat. "That was awhile ago," she teased. "When did you catch on?"

"About the time I turned twenty-six last spring." Lexi slouched and draped a leg over the chair arm, swinging her foot. "Happy anniversary."

"Umm . . . I don't know what to say."

"I talked to Danny this morning. He said if you and Dad hadn't married, we wouldn't exist."

"Good point. Thank you, then. I'm glad you and Danny exist."

"Me too."

"I was just thinking about when I first met Nana. Your dad brought me here for dinner. I actually told her while we were doing dishes that her son and I wanted to elope."

"Really?" Lexi grinned. "I never heard this."

"You know how she is. She made me feel so at home, right off the bat. I could tell her anything. Your dad said I was like a can of soda all shaken up. Nana popped the tab, and I fizzed out all over the place."

Lexi laughed.

Claire joined in. "It was true. I was so excited. They were the family I never had."

"Then why did you elope?"

"Lots of reasons, I guess." How often had she wished she and Max had done it differently?

"You always said it was because you didn't have any money for a wedding, and your parents didn't either."

"Mm-hmm."

"But you could have had a small one so at least Papa and Nana could have come. I bet they would have liked that. They had so much fun at Jenna's."

"*Everybody* had fun at Jenna's."

"Yeah, like half the city."

They exchanged a smile.

Lexi said, "I guess money helps. Who wouldn't have fun with hundreds of people, live music, dancing, free food galore, and an ocean view?" She slowed her swinging foot. "But, Mom, of all places! Why did you and Dad choose Las Vegas? Major yuck."

"It was affordable, and we thought it was really special because we had to leave town to get to it. At least the minister wasn't an Elvis impersonator. Although I think the guy in the motel room next to ours was."

Lexi chuckled. "Seriously, didn't you ever dream about a big wedding?"

Claire shifted in her seat. "No. Yes. No. I guess on one level I did, like most girls. But on another, realistic level, I knew it couldn't happen. It wasn't just the money. You know my mother's condition. Can you imagine . . ." She shuddered even now at the thought of her mom stumbling down a church aisle, clinging to an usher's arm, jabbering slurred words. "And my dad. I've told you, he never hit me or anything, but he never smiled at me either or said anything nice. I truly didn't want him around to ruin my day."

"That's sad."

Claire gazed at her daughter. Her long, straight hair fell across her face. She was slight of build, the opposite of the other three, who always seemed so solid by comparison. Lexi was like a delicate feather, her voice as gentle as the sound of a piccolo.

"Don't you think it's sad?"

From the mouths of babes. "No, Lexi, I always thought it was just the way things were."

"Yeah. I can see that. Sort of like I think it's just the way things were. With my dad."

Claire held her breath. "How's that?"

"He wasn't around much." Lexi shrugged.

"If that's what you remember most about him, that's sad."

"Guess that makes for two sad stories, huh? At least he made it to Jenna's wedding, and on time. Do you want to spend the night here?"

"Are you?"

"Yep. Paquita promised me waffles in the morning. I brought a video. We could make popcorn and watch it?"

Claire heard the little girl's heart in Lexi's suggestion. Her grandpa wouldn't let her win at canasta anymore, but maybe she needed a few cards stacked in her favor. Maybe Claire could ease her sadness a tiny bit. And maybe Lexi could do the same for her.

At the moment, all she wanted to do was curl up into a ball and hope the emptiness inside wouldn't kill her.

Twenty-nine

"Max, you can't keep this up." Neva stood on the other side of his desk, hands on hips.

He leaned back in his leather chair. "You look like you're ready for a fight."

"I am. It's 8:30 p.m. Five women are still here working and crying because you yapped orders at them that they couldn't possibly complete by five o'clock. You've been fussing at staff like that for over a week now. You need a haircut. You're walking around like Quasimodo." She jerked up a shoulder and tilted her head at an awkward angle. "Why didn't you go to the chiro after your little temper tantrum with the tennis racket?"

He could only blink in the face of her barrage.

She straightened her head and shoulder. "You know what I think? I think you're feeling a little sorry for old Maxwell Beaumont. His wife has hurt him, so he's going to lash out at anyone in his path, including his employees. He's hurt his wife and doesn't deserve to take care of himself."

"I'm sorry for the other night."

"You already told me that." She crossed her arms.

"I mean I'm really sorry."

"I know you are. Again, I forgive you for acting like a bozo. Under the circumstances—or should I say influence?—it was a one-time, understandable thing. But now it's time to pick yourself up and climb out of the gutter."

He pinched the bridge of his nose. "Today's our anniversary. I forgot."

When he looked up, she was sitting in a chair, chin propped in her hand, a forlorn expression wrinkling her brow.

"I screwed up big-time." *Way beyond the old "snafu" antics.*

"Did you admit that to her?"

"She won't answer her phone."

"Did you leave a message?"

He rolled his eyes.

"Of course you did." She paused. "You don't want to get blitzed again, do you?"

"No. I want to work until I drop dead."

"That's fine. Go ahead. But your staff is not joining you in that endeavor."

"I don't know what to do."

"Take care of yourself. Shut down the computer, and get out of here. Have you eaten anything today?"

"A muffin." Her advice dangled before him like a hand over the edge of a cliff, ready to pull him up before he slid down any farther toward the jagged rocks below. "Will you have dinner with me?"

"What? You need somebody to keep you company?" The softness on her face removed any sting in her biting question.

"Just for a couple more hours."

She stood. "I was thinking pasta."

They went to Little Italy and sat on the patio in the back of the restaurant.

It was Claire's favorite restaurant for pasta.

At least Max thought it was her favorite. Maybe it wasn't. Maybe she hadn't been real about that either.

The patio was open to the stars. It was a funky place, surrounded by two-story walls that looked like something from an old Florentine neighborhood. An open staircase led up to a second-story door. A clothesline with permanently displayed laundry hung above one corner.

He watched Neva dip a piece of foccacia into olive oil. "Is this Claire's favorite place for pasta?"

Neva looked over at him, the bread in her hand millimeters from her mouth. "I've heard her say that several times. Whenever we've all come here together, she says it is."

"I don't know whether to believe her anymore about anything." He picked up a large piece of bread, jabbed it into the puddle of oil, and crammed it into his mouth.

Neva swallowed. "Want to talk about business instead? It might be better for your digestive system."

"She says she can't be real with me." He spoke around the chunk of food in his mouth.

"Why not?"

He shrugged. "Says I don't want to hear it."

"There might be some truth to that."

He gulped his diet cola. "I'm listening."

"Years ago she and I talked about how she believed a wife was supposed to submit to a husband. It was when you two first started going to church. She was pretty gung ho on the subject. She went so far as to say that if you weren't happy and contented, it was her fault. And she said it with a big smile, like she'd discovered life's greatest secret. Like taking care of you was her purpose for being."

He reached for the bread basket, lifted the napkin, and took out another piece.

"Oh my gosh. Max! You believe that, don't you?"

"Not put that way exactly."

"Put it any which way near that, and there's no way on earth she could be real with you."

"She keeps the peace in our home. She makes it all work."

"Yeah! She wouldn't dare upset the apple cart. She's no wallflower.

She speaks her mind when she wants. But like I said before, I some-times thought she should have nailed your carcass to the wall, because you can be such a bear. Like today at the office. But she couldn't do that, could she? Not under those rules."

"We don't have rules."

"Yes, you do."

"She had an affair."

Neva's eyes widened. She closed her mouth on whatever opinion she was about to render. Her hands stilled at the sides of her salad plate.

"It was a long time ago. You were there. In the early days, when we were losing money hand over fist."

"I knew you two were having problems. Who wouldn't, with their business going down the tubes? But I had no idea . . . What . . ." She went speechless again.

"She gave violin lessons at a music store. She met someone. It was . . . brief. The guilt was more than she could handle. She started going to church. I had no clue until she told me months after the fact. Then I started going to church. The pastor counseled us. I really wanted things to work out between us. We got through it."

"Why are you telling me this now? She's not seeing . . . ?"

"She says no. But . . . who knows?" He blew out a breath. "I don't think I'm hungry."

"Max." Neva reached across the table, turned his hand over, and laced her fingers with his. "You have every right to feel angry and confused, but you will eat."

Is that what he felt? Angry and confused? Well, he could come up with more apropos adjectives, but the point was, he was *feeling*. That should make Claire happy.

Neva squeezed his hand and let go. "Now eat."

He picked up his fork, speared a lettuce leaf, and tried to ignore two suddenly glaring facts. One, he was having dinner, *on his anniversary*, with another woman. And two, the touch of Neva's skin against his burned, as if he'd held onto a blazing match too long.

Thirty

It was after midnight at the hacienda.

Claire brushed her hair in front of the bathroom mirror. She didn't look so good. The highlighted strands of hair struck her as overdone. She should let the color go natural, not concern herself with pretending there wasn't any gray creeping through the brown. Dark circles rimmed her eyes; lines bunched at her mouth. Evidently she'd lost the ability to hide the fact that she was under stress.

Was that progress?

She wore a sleep shirt, one from Lexi's stash of clothes that her daughter kept at the hacienda. It was baggy with big sleeves, loose enough to conceal the turkey-wing arms, five-months-pregnant-like tummy paunch, and cottage cheese thighs. Large velveteen letters splashed a message across her anything-but-perky chest. It read "Hey, Bud, Let's Party."

She should call Max. Of course, he hadn't remembered the date. She'd upset his world, probably more than she imagined possible. Had she really expected him to remember? Who did she think she was, to upset him and then drop in unexpectedly and want "normal" from him? She should call him.

He had left a voice mail. He had apologized. He was sorry for forgetting their anniversary.

For forgetting their anniversary.

Forgetting their anniversary?

She laid the hairbrush on the vanity and felt her insides tighten in anger, the sensation almost frightening in its intensity.

Who was she kidding? He hadn't apologized for his attack. Hadn't even mentioned how he'd once again thrown her past in her face. Did he truly still hold that incident of thirty-two years ago against her? How much longer would he let that wound fester?

And really, how could he accuse her of quitting? *Her?* He was the one who had quit. He'd abandoned them as a married couple. He'd buried himself at work, usually with good old Neva at his side.

Not all that much had changed, had it? Was it even worth thinking it ever would?

She studied the T-shirt again in the mirror and smiled—a grimace that twisted her lips. So Max wanted to hold on to the past? Well, let him. She planned on moving forward.

"Okay, bud. Let's party."

Thirty-one

Jenna strolled with her mom through the dark across Tandy's front yard and giggled. "I can't believe what just went on in there."

Claire snickered. "But you had a good time."

"Yes, Mom, I had a good time hanging out with your weird friends and playing our instruments together."

"Knew you would." She elbowed Jenna. "It's so wonderful making music for no reason at all except to feel sheer joy."

"I felt like when we were on that Alaskan cruise. There were no words to describe what we saw. It was beyond breathtaking."

"That's it exactly. Don't you miss music?"

"We always have music going. Dave Matthews Band, Tim McGraw, Beatles, Ray LaMontagne. All kinds. Once in a while I even sneak in Bach or Telemann, and Kevin says, 'Whoa. That's cool.'"

"I don't mean just listening. I mean creating it yourself. I think about all those years you studied piano and viola. All those concerts. You should take the piano from the house. Squeeze it into your apartment."

"Right. It wouldn't even fit in the center of the living room."

They reached her car parked at the curb. Jenna put her viola case in the backseat. "You know, I never really enjoyed playing that much."

"Really?"

"Really. Sorry to burst your bubble, Mom. But tonight was different. I wasn't uptight about performing. It was fun. Thanks."

"I'm so glad. You're welcome to come again. Two weeks from tonight, same time, same place."

Jenna chuckled. "Wow. Biweekly quintets at Tandy Abbott's condo. A minor in music at UCSD opens all sorts of exclusive doors for me. Is this Dad's hard-earned dollars at work or what?"

"And the best part is no fees and no dues."

"No salary. We could schedule some gigs. Weddings would be nice."

Claire laughed. "That would put you back into performing mode."

"I suppose. Mom, it's so good to hear you laugh."

She leaned her forehead against Jenna's. "You should hear it from this side."

Jenna smiled through a twinge of unease. Why was her mom so happy not living with her dad?

Claire straightened. "Seriously, Jen, I loved having you here. I don't want you to feel obligated, though. You are not responsible for my happiness."

Jenna bit her lip.

"By the way, I didn't invite you to keep me company tonight. I simply knew you'd be an excellent addition. And besides, we couldn't have a quintet without a fifth."

Jenna smiled. "I'll come back because I enjoyed it. And Kevin's life these days is football. I seem to have plenty of free time on my hands."

"You're okay with that?"

"Sure. It's the way it is with a coach during season."

"Great."

"You don't believe me. But really, Mom, I would whine if I weren't okay with it."

"Just meddling—I mean checking." Her mom sighed. "The thing is, I should have been a better role model for you as a wife."

"Are you kidding? You and Dad were Mike and Carol Brady in the flesh. All my friends thought so. Why else did we hang out so much at our house?"

"I know. Compared to some, we appeared to have it all together. What disturbs me now, though, is how I never openly disagreed with your dad. I want you to know that wasn't healthy."

"I sure didn't pick up the habit. Kevin hears my mind no matter what."

"But sometimes . . ."

"Sometimes what?"

"Sometimes you hold back and—"

"What are you talking about?"

"Hon, I don't mean to upset you. I admit, I'm overly sensitive these days. I'm probably overreacting too. The night of my birthday dinner, I heard you give in to Kevin's opinion a few times." She held up a palm. "On-the-surface, insignificant things—"

"Like what?"

"Like about your classroom. What you do with your bulletin boards. Like what you teach, still pushing the old books, like *To Kill a Mockingbird*. He made fun of that, and you didn't tell him where to get off."

"He teases."

"He was putting you down. The point is, you reminded me of myself. And in my case the insignificant added up over the years until I lost track of my own voice. I lost sight of my own passion. I gave up music. I hadn't played my violin for ages until Tandy and I got this group together last year. I just don't want the same thing happening to you."

Her mother's fervent plea subdued Jenna. "How did it happen to you?"

"Slowly. Subtly. I played in the symphony, you know, early on. That was a dream come true. Then we decided to get married and start the business. My little side job wouldn't pay enough to justify the hours spent on practicing. So I quit. There wasn't an opportunity to go back. I did teach violin for a little while, but Beaumont Staffing consumed us those first few years, and then Erik was born."

"The agency always consumed Dad."

"It's his passion. And I adopted it because he was my knight in shining armor. I adored whatever was important to him, even to the point of giving up my passion."

"Well, I haven't adopted a passion for softball or football. I haven't quit teaching to help Kevin coach or mentor a bunch of teenage guys. And my students will still read *Mockingbird* this year."

"Then you're off to a better start than I was. Balance is the key, and I didn't have it. That's what I didn't model. Will you forgive me?"

"Mom, there's nothing to forgive."

Her mother didn't respond for a moment. "Maybe not now, hon. But someday, if you find yourself looking at him to get his approval before you speak your mind, then remember this conversation."

"You didn't really look at Dad—"

"Yes, I really did. Literally as well as figuratively. If he wasn't in the room, I imagined him hearing me." She blew out a breath. "That's what this is all about—finding my own voice again. I know it seems like I'm throwing the baby out with the bathwater by leaving him, but I don't see any other way to do it."

Questions whirled in Jenna's mind. Why couldn't her mom do it from home? How would she know if she found her voice? Was the separation temporary? Did she have a time frame?

But Jenna wasn't sure she wanted to hear the answers.

Thirty-two

"Bravo!"

"That was quite lovely, Ms. Beaumont. Very accomplished."

Claire smiled and lowered the violin, propping it on her lap. "Thank you."

"Thank *you*."

The two strangers sitting in the front row of the auditorium turned from her and conferred quietly between themselves, while Claire pressed the toe of her shoe against the other ankle, hard enough for it to hurt. She wasn't dreaming.

Unsure of protocol at this point, she simply watched the man and woman from her seat in the orchestra pit. Her smile stretched from closed lips to a cheek-aching grin that surely revealed every tooth in her mouth. Her chest heaved as another rush of adrenaline shot through her.

They liked her performance. *They*. People who knew about such things.

The man was the conductor of the San Diego Symphony. The woman was related in some way to hiring and firing and officiating at auditions.

And *they* thought *Claire Beaumont* deserved a *bravo*.

She felt like a schoolgirl soaking up a teacher's praise. She probably looked downright sappy.

The man stood, gave a little wave in her direction, turned, and walked away.

The woman said, "How soon can you join us?"

The adrenaline surge propelled Claire through blocks and blocks of the downtown area. Her skirt swished; her violin case bounced at her side; her feet danced in flats. Every so often a chuckle slipped out.

People, buildings, trolley tracks, and crosswalks barely registered on her radar. She headed toward the water. Still grinning, she finally reached Seaport Village. The festive tourist spot encompassed a myriad of shops and restaurants as well as trickling fountains, a carousel, and a walkway along the bay.

The place was summertime crowded. Like a bee to a hive, she homed in on the book-and-coffee shop, where she ordered some sort of iced coffee drink with a raft of sweet fixings. Outdoors again, she headed away from the shops to where a small peninsula jutted out into the bay. At the first available park bench, she sat and let the view overtake her.

Brilliant sunlight glittered on the water. An aircraft carrier glided under the Coronado Bridge. A water taxi skittered in the distance. Sailboats bobbed. The sky shone, an aquamarine gemstone so luminescent she had to squint her eyes to look at it.

The largeness of it all calmed her until the need to jump out of her skin subsided. At last the grin shrank, and her lungs offered sufficient air. She exhaled a "Whew" and felt a sense of deep gratitude.

So many details had come together to bring about this moment: A reawakened desire to play music . . . Daily hours spent practicing for no apparent purpose . . . The full-time violinist opening with the symphony the day she tried out for a sub's position . . . The courage it took to even inquire, not to mention to audition . . .

On the way downtown that morning, she had twice driven onto freeway exit lanes, intent on turning back, certain she would look like an absolute fool playing, after all these years, in front of professionals. But something had kept her going. And now there she was. Newly hired violinist with the San Diego Symphony.

She sipped coffee through the straw and pulled her cell phone from her bag. Who to call first?

Jenna would appreciate the news. But . . . Claire thought she had maxed out on drawing emotional support from her older daughter.

Probably from Lexi and the guys as well. Not that those three understood her infatuation with orchestras.

Tandy was with clients. Other musical friends were at work.

Indio? No. She wanted to keep her at a comfortable arm's length.

She had other friends. But over the past weeks they had slid into "mere acquaintances." All those women she'd served with for twenty years on boards and committees had floated out of her life just like that aircraft carrier sailing by now. At the mention of "I quit" and "personal reasons," they became hesitant and then unavailable.

Max.

Should she tell him? Did she want to?

Since their non-anniversary conversation in the car two weeks before, she had successfully avoided talking to him. He had left his message, an apology about forgetting the date. It almost prompted her to call him.

It was his only message. Evidently he had successfully avoided talking to her too.

She wished she wanted to tell him.

But he'd always considered her music a waste of time. Even before they married, his disinterest was obvious. "It's a nice hobby for you," he would say. "Do you have to practice when I'm at home?" "You spent how many hours playing?"

Why would she tell him she'd just landed a spot with the symphony?

There really wasn't anyone to share her good news with.

Claire lost interest in the coffee and set it on the bench. Her stomach ached in a familiar way—the way of loneliness.

Most days she could manage it. Most years she had. Life was full. Life was good—

Good grief. Did she live in denial or what? Maybe it was time to face painful truths.

What was good about life? Her parents had rejected her. Her husband had checked out ages ago. Erik lived life in the fast lane. Lexi seemed always on the verge of crumbling. Like Max, Danny worked too much. Like Claire, Jenna kowtowed to her husband but refused to admit it. Indio and Ben probably—and rightfully—hoped their daughter-in-law would get lost. Her friendships were based on societal mores. She had emotionally quit attending church sometime along the way.

And last, she had left her husband. Moved out. Broken her marriage vows. Brought shame on her family. Did not have a clue how to fix things with him. Wasn't quite sure she even wanted to.

Her life was in shambles. It had been for some time. So what that she'd landed a job? Big deal. Nothing mattered, because everything that mattered was gone.

A sense of paralysis crept over Claire. She sat very still, hands clutched on her lap, eyes open, seeing nothing, while panic hovered, eager to pounce if she so much as blinked.

Because no matter how she tried to fix her life, it just got worse.

Thirty-three

Jenna stepped nearer to Kevin and took hold of the arm hanging stiffly at his side. She glanced up at him.

From narrowed eyes to set jaw, he personified every clichéd depiction of an intense football coach watching his players get in position at the start of the most important game of the season. He even wore the school colors, his royal blue sport coat and silver tie.

But his boys weren't on the field. They were at a cemetery, surrounding the casket of a team member's older brother.

Jenna heard a barked command.

Boom!

The three-volley salute erupted. She started at each blast of the rifles.

Boom!

Kevin didn't move a muscle.

Boom!

Jenna remembered how he'd cried last week when they heard the news that Brock Albans had been killed in Iraq. He was a graduate of their school, a member of their community.

Then Kevin quit crying, and life took on a pall. He reported that football practice alternated between grieving sessions and tackling that resembled attempts to slaughter.

She stole another glance at him. His stoic expression hadn't changed. If anything, his features were more set. They could have been carved out of rock.

Intense football coach? Not exactly. Kevin was a Marine. He would not forfeit.

How's my football widow?"

Jenna spun around from the bulletin board. "Kevin!"

Grinning, he crossed her classroom in a few quick strides.

"You scared me!"

"Sorry." He scooped her up in a warm embrace.

"Mmm." She placed her hands on his shoulders and leaned back to look up at him. He wore a jersey with the sleeves cut off and sweat shorts—his workout clothes for warm summer afternoons.

"It's only four o'clock. Aren't you supposed to be at practice?"

"I cut it short." He tapped her forehead. "And not because of what you're thinking."

"What am I thinking?" She played innocent.

"That double practices are insane. That the guys need a break before school starts next week."

"Oh?"

"Okay." He rolled his eyes. "All that might be a little bit true, I admit. But mostly I sent them home because I missed you."

"Well, aren't you Mr. Smooth Talker?"

"I try. And I'm hungry for a big steak." He winked. "Thought I'd pick up a couple on the way home. We can have a quiet dinner and catch up. Okay?"

"And here I was, counting on us falling asleep over pizza and the eleven o'clock news."

"Ha-ha."

He interrupted her laugh with a kiss.

"Mmm. Thanks, Kevin," she whispered. "I've missed you."

"Thanks for understanding, pretty lady."

There was a loud rap on the open door. "Hey!"

She and Kevin turned to see Cade Edmunds, the high school principal.

"No smooching in the classroom!" he shouted.

They laughed at him.

The nearing-forty, balding man didn't crack a smile. He simply waved and continued on his way.

Kevin chuckled. "He's jealous. Bachelorhood stinks."

"I heard—" Jenna caught sight of something as Kevin turned. "What's this?"

"What's what?"

"This." She pulled on his elbow, trying to force him to turn his upper arm toward her again.

He resisted. "Nothing."

She frowned.

"It's a surprise. For later."

"You're bleeding. On your tattoo."

"I'm not . . ." He twisted his head and raised his shoulder. "Oh. Maybe a little."

"Kevin!" She stepped around him. "What is it?"

"A new tat."

"A new—" She winced at the sight of black letters, some with teensy red droplets. They covered a small area, slightly above the eagle and toward his back.

"Oops." He wiped a finger across it. "Missed a spot. I just had it done. At noon, between practices."

"Kevin!"

"I was hoping you wouldn't notice it yet."

"Kevin!"

He touched her arm, and she met his eyes. Under his steady gaze, she willed herself not to squeal his name again.

"I did it for the team. You know how military guys are having the names of their fallen buddies tattooed?"

No, she didn't know that.

"The kids are all gung ho about having it done with Brock's name. Most of them aren't old enough yet. I want to show my support. I mean, some of these kids could be over there fighting in a year. The war just came home to them in an ugly way." He turned his arm toward her. "See? It says 'Brock.'"

"Oh! My! Gosh! I cannot believe it!" She stared at the block letters that looked more like tiny bruises.

"They couldn't believe it either. But, man. What an impact. We connected."

"They've always respected you. They look up to you."

"This is different. I don't know. It's a guy thing, I guess. You can't understand."

"But your arm!"

"It doesn't hurt."

Pain wasn't her concern. Kevin didn't do pain. Her problem was with his marred body. One tattoo, okay. That was the way he came. But now, some stranger's name? As a tribute? As a rallying point for his football players? Teenagers he probably wouldn't ever see again after they graduated?

"Jen." He was doing his sheepish imitation. "They were having twofers."

"What?" Her voice hit the stratosphere.

He hooked his thumbs under the bottom of his jersey and scrunched it up and over his head, keeping it stretched between his arms. "I was kidding about the twofers. But how could I get one name and not the one most important to me?" He turned his back to her and hunched his shoulders.

There, up high between the blades, in flowing, three-inch script, was her name. *Jen.* The *J* was made of double lines, its hook snaking down and under the bone—

"So what do you think?" He turned again to face her, pulling the jersey back down.

"I—I—," she stuttered. What did she think? *That he couldn't have. Really!*

"Did you notice the color?"

Besides yuck?

"It's blue. Sapphire."

Sapphire. Her favorite.

His waggled his brows. "Pretty cool, huh?"

"I don't know what to say."

She had told him the very first night they met. *Tattoos turn me off. They're revolting.* Of course, the two of them had been flirting when she said it, and of course, she fell in love with him anyway. But she had made subsequent comments. Hadn't she? Things like his tattoo was okay, because it was *his* and was only *one*, and it didn't spoil the entire surface of his skin. Hadn't he heard her?

"You're shocked and amazed." Kevin chuckled. "He did a good job, don't you think? I thought the—what's it called?—calligraphy looked appropriate for an English teacher." He cupped her face in his hands and planted a solid kiss on her mouth. "And just think: it's permanent! See you at home."

She watched him walk across the room. At the door he smiled, and then he was gone.

A tickle curled up her spine. His kisses could do that; they could produce a radiating exhilaration. But she didn't think that noun exactly captured the essence of what she felt at the moment.

Thirty-four

A 'Jen' tattoo? That's . . ." Claire cleared her throat, searching for noninflammatory phrases. Her daughter didn't need any encouragement along those lines. "That's creative."

"Oh, Mom. Go ahead and say it. It's disgusting!" Jenna stretched out on the carpet, propping her elbow on the floor, head resting against her hand. "My friend Emmi will think it's the most macho thing in the world. She is so antediluvian! She'll sigh and get all gaga over the fact that Kevin would go through such pain for me. And just imagine! For the rest of his life, the world will know. Or at least everybody who happens to see his bare back—say, people at the beach, walking behind him—that someone named Jen is important to him. Or *was*. 'Brock' is the name of a deceased person. I just don't get it."

"I don't, either, but it probably makes sense to him."

Claire pushed aside a cardboard box and leaned against the wall. They were in Tandy's condo, sprawled on the floor between the entryway and adjoining living room and the old boxes that had belonged to Claire's mother. That afternoon she had finally dismantled the stack. After sifting through a few, she was grateful for a break from the smelly contents when Jenna stopped by unannounced on the way home from her school.

"Hon, why didn't you tell him straight-out that it's disgusting to you?"

Jenna reached for the plate of homemade peanut butter cookies she'd found in the kitchen. "Comfort food really does work." She

136

chewed for a moment, lost in thought. "I didn't want to hurt his feelings. I didn't lie; I didn't say it was great. I could have said, 'Kevin! That is so gross! If it's supposed to speak to me, you missed the mark by a long shot. Emmi will like it, but you're not married to her. And another thing. It makes me feel like I'm some kind of *item* you own, like your baseball card collection. Well, I've got a news flash for you, bud. I'm not, and I think tattoos are ugly.'"

"That's, uh, straightforward."

"Then it's good, right? It's what you've been saying you weren't with Dad, and you should have been."

Aha! Her daughter had paid attention. Claire spoke with caution. "Yes, that's what I've been saying. The trick is how to mix in some tact."

"I could use synonyms for 'gross' and 'ugly.' I'll get out my thesaurus."

Claire smiled. "Mind if I do a little comparison? Oh, come on, Jen, don't roll your eyes. Give me a chance."

"Okay."

"All right. I see myself opening yet another extravagant gift from your dad."

"Like diamonds? I heard you got new ones for your birthday."

"Mm-hmm. And they would still be wrapped up if Tandy hadn't threatened to haul the bag out to the trash bin along with my mom's boxes. Which is why I'm opening them too. Anyway, my reaction would be . . ." She closed her eyes and lilted her voice. "Max! These are perfect." She opened her eyes. "Then I would wear them to the next three social events. And then I would put them in my own safe-deposit box at the bank. I would wonder why he doesn't know, after all this time, that I like plants and earthy clothes and that I only wear this gold chain, a watch, and simple earrings, if any jewelry at all." She bit her lip. "I'm not saying he never gave me anything I liked."

"I know. You've taken some awesome trips. And included us kids on some."

"Yeah. But all that aside, there's a really sad consequence to not communicating openly." She'd adopted Lexi's admonition that, yes, hers was indeed a sad story. Why deny that fact any longer?

Jenna stared at her, speechless, a half-eaten cookie in her hand, apprehension written all over her face. She really didn't want any more marital advice.

But Claire's feet were firmly planted on her soapbox. Her daughter needed to hear this. "The really sad consequence is that I thought by not telling him how I truly felt, I was helping him. It was how I boosted his ego. And my job was to boost his ego, to keep him feeling good."

Jenna shook her head, eyes still wide. "Who says?"

"Books and sermons."

"That's what you were taught? For real? And you fell for it?"

The truth smacked Claire like a sucker punch and sent her flying off the soapbox. Hearing Jenna bring her thoughts to light revealed their absurdity. What a ridiculous excuse, to blame some old teachers and a handful of skewed how-to books for her behavior over the past thirty years.

"Mom, why on earth would you believe such bunk? It's so lame!"

"In all honesty, it was probably more the way I interpreted the teaching."

"But why?"

Why indeed? Her mind whirled. If she had been straightforward with Max about her feelings and opinions, then what?

Then he would have reacted as he did in her car on their anniversary. He would have lashed out. He would have reminded her again and again of what she had done wrong, piling on the guilt.

She looked over at her daughter. "I liked my interpretation. It gave me handles on how to be a good wife, rules to follow. It worked because it kept the peace. Above all, I wanted the peace. The safety. So I guess I truly wasn't doing it to protect his ego. I did it to protect my own well-being." She gestured toward the boxes. "I didn't want to live my mother's life."

Jenna blinked a few times as if filing that tidbit away, maybe in the trash can. "Okay. Moving right along, what would you do differently today?"

Claire sighed. "I don't know, hon. Right now I'm still in over-reactive mode. I want to bite his head off."

Jenna only stared.

"I'm sorry, hon. I'm dumping on you. A healthy person would see that gifts are only symptoms of the big picture. If I was communicating openly about everything with your dad, then gifts wouldn't be such a major deal."

"Well, this is major. Kevin's using up his *skin*. If he gets as many tattoos as Dad gave you diamonds, we're in big trouble."

"You sound like me, going off the deep end. See? That's the sort of thing—"

"Okay, okay, Mom. I forgive you for not being a perfect role model. But I have to figure out what to do with this situation now."

"Oh, Jenna, I can't tell you what you should do. I didn't do it right. If I ever figure out what right is, it might not be right for you."

"Great. That helps a lot."

"Have another cookie." She picked one up for herself. "Tandy and her sweet tooth. I've gained ten pounds in five weeks."

Jenna put her half-eaten cookie back on the plate. "So I should be truthful in a respectful way."

"It's a tall order."

"He'll . . ." She bit her nail. "He'll take it personally if I say I don't really care for this . . . this gift of his, no matter how nicely I phrase it. He might even say other women would love it and that I can be such a princess."

The cookie in Claire's mouth tasted like dirt. Jenna was figuring things out. She didn't need Claire to blast both barrels in Kevin's direction.

"Okay." Jenna took a deep breath and sat up. "I'd better go home and eat steak."

Claire stopped herself from asking Jenna if she even liked steak. She'd challenged her enough for one day.

"Whoa!" Tandy's hands clapped like crashing cymbals. "Claire Beaumont! Are you pushing the envelope here or what?"

She probably shouldn't have told her friend about the conversation with Jenna. "You're way too exuberant over this." Still seated on the floor, surrounded by boxes, she ripped the yellowed, crusty tape from another one.

Tandy leaned forward from her cross-legged position until she was in Claire's face. "But doesn't it feel great knowing you admitted mistakes to your daughter? That is so freeing."

"She left in a worse funk than the one she arrived in. I don't think I helped matters."

"Of course you did. The point isn't to smooth the bumps in her marriage. You can't do that. Being real with her is what she needs."

"I just hope we don't both end up raving feminists with ulcers."

Tandy laughed.

"I'm sorry about these boxes." Claire pulled a stack of books from one. "They reek. Cigarette smoke, must, and mildew."

"This, too, shall pass, as soon as you finish this absurd exercise. Seriously, why don't you just pitch the things?"

"Paying penance for being the firstborn and only daughter?" She shrugged. "I don't know."

"Maybe you're looking for answers. Like why she was looped all the time."

"She wasn't all the time." Claire heard irritation in her clipped words.

"Really?"

"Really."

"When did it start?"

"I don't know."

"When is the first time you remember?"

Claire dug through the box, pulling out knickknacks, papers, books, and clothing, all shoved in willy-nilly by somebody. Most likely her sister-in-law. There were loose photos that made her stomach lurch. George and Louise, young, skinny, and smiling. She'd never met those people.

"Claire, when is the first time you remember?"

"I was eight. I was in second grade."

"Sweetie, look at me."

"Tandy." She kept her eyes downcast and didn't even pretend to disguise her annoyance. "I'm not going there."

"You're already there. It's in those boxes. You lived through that hell once. Why put yourself through it again?"

"I want to find out who she was. You're right. I want to find out *why.*"

"She was sick."

"But why did she take that first drink?"

"Because she had lousy parents too. Just like everybody does to some degree, in some way, shape, or form. We cope; we compensate. If we're smart, we admit they fell asleep on the job, but then, with God's help, we forgive them, and we move on."

Gathering up another stack of junk from the box, Claire said quietly, "I thought I forgave her. Maybe I'm looking for closure in this junk here." She opened a faded manila envelope and removed what appeared to be a legal document. "Maybe I'm— Oh!" Words and numbers caught her eye. She squinted and skimmed over them again. They refused to cohere.

"What?"

"I need my glasses. Where are my glasses?" She flailed about, scattering papers and books. "What did I do with my—"

"Here." Tandy handed them to her. "They were on the table."

Claire slid them on and studied the paper. Her hands shook, and the print bounced.

"Claire?"

"It's a— Oh! I don't believe this! It's my parents' marriage license. And it says . . ." She read it again, did the math again, doubted her own age. "I'm fifty-three, right?"

"Yeah . . ."

She looked up. "Then they got married four and a half months before I was born."

Tandy shrugged. "It was the fifties. If you got pregnant, you *had* to get married. Didn't you know their anniversary date?"

"Apparently not. I thought they got married a year earlier. That's what they said. My mother's obituary gives the year before I was born, because that's what we all thought it was. Dad never corrected us."

"People used to be majorly ashamed of such things. They would lie to save face. Even fifty-three years later."

"No one told me. Not that any of my grandparents were around. Aunt Helen would have thought I was too young to know, and then she died."

"You can punch that empty box with your fists."

Claire's nails cut into her palms. She squeezed them more tightly to stop the tremble in her hands. "I just don't get this. What were they thinking? What difference on earth would it have made to tell us the truth?"

"Maybe they thought they were protecting you. Saving face for you as well as themselves."

"*Pfft.* Like I had any face left to save. My mom showed up plastered at classroom parties, and my dad pretended I didn't exist."

She stared at Tandy as understanding suddenly dawned on her. She could see it light her friend's eyes at the same time. Pain blossomed in her belly. "He didn't want me to exist," she whispered hollowly.

Tandy pressed her lips together and tilted her head in silent, agonizing agreement.

"He did not . . ." Claire pulled the truth from some dark closet in her soul that she didn't even know existed. "He did not want to get married."

They stared at each other.

"Maybe," Tandy said, "maybe he felt trapped."

"Yeah. She could have trapped him on purpose. She used to say she and I were alike, because she couldn't wait to get away from her family either. Only she didn't have a scholarship to some fancy school to help her. All she could do was wait tables and hope some available guy would sit down. Guess Dad was it. He was actually engaged to someone else when they met."

"So he had other plans."

"Yes. I heard that bit of information exchanged during arguments. Mom seemed jealous of the other woman. Then Dad would bring up the fact that he'd planned to go to trade school and then open his own car repair shop. None of that happened because he got married. And, evidently, had a kid right away. Of course, he blamed Mom."

"Of course. The woman is always blamed."

"The wife. The daughter."

"It's not your fault."

"Tell that to the little girl whose dad never said a kind word. Whose mom got plastered instead of feeding her little boys. Oh, God." Claire covered her face with her hands. "I'm not going there. I am not going there."

Tandy's arm came around her shoulders. "Shh, Claire. It's okay. It's okay."

Thirty-five

Pillow talk always worked best with Kevin, and so Jenna waited through the evening before bringing up the subject.

The bedroom lamp was dim, and his eyes were at half-mast when she finally said, "Kevin, I truly appreciate your gesture by getting my name tattooed on your back. But I don't like tattoos. Not really."

He yawned. "Since when?"

Jenna stroked his cheek. "Since always. I've told you."

"I always thought you were joking. I mean, what's not to like? It's art. It expresses who I am. This one expresses my love for you."

"I appreciate the gesture. I really do."

"Yeah, you already said that. So what's not to like?"

"Maybe it's just not my kind of art."

"Okay. But it's mine."

"But your body is mine."

"Huh?"

"You know. All that stuff about becoming one flesh. The pastor explained it at premarital counseling."

"Jen, that was about sex, not tattoos."

"Yeah, well, if I were bald and weighed more than you, would I still turn you on?"

"Of course. You'd still be you. I love you, not your body. Well, I do love your body, but you get my drift."

"What if both my legs were amputated? What if I were in a wheelchair?"

"Hold on a sec. This isn't about art."

"Neither is a tattoo!"

"You're saying the sight of me doesn't turn you on just because I got two new pieces of *artwork* that you can't even see unless I take off my shirt and turn around?"

"It's not artwork!"

"Is that what you're saying? The sight of me turns you off?"

She blinked back tears. "If you get any more, that's what I'm saying."

"So what you're really saying is that appearances are more important than what's inside a person."

"No, I'm not. I would love you no matter what you looked like. But I am not attracted to tattoos. That's all."

"They embarrass you, don't they?"

"Probably. They make me think of losers. Gang members and jarheads."

His face went hard.

Uh-oh. She'd treaded on sacred ground. "You know what I mean. I don't think you're a loser."

"But I am a jarhead."

"You *were*, before we got married."

"There is no 'ex-' in 'Marine.' You married a jarhead with a tat."

She closed her eyes briefly and considered the thought. It was all semantics to her. "Okay, technically, I did."

"Technically and every which way you did. Get over it. You are such a princess." He nearly spat the term.

"I am. I admit it. You married a princess who wishes her husband didn't have new tattoos. Will you please not get any more? Not because I would love you less, but because you love me."

"I do love you, Jen, even when you're a royal pain. And I will always love you, even after you're gray and wrinkly and broad as a barn because giving birth to six kids did a number on you. But I will not promise no more tattoos. I will not be henpecked by someone who can't promise that same kind of love in return. Good night."

He kissed her forehead and rolled over.

Stunned, she lay unmoving. Within moments, she heard his soft snores.

In the ashy lamplight she studied the letters between his shoulder blades. *J-E-N.*

Instead of telling him straight-out her opinion of the tattoo, she had tiptoed around his feelings. If her mom—aka the new Claire— had overheard her, she would have had a cow. The old Claire . . . would have reacted as Jenna had. Maybe the apple hadn't fallen too far from the tree.

No. Stinking. Way. She was Jenna Beaumont Mason, an excellent English teacher who had a voice and an opinion. She wasn't about to make the same mistakes her mom made.

And she wasn't about to succumb to any coach pressure to give his athletes preferential treatment. If any football player dared use a hackneyed expression like "having cows" or "apples falling from trees" in an essay, she'd bench him faster than Kevin could fall asleep.

Early the next morning, Jenna waited at the kitchen counter, arms crossed, watching coffee drip into the carafe. She hadn't slept well at all.

She heard Kevin walk into the kitchen and approach. She didn't turn.

He propped his chin on her shoulder. "Hmm. This shoulder feels a little cold."

She shrugged him off.

"Let's check this one." His chin nudged her other shoulder.

Again she shrugged him off.

"Freezing cold." He stepped around her and leaned on the counter to look at her. "Truce?"

"What do you mean?"

"It's okay to disagree about art. I like Erik, and he thinks that streak of purple paint across a piece of canvas hanging on his wall is nice."

She rolled her eyes.

"Maybe you should have some coffee first."

"I don't need coffee. I need to tell you what I think."

"Jen, you did. You don't like the tattoo. You don't like any tattoos. Message received."

She grabbed two mugs from the cupboard and poured coffee into them. "Hardly." She carried her cup to the table.

He sat with her. "I don't like us being mad at each other. Tell me what I missed."

"You should have known."

He shrugged. "You're a princess. I'm a dumb jock."

"Some days I wonder how we ever got together."

"Me too."

She met the gaze of his navy blue eyes. "You're not dumb. And I'm not so much a princess that I expect life to be perfect. I don't expect that you should do everything my way. We're different, which is probably why we're attracted to each other. But that doesn't give you the right to make fun of my girlfriends or what I teach or how I design my bulletin boards."

"Huh?" He sat back and blinked. "I don't do that."

"You do! You did last night! You told me about the cheerleaders laughing, and you griped about *Beowulf* as though you have to read it yourself, and you called Emmi a nutcase."

"But I wasn't making fun of you."

"What would you call it?"

"Teasing. Flirting. No big deal."

"I'm not one of the guys in the locker room."

"You're not?"

"Kevin!"

He grinned.

"It hurts when you tear me down like that."

"My fragile princess."

"Stop it!"

His smile faded, and he held up a hand. "Okay. Relax." He leaned across the table. "Jen, listen. I love that you're my fragile princess. You know, it makes me feel like some kind of macho hero."

"Well, just walk all over me, if that makes you feel so good."

"I'm sorry. That's not what I meant." His forehead creased until his eyebrows almost touched. "I meant . . ."

"What? I'm listening."

"I meant . . . I love the way your hand feels so tiny and soft in mine. I love that I could punch out anybody's lights if he tried to hurt you. I love that you're the smartest teacher in the school and that the guys think you're hot. I love that you have the chutzpah to make them read *Beowulf*."

All of her indignation took a nosedive.

He picked up her hand and kissed the palm. "Please tell me when I make fun of you. I'm new at this husband thing."

She nodded. "I'm sorry I don't like tattoos."

"Even ones that say 'Jen'?"

"Yeah."

"At least it doesn't say 'Michelle.'"

"Who's Michelle?"

He sighed dramatically, closed his eyes as though remembering, and thumped his hand against his chest.

"You don't know any Michelle."

He sighed again.

"Kevin!" she snapped. "This isn't funny."

He opened his eyes. "Gotcha."

She groaned and laid her head in her arms on the table. That was the problem. Kevin Mason did indeed have her.

Thirty-six

Max spotted Claire across the room and stood. She noticed him and headed his way, sashaying between tables, her mouth a grim line.

Her body language did not bode well for their meeting.

He was at a Starbucks, tucked back in a corner at a table for two. Wavering after nearly six weeks of life without his wife, he'd called her.

Claire didn't walk like Claire. She didn't look like Claire. Not that she looked bad, exactly. She wore something Tandy might have had in her closet, an ankle-length skirt and long-sleeved, unbuttoned blouse over a shirt. All she needed to complete the ensemble was one of those little triangle scarves, like in *Fiddler on the Roof.* A babushka. Totally out of character.

She stopped a couple of feet in front of him, not near enough to touch.

"Hi," he said.

"Hi."

The moment was awkward, no two ways about it.

He attempted a smile.

She attempted one back. An indecipherable upward nudge of the mouth corners, it probably mirrored his own.

He said, "I'm early."

"I noticed." She glanced at the table. "Drinks already?"

"Yeah. Johnny-on-the-spot. Shall we sit?"

They sat.

She touched the clear plastic cup. "What is it?"

"An Americano. You like those, right?"

The outline of the tip of her tongue appeared in her cheek. "What?"

At last she met his eyes. "What makes you think I like it? I've had two in my life."

He felt the flush start in his neck.

"Once by myself. Once with Neva."

He had asked Neva what his wife liked at Starbucks because he himself had never been to the place with her. "At least I knew you like Starbucks."

Claire's stony expression revealed nothing.

"Give me some credit."

She glanced away.

"I'm sorry. Okay? I'm sorry I don't know what you like here."

When she looked back at him, something softened in her greenish eyes.

"Let's start over," he said. "Hi."

After a moment, she replied. "Hi."

"Can I get you something to drink?"

"No, thank you."

He heard his own breathing. In and out. "How are you?"

Her eyes unfocused, as if she were carrying on an internal conversation. He sipped his black coffee and noticed her hair. Though clean and shiny as usual, it was longer and tucked behind an ear. At the top, dark roots contrasted with blonde strands.

The change in Claire was slightly unnerving. Clothes and hair he could handle. But when he'd called her the previous day and left a message inviting her to meet him and then waited all afternoon for her to return the call, Phil pointed out his irritability. Max admitted to himself that annoyance was getting an upper hand. It reminded him of the time several years before when another driver ran a red light and slammed into his car, totaling it. Although he hadn't been hurt, the shock of that moment had stayed with him—that moment of absolute loss of control.

That's how Claire made him feel.

On the phone she'd said yes, it was time they talked. There were developments she wanted to discuss. She hesitated at his offer of dinner, though. He'd scrambled and tossed out the idea of the coffee shop.

Scrambling for Claire was not familiar territory.

At last she said, "I'm well. I got a job."

"A job!"

"Violinist with the symphony. Substitute, but sort of full-time. Someone took an emergency leave of absence the day I auditioned; they don't know how long she'll be gone. My first concert is Saturday. One of the summer outdoor ones, down by the stadium."

"You don't need to work. You don't need money."

Her throaty chuckle was not an expression of delight. "How high shall I jump, Max?"

"Sorry. It's just so . . . so . . . so . . ."

"So . . . what? So not according to your plan?"

"I was going to say uncharacteristic of you."

"I love playing my violin."

"But you haven't. Not for years."

"Life got in the way. I guess it's not in the way anymore."

It didn't take a rocket scientist to figure out exactly what had changed in her life. "Was I in the way?"

She didn't respond.

Tired of their separate lives, he'd vowed to make a supreme effort to listen and not go off half-cocked like the last time. He'd almost blown it right off the bat with that Americano thing. Not a smart move, consulting Neva. He figured he had about half a chance left.

"Claire, you can say it. I won't bite. I promise."

"Yes, you were in the way."

Hearing that it was his fault did something to his gut. They'd been there before. Wait. They? No, he'd always been there. Things were always his fault.

"But," she said, "I'm not totally blaming you. In a sense, I allowed you to be in the way."

He stilled.

"Let me back up. I found my parents' marriage license in one of those boxes we brought back from North Carolina. It turns out they *had* to get married. I was on the way by about four and a half months."

"Really?"

"Yes. They lied about the year."

He shook his head. His in-laws were idiots.

"The thing is," she said, "it explains a lot. Like why my dad resents me. Maybe why my mom drank and why they fought."

"And you felt like it was all your fault."

She stared at him. Her eyes filled up with tears.

"Hon, you're preaching to the choir. Somehow it's my fault my brother got shot down in Vietnam." He shrugged. "BJ's the hero, but I'm the one left to take care of the fallout. Mom and Dad couldn't think straight for six months. I moved home. Made sure they took care of themselves. Handled all the military communications. Not that I did any of it right, according to them."

"You understand."

"Probably not. Does this have something to do with us?"

She nodded. "I told you I don't feel safe with you."

"Except when I was your knight in shining armor."

A smile lit her face briefly. "Right. You rescued me from my unsafe childhood." She paused. "Understandably, I craved peace and security. You offered that. I thought I'd better not make any waves. You might rescind the offer."

"How would you 'make waves'?"

"By causing you to be unhappy. If you didn't like the violin, then

I didn't like the violin. I shaped my opinions around yours. I ignored my wants and needs."

He stared at her. She echoed what Neva had talked about, how in the early years Claire believed her purpose for being was to keep him happy. "You got a little carried away with that submission thing."

"I did. And you let me. But why wouldn't you? It kept the peace in our household."

He let that settle in. "Then we were both wrong?"

"Yes, Max, we were both wrong."

"Okay. And listen, you are not responsible for your parents' mistakes."

"Neither are you for yours."

He smiled.

She tapped her temple. "Head knowledge. My heart still hurts."

The smile fizzled. "Come home. Let me make it all up to you."

She turned and stared toward a window. "You can't make it up."

"Claire." He reached across the small table and touched her arm. "I'll do anything. Talk to a marriage counselor. Take some time off. Whatever. I don't want to live like this, apart from you."

She leaned back in her chair, shifting her arm out of his reach, and studied his face for a long moment. "Whatever? Do you really mean that?"

"Yes, whatev—" What had she said that other time? *Sell. Sell the whole kit and caboodle.* "Whatever within reason."

Her mouth twisted, a quick but distinct expression of disappointment. She understood what he was saying. "Well, there isn't anything you can do, anyway. This is about me."

"No, it's about *us*. It's our marriage."

She waved a hand in dismissal. "We're two separate people. We can't be a real couple until I find me again."

"Until." Max clung to the word as if it were a lone tree sticking out the side of a sheer cliff. His feet dangled a fatal distance above the earth. His heart boomed in his chest.

"The truth is, I'm not sure we're even friends. I hear these sappy stories about husbands and wives who break up and wish they could talk to their best friend about it. But they can't, because their best friend is their spouse."

That stung, but he had no response. He'd never considered Claire his best friend. Phil and Neva were his closest friends. Claire was his wife.

Abruptly she pushed back her chair. "I have to go."

"Claire, wait. What about Saturday? The mayor's wedding."

"I know. I already sent a gift."

"Will you go with me?"

"Max, I just told you my first concert is Saturday."

"This isn't business." He caught sight of her raised brows. Okay, yeah, he wanted to keep channels open with the city by going to the mayor's wedding. "Not totally business. We'll see the Landons and the Greenes there."

"Give them my regards." She stood. "And regrets."

"Claire, please."

"You're pressuring, Max. I can't take that."

He hit his limit. "Well, I can't exactly take what you're doing!" he hissed in a low tone. "Talk about a bombshell out of the blue! What am I supposed to tell people?"

She walked away.

With great effort he remained in his seat and forced himself to take deep breaths. He would not chase after her. He would not grovel. Palm trees would grow in the Arctic before he called her again.

He noticed the plastic cup on the table. Condensation streamed down its sides. Melting ice pushed the coffee against the clear lid. The straw stuck out, no lipstick marks on it. Claire hadn't touched the drink he'd gone to such effort to arrange just so.

Right there in the middle of a busy coffee chain store that he despised, Max Beaumont nearly lost it.

Thirty-seven

W hoa!" Tandy pumped her elbows higher and lengthened her strides. "Again she pushes the envelope!"

Alongside her friend, Claire huffed and puffed and stepped in double time, trying to keep up with Tandy's brisk speed as they rounded a corner.

"You really told Max he was in the way? That it was his fault you stopped playing your violin?"

"Mm-hmm."

Tandy punched the air, her arm raised high. "Yes!"

"Gloria Steinem, here we come."

"Oh, lighten up. I'm not going off the deep end. I'm proud of you for telling him the tough stuff."

"But I'm not totally blaming him. I was at fault too."

"Yeah, yeah, yeah. But still, you did good, girl. You did real good."

Claire ignored the compliment. "Life in general got in the way too. You know how it is with kids. They're wonderful and all-consuming. Something has to give."

"For a season. We haven't been full-time moms forever and a day. Ergo, Max got in the way too. It wasn't just life. I know he never wanted to do concerts with us. You two always seemed too busy with other things."

As they zipped along the blocks, past condominiums and palm trees, Claire thought of how true that was. Max even pooh-poohed her time on the symphony board. Raising money for hospitals and charities was one thing, but for music? For the arts? Forget it.

"Music is a mystery to him. He has no background in it. I guess it just doesn't make sense to him, and he never cared to learn more about it. He resented the time I put into it, time I could have spent doing something productive for the agency or our home. He went so far as to say I acted snooty when it came to my violin. So that's where the need to keep the peace entered in. I eventually quit playing, even for myself when he wasn't around."

Tandy dodged a fire hydrant. "You had it really bad, didn't you? I mean, you lost your own identity. You totally conformed to what he wanted you to be. Just to keep the peace."

"And now, come to find out, it wasn't really peace and safety. Only an absence of conflict. I think I just got tired of holding my breath."

"Claire, why did you hold it for so long?"

In the two days since she and Max talked, she had pondered his challenge: *"Was I in the way?"* And her straightforward reply: *"Yes."* She'd thought about her parents, about her determination not to repeat their marriage.

She said, "I think my life has been lived as just one long reaction to other people. I do and think this or that because my mom drank, because my dad ignored me, because my husband will be unhappy if I don't."

"Eww."

"Eww."

"Guess you'd better forgive them."

Claire halted in the middle of the sidewalk. "What?"

Tandy looked over her shoulder, turned around, and stepped back to her. "Forgive them. They all hurt you, Claire. Don't deny it, but let it go. Don't allow them to define you any longer."

Claire stared at her friend. Her cheeks were as red as her hair, her mouth set in a grim line, her green eyes unflinching in the shadow of a visor.

Tandy touched her arm. "It stinks. I know. But let me tell you. Big-Hair Bimbo from Bishop and Trevor the Toad both would have been long dead by now. If I hadn't forgiven them, you'd be visiting one tough prison mama."

Claire frowned. "You never told me."

"I'm pretty sure I did. It probably didn't click."

"You're strong and independent. You moved on."

Tandy shook her head vehemently. "I forgave them."

"Really?"

"Really. I had to learn how to move on. Now I'm convinced I could live through anything. In a sense, I'm grateful Big-Hair came into my life." She smiled. "Strange, the things that teach us what we need to learn. Nasty women, surprise birthday dinners. You never know, Claire. You just never know."

Forgive her parents? Forgive Max?

Not likely.

Thirty-eight

Saturday evening, her violin and bow in hand, Claire walked onto the outdoor stage. Located at the Embarcadero, the small peninsula jutted out into Mission Bay. The marine air felt warm. Yachts and sailboats glided by. The stage backdrop gave the effect that she was inside a giant concave shell. Before the evening was over, the sun would set, and she would be able to see stars.

It was a glorious setting for a pop concert.

Giddy almost to the point of hyperventilating, she hoped with all her might that she would be able to sit still and read the score. She knew Mozart; she didn't know Gershwin.

How she loved everything about her new venture! The rehearsals . . . the camaraderie with other musicians . . . the music. And tonight! The setting sun . . . the fragrant summer's eve . . . the air crackling with energy from hundreds of people gathered in anticipation of the music, an unparalleled expression of beauty.

Why, oh why had she waited so long? Why had she denied herself this good thing?

Claire found her chair, sat, and smoothed her long, black skirt.

Her girls were in the audience, along with Tandy and friends from their musical group. Kevin was at a ball game. Erik and Danny had wished her well but begged off with other plans. She teased them about filling their music quota years ago by attending their sisters' recitals. They didn't disagree with her.

Max, most likely, was at the mayor's wedding. Not only did his offer of doing "whatever" to get them back together fall short of selling the agency, but it even fell short of supporting her efforts in music by coming to the concert.

So what else was new?

Claire exchanged smiles with other orchestra members as they wove their way between chairs and found seats.

She wondered what excuse Max would give for her absence at the wedding tonight. Surely people were already talking about them. In six weeks she had missed two high-profile social events, one of which she had spent months helping organize. People would have noticed. She imagined he was uncomfortable. She hated putting him in that position. She hated how she was throwing out all the good with the bad.

But, as Tandy remarked, none of that was her problem. To give up her concert for his agenda would be to step right back into the old way of ordering her life around his reactions.

Claire felt a pain in her jaw. She unclenched it. Maybe she was a raving feminist already, sloshing through deep, muddy waters of backlash.

Across the stage, behind other violinists, a trumpeter moved between chairs and music stands. He was a young man, probably a student at one of the nearby universities. She had noticed him at rehearsals but hadn't met him yet. He played with such intensity it was almost painful to watch him. Painful in the way beauty could evoke pain, a longing and aching for something unnamed.

In another lifetime she had known him. Or, rather, one very much like him.

Now the concertmaster stepped onstage. In the split second before the applause began, Claire felt her lungs expand as if great drafts of air were pumped into them. She smiled.

Not only was she done holding her breath, but she was taking in a brand-new one.

His name was Petros Melis, that other one, the trumpeter she had known so many years ago. The man who came alongside her when Max worked twenty-four hours a day. Literally twenty-four hours a day.

They met at Creighton's, in the back corner of the old music shop where the sheet music was shelved. Or, rather, not shelved.

"Excuse me, miss?" The accented voice had come from behind her.

She turned. At first sight, there was nothing particularly remarkable about Petros Melis. He was of average height, with an olive skin tone, large chocolate brown eyes, and dark, curly hair. The mythological Apollo, god of music, did not come to mind—not until later. Much later.

"Yes?"

"Do you work here?"

She smiled. "No. I teach lessons here, but I don't work for Creighton. If I did, this place would not be in such chaos. I still don't understand why any self-respecting musician sets foot in the store. It's enough to unhinge me."

"Unhinge?"

"Unglue." She noted his blank expression. "It confuses me. Music is an orderly language. I would like sheet music filed alphabetically."

"Ah. Let me guess. You play violin, and you play by the rules."

"How did—Well, of course I play by the rules."

"Music is the language of the soul." He pressed a hand to his chest. "Not the head." He tapped a finger against his temple.

"I have a twelve-year-old student who thinks he's a musical genius. He refuses to practice the scales or to hold his instrument correctly. He plays cacophony."

His full lips parted in a grin. "A twelve-year-old hears only cacophony in his soul."

Claire shook her head and turned her back on the stranger. She began to flip through a stack of sheet music lying in an open wooden box set atop a table. Two of her more advanced students needed a challenge beyond what the lesson book offered. Despite the discomfort of feeling unhinged, she knew she would find the perfect piece at Creighton's. He carried the best selection south of San Francisco; that was why everyone frequented his shop.

"Excuse me." The uppity stranger again.

She looked over her shoulder.

"I apologize. I did not mean to offend you. Music is my passion. I—how do you say it?—I am too spoken out."

"Outspoken."

"Yes. Tell your twelve-year-old he must learn the rules. Then he can bend them and create music." He smiled softly. "Can you help me find something? This mess is *unhinging* me."

And that was how it began. At a time when Claire heard only cacophony in her own soul, someone came along who knew how to pull from the din a melody of wondrous beauty.

Thirty-nine

Claire swung her arms in two windmill swoops and clipped along at a quick pace on the sidewalk. "Life feels so good, Tandy."

"It shows." Her friend scurried to catch up. "I've never seen you walk like this."

Claire ignored the comment. "I suppose life shouldn't feel good, though, I mean, given the circumstances."

"Stop sighing, hon. You're entitled to a respite from life as a pit. Forget my question. We don't need to figure out why it feels good now. Just enjoy the positive energy."

"I haven't talked with Max in eleven days."

"That's reason enough for the euphoria."

"Well, it shouldn't be."

"Stop with the 'should' and 'shouldn't' already."

"You're right. I have to keep Max on the back burner for now. I'm determined to figure out *me* before tackling *us*. So in answer to your question . . . music is probably why life feels so good. The impact of playing with the symphony is nothing short of amazing. I feel like I've come home."

Tandy thrust her arm skyward.

"Other things are falling into place. The kids aren't on the phone twice a day asking how I'm doing. Indio and I talk more about guests at the hacienda than my marriage status. She doesn't seem as angry. I'm liking your church more and more. The preacher deals with real issues more than mine does. And there's no pretense."

"Told you so."

Claire laughed. "Well, I guess I wasn't listening."

"Nope, you weren't." Tandy playfully punched Claire's arm. "And what about that real biggie falling into place?"

"I called my dad."

They exchanged a smile and paused at an intersection to wait for traffic.

Claire didn't know if forgiveness entered the picture with her dad. But she had talked to him. She asked him straight-out what the deal was with the marriage license. He confessed to shielding her and her brothers from the truth. He didn't apologize, but he confessed. And his voice changed. The conversation left them in a place they'd never been before.

She and Tandy crossed the street. "And last but not least, I don't notice the lumps in the mattress anymore. But I am thinking of apartment hunting."

"You don't have to. Wait until you're ready to face all that entails. You're a great roommate. Especially since we got rid of your boxes."

"Speaking of Max . . ."

"We weren't."

"I need to think out loud. You can charge me counseling fees."

"Cook me dinner again, and we'll call it even."

"Deal." She slowed her pace; Tandy stayed with her. Like always. Claire wondered why she'd never totally opened up with her before now.

"Speaking of Max?"

"Right. I think I figured out why he's always been so dead set against the symphony. I had a friend who played in it. His name was Petros Melis."

"Oh?"

Claire nodded. "I met him about a year after we got married. I wasn't playing in the symphony. I had quit in order to work with Max and Beaumont Staffing. I was totally inept managing the office. Then Neva walked in one day, wanting a temp job, and just sort of stayed. She whipped things into order in no time and worked for next to nothing. Max was released to go out and sell more. I took a backseat, trying to assist both of them. Again, ineptly."

"Business isn't exactly your cup of tea."

"No. It was obvious Neva had a crush on Max."

"What woman doesn't? He's charismatic and good-looking."

"I still don't know why he chose me."

"Moving right along."

"But it's part of the story, Tandy. I was in the basement of self-esteem. I'd given up music, the only thing I was good at. I was totally incompetent when it came to business. I couldn't even cook very well. Then the money situation got so bad I offered to give violin lessons at night and on Saturdays. Max thought it was a great idea."

Tandy touched her arm. "Let's sit."

Claire noticed they'd reached a park. They headed to a bench.

Tandy said, "Is that when you taught students at Creighton's Music Shop?"

"Yes. He had those classrooms upstairs and a long list of parents wanting private lessons for their children. It was easy to get started. One day I met this guy there named Petros. He was from Greece, here as a visiting artist. He played the trumpet." She smiled. "He was extraordinarily gifted but nowhere near as handsome or magnetic as Max. Still, the thing was . . . we spoke the same language."

"Music."

"Mm-hmm."

"What happened?"

"We connected. We'd go for coffee or drinks or dinner, usually after my lessons. Before he became better known, we'd go to places where there was live music. He let me cry on his shoulder. Max had no idea. We hardly saw each other. Our hours were crazy."

Tandy nodded. She'd heard that part of the story. "He was building the business."

"I had no clue what I'd signed up for. During the day I worked in the office."

"Ineptly."

"Yes. I managed to answer the phone. 'Beaumont Staffing.'" She wrinkled her nose. "And I could hand out application forms to people who came in looking for jobs. Neva did the rest. She took orders from clients and filled them with just the right workers."

"Where was Max?"

"He was out calling on clients. He'd show up at closing time. Then he and Neva worked on the payroll after hours." She shook her head.

"It sounds like a tough gig."

"It was. These past thirty years were nothing like those first two. We were married but not exactly living together." She shrugged. "I was so jealous of Neva. She helped Max succeed in ways I couldn't."

"Did you tell him how you felt?"

"I tried. He usually said things like it wouldn't last forever and did I mind not whining. He got enough of that from clients. When I mentioned the Neva relationship, he would remind me that he was married to me. What was the problem?"

"Hmm."

"Anyway, once I started working at the music shop, I decided I'd made the wrong choice for a husband. Why would I stay with this guy who didn't know the first thing about music? Or care to explore it? Or even pretend to be interested in my passion? At least I attempted to live in his business world." She shook his head. "Petros wanted me to leave with him, go to Greece. In the end I couldn't. Hindsight says I was just stubborn enough to stick by my commitment to Max. I had vowed my marriage would not resemble my parents' miserable situation, and that I would, no matter what, make it work."

"Did Max know about Petros?"

"Eventually. After Petros went back home, I was a basket case. A mother of one of my students noticed. She kept inviting me to church. Finally I went." She closed her eyes briefly. "And I learned that Jesus loved me and forgave me. But I couldn't live with myself until I confessed to Max. It shook him up so badly we went to the pastor for counseling. He helped us see how we were pushing each other away. We got through it. We promised never to leave each other."

"Whew. Max forgave you?"

"Not just like that, but yes. He said he did. I mean, there wasn't that much to forgive. I had a friend I *almost* ran away with."

"Friend?"

"We didn't sleep together. Well, not exactly. I mean, there was plenty of kissing and—Do you want details?"

"No, that's okay."

At last Claire looked at Tandy. She realized then that she'd been avoiding eye contact through the whole story, afraid of seeing condemnation. What she saw now, though, was sheer compassion.

"Max never believed I didn't have sex with him."

"For a guy, that's the worst betrayal."

"Petros and I shared something far more intimate than a physical relationship. Our hearts connected."

"Yeah, I know." Tandy sighed. "Well, I think this explains why Max always avoided going to the symphony."

"You think?"

"Definitely."

"That's what I thought. I'm a little slow."

"Aren't we all?"

Claire's respite screeched to a halt a short time later as she pushed open the gate in the tall privacy fence that surrounded Tandy's back patio. There, on the concrete stoop, sat Jenna, a sea of luggage surrounding her, her eyes like those of a scared child who'd lost her way.

"Jenna!"

"Mom!" Her daughter flew into her arms.

"What's wrong, honey?"

"Oh, Mom! Oh, Mom!" Great sobs swallowed the rest of her words.

Over Jenna's shoulder, Claire met Tandy's gaze.

Suddenly life didn't feel so good anymore.

Forty

Jenna lay in Tandy's guest room on the mattress her mother had warned her about. She said it made camping with tents and sleeping bags sound not that bad at all.

But a lumpy, saggy bed was the least of her concerns.

She felt encompassed in a body cast and propped in front of a television, forced to watch a rerun over and over and over. The show was not *Leave It to Beaver*.

It had started with a phone call.

"Jen." Kevin's husky voice dropped a notch.

She heard two beers in his voice. Hesitancy started with number three. Slurring came at number five. Loudness accompanied shots of tequila. He had a ways to go.

"It was bad. So bad."

"Oh, Kev. I'm sorry."

"These guys. Young guys. Kids. Arms gone. Legs gone. A face . . ."

Tears seeped from her eyes. She'd known it would be bad. Kevin and his ex-Marine buddies had gone to visit the facility for wounded soldiers on the base at Camp Pendleton. Why on earth he and his friends had thought they had anything in common with Florence Nightingale escaped her.

He said, "The thing is, these kids are dying while I sleep with my beautiful wife. I play football with teenagers and teach PE classes to bunches of lazy kids. It's not fair."

"Life is not fair, hon."

"Nope, it sure isn't." He sighed. "Anyway, we're hanging for a while, me and Stead." He referred to Heath Steadman, best man in their wedding. "Wilks, Miller, a few others."

"Okay." She squelched the urge to remind him about the last time he and Stead had "hung" together.

"Don't worry. We're not into getting hammered. We just need to . . . I don't know . . ."

"Decompress?"

"Yeah, something like that."

"I'll put dinner on hold."

"Jen." He exhaled noisily. "I can't think about dinner. I can't think about you holding dinner. Just don't wait for me."

After a calm good-bye, she disconnected and looked at the phone. "Jerk."

He arrived home very late that night, after she'd gone to bed. From the sounds he made, he was sober. Still miffed at his earlier comments, though, she didn't get up or reply to his whispered hello as he climbed in beside her. He touched her shoulder and within moments was fast asleep.

The next morning she should have known. She should have known. He got up before she did and fixed breakfast, whistling the entire time.

It was not his usual Sunday morning routine.

"Jenna, my pretty lady." He wrapped her in a bear hug. "Let's talk before we eat, okay?"

She let him steer her from the kitchen to the front room couch and imagined his apology.

Apology. Yeah, right. Talk about a head in the sand.

"Jen." The corners of his wide mouth curled upward; his eyes danced. "I had to do something yesterday. It's going to change things for us next semester. Stead says you won't understand, but you will."

Her heart pounded in her throat.

"It's good." He scooped her hands into his. "I reenlisted."

"What?" The heartbeats resounded in her ears now, muffling all other sounds.

"I can't ignore it any longer. Ever since the war started, I've known somewhere deep inside myself that's where I belong." He smiled.

He *smiled.*

"*Semper fi.* I have to help. The country needs me. These kids are going off to fight. They don't know squat. I can lead them. I've stayed in pretty good shape, so it won't—"

"You joined the Marines?" She screeched the words. The whole apartment building would have heard. "Kevin!"

"Jen."

"You can't do that!"

"I had to. It's who I am. If you'd seen these wounded guys—"

"You can't! You can't do that! We're married!"

"Come on, Jen. I thought you'd understand. I counted on it. I figured you'd be proud."

"You're a husband! You're not a Marine!"

He laughed.

He *laughed.*

"Hold on, Jen! You know one doesn't cancel the other. Obviously you haven't been paying attention."

She screamed at him. He stopped laughing and shouted back. She called him despicable names, vulgar words she had never said aloud before. He matched them.

She threw clothes and cosmetics and school paraphernalia helter-skelter into bags.

And then he had the gall to say, "You have no clue what loyalty is, do you?"

The tears didn't burst until she reached Tandy's. There they fell fiercely until at last her mom gave her a bowl of soup and one of Tandy's sleeping pills and tucked her into the lumpy bed.

"Honey, I promise you, things will look better in the morning." Her mom shut the blinds against the slanting sun rays and kissed her forehead.

Jenna succumbed to the sleeping pill.

Forty-one

I hope you're happy." Max growled the words, his lips mashed together. His jaw muscle convulsed.

On another day, Claire would have melted in the heat of his anger. Not so now. She propped her hands on her hips. "Oh, I'm happy, all right. As a matter of fact, I'm happy as a lark because my daughter refuses to put up with the likes of her dad in a husband."

"Whoa!" Tandy formed her hands into a T, palm atop fingertips. "Time-out, guys."

Max swiveled his glare toward Tandy. "All due respect, butt out."

The three of them stood in a circle around the kitchen table. Jenna had gone to bed with the sunset, and Claire had phoned Max to give him their daughter's news. He had a right to know. To her surprise, he appeared on the condo's doorstep forty minutes later.

Tandy said, "Hey, my house, my ground rules. There will be no attacking. If you want to tear each other apart instead of console and make a plan, go someplace else to do it. This is about Jenna, not you two." Tandy glowered at him and then at Claire. "Got it?" She turned on her heel and walked from the kitchen, pausing only long enough to pull shut the sliding door between rooms.

Claire pulled a chair from the small table and sat. She really asked too much of her friend. It was time to find her own place.

"Geesh." Max sat across from her. The scowl had not quite left his face. "Sometimes I have no question as to why Trevor checked out of his marriage to her."

A wave of heat surged through her. "Now you're attacking my friend?"

He pinched the bridge of his nose. "In all candor, I'm probably attacking you." He lowered his hand. "You're starting to resemble her. Bold and brassy. It's not becoming. It's not the Claire I know."

"Let's see. The opposite of bold and brassy would be . . . hmm . . . timid and mousey and dependent and controllable."

"Claire—"

"Admit it. You want me to wear beige and—"

"Wear beige?"

"Metaphorically speaking. Be nondescript. And kowtow."

"You've never been timid or mousey, and if you've kowtowed, it's your own fault, and I didn't notice. The point is, we always agreed to present a united front with the kids."

"United behind your opinion. Okay, it's my fault I kowtowed. I hereby officially quit."

"Fine."

"Fine. For starters, I cannot unite with you behind your opinion concerning Jenna and Kevin. He enlisted. He did not tell her he was going to do that. He did not even mention he had any desire to do that. Now, in a heartbeat, she's facing months and months of separation and the very real possibility of him getting injured or killed. What do you expect her to do? Sing the national anthem?"

"He's a Marine, through and through. It's his duty. He was still in uniform when they got married. She should have known him better."

"He could have mentioned his plans to her!"

"How could he? Apparently he didn't know them himself!"

Claire slumped against the back of the chair. No, it seemed he hadn't known them. He'd gone with buddies to visit the Wounded Warrior facility at Camp Pendleton, to offer support to servicemen recovering there from war injuries. According to Jenna, the visit did a number on him and his friends. They proceeded to a bar to take the edge off with a few beers. To reconcile, Jenna said, that world with their own. It didn't happen. He and one of the others reenlisted that afternoon. He swore he wasn't lit at the time.

"Claire, her moving out is not going to change his decision."

"Maybe not, but she will prove to herself that she's not a doormat. That her opinion counts. That all of his put-downs, especially about her teaching, and his disregard for her feelings are unacceptable."

Max blinked. "Is that what it's doing for you?"

She met his somber gaze. "Yes, I think it is."

He opened his mouth and closed it, as if deciding against speaking.

She offered a guess. "No, it's not finished with me yet. I still stumble over the memory of your subtle put-downs and disregard. The second-fiddle position."

"I didn't mean to . . ." He blew out a breath.

She waited a long moment, giving him time to finish the half apology. He didn't.

"Max, I know you didn't mean to, but you did."

He stood abruptly. "This isn't about us. It's about Jenna. And I think you're wrong. You were wrong to teach this attitude to her. Walking out never solves a thing."

With that he went to the door, pushed it open, and walked out of the kitchen. A moment later she heard the front door open and shut. Everything went quiet. Evidently he'd walked out of the condo.

"Yeah, well, you're wrong, Max. Walking out solves one thing right now: we don't have to talk to each other anymore."

Bile rose in her throat.

Oh, what had she turned into? An ugly, foul-mouthed shrew. A horrid woman who felt only anger while her daughter cried herself to sleep and her husband walked out.

Self-loathing flowed through Claire, bending her in two until her forehead lay against the table.

Forty-two

September 9.

It was a glorious summer morning. Royal blue sky. Dry heat thick with the scent of sage. Birds still praising the Holy One.

He gives and takes away. Blessed be the name of the Lord.

Indio laid a bouquet of sunflowers on the ground near the boulder with the carvings and said, "Happy birthday, BJ." Tucking the folds of her denim jumper beneath herself, she sat on a dried patch of wild grasses.

Ben stooped and set a tiny wooden figurine next to the flowers. His bolo tie dangled. "Happy birthday, Son." Straightening, he squeezed Indio's shoulder and then moved aside to lean back against an outcropping of rocks. He hooked his thumbs in his jeans pockets. A puff of wind lifted a wisp of white hair.

Indio smiled softly at him. He gave half a nod in return. It was a gentle exchange of love. How grateful she felt for the sustaining power of that love. Through the years it had indeed divided sorrows.

Indio watched Claire add flowers to the memorial and then sit beside her on the ground. Her daughter-in-law's quiet presence comforted her. The woman had never even met BJ. Never heard his voice, never received a letter from him. Yet she came, year after year, to pay tribute on his birthday.

Indio noticed a crease between Claire's brows and touched her arm. "He'll come."

The crease remained. Claire was blaming herself for Max's absence.

Indio, though, knew he was only late. He could miss family celebrations and recitals and games and even Christmas, but he would not miss the traditional September 9 gathering.

They came for BJ's birthday, just for a short while, first thing in the morning. Not to mourn. No. The keening and wailing was saved for January 10. That was done in private, each in their own way recalling the descent into darkness.

Today they remembered his birth and the joy he had given them for twenty-three years.

The memorial was made of stone and dirt and native plants and sky. Only the carving was man-made. Ben had started it on January 27, 1973, the day the Paris Peace Accords were signed, seventeen days after BJ was declared missing in action. He dulled countless knives and chisels and at long last his grief. Far from the house, on a boulder with a flat face toward the east, he'd grooved out a cross. Later they hired someone to add "Benjamin Charles Beaumont Jr." and his birth date.

They did not want a tombstone. They did not want a death date. Not that one was known. After thirty-four years, they could only assume his remains were in Vietnam.

She had no idea when they'd begun assuming that. Maybe it was the first year Beth Russell didn't show up for the birthday gathering. On January 10, 1973, she had lost a fiancé, not a family member. She moved on with life, married, bore children, relocated to the Northwest.

Indio's grandchildren attended when they were small. As adolescents and then adults, one or another might come, but most often not. The reality of BJ escaped them. He was real for his parents, his brother, and the woman who was to Indio like a daughter.

A movement startled Indio. Max appeared in her peripheral vision, noiselessly stepping up from the long path and now toward the memorial.

She wondered yet again why she had named him after her father, Maxwell James. She should have called him One Who Moves on the Feet of Deer, or whatever the Kumeyaay equivalent of that was.

She watched him. Like always, he laid a stone on the ground. It was about the size of his hand and came from a stash only he and BJ knew of. As children, they'd shared a fascination with rocks and had hidden a secret collection somewhere on the property. To this day he hadn't revealed it, as far as she knew, to anyone. He just always showed up with a rock on September 9.

"Happy birthday, B-Jerk."

B-Jerk and Moron Max. The derogatory nicknames echoed from their childhood. Indio had washed their mouths with soap more than once because of them. It seemed not to affect the love-hate relationship they had for each other.

Max turned to Ben. They exchanged a bear hug. Then he crouched in front of Indio and wrapped his arms around her. "Mom."

His eyes were hidden behind dark sunglasses. As he let go of Indio, she sensed a hesitation in him. But he recovered quickly, leaned toward his estranged wife, and pulled her into a quick embrace. Then he moved to the other side of Indio and sat cross-legged in the dirt. His black dress slacks would need to be cleaned.

Claire touched her hand. "Tell us about the day BJ was born."

She smiled at her. Claire always asked that. And Indio always obliged.

"Fifty-seven years ago, I was just eighteen . . ."

Oh, Ben." Indio's plaintive voice thrummed into a low moan.

"Love." He gently grasped her elbow. "Come away from the window."

Intuitively trusting the wisdom of her husband, Indio let him lead her to her rocking chair in the kitchen corner. It faced away from the window. She sat.

He settled his tall frame on the tiny ottoman and cradled her hands in his.

She returned his gaze, searching his eyes for answers.

In reply, he tilted his head toward her wall of crosses.

With a nod, she acknowledged that there were no answers beyond the choice to leave everything at the foot of the cross. Jesus had died for their pain, for BJ, and for Max and Claire, now arguing outside in the front yard.

God is good. Hallelujah.

Indio said, "They've hardly even fussed at each other in front of us before."

"We could blame the Santa Anas. The wind is kicking up. It's hotter than hot already."

She shook her head. "Not buying that one."

"Okay. They've never fussed like this before because she's never out-and-out disagreed with him before. This is a healthy sign. Remember our rows?"

She winced.

"Indio, it's all right that you made waves in our marriage."

"You say that now."

"Well, I see it now. I didn't appreciate your bluntness back then." He winked. "Back as far as last week."

She shook her head. "I added chaos to our home."

"You kept us real. You know I love our daughter-in-law. She's a wonderful mother, a do-gooder in the community. But her persona as a milquetoast with Max never was admirable."

"She should have spoken up more and not let it fester. Now it's erupting all out of proportion. She always kept peace in their home before. She created a more loving environment than I ever did."

"Want to argue about it?" His eyes twinkled, and he smiled.

"More than we already have?"

"The kids have been our vulnerable spot, haven't they?" He stroked the back of her hand with his thumb.

"And now Jenna. Instead of working through things with Kevin, she just lickety-split follows in her mother's footsteps."

"Indio, Jenna will learn from this and find her own way. I truly believe it's a healthy thing for Claire to let Max have it."

"Maybe she needs to hear that from you. I haven't . . . I guess . . ." She sighed. "I'm so angry at her. I know I haven't forgiven her yet."

"Oh, love, you know better."

"I liked that she kept the peace. Max was so desperate for peace and stability and acceptance."

"You believe that she gave him what you failed to give him."

She closed her eyes.

"Claire is not his mother." He lifted her hand and kissed it. "They will get through this without our interference."

Indio looked at him.

He smiled and peered over her shoulder toward the window. "Well, they're still going at it, but they've moved apart anyway, next to their cars. My guess is neither one is staying for coffee and cinnamon rolls. What do you think?"

"I think you're the most annoying man I've ever met."

"I was talking about coffee and rolls."

"I know you were." She pushed herself up from the chair.

Ben caught her in a hug before she'd gone too many steps. "I love you, Indio."

Coffee and rolls would have to wait. Indio succumbed to the tears she'd been holding back since dawn.

Forty-three

Déjà vu enveloped Claire, a squishy sensation, as if she walked on clouds.

"That's ridiculous." Max stood several feet from her, beside his car in the shade of a large oak.

She saw him through a haze. Perhaps his third—or was it fourth?—repetition of "that's ridiculous" had caused the déjà vu. Perhaps the heat—she stood in direct sunlight—caused the sense of drifting. Or was it the sudden release of thoughts and opinions? They burst from her like water from a fire hydrant, showering him with a deluge of plans he found ridiculous.

"Claire, are you listening?"

"Yes, I'm listening, Max, and I'm tired of it. I told you everything I have to say. Jenna and I are renting a small, two-bedroom house near her school. It's a month-by-month. Nothing permanent. Okay? We move in next week. We're furnishing it à la Salvation Army. She's paying half the rent."

"It's a lousy neighborhood!"

"It's where we lived when the kids were little— Oh! Honestly, Max. You know all this."

"She should go back to Kevin."

"She refuses to. And he refuses to apologize."

"She can move in with me."

"She doesn't want to."

"I'll go somewhere else. Phil has room. You two can have the house."

"I don't want it." The mere thought of living in her home chilled her to the bone. Was it the darkness of accumulated memories? They'd become horrid in light of her new clarity. All those years of the kids growing older, days slipping away like water through her fingers. Max missing one special event after another. The guilt gifts—material things and outings and trips—that she accepted. There was a word for women like her. It was not a nice word.

"You are so stubborn." Max's face reddened, and his voice rose. Perspiration had flattened his blue shirt to his body. Gray-brown dirt clung to his black trousers. He finally removed the sunglasses that kept slipping. His eyes were slits, only the black flashing through.

"I'm stubborn? Me?" Her own voice went up, uncontrollable. "You're the one who can't let something go after thirty-two years!"

"You slept with another guy! While we were married!"

"I did not sleep with him."

"I doubt that. I really doubt that."

"Oh, good grief! Get over it already!" The words shocked her. Those clouds gathered again, surrounding her legs, filling her with airy lightness.

"I'll get over it when you get over it." His voice nearly growled. "You haven't, have you?"

The haze shimmered, blurring her view of him.

"You've always held back a part of yourself."

"That's not true."

"It is. I just now realized it, but it's always been there. An invisible wall you hide behind. Keeping your distance. Letting me get just so close." He raised an arm and wiped the short sleeve across his forehead.

The accusation niggled at her conscience. It felt . . . true. She did keep her distance from him. She did close off a corner of her heart. But it had nothing to do with Petros Melis. Because the real question was, when *hadn't* she hidden herself?

"It hurts too much," she whispered. Her parents, Aunt Helen,

Max. They'd all let her down. Aunt Helen couldn't help it; she'd died. The others—they chose to abandon her.

"What?"

She looked at him. "You would only hurt me. You did hurt me. Why would I let you in?"

"Don't worry. You don't have to let me in. It's over, Claire. I'm done." He turned and yanked open his car door.

Within moments, swirls of dust churned in the wake of his car, across the small parking area and down the road as far as she could see.

The sense of déjà vu vanished. She'd stepped into brand-new territory. For the first time, Max had truly left her.

Forty-four

"Mom, you're welcome to come to brunch with me and Erik." Jenna stood in the doorway of Tandy's small office aka guest room.

"You and your brother don't need to babysit me." Seated on the bed, Claire watched her daughter finger-comb her long hair and gather it into a ponytail. Without benefit of mirror, she deftly twisted an elastic tie around the hair and, voilà, a perfect bun—loose, casual, and lovely.

Claire smoothed back her own hair. "How do you do that?"

"Let me try with yours. It might be long enough. Just a sec." Jenna left the room momentarily and returned with a clear bag of hair accessories, a hand mirror, a brush, and hairspray. She dumped everything on the bed and stepped behind Claire. "When was the last time you had it cut?"

"Nine weeks." The week before her birthday. A week and one day before she'd left Max. But who was counting?

"Maybe you could get it colored so the roots aren't so noticeable."

"Should I?"

Jenna peered over Claire's shoulder. "Yes, Mom, you should."

"I'm trying to go natural."

She went back to brushing her hair. "So have them match the natural color. You need a perkier look than the one you've got going here. I mean, just because your life is a mess doesn't mean you have to show it."

Claire laughed. "This sounds like a hint we should go shopping."

"Mall therapy! Great idea! I can meet you at Fashion Valley this afternoon. Or we'll go together if you want to come to brunch first with me and Erik and what's-her-face."

"Jen, you might try saying her name. Your brother could very well marry Felicia Matthews someday."

"Marriage will not make her good enough for him. The hanger-on of coattails," Jenna muttered, pulling at Claire's hair. "Okay. It's too short to twist up, but this ponytail is great. You can't see the roots as much. Hold on." She dug in her bag and pulled out a silk navy blue scarf.

"We wore those in high school."

"Your point being? There is nothing new under the fashion sun, you know. Just tweaks." Jenna tied the scarf around the ponytail. "There. Perfect. What do you think?" She handed her the mirror.

Claire studied her reflection. Without hair falling about her face, the greenish brown eyes were pronounced. "I look like a scared rabbit."

"You do not. It's a classic style. And more natural than your blow-dry, curling-iron, granny effect."

"Granny effect? Thanks a lot."

"You're welcome." Jenna sprayed the hair into place. "There. A little makeup wouldn't hurt either, Mom. At least some blush."

"Okay, okay."

Jenna plopped on the bed beside her. "Now what about brunch?"

"I'm going to pass on that. I really want to go to church."

"I thought you didn't like Tandy's."

"I didn't. It's growing on me. You probably don't want to come?"

Jenna shook her head. "I need to see Erik. He thinks I've lost my mind. He and Kevin talk." She shrugged. "Maybe I'll learn something."

Claire squeezed her arm. Flippant and carefree as she appeared, Jenna could not hide the sadness in her eyes. Neither she nor Kevin had called each other in the week since he'd reenlisted with the Marines. At the high school where they both taught, they avoided each other. Jenna stayed in her department's wing; he stayed in the gym areas. Rumors flew. They resembled the angst-riddled teenagers they taught.

Still, Claire thought, it beat a lifetime of *"How high, Kev?"* Didn't it?

A short while later, Claire drove into a parking space at the farthest edge of the church lot. Tandy was busy with an open house, leaving Claire to solo for the first time with her friend's quirky congregation. As she had told Jenna, the service and its people were growing on her.

Tandy discovered the place after her divorce. Claire accompanied her a few times; she had not been impressed. Although only about a hundred people attended, their worship time was loud, bordering on chaotic at times. Communion was served every week. Jenna would refer to the dress code as typically So-Cal: shorts, T-shirts, and over-sized print shirts for the men; slacks and summery skirts for the women; flip-flops and Birkies for all. Tears and laughter flowed freely; hugs and kisses abounded.

It was like a church full of Tandys. *What you see is what you get.* Unrestrained emotions and in-your-face sermons ruled the morning.

In spite of the warmth Claire had begun to feel after a service, it was, at times, just a bit too much.

She restarted the car and drove away. There was quite enough of *just a bit too much* in her life.

Claire drove to Oceanside, on the coast, and walked out onto the pier jammed with Sunday crowds. Fishermen lined the rails. Children raced ahead of mommies. Daddies pushed strollers thump, thump over the thick uneven boards. Older couples rode the electric cart "taxi" to and from the fifties-style restaurant located at the end.

Claire stood there, behind the eatery and way beyond swimmers and surfers. Nothing but iron-gray water and steel-blue sky lay before her. Nearby, fishermen leaned at the rails. Families lingered, hoping to glimpse the occasional dolphin or sea lion.

Oceanside was many miles from Claire's life down in San Diego. The women in her social circles would give away a diamond necklace before sharing space with people who caught their own dinner while resting their elbows in seagull droppings. Max's clients did not frequent the military town. Her son Danny lived at a different beach. No, there was not a chance she would run into an acquaintance.

Except the one in her memory.

She had walked with Petros on this pier.

Maybe she should have walked with him all the way to Greece.

Forty-five

That long-ago winter afternoon, as Claire stood with Petros on the pier, a cold, sharp breeze blew. They entwined their arms and watched the sun sink behind dark, puffy clouds on the horizon.

Out-of-the way meeting places had become necessary. Fans occasionally recognized the visiting artist on the street. His life was well documented via local television, newspapers, and magazines. His personality sparkled onstage and at the schools, preschool through university levels. His trumpeting gift mesmerized. And his intriguing Mediterranean appearance wasn't all that bad to look at.

"Claire." Petros intoned that one syllable like a vocal caress.

Before she'd known the real him, she'd fallen in love with his voice. Its foreign cadence and deep richness embodied the most ancient of sounds: music. And, of course, it was music that invisibly bonded their spirits.

"What?" Still laughing at something he'd said a moment ago, she turned away from the railing and faced him. "Petros?" She slid her arms around his waist, alarmed at the shimmer of tears in his eyes. "What's wrong?"

"You are so easy to love."

She shook her head.

He cupped her face in his hands. "Yes, you are. You are beautiful and kind." He kissed her, his full lips a brush of gossamer. "And you—how do you say it? You play a mean violin."

Her throat closed. Max never expressed his love in such ways. He never made her feel loved or even lovable. Why had she ever thought she loved him in the first place? He disdained her music. He cared more for establishing his business than anything.

But they were *married*. She'd vowed to make her marriage work. It would never resemble her parents' ugly version of housekeeping.

But what was she supposed to do with the enormous emptiness inside of her?

Petros traced his thumbs across her cheeks, catching the trickle of tears, and gazed into her eyes.

She shivered, not from the cold air but from the effect of Petros. He touched her at some closed-off place in her heart. No one else had ever come near to finding that place, let alone unlocking it. But Petros held the key. It was in how he made her believe in herself, in herself as a woman. When he spoke affirming words and so obviously desired her, indescribable hope flooded her soul.

Max made her feel . . . inadequate.

"Claire," Petros whispered. "I say it one more time: please, please come home with me. Come to Greece."

"I—I can't."

To her immature, idealistic, proud mind, there were all sorts of reasons why she couldn't. She would succeed where her parents had failed. She would not succumb to affairs or alcohol or other coping mechanisms they'd used. For a time with Petros, she had lost sight of her vow to Max—that she would never divorce. Now she returned to that promise, believing it was the right thing in some cosmic way. And while she might have lofty thoughts, she wasn't stupid: rebounding with a stranger whose native language she did not even begin to speak spelled a worse disaster than pressing on with Max.

She had to tell Petros good-bye. He would take the key to her heart with him, and she would survive, as she always had, before the man from Greece showed her a more beautiful way.

Suddenly Petros kissed her again, deeply this time. Claire lost herself to him. When his lips touched hers, she imagined them on the trumpet's mouthpiece, coaxing, persuading, and seducing. Trills and melodies resulted, breathtaking, powerful, unimaginable. She felt infused with life and beauty and all that was real.

In that moment, it was all that mattered.

Later they warmed themselves in front of a fire, sitting on a lush carpet and sipping hot chocolate. The condominium belonged to one of his adoring fans, a vacation rental she owned on the coast. The woman had made it available to the trumpeter who, in her opinion, desperately needed a few quiet days alone.

Claire said, "Are you sure she won't show up here?"

"She is at least seventy-five years of age."

"That does not make you any less attractive, *Apollo*."

"Stop!" He clapped his hands to his ears.

"Apollo, Apollo."

"Do not call me that! La, la, la!" he sang loudly to drown her voice.

She laughed. He truly disdained the pet name a reviewer had tagged onto him after his first solo with the symphony. "Apollo! Greek god of music! Of light! Of poetry!"

Petros disrupted her banter with kisses—playful ones at first, in between laughs, then slower ones that promised an intimacy they were unwilling to receive from each other.

They lingered there, lying in front of the fire, enjoying the rare opportunity of complete privacy.

"Claire." He nuzzled her ear. "It is time to go."

Max could be home by now. He could begin to miss her . . . after a while. She doubted both prospects.

Petros caressed her chin, holding her face directly beneath his. "It is time to go." His tone was resolute.

But she knew he read her eyes. He knew she would stay the night. And she knew he would not let her.

"Petros, you are infuriatingly honorable."

He gave his head a slight shake. "I am kissing a married woman."

"You understand what I mean."

"I understand that I love you and that you are not free. But I will wait."

"How long?"

"As long as you want me to wait."

Lady. Hey, lady!"

Claire felt a hand on her arm and turned.

"Are you okay?"

She blinked and realized she was doubled over and clinging to the pier's rail. Tears streamed in rivulets from beneath her sunglasses.

A fisherman stood beside her.

"There's a bench over there."

She followed to where he pointed and sank onto a rough-hewn bench that faced the water. A moan rose in her throat. She noticed then the pain in her stomach.

That winter afternoon at the beach had been the last time she and Petros met privately. The symphony and his fans needed him. The staffing business grew busy; Max needed her in the office more. She ripped up the phone number and address of a place she would never see in Greece.

Her guilt grew as well. When all was said and done, she was no better than either of her parents, was she? They'd cheated on each other. They'd hurt each other with a vengeance. She'd done exactly the same to Max, complete with sealing back up that deep place in her heart.

Claire propped her feet against the low bar of the rail and hid her face in her lap.

How long had Petros waited?

Her body shook with gut-wrenching sobs. She wished someone would just throw her off the pier.

Forty-six

Steam becomes you, Jenna, my dear." Erik chuckled, his hazel eyes glinting in the sunlight. "Little curlicues churning from both ears."

"Shut up." Jenna glared across the table at her brother.

"Ooh. Daggers flung from the eyes. That's attractive too. Kevin will be charmed."

"I said shut"—she picked up her water glass and calmly dumped its contents into his Bloody Mary—"up!"

"Hey!" He sopped the red overflow with a napkin. "That was totally uncalled for."

"I don't think so. Felicia is not coming, but Kevin is?" She shoved her chair aside and stood. "You are such a jerk. Oh no!"

At the sight of Kevin on the far end of the patio, she plopped back down. With only one narrow aisle between her and the one doorway, he blocked any escape.

Erik smiled. "You could crawl over the wall. Take the beach route."

"This isn't funny. I swear, Erik—"

"Hi, Jen."

She turned, and her breath caught. Kevin looked good. He looked so good. His eyes locked on hers. His mouth did its lazy, upward-curving thing. He wore a white polo shirt that hugged his shoulders and covered most of his tattoo.

Tattoos. Plural.

She pressed her lips together.

Erik, ever the gentleman except where his sister was concerned, stood up and shook Kevin's hand. "Hi. Have a seat. Sorry about the mess." He moved to the chair nearer the wall, signaling the waitress with a wave of his hand. "Kev, what would you like to drink?"

Kevin sat directly across from her. "Iced tea. Thanks."

"Coming right up." Erik smiled as the waitress approached. "Hi, darlin'."

While they flirted and a busboy cleaned the spilled drink, Jenna pushed back her chair. Being cornered by these guys was definitely not her idea of fun. She wouldn't be surprised if her dad showed up next.

Before she could slip away, Kevin angled his face beneath the busboy leaning over their table.

She read his lips. *I miss you.*

Well . . . maybe she'd stay . . . for a bit.

Erik clapped his hands together. "Okay, kiddos, I'm out of here. Unless you need a referee?"

Jenna rolled her eyes.

Kevin said, "We'll be fine. I think?"

She nodded at him.

Erik got up and playfully slapped Kevin's shoulder as he stepped behind him. "Watch her closely, my man. She's feisty today." He moved to Jenna and leaned over to hug her.

"You will pay for this, you dork."

"Yes, I already gave the waitress my credit card. Brunch is on me."

"Erik—"

He tapped her nose. "Just kiss and make up. You two are my last hope that wedded bliss is possible. Felicia sends her love." He strode off without a backward glance.

Kevin said, "You didn't know I was coming?"

She shook her head. "You?"

"Nope."

The waitress arrived at their table. "Wow. Erik Beaumont is your brother! So what was it like growing up with San Diego's favorite news anchor?"

Jenna hated that sort of question, especially from cutesy, fawning young females. Of course, they were the only ones who asked them. "He was and is and always will be a dork."

She laughed. "Spoken like a true sister. Are you two ready to order?"

Food was the last thing on Jenna's mind. She let Kevin choose first and then said, "Ditto." He usually managed to eat whatever she didn't.

They tiptoed around the subject of wedded bliss and talked about everything else until the server set before them platefuls of bacon, eggs, and Belgian waffles topped with strawberries and whipped cream. In silence, she ate a few berries. Kevin dug in as if he hadn't eaten in days.

At last she laid down her fork. "How are you?"

"Tired of gutting it out and pretending that I'm okay without you. How are you?"

"Tired of being angry."

"Come home?"

She tapped her fingers on the table. "Wait. You're skipping over the apology part."

"Are you going to eat your waffle?" He switched their plates, poured syrup, and forked a bite. "Yeah. I've been thinking about that part."

She watched him chew and swallow.

"The way I see it, Jen, is we're a team. I'm there for you. You're there for me. I don't have to ask permission to throw the ball, because you know me. You know I'm going to throw and you know where."

"Okay, I'm lost. What does football have to do with apologizing?"

"We both tanked the play. You weren't in place to catch my throw. Probably because you didn't understand the game plan." He took another bite.

She waited in silence again for him to continue.

"Remember when we got engaged? My hitch was almost over, but I said the Marines were my family, that I would always be available to serve with them."

She shrugged a shoulder.

"Well, I did say that, exactly, and you said you were proud of me, proud of my patriotism. You said I was a hero. Like a dunce, I figured that meant you understood. I guess I should have explained more. Visiting the base hospital isn't what I was talking about."

"Kevin! We're married! There is a game plan to marriage, and it means you don't make major life-changing plans without discussion."

He shook his head. "It means we love each other so much we support any decision made for the good of others."

"So our being physically together is not a priority."

"Right now it is—"

"Until you go overseas!"

"And then I'll need to know that you're holding down the fort at home. Jen, wives have been doing this for centuries."

"Men go to war, and women wait."

"Yeah, for the most part. I mean, there are some women who go."

She shoved back her chair. "Well, this one's going before that waffle ends up on your head." Picking up her handbag, she stood.

"There you go, quitting again."

"You're the one who quit *us*." She strode away, nearly collided with a waiter, and hurriedly wound her way across the patio. Inside the restaurant she made a beeline for the exit, fighting back hot tears and a string of invectives.

"Ma'am!" Their cutesy waitress popped alongside her. "So does your brother have a special friend?"

Jenna halted near the front door. "What?"

"I'm sorry. You're in a hurry, I can tell." She thrust a piece of paper at Jenna. "This is my phone number. I thought maybe if he doesn't have a girlfriend . . ."

Erik. This was all his fault. If he'd left well enough alone, Kevin might have gotten desperate enough to call her and apologize rather than sit in a public place and talk about football.

She raised her hand, refusing the woman's paper. "I've got a better idea. I'll give you his number." She smiled. "It's unlisted."

Forty-seven

"M ax."

At the sound of Neva's voice, Max looked up from the Sunday newspaper and smiled. "Hi." He folded the business section and rose from his seat, a low-to-the-ground armless lawn chair.

"What is this?" Her wary tone and creased brow above the sunglasses surprised him.

"What's what?"

"This." She gestured at the blanket spread on the grass and the picnic basket beside it. "You said, 'How about a walk at La Jolla Cove?'"

He shrugged. "You got something against food? I found some pâté and Brie and those little crackers—"

"Where's Phil?"

"He couldn't make it. Have a seat." He sat.

She sat in the other chair and crossed her legs and her arms. Her shapely body was easy to admire in the sleeveless blouse, shorts, and sandals. Her body language was easy to read.

"Neva, what's wrong?"

"Why don't you tell me?"

He chuckled. "You're being rather cryptic."

Her glossy lips thinned into a straight line, and she turned toward the ocean.

He was beginning to think this was not such a good idea. *Women.* "You didn't have to come. It's Sunday afternoon; you probably had something else to do—"

She swung back to face him, her eyes flashing. "Of course I had to come! You're my friend. Your wife left you, and three days ago you told her you were done trying to fix the marriage. That translates into 'I could use some help.'"

"I'm sure that's why I called you. I'm sorry if I presumed too much—"

"Max! We're at one of the most romantic places in the county, in this park overlooking a gorgeous ocean and coastline. You've brought my favorite snacks. Phil is not in the picture. My radar just went wild with blips. What am I supposed to think?"

"Picnics are fun?"

She flung her hands in an "I give up" gesture. "Just tell me what's going on."

"What do you want to go on?"

"Now who's being cryptic?"

"All right, all right." He laced his fingers together and tried to put order to his vague thoughts.

Claire would probably call them feelings.

It had all been Phil's idea. He'd suggested the best remedy for letting Claire go her merry way was to start relating to women on something besides a business level. He said, "Who better than Neva?" Everyone knew she was crazy about Max. Why else had she never succumbed to Phil's charms?

That was all news to Max.

But he needed to move on. The empty house drove him nuts. He needed some social time with a female, maybe even in a physical way. He'd never been into flings. Claire was always . . . available.

Not counting the past ten weeks.

He already felt a naturally close relationship with Neva. She was the likely candidate for . . . for whatever.

"Max." Neva stared at him, her sunglasses in her hand. "Just tell me one thing. Did you purposely create this romantic encounter?"

He waited a beat. "Yes."

"To hurt Claire?"

"No. It's not like that. I just wanted . . . just wanted to be with you . . . in a different way."

She puffed her cheeks and blew out a breath. "Can we talk about anything but work, Claire, and the guy I'm dating?"

He nodded.

"Okay, then. Picnics can be fun."

Max's cell phone rang. Seated in his parked car at a curb near the La Jolla Cove, he checked the caller ID. It was Claire.

He cut the engine and flipped open the phone. "Yeah."

"'Yeah'? Hello to you too."

He rubbed his forehead. The glow left over from the hours of pleasant conversation with Neva disintegrated on the spot.

And he'd been wondering if he'd done the right thing spending the afternoon with her.

"Well," Claire said, "I called to say your mom is not doing well."

"She never does well the week after BJ's birthday."

"This is different. She has chest pains. Your dad called to tell me." Why hadn't his dad called *him*?

"Actually, he's not doing so great either. Of course, he practically falls apart if your mom sneezes, but it's the fire too. Not that it's anywhere near, but from on top of the mountain he can see smoke—"

"What fire?"

She sighed her "You're an idiot" sigh. "It's all over the television and radio. It's burning to the southeast. It concerns him because they're expecting a houseful of guests this weekend, and smoke on the horizon is not conducive to a pleasant retreat."

He had no reply. His parents and their Hacienda Hideaway retreat center did not intersect with his life.

"Your dad asked if I could help your mom this week."

"That's why they have Paquita and José."

"They're not full-time. And besides, they're out of town, at their daughter's for something."

"Hmm."

"Your dad never asks for help."

"No."

"He wants her to rest, so I'll go up tomorrow and work around the house." She paused. "He didn't ask for himself, but I'm going to. Can you give him a few hours? He's mending a fence, and the horses need attention. The parking area needs grading."

"I'll send up a couple of temps."

"Max, you know he won't accept someone you hire."

"Well, that's all I can do this week."

"He's your dad. He needs attention. It's not the extra help so much as that."

"Claire, I have things to do. I can't go running up there to hold his hand. He'll be fine."

"You really are a cold fish, you know that? I shouldn't have bothered. Good-bye."

He snapped his phone shut.

Evidently parents and estranged wives never went away.

What more did they want from him? He had given them everything money could buy. He had spent his life seeing to their wants and needs. When did he get a break from hand-holding?

He didn't feel like a cold fish. He and Neva had enjoyed a picnic. They'd strolled the long sidewalk above the beaches and tide pools. They'd bought coffee and chocolate at a small shop and enjoyed them seated on a bench while watching the sunset. He'd felt alive and appreciated.

At least the conversation with his wife answered one concern: would he feel guilty about his time with Neva when he talked with Claire?

Apparently not.

Forty-eight

Indio, I wish you would hire someone to help you."
Claire spoke from her perch on the ladder at the foot of the bunk
beds. Her back was to the room while she tucked sheets into place.

Seated on the other bottom bunk, Indio massaged a tightness at
her breastbone. The pinched-clothespin feeling had been in place
for days now. She supposed it was the combination of BJ's birthday,
Max's floundering marriage, and her age.

Well, God is good, she mused to herself. *Lord, it says in the Bible that
Your grace is sufficient. I take it that means Your goodness and favor are
all I need to cope with all this mess. Right? I sure hope so.*

"What?" Claire said.

She must have muttered aloud. "I was just telling the Lord His
grace is all I need." She chuckled. "And some help from my daughter-
in-law. Not to mention Paquita and José."

Claire snapped a blanket into place, deftly slid its edges under the
mattress, and harrumphed. "José is a smart handyman, but he can't
keep up with Ben anymore. Paquita is a wonderful cook, but she
couldn't climb to the top bunks if her life depended on it. And you
shouldn't. And twelve guests, however infrequent, is too—" She
turned. "I saw that. You're rubbing your chest again."

"I must have pulled a muscle."

"Right. A muscle. Like your heart?"

Indio saw the concern on Claire's face and smiled. "No, not my heart.
The doctor says it's fit as a fiddle, and I should keep chopping wood."

200

"He said that six months ago. You know Max would pay for a housecleaning service to come in once a week or so. More when you have back-to-back weekend guests like this month."

"We could afford a service ourselves. It just isn't necessary."

"Yet." Claire stepped off the ladder and sat on the other lower bunk, facing her. "It just isn't necessary *yet*."

"Okay, okay. It isn't necessary *yet*. But I am not discussing a time-table for *yet*. I refuse to talk myself into *yet*."

Claire smiled. "You are obstinate."

"Bullheaded." Indio returned the smile. "I didn't even thank you for coming today. Thank you for coming."

"You're welcome. You know I love coming to your safe harbor."

"You haven't been around much lately."

"No. It hasn't been much of a safe place for me." Claire lowered her eyelids and gazed toward the floor. "Which is my fault, of course. Seeing you and Ben only intensifies my guilt. And our arguing last week here in the parking lot was so disrespectful. Of all places for me to raise my voice."

"Claire."

Her daughter-in-law looked up.

"We've got enough guilt piled in here to bury an elephant." She rubbed her chest again. "It's high time we mucked it out. Or, better yet, let's just lay it down at the feet of Jesus. You know the whole point of His death on the cross was to forgive us so we wouldn't have to carry the junk around with us."

"I'm sure I've filled my quota for junk left at the cross. Should you see a doctor?"

"No. I just need to get some things off my chest." Her smile felt like a grimace. "So to speak."

"Indio, you don't have to tell me. I know Jesus died for my sins. I know He loves me. But there comes a point when none of that impacts my day-to-day life. Not to mention I'm willfully disobeying God by leaving Max rather than trying to fix things with him."

Indio sighed to herself. "That's between you and God. As far as I'm concerned, I forgive you for hurting Max. But I'm talking about my guilt. Watching you and Max argue just about did me in."

Claire's face crumpled.

"Dear, I don't say that to heap burning coals on your head. It was not your fault." Indio rallied all the breath she could and thrust it into her voice. "Do you hear me? It was not your fault."

Claire's distraught expression turned into one of surprise. "Well, it wasn't yours."

"Maybe it was. I mean, in a way. It wasn't until I was fifty years old that I understood how I wounded Max. I always unconsciously compared him to BJ. And the poor guy always came up short. I hurt him like only a mother can, every which way to Sunday."

"I still remember the morning you came to our house and admitted as much to him. He said he was a hellion and deserved whatever treatment he got."

"Yep. He said there was nothing to forgive. He's in denial, of course. If he doesn't ask God to help him forgive me, resentment toward me will fester in his heart." She shook her head. "But that's between him and God. I can't fix that any more than I can fix your marriage. What I can fix, though, is what's between you and me. Maybe I can give you back your safe harbor here."

Claire watched her expectantly. Indio was reminded of the young woman who used to soak up whatever her mother-in-law had to say on the subject of faith. That side of Claire had faded with age. Had Indio pushed it away? *Lord, I am sorry.*

Indio said, "In all honesty, Claire, I believed that it was your duty to take care of Max in the ways that I failed him. He needed a woman who did not let him down. And when you left him, my head understood why, but my heart condemned you. You had destroyed his home, the safe harbor I had never given him." Her voice caught. Shame flooded her. "I am so sorry that I could ever think such a thing."

Claire opened her mouth as if to protest, but Indio held up a hand. She took several breaths, steadying her voice. "Some would argue that you are wrong to leave him. But I believe you gave Max a crucial wake-up call. He has made work his god. His life is out of order. For you to continue living in that disorder was not healthy for either one of you. Will you forgive me for holding you responsible for Max's happiness? For being angry at you?"

"There's nothing to forgive—"

"There is, Claire. And I desperately need your forgiveness. Trust me, it will break down a barrier between us."

Claire gazed at Indio, her eyes filling. When at last she spoke, her voice choked. "I deserve your wrath over what I've done. But like always, you just welcome me into your heart. You've been more of a mother to me than my own mom. Sometimes I think I married Max because you loved me. And I love you. I'm sorry for letting you down."

Indio moved to the other bed and flung her arms around Claire. "It's all right, child. It's all right."

"Forgive me."

"I do, Claire, I do. Forgive me?"

She nodded, her chin bumping against Indio's shoulder.

"Thank you."

Indio closed her eyes and took a deep breath. She could have sworn that as her lungs expanded, that clothespin popped clean off of them.

Forty-nine

Claire leaned over the island in the middle of the hacienda's large kitchen and propped her elbows on the countertop. Forehead pressed against her palms, she studied the travertine. It was a pretty pattern. Swirls of rust and beige and brown. She had helped Indio choose it when she and Ben remodeled. It was a good choice.

"Mom?"

At the sound of Lexi entering the kitchen, Claire straightened.

"What did Dad say?" Lexi slid open a drawer and began pulling out silverware.

To Claire it seemed her youngest had been asking that question for twenty-six years. *"What did Dad say?"* Of course, she'd had to ask because Dad was never around. Dad's thoughts were always delivered by Mom. Mom filtered what Dad said, added spin where needed so as not to crush the spirit of her all-but-fatherless child.

"Hmm?" Lexi paused on the other side of the island, dinner plates, forks, and knives in hand, on her way to the kitchen table.

Claire sighed loudly. She'd just gotten off the phone with Max.

"That bad?" Lexi's right brow curled up like a roly-poly bug recoiling at the touch of a finger.

Claire realized there was no longer any sense in filtering and spinning. She had probably done more harm than good to Lexi with all her pretense that Max cared.

"I don't think I said good-bye to him. The last I remember was he said you shouldn't have come."

Lexi did the eye-roll thing. Her rendition never quite captured the essence of Jenna's "Who gives a rip" flair. "He just doesn't get it, does he?" She strode off to the table.

"No, he doesn't, hon. But Nana and Papa do, and that's who counts right now." She watched Lexi set the table. "What Dad means, but can't seem to put into words, is that he wishes you weren't here because it makes him worry. The fire is too close."

"Yeah, well, it's also too close to his wife and parents and the house he grew up in!"

"The house doesn't mean anything to him, and we're . . ." Expendable? "We're, um, adults. We should know better. You're twenty-six but still his . . . baby." *I think. I hope.*

A plate clattered on the table. Lexi's petite face contorted like a scrunched-up fist. "Then why doesn't he come up here and help? Papa's out there swearing at his horses. Nana's fretting over her chickens." Her voice rose. "Even Samson and Willow are acting goofy!"

At the sound of their names, the dog and cat lifted their heads from where they snuggled on the braided rug.

"They haven't stopped nuzzling all day. Why doesn't Dad come and say, 'Don't worry. Everything will be fine'? Isn't that what a dad's supposed to do?"

Claire walked over and pulled a shaking Lexi into a tight embrace. "Shh. I don't know, Lexi. I don't know." She really had no clue. After thirty-three years of marriage, the man was an enigma. True, he resented his parents. That was obvious in the ways he ignored them. But what did their relationship have to do with his ignoring his own children and wife?

Holding her daughter close, she eyed the muted television in a corner of the counter. Live video feed shot from a helicopter filled the screen with flames.

On a practical level they did not need Max. The Santa Ana winds had died. The fire was not coming their direction. She and Lexi would spend the night just to give Ben and Indio moral support.

Max apparently didn't know *moral support* from a hole in the head.

Blast it all!" Ben snarled at an old quarter horse that trotted in a wide circle around the corral. "Chester, get over here now!"

The chestnut tossed his head like a defiant teen.

Claire leaned against the fence beside her father-in-law. "That's what Indio said to tell you. 'Get over here now.' Meaning the kitchen. Dinner's about ready."

Ben tugged at the front of his cowboy hat. His eyes were nearly hidden beneath its brim. "Not hungry. Chester's not either. He knows something's up."

"What do you think?"

"That Chester knows what he's talking about." Abruptly Ben turned on his heel and strode toward the topless jeep parked outside the barn. He had no intention of eating dinner.

Claire followed. She squinted as the hot wind swirled dirt in her eyes. Temperatures still hovered above ninety.

It had been a long day at the hacienda. Changing linens, sweeping, scrubbing. Having heart-to-heart talks with Indio. Being mom and dad to Lexi. Claire wasn't all that hungry either.

Ben planted a foot on the running board, swung a long leg over the car door, and plunked himself onto the driver's seat.

"Can I come?"

He gave her half a nod and started the engine.

Within moments they'd left the barn behind in a cloud of dust. As they shot up a steep incline, Claire hung onto the roll bar above her with one hand, the side of the windshield with the other. No road was in sight, but Ben had worn a distinct path through the dirt and dried grass during the past two days.

They were headed to his lookout on the highest point of the property. Indio had told Claire he'd been driving up there almost hourly to check on the wildfire.

Officials were calling it the Rolando Bluff Fire, after the remote area where they believed lightning had sparked it. The latest news reported nearly fifty thousand acres burned. Most of the area was remote and uninhabited. The one community in the vicinity had been evacuated, as well as some rural residences.

The fire was not under control, though, and only 20 percent was contained.

Ben braked and cut the engine. They got out of the car and began clambering up the dozen or so yards of terrain too vertical and rock strewn even for the jeep.

Claire was not an outdoorsy woman. When Erik was two, she'd let him hike to his heart's content in the wilderness surrounding his grandparents' home. His little legs hadn't carried him far—just enough that she was not within shouting distance of the house when she saw her first rattlesnake as it slithered very near her toddler's feet. The next day she began saving money and soon purchased a good pair of leather cowboy boots. Wearing them now, she was glad she always kept them stored at the hacienda along with blue jeans and T-shirts.

Claire said, "I remember climbing here with you and the kids. I think Erik was about sixteen the last time." She always figured out the timing of events by the age of her eldest. She wondered if it was the same with her in-laws and BJ.

"Yep. The Coyote Bluff Fire. That one came the closest."

"The sheriff was at the house when we got back down."

"He'll let us know if we should evacuate, Claire. Don't you worry."

She huffed alongside him. "But you're worried."

"Concerned. There's smoke, and our last good rain was in January. Santa Ana's been blowing for days. S'posed to let up tonight, but the damage is already done. The whole county is one dried-up box of kindling."

Worried, concerned, anxious, whatever. Claire wasn't going to argue semantics. "So what do you think?"

He grunted and climbed the remaining few feet without so much as an audible exhale. Although he seemed fit as a fiddle, he was in a mood, as Indio liked to call it whenever "blast it all" dominated his vocabulary. Or when he quit jobs before they were finished. That afternoon he'd left his big green tractor smack-dab in the middle of the parking area. The grading would not get completed this day.

Claire had always been comfortable to some degree with her reserved father-in-law. He loved his animals and the outdoors and was nothing at all like the dad she'd lived with growing up.

Ben was a thoughtful grandfather too. He never made the kids feel as if they were in his way, no matter what their ages. He had an appreciation for beauty. Before retiring he had been a successful carpenter. His lovely wood creations were everywhere inside and outside the house.

She gazed with him now toward the southeast. Usually the view offered a panorama of jagged mountains the blue-green color of scrub brush. Tonight, though, billowy black smoke encompassed the vista. Although the sky remained blue directly above them, the setting sun to her right could not begin to penetrate the smoke. Two helicopters circled off to one side. The destruction lay on the other side of hills located at least twenty-five miles away, but it was an eerie sight.

He lowered the binoculars. "I think that the wind is good for us, not so good for El Marino and those other communities to the south." He glanced at her. "For now."

"We have the boxes packed in my car." Although her in-laws didn't display family photos, they had plenty of albums and, most important, a small trunk full of BJ mementos.

He nodded. "Thank you for helping out today."

"I'm glad you called me."

He squinted toward the wildfire. "I'm not good at asking for help. Max gets that foolishness from me. We're a lot alike. Can't ask for help. Get tunnel vision. Think we know what's what. That's why we always butt heads." He paused. "It's a healthy thing for you to tell him what's what. Healthy for both of you. No matter what happens, you needed to say it, and he needed to hear it."

Claire's throat closed up. Ben and Indio Beaumont still loved her! More like adopted parents than the proverbial vexations, her in-laws still loved her. They thought she had made right choices! They didn't blame her!

For one fleeting moment, the world was a beautiful, comforting place to be.

Max, please talk to your dad." Claire sat in the dark, on the porch step outside the kitchen. It wasn't the best for privacy, but it was the farthest she could go and still be able to use the house cordless phone. Cell phone signals were nonexistent up in the hills.

"I'm not talking to my dad. It wouldn't matter diddly-squat what I might say to him. His mind's made up."

"That's just it. I'm not sure it is. He's not his usual confident self. I think if it weren't for the horses, we'd leave."

"You and Lexi don't have to stay."

Claire propped her chin in her hand and looked up at the stars. Why was it their daughter understood what Max didn't? No one had to call and convince Lexi to come. She arrived that afternoon and worked in the gardens, fully intending to remain with Nana and Papa to help in any way she could—even if that only meant hanging out at the hacienda, keeping them company.

Claire said, "We do have to stay. They're pushing eighty, and right now they are, understandably, a little concerned."

"Suit yourself. Oh. Sorry." His sarcastic tone undercut the apology. "That's the cold fish talking."

Claire wanted to throw the phone at the large trunk of a nearby sycamore tree. She resisted the urge. Now that she had Max on the line, she wanted to finish the conversation.

He said, "The warm fish says the fire is 20 percent contained, and that was before the wind died down. Santa Reina is in no danger."

"I know." Ben refused to turn off the television or radio. They blared in the kitchen and the barn.

"Then what's the problem?" Max said.

"I have no clue! That's why I want you to talk to your dad!"

"Calm down. You don't want to work yourself into a tizzy just because two old people are unnerved by a fire going the other direction."

"Don't tell me what to do!"

"Why else did you call except for me to tell you what to do?"

Why had she called?

Claire slid her hand up from her chin until it covered her mouth.

No, she hadn't called to ask him what to do. She knew what to do. Either let the eight horses go and then drive down to the city— or trust in the current conditions that indicated all was safe for the Santa Reina area, including the Hacienda Hideaway.

No, she hadn't called so Max could tell her what to do.

She lowered her hand and her voice. It sank to a whisper. "I called because I wanted you to take care of me."

"Then I say stay put. Save Dad from having to round up his horses tomorrow or the next day."

"I meant *here*, Max. I meant I wanted you here to make me feel safe. I wanted you to hold me. I wanted to hear you say you love me and that everything will be okay. I wanted . . . Oh . . ." Why bother to say it again? She wanted him there beside her, to be part of her life. "You know what? There is no such thing as a warm fish. Fish are cold-blooded."

"That's all—"

The line went dead.

And then she smelled smoke.

Fifty

Max punched the Off button on the cordless. Hanging up on him must give Claire a sense of power. She kept doing it.

"Are they all right?"

He turned to see Neva walking across the patio. "They can see smoke. It's the other side of the hills and blowing away from them, but they're goosey."

She stopped beside him next to the pool. "Why don't they just leave?"

"It gets complicated. There are horses, chickens, Willow the cat and Samson the old golden retriever. A houseful of things. My mom learned from Grandma Beaumont to keep important documents and photos packed and in a front closet. Those are probably already in the car." He wondered if the large family photo from Jenna's wedding was off the wall. His mother liked that one. "The dog's rug is in the truck."

"The what?"

"Samson won't jump in the truck bed unless his rug is in it."

Neva smiled. "Did you go through many scenarios like that?"

"A few. The place is too remote. You know, you have a beguiling smile."

She touched his arm.

Her smile wasn't the only thing that beguiled. A clingy, low-cut black dress accentuated her softness.

"Are they all right?"

Max heard the question but let his mind wander elsewhere. For more than thirty years, Neva Martínez-Rhodes had been there at his side. Sure, he'd noticed her attractiveness, personality-wise as well as those feminine curves. He even counted on that luscious package to attract clients—and it did. Which meant, he supposed, that he kept her filed under "Business."

Wasn't that what he had told Claire?

It was true. He had noticed Neva, but he had not *noticed* her.

Until now.

Any out-of-office time they spent together revolved around work. Until now.

During the long day of meetings, their usual banter had taken on a different tone. Or maybe it was different only to him. Maybe it had been there all along.

She offered to bring dinner to his house. His acceptance had been immediate.

And now she was there for his taking. That was made abundantly clear. She'd shown up on his doorstep in that dress, her hair loose to her shoulders, wearing perfume that must have required a special license to buy. He hardly noticed what they ate.

"Are they all right?" she asked again.

"Probably not." He set the phone on the table. "They'll come here. Dogs aren't allowed in Lexi's apartment complex."

She stepped into his waiting arms. "I'll settle for a good-night kiss, then. What's another few days after thirty years?"

He looked into her dark eyes. Had she really been waiting until he was available?

Her body against his felt much smaller than Claire's. Her lips were fuller. As he met them with his own, he allowed himself a lingering moment to imagine what it would be like to spend the night with this very attractive, very feisty woman.

Fifty-one

"Mom!" Lexi's scream ripped through the night's stillness. "Mom!"

Already panicked at the scent of smoke, Claire raced into the house and through the kitchen, following the shouts. They led her back outdoors again and into the courtyard. One glance registered everything: Lexi and the dog ran to the open end of the courtyard, toward the barns. Indio hurried the other way and into the front entryway. She was going to the car, a cumbersome picture frame under her arm.

"Indio!" Claire caught up and relieved her of the family photo that had hung on her kitchen wall.

"Thanks, Claire. The wind shifted. God is good. Hallelujah."

"What?"

Indio's off-centered smile and bright eyes gave her a slightly wild look as they rushed out into the front yard. "He's here, you know. The wind shifted, and now the fire is heading toward us, lickety-split. Phone line is dead. What can we do except skedaddle and ask Him for help?"

If she didn't know better, Claire would have sworn the woman was demented. On second thought, maybe she was. "Whatever. Where's Ben and Lexi?"

"Releasing the horses. The only important thing left to pack is that picture." She pointed to the frame bouncing against Claire's leg.

"Okay, we're all right. We take it one step at a time. No need to panic. There's still plenty of time. It's still miles away. This is just smoke."

Just smoke . . . Then she noticed in the spotlights a flutter of something. Moths?

No. It was ash. Ashes were falling like a fine, dry snow.

Indio coughed, a hacking noise, as if the smoke had settled into her lungs. "The wind shifted *and* picked up speed. It'll do that, you know."

Claire opened a car door, leaned inside, and began rearranging the boxes on the seat. If she wedged the picture behind them, it would be safe. Though then it might block her view out the rear window.

From behind her, Indio said, "Dry as this year's been, the fire could reach Vallecitos Canyon and burn through it quick as a wink."

Claire stilled her hands on a box. Vallecitos Canyon? Hacienda guests who went horseback riding could make it to the canyon and back before lunch.

"Claire, we'd better go help Ben. He's bound and determined to get Chester in the trailer—"

"What!" Claire whacked her head, scrambling from the car. "Ouch! Indio, we can't take the horse trailer!"

"He's already hitched it up to the truck."

Abruptly the front yard went black, as if someone had doused the spotlights. Claire looked at the house. It was completely dark as well. Not even a star twinkled above. Only a feeble patch of light spilled out from the car's interior.

Claire froze. In her mind's eye she traced the path of electrical wires from the house, across fields of scrub vegetation, up steep hills and down valleys, through wooded areas. The lines did not run east toward the mountains. They went west, down into Santa Reina.

Why would power from the west be cut off when a fire burned in the east?

Indio grabbed Claire's hand. "Time for the lanterns and flashlights. Hallelujah."

Claire was not aware of when the wail of sirens reached her. Suddenly they were just there, a distant lament that pulsated in her throat.

She and Indio stumbled through the dark to the kitchen porch where Indio had stashed battery-operated lanterns. Carrying them to light their way, they hurried down the side yard to the barn, the area already lit by the truck headlamps and a number of battery-operated lanterns set around.

Lexi was bent between the big pickup and the horse trailer, disconnecting the hitch. From the truck bed, Samson yipped and jumped. In the shadows nearby, Ben stood in the corral.

Lexi straightened, calling out, "Papa! Let him go!" She shook her head at Claire and Indio.

Without a word, Indio plodded toward her husband.

"Mom, he's lost it. He wanted to start the generator to get the power going, and now he wants to put Chester in the trailer. We don't have time!" The normally soft-spoken girl clearly was losing it herself.

"Lexi, let's not panic. No one has told us to evacuate. It's just smoke—"

"Mom! Where do you think the smoke is coming from? We went up to check on things before I yelled to you." She waved a hand in the direction of the higher ground. "Vallecitos is totally ablaze. The whole rim of Kuphaall Range is on fire. And the wind is doing strange things, going in circles almost."

"You saw flames?"

"Yeah, so we've got to get out of here *now*." She hurried to the driver's side of the truck. "I'm driving. Just leave your car."

Claire's teeth chattered. Her body felt rooted to the ground. Why hadn't the sheriff's department warned them the fire was racing toward the hacienda? It shouldn't have been possible for it to travel so far, so quickly.

She saw Indio and Ben hurrying from the corral, hand in hand. Their shoulders seemed newly bent, as if the crushing weight of seventy-plus burden-carrying years had finally descended upon them.

The truck engine revved, and she saw her daughter high up in the driver's seat, looking smaller and more vulnerable than ever.

Lexi leaned out the window and beckoned to her. "Mom!"

Claire shook her head. "I'll follow you out."

The truck had a backseat, so there was plenty of space for all of them plus the cat she was sure already sat on it. But riding in it would mean abandoning the treasures packed in her car. She didn't care if fire destroyed her car, but she wasn't about to fail her in-laws again. Preserving their photos and the mementos from BJ's short life with them seemed the most important thing she could do.

Claire gripped the steering wheel and drove as close as possible behind the pickup. Lexi's lead foot bucked it along, the back tires shooting up dirt and gravel, the bed fishtailing. Samson stayed out of sight, probably being tossed around. Poor thing. The horse trailer would have long been flung off to a side of the winding lane by now. It had been a good call on Lexi's part to unhook it. Poor Ben. Poor Chester. Poor all the horses. Would they find a way out?

"Dear God, help us. Dear God, help us." Claire's repetitive prayer leaped out between spurts of breath. It was all she could say.

The Beaumont property consisted of a few hundred acres tucked off the beaten path. Like a pair of huge, protective arms, foothills, mountain ranges, and canyons embraced it. There was only one entrance in . . . which meant only one exit out. It was a long, curvy driveway, a ten-minute trip between house and highway, through rough terrain and quiet woods. At the speed they raced, a few minutes might be shaved off.

"Dear God, help us."

The lane met the highway. She mapped out the route in her

mind. A left-hand turn led to a ranch. They would turn right, toward Santa Reina. Before reaching the town, they would come to Estudillo Corners and turn left. They would go down the hill and thirty minutes later arrive in San Diego. Then they would . . .

Then they would what?

Go to Max's house?

When had she started thinking of it as Max's house?

"Dear God, help us."

The truck disappeared in a swirl of dust around a blind curve. Claire slowed for the bend. As she put her foot again on the gas pedal, she saw the truck's back red lights brighten and slammed on her own brakes.

Why were they stopping?

"Oh, dear God."

Straight ahead, visible above the truck and through the swirling dirt and thickening smoke, flames shot skyward—a wall of fire to the right and to the left. Across the lane. That one entrance in, one exit out.

Fifty-two

Max stood in his driveway and, with some regret, watched Neva drive off.

In all honesty, a little relief mingled in with the regret. Sure, a passionate frolic would have been sheer ecstasy. Neva's kisses guaranteed she knew how to please a man.

But if he wanted sex, he could pay for it. Why should he sign up for a complicated relationship? He already had one of those. Becoming intimate with his director of operations would doom him to another one, no doubt about it. He had to work with Neva every day. There'd be no escape when the workday ended. He'd have to really love her to want to go home with her too.

Love? Was that how he felt? *Oh, brother!* Now he was sounding like Claire. How did he *feel*?

Well, he felt like he wanted to hurt Claire, to pay her back.

Was that why he had kissed Neva?

Probably. At least partly. He craved a woman's touch. Neva was in the right place at the right time and turned him on like a match to dry kindling.

He shuddered. *Close call, Beaumont.*

Maybe he should thank God for the fire scare. Without the possibility of Claire and his parents showing up at the house, he easily could have succumbed. This way, though, Neva's departure had been a no-brainer, for him and her.

He weighed the chances of his family showing up. Ben and Indio had stayed at the house with them twice for extended periods—once during the remodeling of the hacienda and once after his dad's surgery. It was the logical choice for them if they had to evacuate. There was plenty of space for guests.

Would Claire stay too?

Weird thought. The state of limbo was driving him nuts. Which could further explain his infatuation with Neva.

His cell phone rang. He pulled it from his pocket and checked the ID. Jenna. Whew. At least he didn't have to disentangle himself from Neva before answering. "Hi."

"Daddy!" Her voice was hysterical. "Santa Reina's being evacuated!" She burst into tears.

"Jen. Jen. Calm down, honey."

"Max." It was Tandy, her tone nearly as distraught as Jenna's. "The wind shifted. Santa Reina's in the path now."

The hacienda lay between Santa Reina and the fire.

A dredging sensation hit Max, a backhoe hollowing out his insides. "Claire?"

"Don't know. Turn on the news, dirtbag."

The line went dead.

Fifty-three

Claire rammed the gearshift into Park, flew from the car, and hit the ground running. There was only one thought on her mind: to get to her baby.

"Lexi!"

Her daughter was already out of the truck, hanging on to the open door, facing the nightmare before them. Claire reached her side, and they clutched each other.

"Mommy." She pointed down the lane.

The world slid into slow motion. Claire felt intense heat as if from a bonfire gone amuck. Her eyes and throat burned with smoke. The scent of burning sage coated her nostrils. Sizzling, snapping, roaring noises filled her ears. Above it all Samson barked.

In light cast from the truck's headlamps, three figures emerged, moving toward them. One of them waved an arm.

"Hallelujah!" Indio appeared in the truck's open door, her arm resting on the steering wheel, legs dangling from the high seat. "It's Shadrach, Meshach, and Abednego."

Claire looked again to the figures. They were firefighters in full gear with helmets, face shields, and breathing apparatus in place. Nearing, they moved things aside, revealing their faces.

"Are you okay?" one shouted above the noise.

"Yeah." Clearly, Lexi fibbed. Claire felt her trembling as much as she was.

"Where does this road lead?"

From the front seat, Ben called out over Indio's shoulder. "To our house."

"We'll have to take the other way out." He pointed a gloved thumb over his shoulder. "That direction's blocked."

"There is no other way."

"Huh?"

Ben said, "Fire's behind the house, coming up through a canyon."

"How far?"

"Five miles."

The three strangers exchanged glances. The one doing all the talking yelled, "We'll check it out. Can you give us a lift?"

Ben nodded. "Climb in front here. But let my granddaughter drive. She knows this road like the back of her hand. Been driving since she was ten." He motioned to Indio to move to the backseat.

Claire's legs shook so violently she began to sink to the ground.

Lexi held on to her more tightly. "Mom!"

"Ma'am?"

Claire's view of slow motion spun into warp speed. The next thing she knew, she was sitting in the passenger seat of her car, next to a stranger who drove it. In the dim light of the dashboard, she saw a black smudge on his cheek. The sight of it brought a sudden balance to her blurred vision. Help had arrived. It really had.

She gulped for air and coughed at the smoke she'd already swallowed.

"Ma'am, why don't you put your seatbelt on?"

Automatically she reached for it. Through the side window, in the blackness of night and smoke, she saw a pine tree perfectly outlined in fire.

"Seatbelt?" Her laugh bordered on hysterical. At least she recognized it, though. That must mean she was still on the controlled side of hysteria. But then, what did she know?

"Are you all right?"

Claire turned to him. "I'm just fine! We're driving through a wildfire, going to a house that's surrounded by fire on three sides, with a canyon on the fourth that's impassible in broad daylight, and I'm supposed to put on my seatbelt?"

He flashed a grin at her. "Yes, ma'am. Safety first."

"Oh, dear God." *Dear God.* Yes. Dear God.

He had sent help. She and Lexi weren't standing down the lane, petrified, watching the fire burn toward them. There was a fireman sitting next to her, and two more with her family in the truck. Indio had recognized them right away. That was Indio, and Claire knew she could trust her.

"So," she said, "are you Shadrach, Meshach, or Abednego?"

He chuckled. "The name's Eddie."

Fifty-four

Crazy with fear, Jenna stood in front of Tandy's television set and watched her brother, the cool TV news anchorman, fall apart on camera.

"Get him off the set!" Jenna shouted.

Beside her, Tandy said, "He's okay, Jen. Look, they're panning away from him."

"Why doesn't he get out of his seat? And that idiot, Felicia! With that idiotic smile on her face! What's that supposed to convey? Empathy? Fifty thousand acres have burned, and she's grinning?"

"Shh." Tandy gave her a one-armed hug. "Shh. It's okay."

At last Erik's shoulder disappeared from view on the screen. Moments before, he and his coanchor, Felicia, had been doing a special update, talking about the Rolando Bluff Fire. About the fifty thousand acres. About the mere 20 percent that was under control. About the sudden wind shift.

And then the "This just in" from her brother. He listened to his earpiece, ad-libbing . . . and, in that honeyed, professional tone of his, informed viewers their reporter and cameraman were rushing to the scene.

And then he said, "Apparently a second fire is now burning to the north. Officials are concerned that it could converge with the original fire—What's that? Yes. Yes. All right. The sheriff's department is ordering all residents of Santa Reina and surrounding areas to evacuate immediately. This is not voluntary. I repeat, all residents of Santa—"

And then no more words came out of his mouth. He just froze, his lips parted, his head cocked to one side, his hazel eyes gazing straight at the camera.

The idiot Felicia, to her credit, filled in his blank. She asked him if that was correct, that all residents were to evacuate Santa Reina and the surrounding area. Erik didn't reply. His eyes didn't even twitch. Jenna knew her brother. In his mind he was projecting the fire's movement. A Santa Reina evacuation meant it was traveling through Hacienda Hideaway land.

Jenna had called her grandparents' house but gotten no response. She called her mom's cell, knowing full well that cell never functioned up in the hills. She had to talk to her dad. Speed dial. What was his—Her thumb missed the keypad. "Oh, God. I can't think straight."

Where was Danny? They should go find Erik. They should—

Her phone jingled. Danny's name appeared on the ID screen.

"Danny!" She shouted his name into the mouthpiece, but there was no answer.

The phone rang at her ear again.

Tandy took if from her. "Let me answer, hon. Sit down. I'll talk to him."

Jenna sank onto the couch. A rushing noise filled her head. The room spun.

They were all burning up. Her mom. Her baby sister. Her grandma. Her grandpa.

She opened her mouth in agony. No sound escaped.

The very worst fire San Diego County had seen in years was roaring toward them. Surrounding them. Maybe it already had.

Excruciating pain shot through her stomach, a knife stabbing over and over. She curled into a tight fetal ball. "Oh, God, please don't let them die. Please!"

"Honey?"

Jenna became aware of Tandy sitting beside her, rubbing her arm.

"Honey, I talked to Danny. He's going to pick up Erik at the studio and head toward Santa Reina. Your dad's meeting them at that park on Poway Road."

"I want to go."

"Listen. I doubt they can get that far. The roads will be clogged with cars coming down from the town and emergency vehicles going up. It's best if we stay put." She tried to smile. "Hey, somebody's got to be here when your mom comes home."

Home. Tandy's condo wasn't her mother's home. It wasn't Jenna's home either.

"I want to go home." At last she burst into tears. "I want to go home!"

"All right. I'll take you to your dad's."

"No! Kevin's my home!"

"Shh, it's okay, hon. We'll call him, all right? We'll just call old Kev. Let's see." She fiddled with Jenna's phone. "I bet he's number one on speed dial, huh? Yep. Here you go." She handed her the cell.

Jenna counted the rings. One. Two. *Oh, God.* Three. *Don't let them die.* Four. *Please.*

"Jen!" Kevin's voice. Firm, solid, assured. Her husband. Her anchor. Her home.

A strangled sob cut off her words.

"Hey, I'm here, pretty lady. I'm right outside the door."

And then Tandy's doorbell rang.

Fifty-five

My great-great-grandfather Charles Beaumont Sr. settled here in 1847."

Claire tuned out Ben's docent tones and hugged her knees to her chest. Seated on one of the couches in the hacienda's large living room, she trembled from head to toe, wondering how her father-in-law could give a history lesson at this point in time. And where was Indio? She half expected her to appear with a tea tray. The two of them slid into hosting mode as if it were a typical Saturday at the Hideaway.

Lanterns lit the *sala*, many of them focused on the framed wall map Ben pointed to. Yellowed and faded, it was a topographical map of the Beaumont property. There he stood, discussing family lore with Lexi and the firemen, Eddie, Zak, and Chad.

Why wasn't Max there?

One of the two younger ones—Zak or Chad—approached her, sidestepping Samson and Willow. The pets paced the room, whining and sniffing, obviously unnerved.

Chad-slash-Zak sat on the edge of the couch. His fireproof overalls and orange jacket with reflective stripes were incongruous in such a setting. "Are you all right?"

"Should I be? There's no way out. You can see that by the map."

"We'll find a way. That's our job."

"You got stuck here."

She had started trembling again earlier when Ben asked about their fire engine and radios. Eddie, the oldest and the apparent leader, said the radio quit working when a leaping wave of flame crossed the road and trees fell. In the confusion they became separated from the truck.

How did firemen lose a fire truck?

He said, "We're not stuck, ma'am, just rethinking strategy." He smiled. His teeth were a brilliant white against the smudges on his smooth face. Sweat had left little trails through one of the dirt spots. He was so young.

"We can't stay in the house." She'd overheard them discussing the four-foot-thick adobe walls and tile roof.

"It's best not to. The exterior won't burn, but if the fire were to get close enough, the thousand-degree heat would burst through the windows, and then we'd be in trouble."

She blinked. The kid seemed excited talking about death and destruction.

Why wasn't Max here?

"Papa!" Lexi cried out, her voice high. "The gold mine! We can go there!"

Eddie said, "Gold mine?"

Ben traced his finger along the map. "My great-grandfather, Charles Jr., refused to include it on the map. He was so mad at his dad, Charles Sr., over the gold business. Senior found gold here in '48. Not much—enough to buy the acreage and build this house. But as the story goes, he wasted his life digging for more that didn't exist. He died down in that mine. Let's see, it's in this area."

"No." Lexi reached up and touched the map. "It's here."

"Lexi, I know—"

"This is a back entrance."

"What?"

"You don't know it?"

Ben reddened. "What are you talking about?"

"The main entrance is too close to the canyon. See?" She pointed at another place on the map. "The fire's probably already in the area. But here, on the other side of those hills, we can get in."

"There's no way—"

"Papa, there is. It's where I find the morel mushrooms. My gosh, don't have a stroke just because we kept it a secret from you."

"Secret or no secret, I told you kids never to go near the mine."

"Papa, I'm twenty-six!"

"I don't care—"

Eddie laid a hand on his shoulder. "Lexi, can we get to it? Can we get inside it?"

"Yes. I know that for a fact." She turned back to the map. "We drive to here. Then hike up, twenty minutes or so."

"Okay, gang," he said. "We have a plan."

A loud whoosh sounded. There was the crash of breaking glass. Something thundered. The floor shook.

And Indio screamed.

Fifty-six

Blinding flashes of red and blue lights shredded the night's darkness. Several police cars were parked at odd angles across the highway, blocking the two lanes that led up to Santa Reina.

A bumper-to-bumper stream of cars and trucks filled the other two lanes, inching down the hill toward San Diego. Impatient drivers honked. People were everywhere, on foot and leaning from open car windows, yelling. Distant sirens wailed.

The whole bizarre scene was like something out of a low-budget disaster movie.

Flanked by his sons, Max stood on the pavement. The noise pounded in his chest. He shouted again to a policeman in a neon-lime vest. "My family is up there!"

"Sir, I repeat." Though he stood only two feet away, the officer had to shout as well. "No one is allowed through except emergency personnel. Santa Reina is being evacuated."

"I'm not going to Santa Reina! I'm going south at Estudillo Corners. I'm going *home*! My wife is there!"

The officer shook his head and waved at a motorist to keep moving.

Max swore. They'd gotten nowhere near to where he'd hoped. The roadblock had stopped them too soon.

"Dad." Danny pulled at Max's arm until he lowered the cell phone he didn't realize he'd put to his ear again. "It won't work."

"Maybe they're close enough now."

"Then they'd call us. Lexi would call me first thing."

He cursed once more. Yes, Lexi would call Danny. The twins' ability to communicate was so eerie, she might not even need a phone.

Erik riffled through his wallet, muttering to himself. He moved toward the policeman.

Max and Danny followed.

"Officer, I'm with the press. I can't find my card, but here's my driver's license—"

"You're that guy from TV."

"Yeah. Erik Beaumont. Can I get through? My cameraman is up there somewhere. I need to . . ." His voice trailed off.

Max held his breath. Gone was the confident, charming TV personality. Danny had told him how Erik froze up on the air earlier as he listened to the reporter relay news of the evacuation.

"Sure, Mr. Beaumont," the officer said. "There's a command center about three miles up the road. There's an area for the press. Where's your car?"

Erik pointed to Max's black BMW parked on the shoulder.

"Give us a minute to clear a path for you." The policeman glanced toward Max and Danny. "News guy only."

Erik inhaled sharply. "My mom's up there, my sister, my grandparents. They're in a house southeast of town. The property backs up to Vallecitos Canyon." He paused. "This is my dad and my brother."

The man gazed at Erik for a long moment. Then he gave a short nod.

They strode to the car. Danny said he would drive and opened the back door for Max.

He hesitated, but Danny was already in the driver's seat, and Erik got into the passenger side, no doubt up front to smooth the way with his television face. Max climbed in the back and slammed the door shut.

It hit him then, a sudden realization that he'd been demoted to old man whose sons had to protect him.

"Erik," he growled. "What exactly did you hear from your reporter when you were on the air?"

Danny and Erik exchanged a look, unreadable in the dark. Still, Max caught its meaning. He and Claire did the same thing behind his father's back.

"Tell me what you know. What did he say that made you freeze?"

Erik didn't respond immediately. "It was a she. Mindy. She and Greg were on the scene." He referred to the cameraman. "Down near El Marino."

"And?"

"And . . ." He looked over his shoulder at Max. "She said they were evacuating Santa Reina because Vallecitos Canyon and the Kuphaalls north of it were burning."

In his mind's eye, Max saw the layout of canyons and mountain ranges and the Hacienda Hideaway. His throat closed.

"And she said that was not for on-air disclosure, because there were a handful of residents in the area who'd had absolutely no warning." Erik turned back toward the front. "Which explains why I froze up. Putz."

Fifty-seven

Lexi drove the truck toward the flames. Claire could see them. Why were they going toward Vallecitos Canyon? It made no sense.

But then, what *did* make sense tonight?

In the backseat of the truck, Claire huddled against Indio, who sat in the middle between her and Ben. Although the windows were shut, the scent of smoke coated every breath. The engine whined as the truck bounced over uneven terrain, at times nearly vertical in its climb.

"Well, we know God is good. He surely is." Indio patted her leg and then went back to petting the cat on her lap.

They hit a bump, and the two firemen up front with Lexi swayed to the left. What were their names? Eddie, the older one. And Chad. Or Zak? Whichever. The third one rode in the bed with the dog.

Except for Indio's occasional mantra about God's goodness, silence filled the cab.

What did one talk about on the road to death?

God, I'm sorry. I don't want to die tonight. I want Lexi to grow old and be happy. I want Indio and Ben to live to be at least a hundred. I want to find my safe harbor. Again. For the first time? I want to know if it's with Max. I do. I really do. I'll talk to him. I'll try.

Claire shook uncontrollably. The brief respite at the hacienda had ended abruptly. The firemen reasoned a large tree had fallen some-where, near enough to send the rumble through the house. Indio had dropped a tray full of teacups, hence the crash of breaking glass.

232

They rushed to the truck with lanterns and water bottles. The car wouldn't make it, Ben and Lexi said.

Which meant the photos wouldn't make it. Which meant BJ mementos wouldn't make it.

"Hallelujah."

Claire tried to close her eyes, to shut out the mountainous horizon lit up bright as noonday, but she couldn't. She felt irresistibly drawn in, that loathsome, typical response to freakish scenes.

She said, "Why are we going this way?"

Indio patted her leg again.

Eddie, next to the front passenger door, looked back at her. His face was in shadows. She felt his eyes on her, though, and waited to hear his voice, the only source of calm she'd found in recent hours.

"Claire, it's the way to the gold mine. To safety."

She nearly laughed again at his convoluted reasoning. First seatbelts and now safety in a treacherous old mine. Its walls had collapsed on Ben's great-great-grandfather and killed him. It had not been worked since. His body was never recovered.

When Claire's children were small, Ben had taken them to the boarded-up entrance. He knew the kids would eventually find it on their own and thought it best just to show it to them and instill in them a horrendous fear. He vowed if they ventured inside, they'd die—either from being buried alive or by his own hand. Evidently it didn't matter. They'd gone off and found another way into the mine.

Ben leaned forward. "Lexi, you have to go north here."

"Nope. Trust me."

"I know my own land!" His voice was a low roar. "Even if I don't know this so-called back entrance!"

Now Indio patted his arm. "Save the bear routine for later, dear."

"Papa, Danny and I found this when we were ten. If you tell him I showed it to you, I swear, you're toast."

Chad-slash-Zak bumped his shoulder against hers. "That was a good one."

Claire could see Lexi's profile by the light of the dashboard. She was smiling.

Smiling?

Evidently the road to death was paved with improbability. Ben sat in the backseat while Lexi drove and mouthed off to him and made bad jokes. Three strangers promised them safety in the most dangerous spot on the property. Indio named them after biblical heroes and breathed praises and made tea.

And Claire . . . Claire thought about moving to Greece.

They all climbed down out of the truck. Claire tumbled from it, legs too wobbly to hold herself upright. One of the strangers caught her around the waist.

"Claire." It was Eddie. "Take my arm."

"I'm . . ." She was what? Fine? Yeah, right. She slipped her hand into the crook of his elbow.

Lexi gathered the cat in one arm and held a lantern aloft in the other. She led the way with Chad-slash-Zak. Indio and Ben followed, Samson beside them, the other Chad-slash-Zak next. Claire and Eddie brought up the rear.

The firemen loomed large in their big coats and helmets and air tanks strapped onto their backs. They carried lanterns. Lights from their helmets also illumined the winding path that led through a grove of trees. The ground before them rose, and at long last the view of fire was blocked.

But the ash fell, and the sound continued, the eerie drone of some dreadful monster eating the earth behind them, steadily catching up.

Fifty-eight

From the recliner, Tandy watched Jenna talk on the phone to Danny. Seated on the couch, she mashed herself against Kevin as if she couldn't get close enough to him. The television was on, its volume low, its screen filled with flames glowing against the night sky. She didn't know if it helped or not to see live videos.

Where was Claire?

Jenna lowered the phone.

"What'd he say?" Kevin asked.

"He thinks . . ." She paused. "No, he believes, truly believes, they're all right. He says he would know if . . ."

If Lexi were dead. Nobody wanted to fill in the blank.

Tandy said, "Yeah. They have that twin thing going, don't they?"

"Mm-hmm. But Dad and Erik might kill each other waiting."

They exchanged an uneasy smile.

"He says Erik used his tarnished charm, and the cops let them in to where the press is, beyond the first blockade. There's no way they'd let us through, though. The traffic is so unbelievable, we'd never be able to see Papa's truck or Mom's car go by. And if for some reason Mom and Lexi's cell phones didn't work, none of us would know when they got out unless we waited for them down here."

"You should go to the house, then."

"Come with us."

"Maybe later. Some friends from church are coming over. Prayer warriors, they call themselves." Tandy had phoned one of them and

explained the situation. Within minutes, she learned that a contin-
gency was on its way. In a previous life she would have eaten worms
before inviting such weirdos into her home. But they were growing
on her.

Kevin smacked a fist against the couch arm.

Jenna jumped and started to cry softly.

Men. At least he hadn't punched her wall. Tandy counted to three.

Kevin disentangled his arm from Jenna's and wrapped her in a
hug. "Sorry."

Tandy leaned forward. "Kevin, I know you want to go do something tangible. The best thing you can do, though, is take her to the
house and don't leave her side." *And while you're at it, un-reenlist, or
you'll lose her.* "Even Marines have to sit and wait at times, right? You
don't just charge the hill."

"Yeah."

"Ooh-rah!"

He gave her half a smile.

Jenna moaned and pushed away from him, her face toward the
television.

Tandy looked at it. A banner with white letters ran across the
bottom of the screen. "Vallecitos what?" She grabbed the remote
and boosted the volume.

"We repeat. Vallecitos Canyon has burned, an estimated three thousand acres. The fire has spread to the north and west along the
Kuphaall range. At this time, we know of several homesteads within
the area. Residents had no warning of the second fire or the wind
shifts. The two fires quickly converged. However, officials believe
that people who had not evacuated earlier would have been on the
alert and noticed any changes in conditions and been able to leave
the area in time."

Jenna ran from the room, a hand over her mouth.

Fifty-nine

Eddie the stranger pried Claire's death grip from his arm and moved away from her.

She sank onto the steep, rock-strewn ground and laid her cheek against a big stone. Was she awake? Maybe not. Hopefully not. If not, then she could awake from this nightmare. She could stop thinking about the monster that now ate its way up through the rocks, devouring the ragged plant life between them.

Her throat burned. Her lungs ached. Her body still trembled in terror and, now, exhaustion. They had hiked uphill, climbing and stumbling over rocks for what felt like hours. The dim lights cast from lanterns and the firemen's helmets did little to light the way. No stars shone. There was no path to follow, just Lexi's insistent "Not far."

She should check on Ben and Indio.

Where was Max?

I love you, Max.

The dog brushed past her.

"Claire." Indio touched her shoulder and sat, holding a water bottle out to her.

She accepted it and twisted at the cap. It wouldn't budge.

Indio undid it for her. She drank.

In silence they watched the others. Evidently they'd reached their destination. Ben, Lexi, Shadrach, Meshach, and Abednego pulled at a pile of rocks that looked like any other pile of rocks against the side of the hill.

Someone let out a whoop. Someone laughed. Someone helped Claire to her feet.

Smoke filled her nostrils.

She clung again to the stranger's arm. He half carried her toward a small opening in the hillside. She heard the others' conversation as if from a distance, their disembodied voices winding through the smoky night.

"In here."

"Lexi! How did you and Danny ever find this?"

"We should cover the opening back up. The heat, if the fire reaches . . ."

"There's a lot of vegetation here to burn."

"Not enough time to remove that."

"Look at this wood frame."

"We'll pile the rocks over it."

Lexi said, "You have to crawl to get inside."

"How far in can we go?"

"A long ways. There's this tunnel, an open space, and then the shaft goes down. It's passable too."

"Where's the other opening?"

"You can't get to it from here."

"It's blocked?"

"It's where the cave-in was. This is the other side of that."

"Lexi." It was Eddie's voice, close by, above her. His was distinctive, an oboe's singular clarity floating on the breeze. "You'll get a medal for this."

She laughed. "Just what I always wanted."

"I thought every young woman wanted a medal. How about a ride in a parade? In a fire truck? Ticker tape and all."

"Try a gift certificate to the mall. Mom, lie down flat. Look. There goes Samson. Good dog! Okay, follow Nana in now."

Claire shook her head.

"It's fine once we get further inside. You can almost stand up. It's just the first dozen feet or so that you have to crawl."

Claire took a step back.

"Lexi." Eddie again. His arms slipped around Claire. "You go first. Let your mom hold on to your ankle. Okay, Claire? Come on. You can do it. You can do it."

He knelt, pulling her down with him. Lexi crouched at the opening, a lantern in front of her, and went down flat. Eddie guided Claire's hand to Lexi's boot.

It moved.

She whimpered.

Eddie grasped her calf. "Go, Claire. Go. I've got you."

"Okay, Mom, here we go. Let's catch up to Nana. Look at her. She's scooting along like she does this every day."

Claire shut her eyes, her death grip now clasped on the boot at Lexi's ankle, and dragged herself along by digging her elbows against the ground. A rock cut on the underside of her forearm. She brought her head up.

It bumped against something solid.

She cried out.

Lexi and Eddie began talking, their voices odd sounding, muffled by the small enclosure.

"So, Lexi, a mall certificate can't be enough. What else can we do for you?"

"How about a weekend in Acapulco? Maybe that's too much. How about a gift certificate to that new restaurant downtown? Did you read about it? Of course, I wouldn't want to go alone."

"Zak's available."

"Now what do you mean by that? Never mind! We're here!" Her boot was yanked out of Claire's hand. "Come on, Mom. You can stand up now. Well, almost. If you're under five-two. Nana fits." She laughed, tugging on Claire's arm. "Mom! Open your eyes."

Somewhere along the way, Claire had stopped breathing. She felt the heavy darkness like thick black tendrils. They coiled all around her, pushing her down, down into the ground, cutting off all light and air.

She'd been here before.

The long-buried scream rose up from a place deep inside of herself. It tore through her lungs, up and out her throat, louder and louder until she had to clap her hands over her own ears.

Sixty

Indio perceived that Claire's screams came from another time, another place.

The ring of terror in them went beyond what the current situation would provoke, dreadful as it was. The Claire she knew would be fighting for survival, fighting for her daughter even more than for herself. This total breakdown made no sense unless it stemmed from some unseen ugliness. Perhaps something from her daughter-in-law's long-forgotten past?

Indio immediately began to pray.

Eddie, the gentlemanly fireman, sat on the ground with Claire, his helmet on the ground. He held her close to himself, like a father would a hurt child, sideways against his chest, with a slight rocking motion, his soothing murmurs lost in her cries.

The cavelike area was small. Talk was impossible while Claire shrieked. Hunched over, they all stood in a compact circle under the low ceiling. Samson huddled at Ben's feet, Willow so close to the dog that she was almost hidden in his fur.

Fear replaced her granddaughter's calm expression. She could face fire, but not her mom's inexplicable breakdown. Zak, the cute fireman, stepped around Eddie and Claire to reach Lexi, and then he put an arm around her.

Chad, the talkative fireman, crouched to pet Samson. He had graciously helped Indio and Ben on the long trek uphill. A couple of times he had placed his mask over their faces, letting them breathe from his tank, and sweet oxygen flowed into them, a respite from the increasing smoke that had begun to make them all cough.

"Nooooo!" Claire screamed.

Indio knelt beside her and placed a hand on the back of her head. She leaned over to speak directly into her ear. "Claire, Jesus is with you. He was always with you. Time does not exist for Him."

Convinced that Claire was reliving a past trauma, she prayed silently, asking God to heal the pain Claire now experienced as if it were for the first time.

At last her daughter-in-law's shrieks dwindled to mewls. She hiccuped and began gagging. With a groan, she pushed herself away from Eddie, leaning forward on her knees.

For several minutes, the only sound was that of Claire being sick. "I'm sorry. I'm sorry."

"Shh." Eddie helped her sit back beside him. "It's okay."

Indio pulled a fistful of tissues from her jacket pocket and handed them to Claire. Claire settled a glazed stare on Indio.

Indio whispered, "God's taking care of it, whatever it is."

"The basement." Her voice was a hoarse whisper.

"Mom?" Lexi pushed her way in next to Indio.

Tears streamed down Claire's face now. "I'm okay." She shuddered.

Lexi frowned. "We have to move on."

Claire wiped at her face, making smudges with dirt and tears. "I'm okay."

"You don't have to crawl anymore."

She nodded.

"Zak says if the fire reaches the opening, the heat might—"

"Got it," Eddie interrupted, helping Claire to stand. "We're right behind you."

Ben lifted Indio to her feet. As the others ducked into a tunnel and filed from the room, he halted, aiming his lantern at a spot along the wall.

At its base Indio noticed a neat pile of small stones. "Oh my."

Ben smiled. "You're thinking what I'm thinking."

"It's Max and BJ's hidden stash! Where he gets a rock every year to put at the memorial."

"Yep. I guess Lexi and Danny aren't the only ones who know about this side of the mine." He wrapped his big hand around hers. "Looking death in the face here, it makes me see what a fool I've been. Why wouldn't the twins tell me about this place? Why wouldn't my own sons?"

"Because you would have tanned their hides."

"For sure. And they would have deserved it in that case. But in other cases, it just seems I've driven them away. I don't allow them to be open with me. Why would Max ever want to confide in me about anything after the way I treated him? When he started the business, I told him he was an idiot, and I haven't given him a lick of encouragement along the way."

She squeezed his hand. It was a night for fighting demons of all sorts.

"And poor Claire. A basement? I got the chills when she said that. You just know she lived through hell as a kid. Probably buried a lot of memories. I should have been more like a real father to her. I've let her down."

"She knows you love her."

"I could have done more." He pulled her into a hug. "Love, if we ever get out of here, so help me, God, I will make it up to all of them."

From behind them came a rushing, thunderous noise.

"Ben! Indio!" Chad yelled from the tunnel entrance. "Come on!"

Ben hustled her toward him.

She questioned the young man with her eyes. He flinched and then gave a quick nod in reply.

The fire had found them.

Sixty-one

Max trudged behind his sons in the semidarkness along the shoulder of another road. Emergency vehicles were everywhere, squad cars, ambulances, fire engines—blocking the way out, filling the parking lot. Up ahead a makeshift lighting system blazed, a white circle in the black night. Traffic exiting Santa Reina was no longer visible.

The police had directed them off the highway to this two-lane. A short bypass of the main road, it led to the Kuphaall Range lookout point, one of those inane Kodak moments that disrupted family trips up into the hills. He'd always voted to bypass the bypass, while Claire waved her camera, somehow communicating guilt in her smile. The kids really didn't give a hoot whether or not they saw some view deemed relevant by film manufacturers. His vote carried the majority, most likely because he was behind the wheel.

Except for a few clandestine gatherings with his drinking buddies as a teen, Max never stopped at the place. One year, though, Claire had made Christmas cards with a photo of herself and their kids standing in front of the stone wall, the deep canyon behind them hidden from view, the mountain vista a blur. It was a good picture. He couldn't remember who'd taken it.

He should be able to remember. He should have been in it. He should have stopped at the point every chance he had driving up to the hacienda with Claire and the kids.

"Dad, you okay?" Danny asked over his shoulder.

"Yeah. Stop asking."

Erik shook his head, obviously in disgust, and muttered something.

An almost irrepressible urge to belt his older son flared in Max. That they irritated each other was no secret to anyone who saw them together. Tonight, though, that subtle undercurrent of antipathy rushed aboveground.

Danny shot a glance over his shoulder at Max. Even in the shadow, he read it as a warning. Danny was probably ready to let them both have it. Max felt as if he was the odd man out, the old man sent to pick blueberries while his sons took care of business.

They reached an outer circle of firefighters. What Max could see beyond them were more, in full gear, talking on radios.

"Press is over there." One of the men turned to them and gestured toward their left.

Max looked and saw a gaggle of people calling out questions to a spokesperson. Cameras flashed.

Erik said, "I'm with the press, but that's not what I want. We have to get to the Hacienda Hideaway."

"Sorry. No can do."

"Our mom's there. Our—"

"Sorry. Now I have to ask you to leave this area. Either join the press or head back down the hill."

Max shoved his way between Danny and Erik. "Look. My wife is up there. My daughter. My parents. I am not going anywhere except up that hill. The Hideaway is southeast of Santa Reina."

"We know that, sir."

"Then let me—"

"They probably have gotten out by now. Go home where they can find you."

"Probably?" Max heard his voice rise. "Probably? That is not an acceptable answer. We're going through."

"Sir, there's no way to get through."

"You're nuts!" he yelled. "Traffic's pouring out of town!"

"I'm not talking about the town. Please, sir, just step aside."

Another fireman approached, older, an obvious superior. "Is there a problem here?"

"His family was at the Hacienda Hideaway."

The older man said to Max, "When?"

"Tonight! What do you mean, 'when'?"

"What time exactly?"

"I don't know!"

"Dad," Danny said, "you talked to Mom around eight thirty."

Max wheeled back toward the new spokesman. "What does the time matter? I don't know where she is! I have to find her!"

"You can't."

"You can't keep me from—"

"I mean you can't. It's not possible to—"

"I will go there!" He was in the man's face now. "It's my parents' house! It's our property."

"Okay." The fireman glanced at the younger one. "Show him." He walked away.

"Show me what?" he yelled after him.

The kid touched Max's shoulder. "Sir?"

Even in his frazzled state, Max noted the pained expression on his face.

"Follow me."

He followed, Danny and Erik with him. They took a circuitous route between trucks and ambulances and firefighting personnel. At last they emerged in a clearing.

It was the lookout point that drew in camera-toting travelers . . . the place where Claire and the kids had grinned for a Christmas card photo that didn't include him . . . the place he and his high school buddies had downed their six-packs while he cursed the hacienda that lay somewhere out there in the distant hills. He cursed it because it symbolized all that was not his: his brother's charmed life and his parents' acceptance.

And now as he gazed out on that scene, the horror of his curses descended upon him with a vengeance, and he roared with the agony.

The entire central portion of those distant hills and the mountains beyond them—the exact area that enclosed the hacienda—was ablaze with fire. All of it. *All of it!*

Max flung himself around and began running. He had to get to his car. He had to get to Claire, to his family. Now!

It took Danny and Erik and the fireman to hold him back.

Sixty-two

Claire shivered mere inches from Eddie. She wanted to curl up in the shelter of his arms again. But the terror had faded, and he was, after all, a stranger.

They all sat in a shadowy chamber of the mine. Hewn out of rock, it was clammy. But at least it wasn't as tight as the first tunnel. Its ceiling was higher than the first opening they'd stopped in, that place where she had screamed.

The image floated through her mind again, the one that had set off the uncontrollable shrieking.

She was a little girl. She crouched on a dirt floor in a root cellar, a small room for storing vegetables in the basement. A bulb hung on a stringy cord from the low ceiling, but a three-year-old couldn't reach it.

Until now. Somehow the screams had split open the long-buried memory. Somehow Indio's prayers loosened the grief she had never vented.

"You okay?" Eddie asked.

She nodded. "A little shaky." Her smile failed.

He smiled for her.

They sat on his turnout coat, a barrier between them and the dank rock and dirt floor. To reach this spot, they'd traversed a steep descent, her hand on his arm.

This irregular-shaped area was the end of the line, so to speak. A pile of rock from floor to ceiling covered much of it. Ben guessed it was the collapsed wall that had killed his great-great-grandfather. Claire wondered if the crushed bones had turned to dust yet.

Lexi had grown quiet, as if her bravado dwindled through that second tunnel. She led them but talked less, except in quiet tones to Zak. Once they'd reached this spot, she didn't move from his side. They sat close together on his coat with the cat. Claire imagined that her daughter felt like she did: safe next to the professional.

The third fireman, Chad, watched over Ben and Indio and wrestled playfully with Samson. Her in-laws huddled under a blanket, one of three they'd managed to bring along with the lanterns and knapsacks. Lexi and Claire were wrapped in the other two.

Claire felt a rush of gratitude for their rescuers. They kept putting her family first before their own needs. In spite of their outer garb, helmets, and air tanks, they'd toted the blankets and knapsacks stuffed with water bottles, crackers, apples, and chocolate.

"You're cold," Eddie said.

"A little." The blanket, T-shirt, and flannel-lined denim jacket were not quite enough to keep her warm in this hole in the ground. "You must be freezing."

He shook his head but rubbed his arms. His light blue shirt had short sleeves. "It was a hundred and five degrees this afternoon."

"Take my blanket."

"No. Thanks."

"We could share it."

"I'm fine."

She couldn't decipher the color of his eyes. They were light. Maybe blue? His face was narrow and youthful, but crow's-feet and a distinct air of maturity suggested he was at least her age. His hair, matted down from the helmet, was brown.

"Eddie," she said quietly, "are we going to make it?"

"Yes."

"Can we stop with the official version? I promise not to lose it again." It wasn't the threat of death that had pushed her over the edge.

"I have no idea." He studied her face for long seconds. "Doing okay?"

"Yes."

"Okay. Truth is, this is a first for me, hiding out in a gold mine with not all that much distance between me and a firestorm burning out of control with absolutely no hope of containment in the next few hours. If the fire or heat doesn't drift toward the opening and catch the wood framework in the tunnel and beyond, yes, we'll make it. If the smoke doesn't settle in here, yes, we'll make it."

Her breath caught. "I really don't want to die right now."

"Me neither."

"Are you afraid?"

"Yeah. You heard the noise when we entered the second tunnel?"

She stared at him. It had been a horrendous roar.

"The fire has reached the path we hiked in on. The temperature up there would melt— I mean, it's unbelievably hot. We've got about five minutes of air left in our tanks. The lantern batteries won't last forever."

"Okay." She blew out a breath. "Let's go back to the official rah-rah version."

He smiled. "Zak and Chad stacked the rocks over the opening, sealing it as much as possible. And we are alive."

She nodded. "What I screamed about back there, it had nothing to do with the fire."

"Do you want to talk about it?"

She glanced at the others. They were all conversing in low tones. Perhaps Indio and Lexi didn't need to hear her story yet. Telling a stranger first might be easier.

She turned to Eddie. "The thought of unloading sounds good. You sure you don't mind?"

"Why would I mind?"

"It's ugly and personal, and you don't know me."

"It's kind of hard to shock a paramedic-firefighter. I've more or less seen it all."

"What do you do with 'it all'?"

"I run several miles a day when I'm not on duty. Eventually 'it all' turns into a determination to help, to do more, to do better." He shrugged. "Then I go back to work."

Gratitude flowed through her again. "Thank you for taking care of me."

"You're very welcome." There was a sparkle in his eyes. "You're . . . pleasant to take care of. And now I've stepped over a line. Ooh-boy. I apologize. That wasn't a come-on."

She smiled. "I like the thought of being pleasant. I accept that as a compliment."

"Okay." He grinned. "So tell me what happened back there. Are you claustrophobic?"

"I didn't think I was." She thought back to their first flight from the house, driving her car behind Lexi, finding their way blocked. "When we met up with you, I was so scared I couldn't think straight. My husband grew up here, at the Hacienda. I knew without a doubt there was no other way out. It's so remote that Ben and Indio had to get special insurance through the state. No private company would cover them."

"No wonder you were scared."

She pulled up her knees and wrapped her arms around them, clutching her elbows. "Later, when we were hiking to the mine, I felt like something was chasing me. I think it was more than the fire. I think it was a memory. I started crawling through that tunnel, and then it was like it caught me."

"You started screaming."

She nodded. "I saw myself— No, it was more than seeing. I *was* a little girl again, trapped in a basement. I know it was a real memory even though I can't remember ever thinking about it before tonight. I must have been three. My mother locked me in a root cellar with no light on. My dad let me out after what seemed like hours and hours. My voice was gone, I'd screamed so much. I don't remember being comforted. My dad yelled at my mom, and he hit her. She kept saying it was an accident. My brother was a baby. I think I just got in the way, and she didn't know what else to do with me. She wasn't a well person."

"Claire, I'm sorry."

"Did you hear Indio praying? She said Jesus was there with me when it happened. I know she believes God is always with us, past, present, future. She says He's in every breath we breathe. I wish I had her faith. I wish I believed I wasn't alone, then or now."

"Hmm."

She noticed his wide eyes. "I thought you said nothing could shock you."

"I admit, this is throwing me for a loop. You're supposed to be on a couch, reliving such stuff with a psychologist, not running from a fire and diving into a gold mine to save your life."

"As my mother-in-law would say, God works in mysterious ways."

"What do you think it all means?"

"I don't know. An old pain has been dislodged. It's like so much of my life recently. I'm tired of pretending things don't hurt. I'm tired of acting like I've got it all together. Of giving the impression that I feel safe and secure. I guess it wasn't just my marriage."

"I'm sorry."

"I don't know exactly what to do with these hurts. I think it's all a process. More painful than I could have imagined, but good has come from it already. I've started to 'find myself,' pathetic as that sounds for a fifty-three-year-old to say. Which is why I really don't want to die right now."

One of the lanterns went out, throwing a new shadow across the dusky room.

Claire jumped. The murmured conversations stopped. Eddie reached for her hand.

She clasped his and scooted nearer to the stranger who offered more safety than she'd ever known before in her life.

Sixty-three

Max shivered in the backseat of his car, under a blanket someone had draped around him. The engine was on, the heater blowing full blast. Danny and Erik sat up front. They wouldn't let him near the key or gas pedal.

"I should have been there," he murmured, half to himself.

The car was parked on the road's shoulder. They weren't going anywhere. Uphill was fire. Downhill was abandonment of the woman he'd abandoned every which way for the past thirty-three years. He would die before going downhill.

"I should have been there."

In the distance, reporters still waited for news; emergency workers still commanded firefighting efforts and waited to go in and rescue people. Mercifully, the Kodak-moment view remained hidden from his sight.

But he knew it was there—the blazing hillside, the canyons, the mountaintops . . . with his child, his parents, and Claire somewhere in the middle of all those flames.

"I should have been there." His voice choked.

"Dad." Erik sighed. "Please stop saying that. We all should have been there. We all know Papa gets the heebie-jeebies if there's a fire anywhere in four counties. We all know he and Nana need extra help around the place on a good day."

Danny said, "Leave it to Mom and Lexi to jump in while we sat back and twiddled our thumbs. At least Jenna hadn't gone up yet. Did you know she was going? Soon as school was out, but there was some special faculty meeting that kept her late. Then Mom told her not to come. If anyone could talk Papa into leaving the horses, it was Nana, and they didn't need another car up there."

Max said, "I didn't know any of that."

His sons exchanged a look.

"You're right," he declared loudly. "You are absolutely right."

They turned to face him.

"That I don't know jack. But I'll tell you one thing I do know. I am not going to let your mother go. She's the most important thing that ever happened to me, and I swear I will not let her go. Do you hear me?"

Danny reached over the back of the seat and grasped his knee. "We hear you. Just relax, Dad, okay? We can't do anything right now except wait."

There was a tapping on Erik's window. He slid it down. "Hi."

"Hi." It was the fireman, the young one, checking on them again, as if they were his special assignment or something.

Max figured it for one of two reasons: either Erik's semifamous television status . . . or the fact that their situation was hopeless. Or maybe it was both. When this was over, the world would know the Beaumonts had lost half their family along with the old homestead, and—just imagine—the good-looking talking head could describe how great these guys were.

Noel—they were on a first-name basis now—leaned through the open window. "Has your sister heard anything yet?" He referred to Jenna, at the house now with Kevin.

Erik said, "No."

"Okay. Well, we have some news. Not sure what it means exactly."

"What?" Max's volume hit whisper or shout; there was nothing medium about it.

Danny squeezed lightly on his knee.

Noel said, "We're missing three guys. The last we heard they were just south of Estudillo Corners, on the east side of Reina Road."

Silence filled the car.

"The fire jumped around. Trees fell. They got . . . separated. We lost radio contact."

Danny said, "The road runs southwest there, to a neighboring ranch. Maybe . . ." His voice trailed off.

"That's where things went wild. We're thinking now a third hot spot developed to the south. It's the only explanation."

"How? It doesn't make any sense."

"It happens. Where does Reina Road meet the drive to the Hideaway?"

Max said, "One point two miles southeast of the Corners."

"And that's the only way in?"

And out. The words hung in the air.

Nobody said anything. There was nothing to say. They all knew it was the only way in and out. They all knew fire burned between it and Reina Road.

Noel said, "Is it a real hacienda? The old adobe kind? Red tile roof?"

"Yeah."

"Those thick walls don't burn. Roof would be good. Unless it's got wooden eaves. Fire would go inside through those. If it got close enough. But if it doesn't get too close, the eaves are protected, and the heat wouldn't be sufficient to shoot through the windows—"

"Shut up!"

"Dad!" Danny was in his face now.

"Tell him to shut up!" Tears sprang from his eyes.

"Dad!"

"Tell him to shut up!"

Above the noise of his own blubbering, he heard the window hum its way up and close.

Sixty-four

They turned off all but one lantern to conserve the batteries. The shadows deepened, and with them, fear crept in, a palpable thing.

Claire moved nearer Eddie. They leaned back against the wall, their shoulders touching, her hand on his arm. Only the stranger's solid physical presence kept her from falling again, down into that abyss.

On the other side of her, Lexi and Willow sat beside Zak. Beyond them was the tunnel opening. Indio, Ben, and Chad—Samson's head plopped on his lap—rounded out the half circle. Then came the pile of crumbled rock and dirt, a reminder that death had visited before in that place.

Except for Indio's occasional soft humming, they all remained silent.

For Claire, as the long minutes ticked by, hope played a game of tag with despair. Would the fire miss them? Or would death creep down into the gold mine?

She thought of Max, Erik, Jenna, and Danny. How she ached to hold them all! To tell them how much she loved them. What must they be going through right now, not knowing if the rest of them were dead or alive?

Max . . . Did he worry for her? That would be a first. She couldn't imagine it. In an odd way, he was so much like her father: aloof, disconnected, his heart sealed off. Why had she never seen the resemblance? Why had she glommed on to a man who did not have the strength of character not to abandon her? She should have known.

"It's okay," Eddie whispered, tracing her cheek with his thumb, pushing aside the tears that now fell silently.

She turned slightly and pressed her face against his shoulder, holding her breath, stifling the cry that built up in her chest.

Eddie put his hand on the back of her head—firm assurance from a stranger that he wouldn't leave her.

Why wasn't Max there?

Sixty-five

At three in the morning, Jenna's tears quit. They didn't falter; they just quit. She didn't have any more available. The well had gone dry. Or wherever it was tears came from.

She thought she'd cried a lot because Kevin rejoined the Marines. That was nothing compared to images of her mom, her sister, and her grandparents being burned alive, being turned into ash.

"Jen?" Kevin stirred beside her on the couch where they lay together. "You're shivering."

"We have to go. We have to go. I am not sitting here any longer! I've got to get to Dad. I've got to get closer to them, Kevin. I've got to get closer."

"Shh, shh." He kissed her forehead. "Okay. Let's go."

Tears stung again.

He was so precious to her.

Daddy!" Seated in the back of the car, Jenna clutched her father's arm. "Oh, Daddy!"

The sight of him panicked her. He was a wreck. Tears streamed down his face, and he couldn't talk coherently.

She cried, "They'll be okay. They'll be okay! Danny knows. He just knows."

Her dad pulled her into an embrace, squeezed tightly, and cried against her shoulder.

Through her own tears, Jenna soothed him as best she could. Through the window she saw Kevin with her brothers, drinking the coffee they had brought from the house.

She and Kevin had talked their way through the roadblock. Danny had told her on the phone to mention "Vallecitos Canyon." The phrase worked like "Open sesame," a magical command that moved police cars and softened stern tones.

There was still no word. Firefighters were missing. Her family was missing. Distant flames raced down the mountainside toward Santa Reina, lighting up the predawn sky like noonday.

Sixty-six

They were down to one working lantern.

Claire held Lexi tightly to herself. She kissed the top of her head and shuddered at the thought of total blackness.

Zak and Eddie had gone up through the tunnel to check on things, using the lights on their helmets to illumine the way. Indio sang softly, choruses and old hymns about God's faithfulness. Ben and Chad stood, stretching upright as far as they could, their hands pushed against the ceiling. They joined in with some of the familiar verses. Claire hummed to herself now and then when she had an extra breath.

"Mom, I think I'm okay with dying. Nana tells me often that Jesus loves me. But I really don't want to go yet."

"Of course not, hon. Jesus understands. You're still young."

"It's not just that. It's like, I mean, He's very real tonight. More real to me than ever before. And what have I ever done for Him? Not a whole lot." She sighed. "I suppose He hears this stuff all the time from people when they think they might die at any minute." She raised her voice to mimic. "'Oh, just let me live, and I'll do whatever You want from now on! I swear I will!'"

"Probably."

"Nana reminded me that I don't have to be perfect. He just wants me to be real with Him. He wants me to trust Him with my life."

"Nana always has the best advice." Nana as well as those teachers and pastors who had influenced her at church so many years before.

In spite of some confusing lessons on marriage, they opened up to her the world of God's love and forgiveness, a merciful place of peace.

"Lex, when we let God be head of our lives, everything is right, even when it's all going down the tubes. Like tonight."

"Are you making crazy promises to be perfect and do better?"

"Oh yeah. First thing I'm going to do is make you chocolate chip cookies, because I haven't for such a long time."

Lexi giggled. "Sounds good to me."

She smiled. "But I realize I've tried my whole life to be perfect. And you know what? It hasn't worked. I think I'll listen to Nana, too, and just try to be real, especially with God. A night like this one puts things in perspective."

"That's for sure. Will you go back to Dad?"

Claire stilled. "I—I don't know. That may depend on him. If he can live with me being real, that would be a good starting point to work from."

"It's not about rules, is it? Even no-divorce rules."

"I suppose I still believe God doesn't want us to divorce. But . . ." The little girl from the basement grabbed hold of her emotions again. What was it? A hurt. An agonizing pain. Terror beyond words.

"But what, Mom?"

"Earlier, when I was crying . . . I was reliving a time when I got locked in a basement." She told her daughter the story.

Lexi sat up and peered at her in the dim light. "That's awful."

"Yes, it is. My parents abandoned me. In other ways, your dad abandoned me. I've never felt safe and secure, not really. I know I need to forgive them and him. I know God helps with that sort of thing. But still it hurts so much. I don't think that forgiving means I have to live within the old parameters that allow them to do it to me all over again." She blew out a breath and thought for the umpteenth time, *Max should be here.*

Lexi squeezed her hands. "I love you, Mom."

"I love you, honey."

She saw movement behind Lexi. "Ah. Our heroes return."

"Good news!" Eddie crouched in the center of the group, grinning.

Zak raised a fist toward the ceiling. "Yeah! The fire has passed!"

Everybody cheered, Samson barked, and Chad whistled.

Indio said, "Yes, God is so good."

"Amen," Eddie said. "We crawled out to the opening and couldn't hear a thing. Couldn't see any flames. But the stones over the entrance are hot to the touch. More than likely our path is full of ash and cinders. So unfortunately, we need to hang out in here awhile longer, give the earth time to cool."

Ben asked, "How long?"

Lexi laughed and stood up. "Papa, he just told us we're not going to burn to death tonight, and you're concerned about how soon you can check on the damage and look for Chester?"

"Yeah. What's wrong with that?"

"Give it a rest. Let's celebrate the moment."

Indio clapped her hands. "She's right. We'll eat dessert first. Chocolate before apples!"

She unpacked the food they hadn't been interested in earlier, and Lexi distributed it. Eddie sat back down next to Claire, removing his helmet.

He said, "Good news, huh?"

"Yes." She shook her head. "But it's so horrible not being able to reach my family and tell them. I can't imagine what they must be going through!"

"There's nothing to be done about that. Just imagine the sweet reunion. Focus on that; otherwise you'll get an ulcer before we get out of here."

She tried to imagine it. Max would blame her for being at the hacienda. Jenna would be an absolute mess, inconsolable. Had she called Kevin? Danny and Erik would be exhausted and irritable, unable to handle their emotions. The sweet part wasn't coming to her.

She sighed. "It'll be awful out there."

"Yes. The devastation will be worse than anything you've ever seen. But the earth replenishes itself. Buildings can be rebuilt."

"Actually, I was talking about the awful impact on my family. What about yours?"

"Well, I told you my ex-wife lives in Washington. She won't know. Hopefully our two grown children in LA haven't heard either. They probably assume I'm fighting the fire, but the department might not notify them yet that we three are missing. My special friend, Sheila, knows I'm at the fire. I can only hope she hasn't gone to the station and found out."

"I wish my family didn't know. It's not like they can do anything. It seems cruel if your kids or friend would be told."

"It's a cruel world."

"I'm starting to feel safer in here. I'm not sure I want to go back out there."

He smiled. "Everything is going to be all right. And that's not just the official rah-rah version."

It clutched at her again, a gnawing sensation in her stomach. Fear paralyzed the little girl who craved safety.

"Claire, what's wrong?"

"I'm so afraid."

He touched her arm. "We're really going to be fine. And you're going to be just fine reuniting with your family."

"What if the lights go out?" She heard a childish whimper in her voice.

Eddie squeezed her arm. "Don't worry. I'll stay with you, lights or no lights, in or out of this mine, for as long as you need."

Sixty-seven

Indio watched her daughter-in-law fall apart again, quietly this time, her face turned in to Eddie's shoulder.

Once more, Indio asked God why He had brought along a stranger to offer comfort instead of Max.

"Is there more chocolate?" Chad asked.

Indio smiled and handed him an unopened bar of Cadbury's dark. He was a sweet young man. Obviously churched, since he knew the words to all the hymns. Samson had loved him at first sight.

Ben polished an apple against his flannel shirt. "We're just like the Israelites in Egypt. We got passed over tonight. The angel of death saw the entrance to the tunnel and just kept on going. I wonder what he saw on our doorpost that sent him on his way."

Chad bit into the chocolate. "I left a prayer there. I bet we all did."

Indio grinned. "Yes, I bet we did. Hallelujah."

"Nana," Lexi said. "How did you know?"

"Know what?"

"That we'd make it?"

"I didn't."

"You kept saying things like 'Hallelujah.'"

Indio shrugged. "God is God. Glory belongs to Him—no matter what. It's my job to give it to Him—no matter what. You know how Job in the Bible lost everything? When he whined about it, God asked him if he hung the stars in the sky. God comes through, even if it's not how we think He will or how we want Him to."

Ben said, "At least He gave us a clue. Three clues. Shadrach, Meshach, and Abednego showed up just when we needed them."

"Yes. And I'd like to have them all over for dinner soon. Chad, you'll bring your wife and baby? Zak, you come too."

They stared at her, silent, odd expressions on their faces. Ben's jaw worked slowly at the bite of apple.

"What?" she said.

Lexi inhaled sharply. "Oh, Nana."

Ben slid near her and put an arm around her shoulders. "Love."

"What?"

"The fire. Most likely it hit the house. We might have a roof and walls, but nothing else."

Lexi whispered, "No gardens."

Something snatched Indio's breath away.

She hadn't thought about the aftermath. She had been so focused on the moment, so intent on prayer—for their safety, for Max and her grandchildren, for courage and peace for them all—she hadn't imagined her home being destroyed.

She looked up at Ben.

He kissed her forehead.

God is God. God is God. God is good.

"Well. Hallelu—" Her breath released only syllables before Ben's shirt was soaking up her tears.

Her home? Her grandmother's woven rug. The chair her father made. Her mother-in-law's china. The old buffet and shelves and antiques handed down by Ben's ancestors. His beloved barn and workshop.

The parking lot? Claire's car with the photos? Her babies at every stage, infancy to teens . . .

Oh, Lord! I can't. I can't sing praise. How do You expect me to—

The horror consumed even her thoughts.

Sixty-eight

A charcoal grayness seeped into the area. Only this subtle absence of midnight black suggested dawn had arrived.

Jenna stood next to the car, her arm entwined with her dad's, grateful for Kevin's foresight to bring winter coats for them all, a thermos of coffee, and travel mugs. Still, she shivered. Kevin, Erik, and Danny stomped their feet and huddled together. Their breath frosted the air. Such extremes in the desert climate.

But no one wanted to sit in the warm car and be removed even one step further from the situation. Even Erik didn't linger with the group of journalists who got fewer updates than her family did. The firefighter named Noel informed them frequently of the latest—which hadn't meant a thing, really.

Max had calmed to the point of being an automaton. Jenna wondered if he was in shock. Maybe she should find a medic to look at him.

Noel approached again. She felt her dad stiffen and heard his ragged breathing.

The fireman stopped near Erik. "The helicopters are out now. They'll survey the area. They'll head to the Hideaway property first." He turned and walked away.

No one said anything. They understood that this was it.

The Rolando Bluff Fire was already being referred to as one of the worst. Over a hundred fifty thousand acres had burned so far, fifteen hundred homes. Three people had died. The Santa Anas spread it.

When those winds stopped blowing, "they"—those faceless people in the know—had said it was basically over. Said it would be contained soon. Santa Reina was on nobody's radar.

Then the wind gusted from the ocean. A second fire erupted and met the first. Either a third one complicated the whole picture, or flames had simply jumped to encircle people who could not be alerted.

The fire shouldn't have gone the way it did, advancing miles and miles from the origin and into places fueled only by scraggly mesquite and sagebrush and piñon pine. Even the hills surrounding the Hideaway supported little vegetation. The mountains beyond were all *rock*. What was there to burn?

Erratic winds came and went and came again, tearing apart all predictions of what they would do. Communities were caught off guard. Residents of housing developments. Rural dwellers. Ranchers. The Hacienda Hideaway . . .

The ancestral homestead was old and austere, but a cherished piece of living history for Jenna. She remembered the first time she'd read H. H. Jackson's novel *Ramona*. The fictional hacienda and grounds leaped off the pages. Jenna knew the place. Her grandparents owned it! Her imagination took flight. The Beaumonts were the Morenos, the fictional family who lived in the house.

The book sealed her love for literature and energized her ambitions for teaching it. She was twelve at the time.

But now . . . Now she couldn't give a flying fig about the fate of the Hacienda Hideaway.

The minutes dragged. Jenna had no idea how many. There was an eerie, ashy feel in the air beneath a yellow sky overcast with something other than its normal clouds. All the lights around the encampment stayed lit.

The cameraman from Erik's station found their little group standing by her dad's car. She watched her brother talk with him. Erik's impudence had been totally wiped from his demeanor. His expressive eyebrows didn't budge. Scrunched lips replaced his easy smile. The camera guy left, disgust written all over his demeanor.

Erik stepped nearer Danny. "He wanted to make us the morning news. I told him where he could store his camera."

Noel, their fireman of few words-slash-personal liaison, strode toward them again. Danny told Jenna that at first he had been chattier. That was before their dad nearly bit off his head. Now his face remained passive.

"The helicopters made their first pass over the property. The fire is smoldering, but it's out. The house is standing. Nothing else, though. Burned outbuildings, vehicles. No one has been spotted. We should be able to move in on the ground later this morning. Meanwhile, the copters will pass over again, soon as they check on some other areas."

Jenna wondered if they'd send someone besides Noel if the news really meant anything.

Sixty-nine

M om!" Lexi's hollow voice drifted down through the tunnel. "Come on!"

Claire crossed her arms at her waist and tried to smile.

Eddie chuckled. "You know, the worst really is over."

They knelt on their haunches under the low ceiling. Only the two of them remained inside the gold mine. Directly in front of them was the entrance to the narrow passageway that led up and out. The light from Eddie's helmet flickered.

He said, "After what you just went through, you're able to conquer anything."

"Not that." She dipped her head toward the tunnel and winced at the vivid image of being squeezed on all sides, of tumbling into a dark void, where little girls cried alone in basements.

"Claire, you can. You're not alone. I'll come behind you. Chad's at the other end. He'll crawl in to meet you. Trust me. I said I wouldn't leave you."

She gazed into his eyes, nearly lost in the shadows.

"You already faced this memory, remember? And you won." He tugged at her arms until she uncrossed them, and then he held her hands. "You won."

"Mom!" Lexi called again. "I'm waiting for those chocolate chip cookies you promised to bake!"

Eddie laughed. "Let's go." He guided her, helping her duck her head into the opening. "Chad! We're coming."

A voice called back, "I'm here! It's me, Claire."

Ben.

"Come on, honey. Let's go home. Stretch out your hand, and I'll grab it."

Her father-in-law waited for her at the other end.

She lay flat in the dirt, her forearms pressed against it. "Eddie?"

"I'm here."

She felt his hand on her leg.

"Go ahead."

She inched along like a worm. Eddie kept up a steady stream of talk behind her. Lexi sang loudly, "Well, I stuck my head in a little skunk's hole, and the little skunk said, 'Well, bless my soul!'"

At last she felt the tips of Ben's fingers.

She focused on the men who stayed with her. She focused on her daughter's silly singing. She focused on the other voice. "You can do it, Claire!"

And then she was lying facedown in ash, and someone was helping her to her feet.

The forced chatter had been all for her. Once Ben released Claire from his bear hug and the cheers died, all talk ceased. She immediately saw the reason for their somber faces.

The landscape before them was not the one they'd traversed the previous night. If someone told her she'd been transported to the moon, she would have believed them.

Maybe they had, after all, died. Evidently every other form of life had.

A sickly yellow light emanated from the sky. Something heavier than clouds filled the atmosphere. It was so thick it swallowed all sound. No birds chirped. No insects thrummed.

Where they stood was a steep incline. The stones they'd climbed up and over last night and the ground beneath were black. Where she should have seen trees in the distance, she saw giant broken match-sticks and wisps of smoke.

Eddie crouched in front of the entrance and inspected it.

A wave of nausea rolled through Claire. The opening was, liter-ally, a small, square hole hewn impossibly out of rock on the hillside. Last night she hadn't been able to appreciate the full effect in the shadowy light of lanterns—else she never would have crawled into it. How the firemen in their gear and the knapsacks had fit through, she had no idea.

Eddie traced the wood slats that framed it. They were charred. "It came close."

Chad chuckled. "That's the understatement of the century."

Indio whispered, "Oh my."

Horror engulfed Claire. Its weight pressed at her like giant hands on her shoulders. She sank onto the nearest rock, propped her face against her hands, and burst into tears.

Seventy

They've been spotted." Noel, the fire department's spokesman, said nothing more. He just stood there.

Max pushed himself away from the car and moved. He made it all of three steps before Kevin threw an arm across his chest.

Max had no voice left to object, but he swore to himself if that moron Noel did not finish what he'd come to say, he would knock him to the ground and get him in a choke hold and keep him there until he guaranteed the kid would never speak again.

"The helicopter can't set down near them yet. Ground's too steep and rocky. But they're walking in the general direction of the house. So." He smiled. "Great news, huh?"

Max wrestled against Kevin's arm.

Erik said, "Maybe. Who exactly is 'they'?"

"Oh yeah." Noel shook his head. "Sorry. Uh, seven people."

"Seven?" Max's three kids cried in unison.

"Three are obviously firefighters. We're sure they're the guys we were missing."

Kevin tightened his hold around Max.

"And," Noel said quickly, seeing Max's movement, "and an older couple, tall man with white hair, a short woman, hair braid. A skinny woman with long hair, carrying a cat, and a woman with shorter hair. And a dog was with them. Probably a golden retriever. They all waved. I mean, the people did."

For one long moment, nobody said anything.

Then the laughter and tears and shouts and hugs began.

Relief flooded through Max, as strong as a physical sensation. It gushed, shoving out the weight of despair that had nearly suffocated him through the awful black hours. Light and warmth exploded in his being, and he could not contain the joy.

Joy?

No doubt. That was it. His family was safe.

He leaped into the air like a jackrabbit.

Sudden compassion for Noel filled him. The guy was his new best friend. He bounded over to him, grasped his head between his hands, and planted a kiss on his cheek. "I'm gonna write you into my will!"

Seventy-one

At long last, hours after emerging from the mine, the survivors neared the hacienda, speechless and exhausted beyond measure.

Claire wondered again if she had died. She couldn't remember much of the hike except the conscious effort it took to put one foot in front of another and then to do it all over again. And again. And again.

They'd lived through the fire, but the blackened earth and yellow sky nagged at her. Death hovered all around.

She remembered reaching Ben's truck. Nobody said a word. They all just gazed at the twisted hunk of metal that had carried them most of the way to safety the previous night.

Now and then a helicopter whirred overhead, tracking their progress. Once it seemed about to land. It only stirred up a windstorm of ash that swept particles into their eyes and made them cough more.

"Oh . . ." Lexi groaned.

Everyone slowed. Claire looked to where Lexi pointed. The parking area lay directly before them. There were three burned-out vehicles: the tractor and her and Lexi's cars. Thinking of the treasures she'd packed in her trunk and backseat, she reached out and slipped her hand into Indio's.

They moved on. Moments later the house came into view. It still stood. Black streaks marred the white walls, but it still stood.

It just didn't have any windows.

Indio moaned.

Eddie spoke. "We'll go in first."

Ben heaved a breath.

Claire said, "We're right behind you."

His soft smile poured courage into her. Whatever lay ahead, she and her family were not alone.

The shocks hit her in waves, one scene after another battering at her psyche.

Charred, twisted, melted, unidentifiable things. Glass, draperies, and blinds gone. Ash where rugs had lain. Buckled floors. The inner courtyard devoid of flowers and plants, furnished with chunks of burnt wicker.

She ached for her in-laws as they surveyed shadowy room after room. Ben and Indio seemed to shrink before her very eyes. The life they'd known for nearly sixty years had vanished overnight.

She cried with them as they realized one loss after another. It seemed they had felt total devastation at the sight of her car, with its contents of photos and mementos obviously destroyed. But the pain now deepened beyond measure.

Alone in the courtyard, Claire hugged herself. Why had this happened? What was the point? Ben and Indio did not deserve this. Something besides the physical had been eradicated. The sense of history was gone . . . of the first Beaumonts forging a home in the wilderness . . . of the generations that followed—good and bad, but still an unbroken thread that held the spirit of the place together.

"Hallelujah!" Indio's shout came from the kitchen.

Claire rushed inside.

At the far end of the room, her in-laws stood near the blown-out window, silhouetted in the strange light that wasn't exactly natural light.

Indio laughed, her hands raised in the air. "God is so good. Take a look at this!"

Ben hooted. "Ain't that something?"

Claire walked toward them and followed their gaze to the side wall.

Indio's wall of crosses was completely intact . . . as was the small table alongside it . . . as was the book atop the table.

Ben reverently lifted the thick, old family Bible with both hands and whispered, "Ain't that something."

Tears now streaming down her face, Indio covered her mouth and whispered, "The Lord giveth and the Lord taketh. Blessed be His name. His Word is all we need."

Claire wiped her eyes. They would grieve the losses, but in the end they would still trust.

She wished she had their faith.

The medics insisted on examining all of them.

Claire didn't have the energy to protest and waited her turn on the railroad tie steps on the terrace above the parking area, sipping from a water bottle. Ben and Indio were inside the ambulance; Lexi and Chad and Zak leaned against it.

Eddie draped a blanket around her and sat down.

"Thanks," she said.

"You looked cold."

"No. My teeth always chatter like this."

He put his face close to hers. "What's your name?"

"Huh?"

"I'm back on duty." He touched the side of her face. "Tell me your name. Please."

"Why?"

"Because you just went through the worst imaginable night." He gently took the bottle from her hand, set it aside, and pinched the skin on the back of her hand.

"Ouch."

"Sorry. My technique wanes after such nights. See the skin sticking up? You're dehydrated." He gave her the water. "Drink up. Now what's your name?"

"Claire. Beaumont. What's yours?"

"Edward James. Where do you live?"

"I told you. And you live in Vista."

"Do you feel dizzy?"

"Floaty. So how come these steps didn't burn, Edward James?"

He narrowed his eyes at her. "Don't know, and let's not change the subject. Another ambulance will be here in two minutes. You're first in line. Take another drink."

She sipped from the bottle. It hurt to drink. The water trickled down her raw throat.

"Your family is headed here, too, right behind the ambulance."

"Here?" Earlier talk indicated they would not be able to get through.

"Yeah. The roads are opened up. The fire is contained to the north. Santa Reina is out of danger. Anyway . . ." He paused, his face toward the horizon. "Things are going to get crazy now."

She studied him. Like the others—and, she imagined, like herself—his face was smudged, his eyes bloodshot and rimmed in dark circles, his appearance disheveled. Punch-drunk with exhaustion, he laughed one minute and became deathly silent the next.

His tired eyes returned to her. "Claire, your daughter saved our lives."

She nodded.

"Don't let her forget that."

"Okay."

"And you're alive. Don't forget that."

She frowned, not understanding him.

"I mean, the past is dead. That memory you saw? It's over, and you're a beautiful, intriguing woman with your whole life ahead of you."

"O-okay."

"You said some things that, well, that made me think— Let's put it this way. Take care of yourself, and if you need anything at all, I'm there for you."

Unsure of what he said, she cleared her throat and probed. "'There.' You mean Vista?"

"Right. Number is in the phone book."

She stared back at him for a long moment. "Okay."

Lexi whooped.

Claire gazed down the lane. At the last curve she saw them. An ambulance, lights flashing. Then Max's car. Behind it, Kevin's SUV. Dust flew everywhere as they sped closer.

Lexi yelled and jumped wildly about, waving her blanket-covered arms.

Claire felt no relief, no joy. Had her heart dried up as well as her throat? Maybe it had dehydrated itself through the night's long ordeal.

She didn't even feel anger toward Max for missing—by his own choice—the worst experience of her life.

She felt nothing.

Seventy-two

Max yanked on the car's back door handle before Danny braked.

"Dad!" The car skidded to a halt. "Wait—!"

Max was out the door. He spotted Lexi, already at Danny's open door, waving across the car to him.

"You're okay?"

"Yeah."

"Mom?"

Lexi pointed as Danny scooped her into his arms, both laughing, whooping, and hollering.

Max stumbled across the gravel, straight toward Claire. The scene before him scarcely registered as he rushed past. His father's face peered through the open doors at the back of an ambulance. From a second ambulance, the one they'd followed in, medics emerged. The hacienda loomed in the desolate landscape, gaping black holes where windows had been.

Claire sat on the terrace steps, waiflike, engulfed in a blanket, hair matted, tear tracks on her cheeks, eyes wide.

He collapsed beside her and enfolded her in his arms. "Oh, Claire! Oh, Claire! My sweetheart." Rocking gently back and forth, he kissed her head, pressed it against his chest, and sobbed. "I thought I'd lost you. I thought I'd never hold you again. Oh, Claire, I am so sorry, so sorry for everything! Please forgive me. Please forgive me."

Her body convulsed.

"Are you hurt?" He tilted back and caressed her cheek. "Are you all right?"

Blank, unfocused eyes gazed at him. Her chapped lips parted slightly. "You." Her whisper rasped. She swallowed with obvious difficulty. "You weren't there."

He pulled her to himself again. "Oh, honey. I am so, so sorry."

Another tremor shook her body.

Dear God. Help me! Help me win her back.

His prayer sprang out of nowhere. He was at the bottom now, calling on a God he wasn't sure existed.

Claire's tone had revealed no malice, no anger. She'd simply stated the fact that he wasn't there as she would state the fact that the day was warm. The information made no impact on her whatsoever.

She wasn't going to forgive him.

God was the only answer. If He existed. If He cared.

Wordlessly, Max held Claire more tightly, swaying back and forth, back and forth . . . just as he'd held the kids when they were little and got hurt . . . as he'd clung to a pillow the night he learned his brother was missing in Vietnam.

Oh, God!

"Sir, excuse me. Sir! Please."

He looked up and through his tears saw a young woman with a stethoscope around her neck, leaning toward him. Her gloved hand was on his shoulder.

"Sorry, sir. We need to examine her."

Max released his hold on Claire and wiped his eyes. "She's all right, isn't she?"

"Yes, she should be just fine. She hiked all the way out of there. But we want to check her vitals." She knelt before Claire. "Hi, there. My name's Annie. What's yours?"

She blinked, that dazed expression still on her face. "Claire."

"Nice to meet you, Claire. Can you walk to the ambulance? We parked it right here, three steps away. Hold on to my arm."

Wiping tears from his own cheeks, Max watched them move away and stood to follow. His legs wobbled, and he grasped the rail to steady himself.

"She'll be fine." A nearby voice surprised him.

He turned and saw a man standing a few feet away, his face smudgy like Claire's. A fireman.

"She's dehydrated," the man said. "I kept trying to get her to drink more, but . . ." He shrugged.

"Who are you?"

"Eddie." He stepped to him and thrust his hand forward. "You must be Max."

Max shook the hand, confused.

"I'm one of the firefighters who was with your family," the man explained.

"The three missing guys!"

Eddie smiled in a tired way. "Yeah."

Max grabbed his hand again and shook it heartily. "Thank you for saving them!"

"No, thank you. It was your Lexi who saved us."

"Lexi? What did she do?"

"Let her tell you about it. You're one lucky man to have such a family." The tall, lean firefighter straightened and spoke toward an approaching medic. "Yeah, yeah, I'm coming."

As he limped away, Max sought out Lexi. She was in the middle of a group hug, surrounded by Jenna, Erik, and Danny. The four of them laughed and danced like a group of silly toddlers. Kevin knelt beside Samson, grinning as the dog licked his face.

Max lumbered over to them, desperately longing to laugh and dance and hug the dog.

Danny spotted him and moved aside.

Max enveloped Lexi in a bear hug. "My baby. My baby."

She embraced him silently.

"Hey." He held her at arm's length. "I heard you're the hero."

Lexi smiled. "Heroine."

Max tucked a long strand of her hair behind an ear. "Heroine. I'm so proud of you."

"All I did was take us to the back entrance into the gold mine. We spent the night in there."

"The back—" He laughed. "No way. How did you know about that?"

Words gushed from his youngest, the most reserved of his four. He saw a sparkle in her green-brown eyes as she described the long ordeal. She clung to him, her face animated, first with joy and then, after a time, with fear.

When the tears began, he pulled her close again.

I should have been there.

Hugs and smiles and tears continued to be exchanged among them all. The kids crowded at the rear of one ambulance. Claire was inside of it, out of sight. Max went to the other ambulance to greet his parents.

To his chagrin, they appeared more shaken and feeble than he imagined. Considering their age and what they'd been through, it shouldn't have been a surprise. But still, he thought, overnight? Ben and Indio Beaumont were not frail people. His mother liked to think of herself as a squaw in the image of her grandmother, a robust woman who'd worked until the day she died at the age of one hundred and three. His dad boasted about his rugged stock inherited via some Brit named John Beaumont, who sailed to the new world in 1635. Not to mention the great-great-grandfather who'd clawed his way through rock into a gold mine and built the estate out of nothing. Pioneers, every last one of them.

"Dad." Max embraced his father.

"Max." Ben's voice caught. "Max. We made it."

"You made it." He leaned back to look at him. "How are you?"

"Okay. They want your mom in the hospital, just for observation.

She's hooked up to an IV. Dehydration. Her blood pressure's gone haywire."

"How about yours?"

"Just great." His smile faltered. "Got the sap snuffed clean out of me, though."

Max drew his dad to himself again and squeezed.

I should have been there.

Claire was gone. His family was gone.

Panic wrenched Max around in a circle. He spotted the kids moving toward the house, Erik bringing up the rear.

"Erik!"

He turned.

Max held his hands out in a gesture of helplessness.

His son jerked a thumb toward the second ambulance. "She's still in there."

Max blew out a breath and walked to the vehicle. Through the opened back doors, he peered inside.

Claire lay on a stretcher, covered with a blanket. The medic named Annie held her wrist. The fireman named Eddie held her other one.

Max climbed inside. Claire's eyes were shut. Her jacket was off and her bare arms exposed. A blood pressure cuff was attached to one, the line from an IV drip bag to the other.

"Hi," Max said.

Eddie looked up. "Hey, Max."

"What's wrong?"

He exchanged a glance with Annie. She said, "She'll be fine. Won't you, Claire?"

His wife murmured something through dry, colorless lips.

"Right." Annie gestured with her head at Eddie.

He moved toward Max, indicating they should get out of the vehicle. Once on the ground, they stepped away from it.

Eddie said, "She'll be fine."

"I heard that already. What's wrong?"

"She's in shock, most likely from dehydration. I know she didn't drink much through the night. She couldn't this morning; the water ran out early. We had fruit, but she didn't eat. Another reason she would have lost more fluid than the rest of us is because she vomited."

Max closed his eyes briefly.

"I don't know if tears can be measured, but she cried enough to fill . . ." Eddie cleared his throat. "She'll be fine."

Max felt the backhoe again, digging, digging, digging away at his stomach. He locked his knees in place before he keeled over. This stranger knew what Claire had or hadn't eaten and drunk. He'd seen her be sick. He'd seen her cry so much, he questioned if shed tears could pull excessive fluid from the body that was lying spaced-out on a stretcher.

"She'll be fine," Eddie repeated.

"Will be. What about now? How is she right now?"

"Well, she's conscious, but exhausted. Nobody slept, of course. The hike just about wasted one of my guys, and he runs marathons. Your parents are in amazing shape." Eddie took a deep breath. "Her blood pressure's too low, her heart rate too high. The IV will help. They'll transport her to the hospital. The doctor will want to keep her there until she's stabilized. I should have made sure she drank. I should have noticed her condition sooner."

"No, it was my job." Max shook his head. "I should have been there."

For his parents. For his daughter. For his wife . . . *I should have been there.*

And yet he hadn't been.

Seventy-three

The Beaumonts filled up a large section of the emergency room. Claire observed them from her bed. They were a noisy bunch, moving in and out of exam rooms, milling about in the aisle.

Hospital personnel kept saying, "Excuse me," to Erik, Danny, and Kevin. Max and Jenna gave thinly disguised suggestions in their usual "I'm in charge" voices. Ben kept talking about the Passover to anyone within earshot. Lexi asked every nurse she saw about the three firefighters. Indio reminded her of their true names: Shadrach, Meshach, and Abednego.

Claire wished she could slip back into her fog.

Events up at the hacienda remained a blur. Her last clear picture was of Indio's intact wall of crosses. She'd sat on the steps, talked with Eddie, and felt reality slowly slide away. She vaguely remembered her kids peering into the ambulance, calling out to her, crowding and buzzing like a swarm of bees. Claire tried to reassure them not to worry by emitting a croaky "I'm fine!" until Annie, the kind paramedic, shooed them off. Claire immediately succumbed to that floating sensation she had described to Eddie. Details of the ride down the hill and entry into the hospital were all lost in a haze.

Now, slowly, she had emerged from the fog.

The doctor proclaimed that Lexi and Ben had passed inspection and could go, but he insisted Claire and Indio remain overnight for observation.

Indio protested. She wanted to stay with Ben. The doctor rattled off her vitals, explaining how precious few points she was from kicking the bucket. He further described how her insides were shriveling up like peaches in a dehydrator. Then he made a sucking noise, his mouth pursed and wrinkled.

Kevin, Erik, and Danny thought the guy was pretty funny. Lexi turned her back on him and convinced Indio that they would all take care of Papa at the house. Her words put Indio at ease.

The swarm of bees, which now included Max and Ben, accompanied Claire and Indio upstairs to a room with two beds. Jenna burst into tears over their hospital gowns and stark surroundings. She promised to pack nighties and cosmetics for her mom and grandma; Kevin promised to deliver them to the hospital.

Claire was content just to wash her face with soap and water. It didn't matter what she slept in or that her hair smelled of smoke.

Eventually the young people were ushered out, Ben in tow. Claire overheard plans for dinner and talk about dibs on showers and on the few beds still available at the house. Evidently they all were staying, these siblings who didn't even see each other on a monthly basis.

Max did not leave with them, and another disagreement ensued. He informed a nurse that he was spending the night in plain sight of his wife and his mother. The sweet-faced woman wasn't crazy about the idea.

In the midst of the argument, Max's phone rang. Claire recognized the ring. "You've Lost That Lovin' Feeling." It was a joke, rooted in an office party the previous year. The party involved karaoke and Neva and that particular song and Max refusing to sing it with her. Everyone booed until he finally got up and sang.

Claire had smiled through the whole evening, not flustered in the least.

Soon after that night, his cell phone was programmed to play the tune as the ID ring for Neva's calls.

Max answered it now. "Hi . . . We're doing great." He filled in details. "Claire and Mom have to stay overnight, but they're just fine."

He listened for a while. He gave instructions concerning a second-shift manager. He said good-bye. "Neva sends you her love."

Since when would Neva send her love?

The nurse plucked the phone from Max's hand. "If you think you're staying, this is staying with me."

Winsome Max smiled and shrugged.

It also didn't matter to Claire where any of them stayed.

She obsessed over the odd sensation of her organs shutting down. She imagined them shrinking, curling up to resemble dried fruit. When would her heart go? Would it go for lack of water or for other lacks? Lacks of words, emotions, thoughts, dreams. Would that do it?

The nurse offered her a sleeping aid.

She whispered, her throat raw, "Please." She swallowed a pill. "The firemen?"

"Here and gone. They're fine."

The fog, thicker than the last one, welcomed her.

Seventy-four

Hallelujah." Indio's tone had lost its typical forceful delivery. She nearly whispered her favorite word from the backseat of Max's car. "We are out of the hospital."

Claire turned halfway around from the front seat and reached back to squeeze Indio's hand. Her mother-in-law appeared the worse for wear. Claire ached for her, for the loss of her home, for the excruciating endurance test of the fire, for the experience of being poked with needles and spending the night in the hospital without Ben.

Evidently Claire's heart hadn't shriveled up. When she awoke, it felt quite heavy.

"Dear." Indio smiled. "We will get through this."

Claire nodded and turned again to the front.

Beside her, Max drove. He said, "They say this sickly gloom might last a week. Jenna and Kevin's school is closed. Most of them are."

Ash fell like a fine snow and covered everything. Traffic was light, uncharacteristic for a weekday morning. Side streetlamps glowed.

She said, "It's so eerie."

"Yeah," Max agreed. "It makes me feel like I'm in the middle of a bad disaster movie." He glanced at her. His eyes were puffy, his face haggard, his clothes a wrinkled mess.

He'd spent the night in a recliner in their room. The nurse couldn't find a cot for him but had furnished a blanket and pillow. He hadn't slept well.

"You've lost that lovin' feeling . . ." His phone rang out.

Claire's heart went heavy again. With a start she realized it had lightened momentarily when a connection flashed between her and Max. Her glimpse of a caring husband released the weighty load.

Then his phone rang.

And now he answered it.

"Excuse me." He pulled it from his pocket. "Hello . . . Yes . . . No . . . Just on our way home. I'm not coming in today . . . Have Phil look into that . . . Really? Okay . . . I'll call you later. A long, hot shower is about all I can think about right now." He closed the phone. "We're getting calls already for workers for all kinds of fire-related situations. Turns my stomach thinking we'll benefit from this tragedy."

They rode in silence, through stoplights, onto a freeway ramp.

"Claire, would you hand me my Bluetooth, please?" He referred to his phone's earpiece, the gadget that allowed him to talk without letting go of the steering wheel. "It's in the glove compartment. I have to touch base with—"

She tuned him out. No reason not to return his favor in like manner.

The buzzing swarm of busy bees greeted them outside the house. "Welcome home! Welcome home!"

Claire couldn't help but smile at the wild sight.

Max put his arm around her shoulders. "We do have a colorful bunch of kids, don't we?"

"Mm-hmm. They must get it from their grandparents. Look at that."

Ben pushed others aside to reach Indio. Barefoot, he wore a fancy green silk shirt that had to have come from Erik's closet, and too-short sweatpants, probably Danny's. With a loud hurrah, he scooped up his wife and carried her across the threshold.

Max chuckled.

"They're such special people," she said. "All night long your dad was this solid presence, and your mom kept our spirits up. I don't understand why they had to go through this." She brushed tears from her eyes. "Guess I got all rehydrated. Now I can cry some more."

He kissed the top of her head. "Do you want to tell me about it?"

"I just want a bath. I promised Lexi homemade chocolate chip cookies. We don't have any clothes that would fit Nana. None of us have driver's licenses or credit cards. All the photographs are gone. The mementos. Books. Your dad's truck. We need to—"

"Claire, shh." He pulled her to himself. "Shh. It's okay. Everything is okay."

She didn't believe him. He had left her as recently as ten minutes ago with his phone conversations in the car. He would leave her again. He was not there for her Monday night. She had closed herself off from him years ago. She had hurt him, and he hadn't forgotten.

A fire did not sweep history under the rug.

But for now she clung to him and to their masquerade.

Bear hugs and coffee and conversation welcomed Claire into the kitchen. No one was going to work; they promised to shop for Nana and Papa's immediate needs and to cook dinner. Jenna told her in no uncertain terms to take a break from being "The Mom."

By the time she finished a long, hot soak in the bath, everyone had scattered. She turned off the television, with its blare of continued sad news, and went into the backyard. Miles from the fire that was now under control, the yellow gloom and smoky scent persisted. Ash dusted everything and slimed the surface of the pool with a gray film. Where someone had swept the patio, charcoal black streaks remained.

She should go indoors and get away from the reminders. But she craved the wide sky and green grass and yellow flowers. Wrapping herself in a blanket, she sat on a lounge chair and fell asleep.

The sound of the sliding door opening woke her. Tandy and Max walked from the house. What an odd sight, she thought. Side by side, cordial expressions on their faces.

Claire stood to hug Tandy.

"Oh, Claire," she cried. "Thank God. Thank God."

Claire smiled and nodded through her own tears.

Max set a bottle of water and a travel mug on the table beside her. "Ta-da. Latte. Two shots of espresso, 2 percent milk, frothed to perfection. I made it myself."

Tandy said, "I watched him. He really did."

"Thanks."

Max said, "Be sure to drink the water. Can I get you anything else? Jenna and I are going to the market in a few minutes."

She settled back onto the chair. "I don't think so."

"Okay. Call my cell if there's anything you want." He leaned over and kissed her forehead. "Be well."

More strange developments—the kisses, the hovering. The market?

As he walked away, Tandy pulled a chair nearer hers and sat down. "How you doing?"

"Tired of being asked that question."

"You've only been home for a few hours. You can't be tired of it yet." She leaned her head back against the chair. "How's Indio?"

"Napping with Ben in the guest room."

"Claire, do you want to talk about it?"

"It was so awful."

Her friend said nothing.

Claire swung her feet to the ground. "Let's go bake some cookies."

To Alexis!" Amid family cheers and the clanking of spoons against water goblets, Erik raised his glass. "Long live our heroine!"

Jenna said, "May she be granted much prosperity."

"And health," Danny added.

"And Zak, the fireman." Erik grinned.

Lexi wadded up her linen napkin and threw it at him. Everyone laughed.

Claire smiled. Seeing her family gathered around the dining room table felt like a salve on her still-open wounds. It was Christmas and birthdays all wrapped into one giant celebration.

The house was filled with life as never before. Except for a trip to the grocery store, Max had been there all day. Erik, Danny, Lexi, Jenna, and Kevin had been in and out but planned to spend another night. That meant couches for her sons, but they said they didn't mind. Of course, Ben and Indio, Samson, and Willow had nowhere else to go.

Claire ached especially for her in-laws, but they exchanged frequent smiles and spoke only thoughtful words of gratitude that they were alive. Indio's hallelujahs punctuated every other sentence.

"Claire." Max winked at the other end of the table and in the midst of the rowdy talk mouthed the words "Drink up."

She gazed at her full glass of water. Yes, she should drink up. And she should drink in the moment, flood her soul with the goodness it offered.

Because it was fleeting.

Seventy-five

Max sat on the edge of their king-size bed and stroked Claire's hand. She was curled on her side under a mound of covers.

Other than their brief moment on the front lawn that morning, this was their first chance to be alone.

The truth was, she scared him. Her reactions were slow, her smile hesitant, her eyes not always focused. The magnitude of what had happened was not lost on him. She had nearly died in a fire. She endured an inconceivable night fleeing from it. And now, through no choice of her own, really, she was back at her house with her husband, both of which she had left two months ago.

"So," he said, "welcome home."

She blinked, a long, slow drifting of her eyelids.

"Crazy day, huh?"

"Mm-hmm."

"Claire." His throat tightened. "Please talk to me. That fireman, Eddie, he told me you were sick, that you cried a lot."

"I don't want to talk about it." Her voice was still a hoarse whisper.

"I need to hear about it."

"Ask your dad."

"I want your version."

"Max, you know my version."

"I don't know—"

Her gaze cut him to the quick.

Yes, he knew. "I wasn't there."

She shut her eyes, pulled her hand from his, and slid it under the pillow. "I needed you so badly. I called you, and I asked you to come, but you didn't."

"I'm sorry."

"I know." Her breathing grew deep. She had taken one of the sleeping pills the doctor sent home with her.

Now, as tears seeped from his eyes, he watched her drift into sleep and travel far from him.

He had absolutely no clue how to make it up to her.

Max surveyed the guest room. Originally Jenna's bedroom, it was fairly large, with space for extras, including two upholstered armchairs and a desk.

"Son." Ben chuckled from a chair. "You don't have to tuck us in."

Max shifted his weight to the other foot and glanced at the silk flower arrangements and the floral bedspread. Except for Claire's office, it was the one room in the house she'd decorated without regard to his opinion.

He said, "You're comfortable enough? It's a little froufrou in here."

"Beats the heck out of an ash heap."

"Yeah. I suppose so." He crossed his arms. "Do you want me to talk to the insurance guy?"

"I think I can handle it."

"Let's visit the truck dealer tomorrow. Get you some new wheels. Cash flow is not a problem, you know. I'll help."

"I appreciate that, but it can wait. Jenna said their school is closed for the rest of the week. She offered me her car. Guess who I just talked to."

"Who?"

"Kennedy." Del Kennedy was a rancher to the south of the

Hideaway boundary line. "He's got my horses. Found them this afternoon. All except Chester."

"I'm sorry, Dad."

"There's a lesson in there somewhere. Chester's the one I hung on to, thinking I could save him. Then he's the one I lose." Ben shook his head. "The sheriff said he'd keep an eye on the place, but we should go and sift through things soon. And your mother wants to get her crosses."

"I'll come with you."

"Max—"

"Dad, I should have been there for you. I'm sorry I wasn't. I'm here now."

"Sit down."

He sank onto the foot of the bed.

"Listen." Ben leaned forward, resting his arms on his knees and lacing his fingers together.

Max willed himself to be still, to look directly into the blue eyes that had, more often than not, condemned him his entire life.

"Son, none of this is your fault. The house would have burned if you'd been there. We easily could have stayed too long if you'd been there. Hindsight, the back entrance to the gold mine was our only escape, which you would have thought of—maybe even before Lexi did—if you'd been there. But she got us there safely without you."

"But I could have helped in other ways."

"Yes, you could have. But it's over, and we're all fine. Just a little worse for the wear."

"I'm sorry."

"I forgive you. Will you forgive me?"

"And me?" Indio entered the room and shut the door.

Max watched her walk over to his dad. She draped her arm over Ben's shoulders. They looked at him expectantly. He intuited their drift.

"Guys," he said, "we've been here before. You're sorry for placing

BJ on a pedestal and not me, even though, given our two characters, it was a perfectly natural thing for you to do. It's over and done with. I told you years ago that I forgave you."

Ben said, "This is a little different." His smile was sad. "Blame it on foxhole epiphanies."

"What's that?"

"Sitting in a hole in the ground, wondering if fire and smoke would do us in."

Or sitting at a lookout point, wondering if I would ever hold Claire again.

Ben went on. "The other night, we thought a lot about death. You know our faith. You know we don't fear going to meet our Maker. But . . ." He threw a sidelong glance at Indio. "I deeply grieve how I've pushed you away."

Max stared at his father, unsure he'd heard correctly.

"Son, you dragged us through a lot of manure over the years. You can't lay all the blame for that at our feet. At some point you became responsible for your own choices. I forgive you. We forgive you. We hope you can forgive yourself. And I . . . I hope you can forgive me, because your choices were rooted in the way I treated you."

His mother wiped at the corner of her eye. "And in the way I treated you. I am sorry."

Max's throat closed up.

Indio said, "Yes, you told us years ago that you forgave us. But, well, it's been obvious you haven't. We don't hold that against you. It's for your own sake we hope you can truly forgive us."

Their words resonated within him. It was all true. They'd admitted they were wrong in how they'd treated him, how they compared him to BJ, how they expected more from him than he could deliver. He'd glibly offered forgiveness and then, for twenty-five years, abused their confession. He took it as vindication for his own behavior. He was above reproach. He was righteous. He didn't need them.

He'd been such a fool.

"Oh God, help me." His voice broke.

Ben nodded. "Yes. Exactly."

Max sat alone on the patio, in the dark. No stars shone; the strange, smoky cloud cover still blanketed the sky. Oddly, it did not matter. For the first time he was seeing his own version of starlight.

He had been in the dark forever, his mind filled with a smoky gray blanket that obstructed his view of reality. Now, after unprecedented tears and a true heart connection with his parents, it was lifting. He could see life as it was, not as how he imagined it to be.

He had held life at arm's length. Feelings did not exist because he never peered close enough to see them. In truth, the emotion that fueled his life was fear. He feared losing Claire, his children, his business. He feared the pain that always accompanied the mention of BJ. He feared being a disappointment to his parents. By living out of his fears, he had let everyone down, himself included.

The fire had thrown all this in his face, forcing him to acknowledge it . . . for a brief period. But with everyone's physical safety had come a release from that pressure. No need to address it—they could all happily revert to the status quo.

But no one had cooperated with him. One look at Claire and he knew there was no going back. One look at the kids and he knew the fire was not the only thing that haunted them. One conversation with his parents and he knew they weren't about to let go of him.

As his mom and dad freely admitted their faults, Max began to admit his own. As they told him again about God's unconditional love and forgiveness, he began to hear them as if for the first time.

And something broke. It hurt. It physically hurt inside his chest. His mother said it was the cracking of the defenses he'd built up around his heart, an icy hardness that feelings could not penetrate.

Well, they were penetrating now.

He fell to his knees and let them come. Fear, anger, remorse, hatred, pain, frustration, pride, doubt. Sobs erupted from deep inside his belly as he regretted every single incident he could recall.

After a time, other feelings came. Love, forgiveness, hope. Faster and faster they came now, engulfing the ugliness. Tears that stung like fiery darts softened to warm, liquid pools that cleansed inside and out.

His knees ached. He smiled at the realization. He was going to be okay.

"Thank You, Lord. Thank You."

Late that night, Max slipped quietly into bed, keeping a large space between himself and Claire. She was in the same fetal position he'd left her in hours before.

He felt horrendously drained in every way.

"I feel, hon," he whispered to her back. "How about that?"

It wasn't what he would call an enjoyable situation. He would give anything to retreat into his comfy, icy shell again.

Almost anything.

After asking God for help, crying with his parents, extending and receiving forgiveness, there was a hint of—corny as it sounded—sunlight in his soul.

He wasn't so sure he'd trade that in.

Seventy-six

Max awoke to his cell phone's ring. The tune indicated the call came from Neva. He reached over to the nightstand and grabbed it. The clock read seven ten.

"Morning."

"Yo, boss."

Beside him, Claire stirred.

Neva asked, "Are you awake?"

"No."

"Okey dokey. Call. Soon. It's a zoo here already. Bye."

"Bye." He folded shut the phone. "Sorry, hon."

"She couldn't wait at least until eight?" Claire had recognized Neva's personal ring.

Max exhaled carefully and pushed himself up to a sitting position. "There's a lot going on in the wake of the fire."

"Ain't that the truth."

Her face half hidden in the comforter, he couldn't make out her expression. The unusual dusky morning light didn't help. "How are you?"

No sound from her.

"Go back to sleep if you need to."

"Please don't tell me what to do."

Max shut his eyes. It was obvious how she was. Angry.

He thought about the sweet time with his parents the previous night. They'd communicated as never before in his lifetime. Confessions of wrong attitudes. A clearing of the air. A meeting of minds and hearts. True forgiveness, given and received. Sunlight in his soul.

"Claire, please forgive me for not being there for you through the years. Please give me a chance to make it all up to you."

"I don't need another piece of jewelry."

"I'm not talking about things. I mean I want to be there for you, always, in every way you need."

"Why didn't you come?"

"What? When?"

"When do you think? Your daughter and your parents and your wife were almost killed on Monday night. That would be the 'when.'"

He really wanted a cup of coffee. "I honestly thought you were fine. According to the news, you all were fine."

"Did you ever think that even if the fire didn't come our way, we weren't fine? Your parents are old, and—in case you haven't noticed—I've been a basket case since July."

"I'm sorry."

"What on God's green earth was so important Monday night that you couldn't take a couple hours to run up there? Football? . . . Oh." She inhaled sharply. "Were you with her?"

He went still.

He sensed Claire become even more still.

At last he said, "It wasn't like that—"

"I moved out. I left you." She threw the covers back and swung her feet to the floor. "In some circles, I guess that gives you permission to see other women. I can't stay here." Without a backward glance she hurried toward the bathroom.

So much for sunlight in his soul.

Max avoided eye contact with Claire in the kitchen. It wasn't difficult given that the television blared and seven other people were fixing themselves breakfast. He made small talk and ate whatever his kids offered. An omelet, a bagel, and fruit made their way to his plate.

Later, while shaving, he realized what a pathetic picture he made of tiptoeing around his wife. In the hopes of delaying her wrath, he behaved like someone ready for the loony bin.

His hand slipped, and the razor nicked his chin.

What was that about sunlight in his soul?

He stuck a Band-Aid on his face, dressed for work, and found Claire alone outside, sweeping the patio.

"Claire."

"You're going to the office." Disbelief filled her voice.

"I have to. We can't exactly shut down like the public school system." Too late he heard his snappish tone and swallowed it. "There's just a lot going on."

She propped the broom against a chair and looked at him. "There's a lot going on here, too, with your family."

"What do you expect me to do?"

"Nothing. That's what I learned Monday night, anyway—to expect you to do nothing. Then I won't be disappointed. We can take care of each other like we always have, without you here."

"Why in the world do you think I go to work if it's not to take care of my family?"

"That is not the point. I'm talking about things money can't buy." She stepped nearer him. "Max." Her tone grew soft and yet self-assured. "I truly do respect and appreciate how you've been our provider. I always have. It's one reason it was so easy to fill in where you couldn't. Your plate was full. But listen. Your family is hurting today, and money won't speak to that. Only your presence—constant and not in between phone conversations—will help."

He stared at her, at the stranger she had become. It was her confidence now that scared him.

She said, "I lived through the worst night of my life without you. Now I know beyond a shadow of a doubt that I can live through anything without you."

"Claire, I love you. I need you."

She picked up the broom and resumed sweeping.

"I'll be home as soon as I can possibly get away. We'll talk then. Please, Claire. Okay?"

She looked up, gave him an odd smile, and pointed at her throat. "Hurts to talk much. Good-bye."

Frustrated, he stomped through the house and into the garage, her words echoing in his head. As he pulled from their drive onto the main road, he heard the finality in how she'd said, "Good-bye."

She easily could have said, "Have a nice life."

At a stop sign he hesitated. Should he turn back? Could he be the kind of father and husband and son she wanted him to be?

Then he thought of the chaos at the office, of the loss of stature and revenue for his company if he didn't take care of certain things only he could take care of.

Behind him a driver honked.

Max drove through the intersection, toward the freeway, toward Beaumont Staffing.

Seventy-seven

Jenna sat on a chair in her parents' bedroom and watched her mother dig through a dresser drawer. "Mom, I can stay and help you."

"No. Thanks. I'll be fine. Nana and Papa will appreciate your help at the hacienda. I'm just not up for going there . . ." Her voice trailed off, and a dazed expression crossed her face.

Jenna's stomach lurched at yet another sight of her mom falling apart. "Do you want to see a counselor or someone? You've been through a traumatic experience. It wouldn't hurt Lexi, either, to talk with a professional."

"Maybe. Later. Right now I just want to rest."

"Then sit still, for goodness' sake."

Claire glanced up. Her face was gray and drawn. "I have no ID, no cell, no credit card, no car. I can't even remember where I left my purse. House or car? I don't know. Not that it matters where it burned, but isn't that crazy?"

At the sound of hysteria in her mom's voice, panic clutched at Jenna. "It doesn't matter, Mom. You don't need any of that stuff yet. We'll take care of it later this week."

"I— Oh, good. Here's my passport. People use passports instead of driver's licenses, right?" She pulled things from the drawer. "A Visa card. I can rent a car. Great. My old glasses. Not as cool as the Donna Karans—"

"Mom!"

"What?"

"What are you doing?"

Claire shut the drawer, card in one hand, eyeglasses in the other, and sat on the bed. Her cheeks were bright pink now.

"Mom, Dad's taking care of everything. Why won't you let him?"

"I can't."

"Why not?"

"Jenna, the traumatic experience didn't change anything between us."

"Oh my gosh! It did so! It changed him! You should have seen him, Mom. He sobbed like a baby that night."

"Mm-hmm. So did I. He could have been there."

"You're leaving again, aren't you?"

"Not again. Still. I'm picking up where we left off. We're separated. I'm finding my own voice. I'm finding my safe harbor."

"That night changed things between me and Kevin. We're each other's safe harbor."

"Honey, I know. I'm proud you did the hard thing and told him how it hurt you when he reenlisted. It's what I should have done at your age."

"I don't want to go through life without him, even if he is sent overseas."

Claire nodded. "I'm glad you're back together and working things out. You're becoming a team. Your dad and I should have been one, but I let him take away my identity by not speaking up. I blame me, not him."

"Then why are you leaving?"

"Because now I'm speaking up, and he doesn't want to listen."

Jenna bit her lip. "Are you going to Tandy's?"

"Just to pack my things."

"Where will you stay? Not in that awful house we rented! Let the owner keep the deposit. There's no furniture, and there's rust in the bathroom sink!"

"Well, I could stay there, but since I don't have a roommate, I think not." She shrugged. "Tandy will take me to a car rental place this afternoon; then I plan to go to the coast and find a motel room."

"A motel room!"

"I need to be by myself for a few days. Honey, please don't cry."

"Dad's trying!"

Claire pressed her lips together.

"You could at least give him a chance!" With a sob Jenna hurried from the room.

Her mom had totally gone off the deep end this time.

Seventy-eight

Claire carried her violin case and pulled a wheeled suitcase down Tandy's hall. *Only three more feet and I'm out of here.*

If Tandy would ever budge. She had picked Claire up at the house and taken her to rent a car. Claire went to her condo and packed her things. Now ready to leave, she found the exit blocked by her friend, arms crossed, legs wide.

"Claire." Tandy flicked her fingers beneath one eye, then the other. "You shouldn't be alone right now."

"Please don't go sappy on me."

"I can't help it. Forty-eight hours ago I thought you were dead. I thought Lexi and Indio and Ben were dead. So did everybody else. How do you expect us to let you out of our sight already?"

"Me out of your sight? So it's you who shouldn't be alone, not me."

"Same difference."

"Tandy, give me a break. I just went through this with my kids. I can't take care of you all!"

"We need to comfort each other. Sort of a group decompression."

"You know, I'm the one who thought I was going to die. I'm the one facing ghosts."

"All the more reason not to go it alone. You've heard my pastor speak. He's compassionate and wise. He'd be over here lickety-split if I ask him."

"How many ways can I say this? I do not want to talk to anyone!"

"Till when?"

"I don't know till when! I told you, I'll be at that Villa place in Oceanside. They have telephones. I will get a new cell phone as soon as possible. I am not going anywhere else."

"I'll come over and take you to dinner tomorrow night."

"No."

"Max needs you."

"Ha. Right. Ben was telling me yesterday about 'foxhole epiphanies,' how fear makes you see things differently. They can help you set things right, or they can cause you to make worthless promises. Max's epiphany falls in the latter category. He'll get over it. He already did. He went to work."

"I really think he's changed."

"Tandy! Get off my back!"

She flinched as if Claire had slapped her. "You've turned into a selfish witch."

"Thanks."

Tandy moved aside.

Claire went to the door, yanked it open, and strode through it without a backward glance. She heard it click shut behind her.

Claire's throat felt scraped raw.

As it should. She'd shrieked and cried and gotten sick in the gold mine. She'd inhaled smoke and ash for days. And to top it off, she'd just yelled at her best friend.

On the balcony of her hotel room a block from the beach, she pulled on her jacket and settled into a chair. Ash was not falling here. The sky remained overcast, but it was a normal gray, not that ugly yellowish tint. The sound of muffled ocean waves racing to shore reached her ears. Their constancy soothed her nerves. She gulped in large amounts of clean salt air.

Poor Tandy. She'd gotten the brunt of it all after Claire managed to hold herself together with her family.

Jenna's emotional reaction in the bedroom when Claire searched for money and cards had convinced her she needed to talk to her other kids before leaving the house.

Max was at the office. Of course. Ben and Indio were sequestered in the guest room. Jenna and Kevin disappeared outdoors somewhere. Claire approached Erik, Danny, and Lexi on the drive in front of the house. They were preparing to go to the hacienda with their grandparents.

Lexi said, "Mom, you don't look ready for this."

"I'm not. Actually . . ."

Danny caught her eye. She suspected he knew already, not because Jenna told him, but because he noticed things better than his siblings did.

"Actually," she said, "I'm not ready for any of this. I guess I'm still shell-shocked. This reunion is wonderful. All of you staying overnight here has meant the world to me. But tomorrow or the next day, you'll get back to your regular lives."

Danny said, "Mom, he's trying so hard."

She held up a finger. "Let me finish. You should get back to your regular lives. My regular life, three days ago, wasn't here. I was in the middle of finding my own voice again. I have to—" Her energy gave out at that point. She'd told them she was leaving. It was all she could say.

But Lexi nodded. "You have issues to deal with, like that thing in the gold mine. Abandonment. Feeling safe and secure."

Grateful surprise flooded through her. Lexi had grown by leaps and bounds through that night. "Exactly."

Lexi smiled and gave her a thumbs-up.

Claire turned to her eldest.

Erik shrugged. "Do what you gotta do."

Claire's throat caught at the defeated expression on his face. The night had done something to him. It had muted him. There he was, living with a great special feature story for his evening news, and he refused to allow any reporter or photographer to interview his family.

Already the news was old. His station and others, as well as the newspapers and *People* magazine, had gleaned what they needed from Shadrach, Meshach, and Abednego. She was glad not to be included and trusted that Erik would recover after a time.

"Mom." Danny's tone challenged. "Why not give Dad another chance?"

Toxic words spewed forth. "Because he gave up his right to another chance when he chose to work on Monday and spend that night with Neva instead of coming to the hacienda."

She shouldn't have said that.

But she had, and it was the truth, and there was no taking it back. Let them discuss it with their father.

Claire shut her eyes now.

Maybe she'd always been a selfish witch, really, deep down inside. If that were true, she might as well stop trying to hide behind nicey-nice smiles and agreeable words.

It seemed she'd already stopped doing those things. She'd spouted off to everyone—everyone she supposedly loved. She'd alienated them. And now there she was, spending a large chunk of her husband's money—which she claimed wasn't important—on a beach motel and rental car. She would eat at restaurants and buy books and make long-distance calls to her kids. Of course, if they didn't answer, there'd be no charge.

One person would answer, though. He'd promised he'd be there for her. He'd said his number was listed in the phone book.

Seventy-nine

"Alone at last." Kevin set a gym bag on the floor and shut the apartment door.

Walking toward their kitchen, Jenna threw him a weak smile. She was exhausted every which way. They had spent most of the day at the hacienda with her grandparents, Erik, and the twins. They sifted through the fire's aftermath, finding very few salvageable items. It all had been too sad for words. Even Papa had wept, more for the loss of chickens and his favorite old horse than for the material things in the house. Nana mourned little—except for the photos, the mementos, the only tangibles of her lost son.

Then, back at her dad's, they ate pizza, one last meal together before going their separate ways. Of course, her mom had already gone her separate way.

Yes, it was all too sad for words.

Now she was home for the very first time since before the fire, since before she'd gone her own separate way and moved to Tandy's.

She stepped into the kitchen, stopped dead in her tracks, blinked, and screamed, "Kevin!"

Dirty dishes and glasses lay everywhere—in the sink, on the countertops, on the table. Empty chip bags, boxes of crackers and cereal, and more sat all over the place. A potted philodendron in the window was brown. Not yellow or weepy green, but brown and crusted.

"Kevin!"

"Whoops. Sorry. I didn't have a chance to—"

"I can't believe this!" She circled the small area. "My poor philly. Nobody kills a philly. Oh. My. Gosh. Look at that stovetop!"

"Jen."

"What?" she snapped and looked up at him.

"I missed you."

"What does that have to do with living in a pigsty?"

"I'll clean it up."

"You got that right."

"Tomorrow."

"You are not a slob. My gosh, you're a Marine. You get on me for not being tidy enough. And look at this! Unbelievable."

"What can I say? I lost my head. I couldn't think straight without you here. I couldn't eat or sleep."

"It looks like you ate plenty."

"I didn't eat right. Mostly junk food."

She stared at him. He wasn't doing his little-boy, oh-shucks-ma'am routine. He was admitting what she meant to him.

"Because I wasn't here?"

"Yeah." He shrugged. "You saw your dad Monday night at the lookout point? I wasn't in that bad a shape, but close to it."

"Oh, Kev. You never let on at school or at that brunch Erik tricked us into."

"Right. And lose macho face? A guy doesn't go around saying, 'Boo-hoo. I'm falling apart because she left.'"

"They do in songs."

He smiled. "Hey! Wait a minute. Back up. Did you hear what you said?"

"What?"

"You called me a Marine. Present tense."

"I did not."

"You did. Come here, pretty lady." He took her hand and led her out of the kitchen. "Let's get out of the pigsty. We need to talk."

They sat on the couch. For a long moment they only stared at each other. In all the hubbub of the past few days, Jenna didn't remember really looking at him. There hadn't been a spare moment to be alone.

She touched his bristly jaw. "Did I thank you for coming to Tandy's Monday night?"

"Yes."

"You've been my rock this week. You were just there all the time, helping everybody. You never complained. You always knew exactly what to do."

"I love your family."

"It's not my family. It's ours."

"Okay, our family. As long as I don't have to change my name to Beaumont." He smiled. "Welcome home."

"Thanks. It was good to all be together, in the same house, but, whew." She batted her eyes. "This feels so incredibly good to be home. With you."

"We're each other's home, aren't we?"

"Yeah, we are. Being away from you was the worst." She smiled. "And I hated living at Tandy's. I mean, it was all right. Except for her lumpy mattress and the long drive to school. Not to mention having to check in with two moms all the time about my schedule."

"I'm sorry."

"Well, I could have gone to Dad's. That would have been more comfortable—"

"I don't mean I'm sorry about Tandy's. I'm sorry, Jenna. I'm sorry for not discussing with you my decision to reenlist."

She leaned toward him. "Can you repeat that? I'm not sure I heard correctly."

He caught her in his arms, turning her until she was across his lap facing him. "Only if you repeat what you said."

She giggled. "I did not say you are a Marine, present tense."

"You did." He pulled her close.

His navy eyes blurred before her. She became acutely aware of how close his mouth was to hers.

"On second thought," she murmured, "maybe I did."

"I love you, and I am sorry I hurt you."

"I love you, and I am sorry I hurt you."

He brushed his lips over hers. "Does that mean you'll clean up the kitchen?"

"No way."

"Jen, I promise to try to talk more about things with you. I'll try to remember that besides being a Marine—present tense—I'm also your husband, present tense. Will you forgive me for not cluing you in on my decision before I made it?"

She studied his face, drinking in the familiar angles and markings, pushing aside the realization that they still did not agree on what happened. "Cluing" her in on his decision was not exactly all she wanted. They should have discussed the idea for a long, long time. Her opinion should have been given full consideration.

But . . . maybe this was where give-and-take came into play.

"I forgive you, Kevin."

"Thank you." He kissed her. "But I might mess up again. Wait. Knowing me, that's a given."

She nodded. Of course he would. Of course she would. "That's life."

"I mean, I'll screw up on purpose."

She pushed back to see his face better.

"Just so we can make up again."

She watched his lazy grin emerge, one corner of his mouth lifting at a time. The thought struck her that she would not see him for long periods of time. That they would again separate and make up, so to speak.

"Jen, I was kidding. Don't look so sad."

"You're leaving. Because you're a Marine."

"Yeah." He drew the word out, as if he didn't follow her reasoning.

"Not for a while, though. Hey, pretty lady. Will you stick by me, even when I make you sad?"

She saw the worry in his eyes. He feared the unknown future as much as she did. He needed her as much as she needed him.

She said, "I suppose 'sad' comes under the category of 'for better or worse'? Which means I already promised in our wedding vows to stick by you, but I didn't. I'm sorry."

"It's okay. You did what you did because you thought I wasn't sticking by you."

"But I'm sorry."

"I forgive you. It all turned out for good. I think we learned a lot about each other, about marriage."

"Yes."

"Uh-oh. I just had another thought. Enlisting means a pay cut. You'll remember the 'richer or poorer' part too?"

An almost unbearable weight of sadness pulled the corners of her mouth downward. It had nothing to do with money. She forced a smile and nodded.

Kevin pulled her close again and held her tightly to himself.

For one brief moment, she wondered if the pain of sticking by him would be worth it. If she got up and left right now and never looked back, she would not have to say good-bye and hello, good-bye and hello, over and over and over. She would not have to try to fit into the parameters that defined the incomprehensible being called a "military wife."

She pressed her face into his shoulder and wondered when life had gotten so hard.

Eighty

In the evening twilight, Max stood on the patio, hands in his pockets, rocking on the balls of his feet, appraising the damage to his yard and pool.

Fighting off a migraine.

Danny kept him company. He and the others had spent the afternoon at the hacienda, returned to the house, and ordered in pizza.

"The others" meaning everyone except Claire. Claire never would have ordered in pizza. She would have cooked for them. She was a great cook. And she was gone. Again. Still? Whatever. It was for good this time. He felt it in his bones.

"Dad, can you hire somebody to help clean this mess?"

"Hmm? Oh yeah, I'll hire some temps. It hardly seems like much, though, not compared to the hacienda."

"That's for sure. I'd help you, but I have to get back to work tomorrow. I'm going home tonight."

"Understandable. Thanks for all you've done. It was good to all hang out here together, huh?" He smiled.

"Yeah, it was. I'm taking Lexi home too."

"Aw, you're all abandoning me," he teased. "First Erik, Jenna, and Kevin. Now you and Lexi."

Danny didn't respond for a moment. "Did . . . uh . . . did Mom or Nana tell you about Mom's incident in the mine?"

"What incident?"

"Lexi said Mom had this sort of flashback thing. They were in that space just beyond the entrance tunnel?"

He nodded. He knew the mine's back door and wasn't all that surprised to learn the twins had discovered it on their own.

"She said Mom screamed and cried for, like, twenty minutes."

Max stared at him.

"Nana prayed. Later Mom told Lexi what happened. She was reliving a time when her mom locked her in a root cellar. She was three years old. Her dad eventually found her, then beat up her mom."

Max cursed under his breath. "I swear those two take the cake for being supreme idiots."

"And . . . well . . ."

"Well, what?"

"The point is, those supreme idiots abandoned Mom. And she feels abandoned by you. Basically that's what she's been saying for months."

"You're all psychiatrists now?"

Danny turned toward the pool, clearly disgusted with Max.

"Son, I'm sorry." The words came quickly to him. He was so tired of hurting people. "Okay. I can see how it could make sense. Your mom felt abandoned by me because whenever business was my priority, it would appear to her that she wasn't. Given her history, she would be especially sensitive to abandonment issues, even if she didn't analyze exactly what was going on."

"Maybe it's not just your prioritizing the business."

He waited.

Danny looked at him. "What were you doing Monday night?"

Kissing Neva. "Making a dumb mistake."

Danny chuckled softly, a sound of surprise. "Wow. That's gotta be a first, you admitting fault."

"I suppose." Max rubbed the back of his neck. "Trust me, Danny, I know I've made countless mistakes. Now it's time to rectify them."

If it wasn't too late.

Hey, bud." Phil rapped his knuckles on Max's desk.

"Huh?"

"Why don't you go home? You zoned out on us again."

"Sorry. I'm fine."

"Shoot, Max, you're not fine, and you shouldn't be fine. Right, Neva?" He glanced at her in the other chair across from Max's desk.

"Right," she said. "You have family matters to attend to."

He gave a sad smile. "My parents are older than they look. I should go with them to buy a vehicle."

"Then go," Neva said. "Nothing needs your immediate attention here. We've gotten by without you for most of the week. Missing Friday afternoon isn't going to hurt."

He closed up a file folder. "You're right."

Phil stood. "Anything I can do, besides the obvious?" He took the file from Max's hand.

"I don't think so."

"Okay. Then I'll get to this and see you next week."

"Thanks." Max watched Phil leave his office.

Neva remained seated.

He looked at her.

She looked back at him, her face unreadable.

He said, "I get the feeling something does need my immediate attention."

"I'm resigning."

Max wouldn't have guessed he could feel any more hollow than he already did, but her words dug a new hole.

"I'll wait until you're on your feet again. You do have a lot on your plate personally. Not to mention the city is falling apart, and everybody needs temporary help."

"Why?"

"The fire."

"I didn't mean why the need for workers."

"I didn't either. Let's call it The Fire, capital letters. It changed everything between us. I was going where I swore I would never go with you. I love you, Max. I always have. But I should have kept quiet about it. The Fire showed me you're not mine to have. It melted you, and now the truth shows: you won't leave Claire. Even if she leaves you, she'll always be with you. I can't stay here knowing that."

"I—I—"

"You have nothing to say." Neva stood. "There isn't anything you can say. Except that you'll write a great letter of recommendation for me." She smiled in a sassy way.

Before he could gather a coherent thought, she was out the door.

Women. The most untrustworthy species that ever walked the face of the earth. Every single one in his life had walked out. That chick in high school. His mom. Neva. Claire. Why did they all leave him? What was it about—

About him? Talk about slow on the draw.

"Okay, God. I get the picture. It must be my fault. I let them down. Fine. I take responsibility."

Max closed his eyes. The words were on the tip of his tongue, but he resisted.

And then he wondered, what did he have to lose? A little face? Did that really matter after losing the most important woman in his life?

"Evidently I have abandonment issues too. God, help me to forgive Claire and Neva and my mom and any others." He took a deep breath. "And please, God, forgive me for how I've hurt them all."

Eighty-one

Claire slept for three days at the hotel. On Sunday evening, she called Eddie, the fireman. A short while later, they met on a sidewalk outside a book-and-coffee shop.

"Hi."

"Hi."

An awkward moment passed as they stared at each other.

He grinned crookedly. "This is like some kind of weird blind date." He held open his arms. "It shouldn't be, should it?"

"No." She sighed and stepped into his embrace.

He was taller than she remembered. Lean. Sinewy. His cotton polo shirt smelled of fresh laundry, his arms of soap.

The stranger again—offering safety and security she could find nowhere else.

They sat across from each other at a small corner table, coffee mugs in hand. Classical music played softly in the background. Scattered about the store was a hodgepodge of people at other tables and on couches and upholstered chairs, with friend, book, or laptop. Paintings by local artists adorned the walls, some of them pastoral, some of them angst-ridden.

Eddie said, "This is a great place. I've never been here before."

She nodded. "It's comfy. I found it a few years ago."

"So." His eyes zeroed in on hers. "How are you?"

"Confused, angry, exhausted. Wondering if I'm on the verge of a nervous breakdown. Did I mention angry?"

"Hmm."

"Sorry, that sort of slipped out by itself."

"No, it's fine. I was just thinking you look prettier than I remember. Probably because you washed the smudges off your face and combed your hair."

"Now I know why I called you. You lie quite well."

He laughed. Crow's-feet crinkled around sky-blue eyes. His mouth was wide in a narrow face. Now that his cappuccino-brown hair wasn't mashed down from a helmet, she saw that it was wavy.

"It's the truth," he said.

She narrowed her eyes, the ones that carried bags so large she hadn't even bothered with makeup. It wouldn't have helped. "I have to warn you. I'm into being abrasively real these days."

"I'm okay with that."

"I keep upsetting people."

"No problem."

"Then let's get something straight. I'm a mess and I look it, and I don't care. I am not capable of saying a kind word, and I don't care."

"I still think you're prettier than I remember."

She puffed out a sound of disbelief.

"You will get through this." His gentle voice and demeanor melted her defenses. The words of hope echoed Indio's.

She plunked her elbows on the table and pressed the heels of her hands against her eyes.

"Hey." He pried off one of her hands and squeezed it. "It's okay. Did you know disaster survivors get together in support groups? Just like we're doing, so they can vent and laugh and cry and connect on a level that's impossible with anyone else who didn't experience what they did."

She sniffed and lowered her other hand. "I'm sorry."

"Don't be. I'm really glad you called. When Zak told me he and

Lexi were having dinner tonight, I was hoping he'd invite me and she'd invite you. He didn't catch on to my hints. I guess a support group wasn't what he had in mind."

"Zak and Lexi? Dinner?"

"You didn't know?"

She shook her head. "I moved into a motel on Thursday. I needed to be alone."

Concern registered on his face. "Claire. This isn't the time to be alone."

"I'll give you the short version." She explained the current status of her marriage.

"I'm sorry."

"So I haven't talked with anyone for a few days. Is Zak a nice guy?"

"Yeah, he is. I've worked with him for about three years. You can trust him with your daughter. And you're changing the subject."

"Yep. Enough about me. How are you?"

His eyes crinkled again, and grin lines deepened around his mouth. "Way better than you."

"Well, aren't you special?"

His laughter filled the shop and turned contagious for other patrons. Even Claire joined in, one giggle at a time.

"I've been in some serious fires." Eddie grew somber. "I never came that close to dying, though. It started to sink in when I saw Indio's wall of crosses. It was one of those 'whoa!' moments."

"And their Bible not burning?"

"It wasn't so much that; I've seen that happen before. I chalk it up to another example of weird phenomena that happen with fire. Amazing, yes. But this was different. I saw that paneled wall with wood frames and crosses and whatnots hanging on it, right next to a blown-out window where incredible heat came roaring in, and nothing was burned? Now we're talking beyond weird phenomena."

Claire recalled the blackened, melted kitchen and Indio's corner. It nearly glowed in contrast to the rest of the room.

He said, "It was like God saying, 'Hey, you, the bozo firefighter, pay attention.'"

"The wall is special to Indio. At the dinner table a few nights ago, she said it was her gift to Jesus, and that on Monday night, He gave it back to her."

"Wow."

"Yeah. He's very real to her. A real Person who lives inside of her."

"What about for you?"

Claire's mind spun back to a time when she wept at an altar, in sorrow and in joy. "Thirty years ago I asked Him to live inside me. That was good and wonderful, and He turned my life around. Then . . . I don't know. He got me squared away, and life was fine. I loved being a wife and mom. I enjoyed being involved with schools and community things. I kept all the rules the best I could. Took the kids to church, didn't swear, didn't lie about big things, didn't drink or smoke, didn't gossip, didn't steal or commit murder, didn't take over for Max as head of the family. What are you grinning at?"

"You just described what I learned as a kid—except the part about not taking over for Max. I don't remember that rule."

"Ha-ha."

"You were saying?"

"That I kept all the rules." She thought a minute. "I still pray, because I believe God exists. I know He saved us Monday night. But He's not very real to me."

He nodded.

"I broke that last rule big-time a couple months ago. I usurped Max's position by giving him an ultimatum."

"What'd you say?"

"Choose me or his agency."

"Ow. That had to hurt."

"It did. Ben and Indio and my friend Tandy tell me that Max

needed to hear some hard truths. They say it's all right I did that. I don't think it's all right with God, though. I mean, I've single-handedly dismantled my family."

"'Single-handedly' is a big word. I'd say you're probably giving yourself way too much credit on that one."

She shrugged.

"Well," he said, "I chucked the whole religion thing when I was a teenager. But seeing that wall the other morning sure brought me up short. I've been asking myself ever since, if God is real, what does that mean to me?" He paused. "Did you know a dozen firefighters were injured in the fire and eight people died?"

"Mm-hmm."

"The ones who died were in a similar situation to ours. The fire encircled them like it did us." He snapped his fingers. "Why them and not me? It's not fair. It doesn't make sense. Unless God is real and for some reason chose to give me a second chance at life. Which begs the question, what do I do now?"

She had no reply. Obviously she'd blown her second chance, bailing out on her family.

"I didn't come up with an answer. It's probably a step-by-step thing." He tilted his head, eyeing her with a peculiar expression on his face.

"What?"

"Have you eaten dinner?"

"Uh, no. I haven't been hungry. I should get going, though. It's late, and I'm tired."

"How's your anger and confusion?"

She smiled. "Less than when I arrived here, thank you."

"What was the other thing . . . Oh yeah. On the verge of a nervous breakdown. Still there?"

"Uh, no."

"Then this was a successful support group meeting. We can do it again, if you'd like." There was no pressure in his kind voice.

A sense of peace settled about her, lessening even further the anger, confusion, and anxieties she arrived with. But she knew the respite was momentary. The unsettledness would return, because her life truly was a mess. One fiery night didn't fix anything; it only complicated things.

Except she'd met this safe harbor of a fireman.

"Yes," she said. "I'd like."

He grinned. He had a very nice grin, an ear-to-ear, jovial expression.

Maybe Eddie was indeed a hero of biblical proportions.

Eighty-two

Late Friday afternoon, in the parking lot of a semi-dumpy motel in Oceanside, Max stood beside a brand-new Volvo—pearl white, with a sunroof and a butter-soft, white leather interior.

He held the keys out toward his wife.

Claire stuffed her hands into the pockets of a ratty green cardigan sweater that hung halfway down a long brown skirt.

"Max, I told you on the phone. I don't need a car."

"Your car was totaled in the fire."

She gave him a withering stare.

He said, "I realize this is not news to you, but this car costs less than your rental."

"I was planning on getting one myself. Next week."

Her words struck him as ludicrous. She'd never purchased an automobile in her life. She wouldn't know the first thing about what was a good deal, let alone the ins and outs of financing. Could she even get financing? It wasn't like she received a paycheck.

But he kept his thoughts to himself and his face passive. He was here to make amends, not to point out her mistakes.

"I can do it," she said.

Uncanny how she could read his mind.

"I can do it all by myself."

"But here." He offered the keys again. "It's done for you. Try this car for a while. If you don't like it, we can trade it in." What was not to like? A shiny new luxury sedan with all the trappings—

"I don't want any more guilt offerings from you."

He lowered his hand. "That's not what this is. This is simply a set of wheels, a practical thing that you need. Claire, I can't ever make up for what I've done and not done. Please just let me take care of your necessities. No strings attached. There are new credit cards and a checkbook in the glove compartment to replace the ones lost in the fire."

"Is that supposed to make me feel safe?"

"Yes!"

She opened her mouth, seemed to reconsider whatever the retort was, and closed it.

Claire didn't look so good. Her face was pinched, her hair unkempt, the bohemian-style clothing odd. Well, odd for the woman he knew. Or thought he knew.

He felt as if his heart would break on the spot. "Are you sleeping?"

Again she hesitated to speak.

"Eating?"

"I'm doing all right."

"Please come home. Let's go to a marriage counselor and straighten this whole thing out."

She scrunched her lips together.

"Give me one reason why not, besides selling our livelihood."

"I rented an apartment. In Vista. I'm moving in tomorrow. And I applied for a job at Macy's. The symphony alone isn't enough to make ends meet."

He stared at her. "Why?"

Anger flared in her eyes.

"Okay, okay. I know why. You've told me. You want to play first fiddle. You want to find your own voice again. I understand now! Last Monday night the thought of losing you made me want to die. Yes, I want you to play first fiddle, whatever that means. I want to hear your real voice again."

Her shoulders sagged, and she gazed beyond him.

"Claire, how do I win back your heart?"

"These past few days, I . . ." She paused, still not meeting his eyes. "My heart shut down Monday night. There's nothing you can do."

"Don't give up on us! We just need some time and some help."

She looked at him. "You burned your bridges. I can't trust you. You've never been there when I needed you. Never, ever. You were late to all three births. You weren't there when I woke up from my hysterectomy. You convinced me I wanted to get married in Las Vegas. You weren't there to help me when Erik broke his arm or when Danny had pneumonia. You missed my birthday dinner in July."

Fear and anger crashed over him. "That's right. Blame it all on me. You know what I think? Your heart shut down a long time ago."

"Like I could keep it open with you."

"Just take the new car and give me the keys to your rental. Save me a few bucks."

"Fine." She pulled keys from her pocket.

They quickly exchanged sets. She pointed to an ugly blue car and walked away.

Ten minutes later, sitting in the crush of five o'clock traffic on the 78, Max got a whiff of Claire's perfume. Donna Karan's Cashmere Mist. He knew the exact kind. How many husbands could say that?

It permeated the car, overpowering even the strong scent of cheap air freshener. It was as strong as if she sat right there beside him.

He lowered all four windows and deeply inhaled exhaust fumes.

Max scarcely tasted the dinner his mother cooked.

Three of the kids had come—the twins and Jenna and Kevin. Erik couldn't make it; he was back on the news that night, his first broadcast since the fire. His boss hadn't been too happy with Erik's disinterest in reporting how his family survived.

Of course, Claire hadn't come.

Jenna said, "I talked to Mom yesterday. She's moving into an apartment tomorrow. She said you're helping, Lexi. Want me to pick you up?"

"Yeah. Thanks. I guess Tandy's coming too."

"I heard. I guess they made up. Can you believe she called Mom a mean witch?"

"Knowing Tandy, I'm surprised she kept it that clean."

They laughed.

Danny shook his head at Max. "Girl talk." He turned to his sisters. "Mom doesn't have any big stuff to move, does she?"

"Not yet. A mattress and bed frame are being delivered." Lexi winked. "You can skip it."

Max listened with one ear. The banter struck him as weird. There they sat, discussing their mother's home—some apartment in another community that had nothing to do with him, their father, her husband. Lexi carried most of the conversation. Strange when, in the past, on a good day, she barely got in three sentences among her siblings. It was as if the fire had burned away whatever wall had closed off her true heart.

To his surprise, he realized it was the same with all of them.

Lexi jabbering like a magpie.

Jenna moving back in with Kevin.

Kevin apologizing to Jenna about reenlisting without telling her first.

Danny courageously confronting Max with hard truths.

Erik quieting.

Max's parents asking his forgiveness.

And him . . . He knew beyond a shadow of a doubt he would do anything for Claire.

Anything.

Jenna interrupted his thoughts. "Okay, Lexi, I've waited long enough. You're not going to mention it, are you?"

"Mention what?" Lexi tossed her hair over her shoulder.

Indio laughed. "He's awfully cute."

Ben shook a finger at her. "You promised."

"Well, he is."

"This is Lexi's business."

Danny nearly choked on a drink of water and spit it back into the glass.

Max said, "What? Who's cute?"

Jenna rolled her eyes. "Zak."

"Zak who?"

Lexi tossed her hair again and batted her eyes in an exaggerated way. "Zak the fireman. My hero."

Indio said, "I still like Chad the best, but that's all right. He has a wife and baby. Zak is nice too."

Ben growled. "Indio."

Kevin said, "I guess Lexi's idea of Mr. Stud is not the same as yours, Nana."

Everyone laughed, except for Max.

He said, "Zak. Uh, he's one of those three who were with you that night."

The laughter intensified.

"What about him?"

"Lexi!" Jenna cried. "You didn't tell Dad?"

As if his youngest ever told him anything.

Lexi shrugged.

"Chicken." Jenna turned to Max. "Lexi went out with Zak for dinner Sunday night."

Lexi cleared her throat. "Wednesday night too," she whispered. "Movie *and* dinner."

There was more loud laughter.

Max pasted a smile on his face, one of the gang.

He wondered how to get back into the loop he'd bypassed for thirty years.

Eighty-three

Claire flipped on the coffeemaker in the galley kitchen of her new apartment and turned around to face her friend. "Tandy, I want out."

"You're nuts."

"Thank you for that vote of confidence."

"I mean it. You are nuts. I know a good shrink. He's also my pastor."

"Stop trying to fix me. Just be my friend."

"Hey, those two go together, you know? Friendship and fixing. You need help. Who else is going to tell you that?"

"I need someone to say it's all right. That's what I did for you."

"My husband wasn't begging for forgiveness and falling all over himself to take care of my needs. Claire, why can't you give Max half a chance to prove he's changed? It's only been a few weeks since the fire."

"I forget why I'm talking to you again."

"Because you know I love you enough to talk straight. I refuse to allow this fit of self-pity to continue. Yeah, so what, he missed out on most of the past thirty years? Maybe you've got thirty more with him. You make a good team. Forgive him, and get over it."

"And go back to being mealymouthed, and asking him how high I should jump, and giving up my music, and waiting for him not to come home for some event?"

Tandy clamped her mouth shut.

Claire opened a cupboard and grabbed two mugs from a mostly empty shelf. She owned a total of four mugs—two more than she needed, but they came four to a box. She clanked them on the countertop.

"Claire, I am not saying to go back to the old ways. I'm saying try a new way *with* Max, not without him."

She shook her head. "I can't trust him to try a new way."

"Can't or don't want to?"

"He'll get over this so-called change. He's upset because of the fire. Once it sinks in that his family didn't die while he refused to help, he'll be okay."

"Then give it time. Give him six months to either get over it or not."

"I don't have six months."

"You're making a huge mistake."

"Well, it's my huge mistake, not yours." She picked up the carafe and poured coffee into a mug. It sloshed over the sides. With a muted cry of frustration, she banged the carafe against the ceramic-tile counter-top and watched a crack zigzag up its side.

Wordlessly, Tandy put an arm around her shoulders and held her tightly.

Claire huddled on the bed under a pile of blankets and hugged the stuffed lion with all her might. She shivered uncontrollably. The clock's green dial read 1:18 a.m.

The nightmares were getting worse, more intense. They lingered in the daytime. Even when she talked with others, she felt the shad-ows—as if she still sat alone in that dark hole of a root cellar.

Why would anyone love her? Her parents obviously hadn't.

Why would Max want to be married to her? He was right. She blamed him for everything, when she was the one who'd cheated on him all those years ago, making Petros her confidant. Now she was confiding in Eddie as though he was a better friend than Tandy. It didn't seem to matter that he had a steady lady friend and she had a husband.

She'd been a lousy mom, pretending life was all sunshine and rainbows. The kids didn't stand a chance, expecting the same in the real world as adults.

She had too much money, too many things. She didn't deserve diamonds and a huge house and a brand-new Volvo.

She'd left her husband.

To top it off, she couldn't sleep without a heavy-duty pill.

She reached for the bottle and took the last one. Tomorrow she'd see about refilling the prescription.

She'd be fine. She would be just fine. What she needed to do was get on with her second-chance life.

Getting the apartment was a huge first step. The job was number two. She'd start on number three tomorrow.

And then after that, for sure, she would feel safe.

Eighty-four

Max heard a step and looked up from his desk. A stranger stood in the open doorway of his office, knuckles poised to rap on the wood.

"Maxwell James Beaumont?" the young man said.

The air shimmied before him, like heat waves rippling above the desert floor.

"Yes."

The kid stepped across the room, handed him a large envelope, and left.

Max knew what it was. He felt the floor might swallow him whole.

"Max."

He focused again on the doorway. One of the staff ladies stood there. He couldn't think of her name.

"You okay?" she said.

"I need to be alone. Shut the door, please."

After a moment's hesitation, she did what he asked.

He read the return address. The female attorney's name was familiar. Tandy had used her services.

Max laid his face on the desk.

"Dear God, please don't let this be happening."

Max sat with his father in the gazebo at the far corner of the backyard. Night had fallen. Low-to-the-ground solar lamps lit the path.

334 SALLY JOHN & GARY SMALLEY

Strings of twinkle lights crisscrossed the ceiling and cast a soft glow. Claire loved her twinkle lights.

"Son." Ben tamped down the tobacco in his pipe. "I've been thinking."

"I've been thinking, if Mom sees you with that thing, you're in big trouble."

Max really didn't want to hear his dad's thoughts. Claire was filing for divorce. Somehow he had made it through the day. Somehow he'd told his parents. His mother cried quietly.

The world would never be the same. He didn't want to talk about it.

Ben chuckled. "I figured your mom would blow a gasket when she heard that the one thing I thought to stuff in my pocket the night of the fire was my pipe. But she didn't. 'Course, we were in the mine when I told her. Then Chad said she had probably inhaled enough smoke to equal a lifetime of pipe puffing."

"And she likes this guy?"

"Yep. Go figure. It was the fire. It sure did put a lot of things in perspective. We're just glad to be alive. Other things don't matter like they used to." He lit the pipe.

"I couldn't agree more, Dad."

"Hmm."

Max watched him get the pipe going. The soft night breeze carried a hint of cherry vanilla.

After a few moments, Ben lowered the pipe. "Been thinking about marriage. Yours and Claire's. Mine and your mother's. How we got to fifty-eight years. You know, we almost didn't make it this far."

Max shifted in his chair. "No, I didn't know that."

"Guess you wouldn't. I never was much of a sit-down-and-explain kind of dad, was I? That wasn't the manly Beaumont style. Leastways I didn't whack you over the head all the time, like my dad did with me. The first time I hit BJ, your mom packed her bags."

"Really?"

"Yep. She didn't care much for my dad. Said she sure as heck didn't marry him."

Max's overriding memory of his grandpa was one of extreme fear. He remembered a distinct sense of relief when he was eight and the old man died.

Ben said, "We reached a compromise. Paddling your behinds was okay, but never when I was angry and only under certain circumstances. So we got through that milestone. Next time she packed her bags, it was over my mother meddling in our affairs and me not taking Indio's side. There were other situations, but you get the drift."

"This is all news to me."

"'Course it is. You were too young to understand. Later you were too busy with your own life, rebelling and working and meeting Claire."

"I suppose." He thought about the stories he'd just heard about his mom. "Were you always in the wrong?"

"Not always." Ben grinned around his pipe stem. "But mostly."

"Dad, I already know I'm in the wrong. I don't blame Claire for any of this."

"Don't be too quick to let her off the hook. It takes two to tango, as they say. But there's a way through all the muddle."

"At this late date? Doubt that."

"And don't be so quick to give up." His father lowered the pipe. "The secret your mother and I have learned is to make each other feel safe. So safe we don't have to hide anything. We can be mad, sad, happy, and say whatever we want, even if it's wrong, because we know nothing can kill our love for each other."

Max rubbed his forehead. It was what Claire had said.

"We didn't get here by accident. We had to make some conscious decisions along the way, set some goals. They're kind of like promises we make over and over."

Max sighed to himself. Apparently his dad wanted to be the teacher he had never been. Okay, he'd bite. "Promises like what?"

"Like we promise to believe God loves us and cares about every detail. When we're seeing life through that belief, all is right with the world. Down-deep-inside sort of stuff like emotions get put in order. It's not up to your mom to make me happy. That's between me and God. If my eyes are fixed on Him, I'm okay. Same goes for your mom."

He was talking about feelings. *"How does that make you feel, Max?"*

"The hardest promise we ever learned to make was when the bad times come, we don't give them the power to destroy us."

"BJ." His brother's disappearance in Vietnam was the worst imaginable difficulty his parents had ever faced.

Ben lowered his chin in a half nod. "Another thing we promise is to honor each other. I try to call your mom 'love' often. It reminds me that she's more important to me than the hardware clerk I'm so polite to."

Max nodded.

"Your mom and I try our darnedest to be like Jesus. Even though He is God, He decided to put some skin on so people could recognize Him better. He gave us His all just to prove His love. I try to give Indio my all. I choose—because I don't always feel it—to focus on her. I choose to show her in any way I can that I love her."

"So these promises that you live by—do they explain fifty-eight years of marriage?"

"Darn right, they do. Bottom line, Max, they make safety and security."

"That's a strong statement." He exhaled wearily. "Hindsight is a marvelous thing."

"Yes, it is. And you can have all mine, no charge." Ben pointed his pipe at Max. "Don't let her go."

"It's not my choice. She's the one ending this marriage."

"But isn't there a six-month waiting period?"

"I'm sure I could prolong it even longer if I contest it. But I don't see any sense in dragging things out. She can have whatever she wants."

"That's not my point, Max. I'm saying take the next six months and shower your unconditional love on her. Make her feel safe and secure when she's with you. Don't let her get a whiff of blame coming from you. Soon as she feels secure enough, she'll come 'round to taking responsibility for her part. Win her back, Son."

"Kind of tough, considering we don't live together, and she doesn't want to see me."

"Don't make excuses. You'll figure it out." Ben smiled. "You got all that hindsight going for you."

Eighty-five

The hauntingly beautiful Brahms Quintet still rang in Jenna's ear as she packed up her viola and set it by Tandy's front door.

The other members of the music group had left, except for her mom and Tandy. They'd just finished a session. Her mother's quirky friends were growing on her. They still balked at her idea of scheduling a gig, but she didn't mind. She'd fallen in love with the making of music as never before.

Similarly, she had fallen in love with Kevin as never before. She unabashedly flirted with him in the halls at the high school and never missed a football game or failed to cheer for the coach. His plans hadn't changed. He was still a Marine and was still leaving her. But at least they talked about it, and at least he wouldn't report for duty until January. That was months away.

Was she becoming like an ostrich with her head buried in the sand?

The thought snuck up on her at odd moments. She cast it aside by remembering the long night she spent wondering if half her family was alive or dead. The trick was to live in the now, loving them all and being loyal.

Always the fire. She could delineate her entire life by the before and after of The Fire. The "after" only covered four weeks now, but it accounted for the most significant changes in her twenty-eight years.

Humming to herself, she found her mom and Tandy in the kitchen, giggling about something. She smiled at the sound of her mom's laughter. It happened too rarely. Would she ever settle things with Max? Jenna could not understand their lack of reconciliation. At least her dad hadn't up and joined the military and abandoned the family.

Claire said, "Well, ladies, I have to go. Early morning tomorrow. It's inventory time at the store."

"No time for a cup of coffee?" Tandy said as they hugged.

"No, thanks." She picked up her handbag.

"Jen?" Behind her mom's back, Tandy raised her brows in a quick up-and-down motion, an obvious prompt for Jenna to stay.

"Yeah, sure. I have a few minutes. Kevin's not home yet."

After Claire left, Jenna sat at the table with Tandy. "What's up?"

"How are you?"

"Great. I already told you. What's up?"

"I worry about your mom."

Jenna studied the woman she sometimes called her "other mother." The redhead was a fireball of energy. As little girls, Jenna and Tandy's daughter had explored the canyon behind their houses. Hours later, after the police had found them, Claire had needed a sedative. Tandy laughed, fed them junk food, and wanted to hear all about their adventure. Tandy was not a worrier.

"Mom looks good. There's color back in her cheeks. She adores her new job. She's busy with the symphony. She's got furniture in her apartment. She seems calm. Settled. She's not taking the sleeping pills anymore."

"She is definitely progressing. I think she's discovered her 'own voice,' the one she kept saying she wanted to find."

"Then why are you worried?"

"She won't talk to me about your dad."

"Yeah. She is avoiding that whole subject. I figure she needs more time. It's only been a month since the fire. That seriously set her back."

"How is your dad?"

"Mellow." Jenna snickered. "Max Beaumont, mellow. Do you

believe it? He sometimes gets this faraway look in his eyes, but mostly he's in the moment. Totally unreal."

Tandy smiled.

"He hasn't missed a dinner with Nana and Papa in weeks. I wish Mom would . . ." She didn't finish the sentence. She wished so much: that her mom could see him now, give him half a chance, spend a little time with him, at least talk to him.

"Yeah," Tandy said. "Me too."

Eighty-six

Friday afternoon, in the attorney's office, Claire twiddled her thumbs and counted the feminine touches that adorned the pretty room. Three vases of silk flowers on the desk and bookcases. A crystal bowl of potpourri. Another filled with wrapped peppermints. Embroidered throw pillows on the love seat. Flocked rose-patterned upholstery on two chairs. Framed floral prints. Family photos on the credenza.

She pressed a hand to her stomach, the serene ambience totally lost on her. Could a prisoner on death row feel any more intimidated or remorseful?

Why were there papers to sign already? She'd only filed for divorce five days ago.

"Claire." The smiling lawyer entered the room, her hand extended. "I'm so sorry to keep you waiting."

Claire shook her hand and tried to smile.

Gloria Tinley shut the door, swept around the large oak desk, and settled into her chair. She was a large, confident, steel-gray-haired woman with a reputation for taking husbands to the cleaners.

Claire didn't want to take Max to the cleaners. She didn't even want anywhere near half of their property. Tandy had found the lawyer when she divorced Trevor. Tandy had been immersed in revenge, and Gloria did not disappoint. Claire just wanted out, but for convenience' sake she chose the path already laid to this woman's door.

Gloria chatted about traffic and weather as she rearranged file folders on the desk.

Claire said, "I didn't think Max would contest this."

"As I said, you never know. True colors aren't always what we perceive them to be until we shove someone into a corner." She pulled a folder toward herself and opened it. "Be that as it may, your husband is not doing any contesting. Not yet anyway." She glanced down at a set of papers and then looked back at Claire. Rhinestones sparkled from the silver frames of her glasses.

"Claire, Max is selling Beaumont Staffing Agency."

Selling . . . The words made no sense. "What?"

"He wants to sell the agency. Technically, because the two of you own it, you're both selling the business. You both need to sign the papers."

She stared at her. Thirty-three years ago she had signed a paper that made her co-owner with Max. She hadn't given it a thought since.

"Claire, I don't know why he's doing this, but obviously you'll get half of the proceeds, sooner rather than later. Actually, this will probably all happen long before the divorce."

"He's selling it now? As in right now?"

"Yes, as soon as possible. To . . . let's see." She read from the paper. "Philip Singleton. For an extremely large amount of cash up front as well as scheduled payouts over a number of years, adding up to, um, several millions of dollars. Max will be retained as a consultant for twelve months."

Claire put a hand to her mouth. As the enormity of the news sank in, she felt a cry building in her chest.

Gloria said, "I recommend you give this some thought. Take as long as you need, a week or two. I'd like to study the terms. At first blush I'd say this is a more than fair selling price, but that's only a guess. Do you have any questions?"

She shook her head.

"You look very surprised."

She nodded.

"I believe it's a good thing. You'll get money right up front."

Claire lowered her hand and grabbed a tissue from a box set strategically in front of her on the desk. She pressed it to her eyes.

"Are you all right?" Gloria's steady voice sounded far away.

Oh, dear God. Not now. Not now!

"Claire, would you like us to call someone?"

Again she shook her head. "I know—" Her voice was a low whisper. She took a deep breath and looked at Gloria. "I know why he's doing this."

"Why?"

"Because I asked him to."

In another lifetime she had asked him to.

Claire stumbled from the attorney's office. After several moments of staring blankly at the big parking lot, she walked through it, up one row and down another. She had no clue where her car was.

At last she found it. The brand-new car that she didn't need, want, or deserve.

She popped the locks remotely and got inside. Her hand shook so badly, she couldn't insert the key into the ignition. She sat. Her whole body shook.

She dumped her purse upside down. Its contents scattered over the passenger seat. There was her cell phone. Should she call him?

No. She was coherent enough to realize she had nothing to say to him.

Was she capable of driving? Should she call someone for help? Tandy or Jenna? *Meet me. I can't drive. I can't think straight. I don't know what to do!* She would frighten them. She was frightening herself.

What about Eddie, the stranger who'd been feeding her soul with simple acts of kindness? Coffee and conversation. There was none of the pressure she sensed from Tandy or her kids. Occasionally he shared words of wisdom gleaned from the Bible, which he was reading for the first time in his life. There were no strings attached, like the ones she tied to herself whenever Indio spoke of God's truth—strings that convinced Claire she wasn't good enough for Indio's son.

Help! I'm losing my mind. She would sound like a lunatic to Eddie.

No, she needed to be alone to think through what Max had just done. She had to come to terms with the fact that he'd presented to her exactly what she had wanted.

Three months ago. A lifetime ago.

Eighty-seven

Max drove several car lengths behind Claire. They headed west.

Maybe he should have intervened. He'd watched her in the parking lot outside the lawyer's office, obviously distraught, unable to easily locate the car. Then she had sat for a long time. He'd been near enough to see the tears glisten on her cheeks.

But he waited. He didn't want to intrude. She would feel pressured to respond.

The truth was, he didn't feel ready to hear her response. What if this, his ultimate sacrifice, wasn't enough?

And so he followed her in his car, like some undercover cop hoping to be led to the prize. Maybe she would call him, and he could say, "I'm right here close by." That was how Kevin won back Jenna. He'd been right there when she needed him.

Maybe Claire would go to their house, and he'd arrive immediately, and they could talk all night long. She'd like that, wouldn't she, his availability? It was one of those things he'd never given her.

She turned toward La Jolla.

Friday afternoon traffic thickened the closer they got to the coast. Stop and go. Stop and go. Merging. Red lights. Green lights. He lost sight of her car.

Max assumed three things: Claire would not be shopping in the downtown district. Nor would she be eating there. She would go down to the cove to walk or to sit at an overlook. She liked it there.

He only hoped she would not be meeting someone.

Like he had.

The memory of his picnicking with Neva at this place horrified him.

Lord, I'm sorry. Help me find her. Please.

He'd been praying frequently in recent weeks. Living with his mother was to blame. Her brush with death had loosened her tongue more than ever about God.

Max drove along the cove area. Even on a late October afternoon, there were no available parking places. Year-round the world gathered to picnic, stroll, jog, swim, watch a sunset, throw a Frisbee.

He didn't spot Claire's car. At last he turned uphill and finally found a slot to park in a couple of blocks away. He got out and walked.

At the sidewalk above the ocean, he paused. Would she go left or right?

With a prayer on his lips, he veered left.

Weary beyond belief, Max had almost reached the farthest end of the long, winding sidewalk above the ocean. He would have to backtrack.

And then he saw her.

Nearly out of sight, she sat alone on an outcropping of rock. A narrow path led to it, several steep feet down from the grassy area. The path continued past her, to the bottom, where waves crashed against the rocks.

The sun was already hidden behind low clouds on the horizon. Seated on a blanket, Claire wore a long skirt, a light blue denim jacket that didn't appear to offer much warmth, and a long knit scarf around her neck. She hugged her knees. Her forlorn expression made her look like the loneliest person in the world.

It was time.

"Claire."

She continued staring toward the ocean.

He called out louder, "Claire."

Now she looked up over her shoulder and saw him. Her eyes widened. Her mouth formed an O.

He held out his hands, palms up, in silent offering.

Above the noise of the surf, he heard her moan. She lowered her face, hiding it against her upraised knees.

Max scuttled down the path, nearly sliding in slick-soled loafers. He reached her, sat down with his back to the water so he could face her. His arms ached to hold her, but he hesitated, again not wanting to intrude where he was not welcome.

She looked up at him, her eyes nearly swollen shut, tears seeping from them. "You can't do this."

He knew what she'd learned at the lawyer's office. With a rush of gratitude, he realized she understood. Selling the business was his ultimate sacrifice.

"Why can't I do this, Claire?"

"Because I can't take it from you."

"You're not taking it. I'm giving it."

"Oh, Max!" She broke down completely and could speak no more.

He wrapped his arms around her, his own tears falling freely on her hair.

Eighty-eight

When her cries subsided, Claire raised her head so she could see Max.

He lowered his arms, and she straightened. His cheeks were damp, but he smiled gently.

"It's too much," she blubbered.

He pulled a handkerchief from his pocket and dabbed it against her face. "Shh."

"I can't make you give up your life."

"Claire, sweetheart, you're not making me do anything. I'm done. I don't want the business anymore. It's kept me from you long enough."

Her throat squeezed nearly shut again. "I'm so sorry."

"No, I'm sorry. I'm sorry I never understood before."

"I can't take this. I don't deserve this. I've hurt you so much."

"We've both hurt each other."

"I held back, just like you said. I kept my heart closed off."

"You had to protect yourself. You had no reason to trust me."

"But I blamed you for my friendship with Petros. I thought I had a right to turn to him because I couldn't turn to you. I am so sorry."

"It's over."

Through blurry vision, she looked into his brown-black eyes, those dark pools she'd fallen in love with so many years ago. The dimple in his chin had deepened. She used to kiss it. There was more white than she remembered in his black hair, especially on the sides.

Was he truly changed? Could she trust him with her whole heart? How could she know?

There was only one way to find out.

"Max, I'm doing it again." She bit her lip.

He blinked. "Doing what?"

"Connecting with someone because he pays attention to me."

Max pressed his lips together.

"He's one of the firemen from that night."

"Eddie?"

She nodded. "We talk, like a support group. He has a sort of steady lady friend, but still. Our friendship is turning into this deep emotional attachment just like before."

"Like before. You didn't get what you needed from me. It's my fault."

"No, it's not, Max! It's mine. Let me take ownership of my decisions. I can't blame you anymore. I can't blame my parents anymore."

He took a deep breath. "Do you love him?"

"I don't love anyone!" The awfulness of what she'd confessed raked through her and ripped open deep hurts. She cried out, "I'm so horrible. So ugly."

Max cupped her face in his hands. "Shh, sweetheart."

Sweetheart again. The word touched her deep inside, a warm balm flowing over wounds. It soothed and softened.

"You are so beautiful, inside and out. You'll always be beautiful and precious to me. I love you, and I forgive you. No matter what you've done or not done, I forgive you."

"How can you?"

"How can I not? Jesus forgives me."

She felt her eyes widen.

"Yeah, I really said that." He smiled. "It's finally making sense, how stupid I've been, all the wrong choices I've made, how God loves me anyway, even though I don't deserve it. Will you forgive me, though, for everything? I've shut you out of my life. I don't want you out of my life any longer. I want you in it. Can you ever forgive me?"

Her forehead against his, she whispered, "I forgive you."

"Thank you." The words gushed as if a dam burst deep in his soul, releasing a flood of gratitude and hope.

They sat for a long moment in silence.

"Claire, I want to take his place."

The tears welled again.

"Can I do that? Will you let me take Eddie's place? Will you let me earn back your love?"

"Ohhhhhh." It was a drawn-out sigh. "Oh yes."

They walked through the twilight to her car. Max touched Claire's arm whenever they stepped up and down curbs.

She couldn't recall him ever doing that.

But she didn't want to go there, into the past. She wanted to linger in the newness of her husband's love and forgiveness. Undeserved. That was Jesus's way. She'd forgotten.

"Claire, what's next? Where do we start over? How do we start over?"

"I was just thinking how safe I feel. It's like I'm wrapped in a safe, cozy, snuggly cocoon. I don't have to come out yet, do I?"

He chuckled. "We are at your car. I think we have to decide at least what we're doing tonight."

She leaned against the car and looked at him.

"What?"

She smiled. "I'm waiting for you to tell me what we're doing tonight."

He groaned. "I'm that bad."

"Yes, you are. Or were, anyway."

"Let's go for 'was.' I was that bad. I always dictated what we should do."

"Not always, but often. And I often sat back and let you."

"Here's a new thought, then. I honestly don't have a clue what to do tonight."

"Thank you."

"You're welcome. It's a start, anyway, huh?"

"Yes, and a good one. Maybe the next step is to figure out how we feel. You go first. How do you feel?"

He stuck his hands in the pockets of his sport coat and rocked on his heels, his mouth a straight line, his eyes focused beyond her shoulder.

She waited again, intuiting that the key to any future together lay in the breaking of old habits. Would he belligerently shut her down? She hoped not.

He stopped moving and gazed at her. "Okay, here goes. I feel deeply happy. I feel infused with gratitude for what's happening between us. And I feel intimidated, so much so, I could almost give up right off the bat."

She stared, her eyes nearly bugging out now.

He grinned.

"Hmm," she said.

His grin widened until his eyes were slits.

"You just talked about your feelings. God must be real."

"Yeah," he said.

She smiled. "Why are you intimidated?"

"Good grief. I'm competing with an honest-to-goodness knight in shining armor. I mean, this firefighter saved your life. That's a tough act to follow."

"Lexi saved us, Max. We didn't need those guys."

"Really?"

"Really. And besides, you're full of knight material. Remember I thought of you in that way because you rescued me from my family?"

"I'd forgotten."

"And what do you think this act of selling the agency takes? Knightly stuff, for sure. Not to mention you found me this afternoon. How did you find me, by the way?"

"I followed you. My lawyer learned that you'd be at your lawyer's this afternoon. I waited in the parking lot, hoping you'd call me on the cell and I could just be there, lickety-split. That'd be a first, wouldn't it?"

Where had this man called her husband come from?

"Your turn, Claire. How do you feel?"

"Shell-shocked. I want to stay in that cocoon for a while."

"Is there room in it for two?"

A knot tightened in her stomach. "No."

"That's okay."

She winced.

"It's okay. I have to earn your trust. Right?"

She nodded. "Tonight I want to go sleep in my little apartment. Tomorrow . . . well, we'll have to see what tomorrow brings."

He stared at her, his face unreadable. "I can't whisk you off to the castle?"

She shook her head.

"All right. If this is what a knight would do . . ."

"Max." She pushed herself away from the car and slid her arms around his waist. "You're not competing with anyone."

He held her close.

Her cheek against his chest, she whispered, "And please don't give up on me."

"Never, Claire. Never."

Eighty-nine

The day after Max flabbergasted her with his plan to sell the business, the world spun in a different direction for Claire. She was on sensory overload. The sun was nearly too bright, colors nearly too vivid, people nearly too real.

He invited her to dinner. She invited him to her symphony concert. He went, and they ate a late dinner afterward. He wanted to spend the night with her. She said no. He pressed, but only momentarily.

She needed time. Not to decide whether or not they could love each other again, but to wait for the love to sprout again and for the trust to send down roots and take hold.

Two days after Max flabbergasted her with his plan to sell the business, she called Eddie. They met at the beach.

They walked. As usual with their informal support-group style, they explored residue that still clung to their hearts, hiding like the ash in out-of-the-way places and surprising them when they discovered it. Odd dreams here and there. Questions about eternity. Fears over silly things.

After a bit he said, "Okay, Claire. You're holding back. What do you want to tell me?" He read her like that.

"Residue. Max and I reconnected Friday night."

He looked down at her. "Whew. That's wonderful."

"I think so. I'm not sure yet, but I think so."

They walked in silence for a while.

"Eddie, I can't keep meeting with you. I don't know what it's like for you, but for me . . ." Her voice cracked. "I'm getting . . ." Another surprise. She hadn't expected to cry.

"I know."

She glanced at him.

"It's mutual, Claire. Let's sit."

They turned up from the ocean's edge and sat in the sand. It was a sunny, late October day, but not hot enough to entice beachgoers. The place was nearly empty.

He smiled. "I should know better. I mean, the circumstances we met under were pretty wild. Support groups are great, but these aftershocks will continue to lessen. Once they're gone, then what would we have between us?"

"An emotional connection unlike we have with anyone else."

"You're not supposed to say that."

She smiled. "The fly in the ointment is I'm married. And now I think I might want to stay married."

"I don't want to interfere with that."

They turned to look at the ocean.

She said, "So how is Sheila?"

"Well. We may be going our separate ways."

"I'm sorry."

"No, it's okay."

"Did I—"

"It wasn't you. It wasn't us. It's just time." He reached into the pocket of his jeans and pulled out a paper. "I wanted to read something to you. It's from the book of Joel."

Eddie had continued studying the Bible.

"Just some bits and pieces I liked. 'For fire has devoured the open pastures and the flames have burnt up all the trees . . . Surely a day of darkness and gloom is upon us . . . a blackness spread over the mountains.' There's more stuff about fire and other terrible things. But here, listen to what comes next: 'The Lord says, turn back to me with your whole heart.' And 'Turn back to the Lord your God; for he is gracious and compassionate.'" He looked at her. "I don't understand it at all. But it makes me feel like God is available."

"He loves us."

Eddie nodded. "So I guess I'll go find a Bible study group next. Kind of like a support group, I bet." He smiled and held out his hand to shake hers.

She put her hand in his. "Thank you for everything."

"Thank you, Claire Beaumont." He stood. "Be sure to invite me to Zak and Lexi's wedding?"

She laughed. "If that happens, of course you'll be invited. And knowing Indio, she'll have all three of you up to the hacienda for dinner as soon as the kitchen is open."

His eyes held hers until she had to glance away. "Well, Claire, I do wish you all the best. Bye." With a wave, he took off down the beach, his strides long and confident.

Claire felt a new lightness in her heart. He had been a good friend in a time of need. But she didn't want to need any man right now. She wanted only to turn back to God and need Him. After all, only He had the power to truly take care of her. She'd lost sight of the truth, of the gift Jesus gave by dying for her sin. It meant everything was right between her and the Creator of the universe.

Imagine that. The Creator.

No matter the dreadful things she had done or thought, no matter the good things she had failed to do or think—she was right with God. No matter any less-than-perfect choices she would make in the future—forgiveness was just an "I'm sorry" away. There, in God's love, lay her safety and security.

Imagine that.

"As Indio would say, Well, God is good. Hallelujah."

Ninety

Shall we sell it, love?" Ben swung an arm around Indio's shoulders.

She leaned into him, her eyes fixed on the deplorable sight of the hacienda before them. They stood in the courtyard, in the cup of the U. Blackened walls rose on three sides. In its center, the tiered concrete fountain lay on the cobblestones, split into many pieces. Where plants and flowers once flourished, ash piles shifted in the breeze.

She said, "This is like standing inside a charcoal grill."

"You didn't answer my question."

"You were serious?"

"It's been seven weeks. We need to decide something."

"Who would buy it in this shape, and especially now, without a second entrance?"

"The horses made it. Kennedy and I talked about blasting a trail through the boulders in the south section between our properties. It wouldn't be a road, but it'd be enough of an option. Better than the one we had."

Could have, should have. That night was over. "Ben, I can't imagine selling this place. It's our life. It's the Beaumont heritage."

"Max is giving up the same by selling his business. It's time for a new start for all of us."

Indio sighed. She hated the thought of losing the hacienda. "No more Hideaway retreats? We had guests booked for almost every weekend through Easter. Those poor people, missing out."

"Truth is, the thought of keeping up this place and entertaining guests makes me want to go take a nap. I feel as burned out as this courtyard looks. You know, I am almost seventy-nine."

"You saying you're ready for the nursing home?"

"No."

"Well, where would we live?"

"I don't know."

"With Max? He says we can stay as long as we like."

"Good Lord, no. He really is a chatterbox, isn't he? Can hardly get a word in edgewise these days."

She chuckled. "I guess he's making up for lost time with us."

"I sure do miss the quiet up here and my horses. Maybe we could park an RV in the yard and live in that. Leave the house as is. Just build a new barn."

She poked him in the ribs. "You're a rambling, growly bear today, Benjamin Beaumont, and that makes *me* want to go take a nap."

"I'll call a Realtor tonight. See what we can get for this place. What's that woman's name in Santa Reina, the one from church? Isn't she a Realtor?"

"Oh, go soak your head." Indio moved out from under his arm and marched through the yard. "I'm getting to work."

Out in front of the hacienda, Indio reached Ben's new truck. She was grateful the burned vehicles had been towed away from the lot.

She lowered the back hatch and reached into its bed for a broom. Although they'd hired a professional group to clean up the fire's aftermath, she wanted to go through the kitchen some more. She kept finding salvageable things, all the while trying not to think of what had been lost that night—especially the photos and keepsakes in Claire's car. *Ben saves his pipe, and baby mementos get incinerated.* She questioned God's sense of fairness as never before.

"Mom, need some help?" Max spoke from behind her.

She turned to see him and Claire approach from the side yard. "Thanks."

He started pulling brooms, shovels, and other cleaning items from the truck. "Want all of it out?"

"Yes, please."

Indio eyed her daughter-in-law. She prided herself in not butting into the affairs of Max and Claire. She'd kept a muzzle on her mouth the past three weeks, reminding herself that the couple had to find their own way back to each other, outlandish as their behavior seemed to her.

Claire still lived in her apartment, like some misguided feminist who felt the need to prove her independence. She and Max met often for lunch or dinner. A more peculiar setup Indio could not imagine, but it was having an effect. The defensiveness Claire had worn like a neon sign was fading. She'd grown softer. There had been no talk, though, of her returning home.

Overcome by a sudden sense of despair over her house and her husband, Indio could not let go of her last hope: that Max and Claire would reconcile. The muzzle broke off, and the words tumbled out.

"Claire, are you all right?"

Her daughter-in-law blinked a few times. "No, not really. We're going up to the mine. Max wants to pile the rocks over the entrance."

Indio thought of Claire's screams that night, her intense terror, her inability to easily crawl back out. "You don't need to go with him."

"And I can't pretend it didn't happen." Claire smiled gently. "You're supposed to tell me to go face my fears."

Indio nodded.

"Mom." Max handed her a broom. "Are *you* all right?"

"No, I guess I'm not either."

Claire said, "This is really hard on all of us, but the worst part is you've lost your home."

She nodded again.

"We'll be back to help in a bit," Max said. "Where's Dad?"

"In the courtyard. He's talking about selling the place."

"No way!"

"Oh no." Claire's face showed her disappointment.

"He'll get over it." Indio shooed her hands at them. "Now run along. Don't worry about us here. Take all the time you need."

Max gave her a quick hug, and they climbed into the truck.

She watched them drive off, a prayer she said often these days on her lips. "Lord, bring them back together."

Carrying her broom across the yard, she was struck with the need for more prayer.

"Okay, Lord. I'm listening. Yes, I admit it. I have a hankering to leave my husband until he sees the light. I do not like this idea of selling one bit. Maybe he could woo me like Max is wooing Claire, until I see the light." She laughed aloud. "Lord, bless us all. We're never going to make it without You!"

Ninety-one

Max held his hand out to Claire as they walked through what had once been a grove of hardwoods. Now it was a black and gray scene of broken, charred tree trunks and bare limbs.

She slid her hand into his.

He thought he might have to sit until the mushiness receded from his legs.

Claire didn't always take his hand. Three weeks ago, when they'd first started this odd dating relationship, she avoided physical contact with him. They'd advanced to hand-holding and chaste goodnight kisses. In the truck, she had moved across the bench seat until their thighs touched.

Progress.

He had begun writing her notes. Love notes. Chatty notes. Thinking-of-you notes. Things he had never thought to tell her before. He mailed them. He mailed her cards, too, sappy ones and funny ones.

Like a flower bud in the warm sunshine, she began to unfold. Almost daily he discovered something new about her. He hadn't paid attention for a long time, but if anyone had asked a month ago what she was like, he would have said she was confident enough, though not the in-your-face type. She could even be a bit of a pushover.

Forget that.

One night she asked, "What if there hadn't been a fire?"

He was ready for that. "Then God would have had to use a different two-by-four to get my attention."

Another time she said, "So what's the deal with Neva?"

He wasn't ready for that one. "She resigned."

"Why?"

He cringed.

"Max, I told you all about Eddie. I even told you I met with him on Sunday."

"But I . . ." He swallowed. "I kissed her."

Claire winced.

"And I wanted to spend the night with her to hurt you, but I didn't. I'm sorry."

"So why did she resign?"

"Because, she said, she loved me and couldn't continue to work with me, knowing I would always love you."

Claire nearly snarled. "Like she didn't suspect that for the past thirty-plus years?"

He shrugged.

She narrowed her eyes in a "told you so" glare.

Yes, he agreed silently. Claire had always sensed that Neva loved him. How did women know this junk?

"So when is she leaving the office?"

"After Christmas. First of the year."

"Anything else?"

He tilted his head back and forth. "Kisses. A picnic. A dinner. I'm sorry."

Claire hadn't kissed him good night after that conversation.

But they were making progress.

Max, look." Claire stopped near a blackened tree and pointed to the ground.

"Where?"

She crouched, pulling him down beside herself. "There."

Her nearness distracted him. He felt like an adolescent. He wasn't all that comfortable with feeling like an adolescent.

"Look. It's green!"

He saw it then, the slender sprout of a plant, poking through thick debris. "Wow."

"Yeah, wow." She smiled at him. The new shine in her green-brown eyes caught his attention. Flecks of topaz sparkled. They hadn't always been there, he was sure of it.

She said, "Kind of like us, huh?"

He raised his brows.

"New life springing through old, dead stuff."

He grinned. "Yeah. Yeah. I like that."

She kissed his cheek.

She didn't often kiss him.

He pulled her to her feet before he suggested they remove their clothes. They hiked in silence for a while.

"Max, what do you think about your dad selling the hacienda?"

"He mentioned the idea to me the other day. I think it's just his way of coping. There's so much to be done, it overwhelms him. I sure would hate to see him give it up."

"It's an extraordinary place."

"Yes, it is."

"Are you still okay with giving up the agency?"

He smiled at her. "Oh, sweetheart."

Her face went all soft.

And the mush hit him again.

He'd borrowed from his dad's idea of calling his mom "love." Max had given Claire her own special endearment, not the old "hon" he used indiscriminately with females. The new moniker worked just as his dad said it would: Claire adored it when he called her "sweetheart." He sensed that she received it as his way of telling her she was more important to him than anyone.

She said, "Did you have something to add?"

"Hmm? Oh yeah. Yes, I am still okay with giving up the agency."

She nodded.

He hadn't held back. He'd confessed his doubts to her, described the agony of letting his baby go. But his choice was clear: the business or her? It was a no-brainer.

They'd signed the papers to sell to Phil. Next week they would be paid a lot of money. Arrangements had been made to deposit half in his account and half in Claire's new savings account. Her idea.

Every once in a while, a fearful thought stabbed him. Would she take the money and tell him to take a hike?

Ridiculous. But unsettling nonetheless.

Probably right where she wanted him.

They reached a steep incline covered with boulders of all shapes and sizes. Claire let go of his hand and started to climb.

He grasped her elbow to stop her. "Claire, are you sure about this?"

She looked back at him. "Is my knight in shining armor with me?"

He smiled. Talk about nicknames. He liked that one. "Right here."

"Then I'm sure. Let's go."

Ninety-two

Claire watched Max pile stones in front of the gold-mine entrance. He wore blue jeans and a brown T-shirt. The muscles in his biceps and forearms bulged with each hefting of a large rock. The sun beat down on the back of his head and accented the salt in his pepper hair. It would turn all white someday, like Ben's. Perspiration glistened on his neck.

When was the last time she'd noticed him as a flesh-and-blood man?

She shut her eyes. The insides of the lids were bright.

For so long she had considered him the source of all that was wrong in her life. She blamed him for her inability to stand on her own two feet. She blamed religious teachers for garbling the precept of submission and making her think she had to lose her identity in Max's. She blamed her parents for a crummy childhood that did not equip her to stand on her own two feet in the first place.

Lord, I'm sorry for it all.

It was time, as she had told Max weeks ago, to take ownership. Now she knew how.

She opened her eyes. "Max, wait."

"Hmm?" He turned to her.

"Don't close it up. I want to go inside."

Concern wrinkled his brow, and his shoulders heaved, but he didn't say anything.

"I have to finish it."

"I'll come with you."

She shook her head. "Just wait for me."

Claire crawled and, where the tunnel fit tight as a sock around her body, inched along on her stomach.

They hadn't brought flashlights. With each forward move, the sunlight diminished.

She was going into total darkness.

And the memory came again.

She didn't fight it this time.

"Jesus, Indio said You were there. She said You are outside of time. Help me believe that. Help me stop believing the lie—that lie rooted in the past that says people who love me will always shove me into a dark cellar and leave me there."

A wave of nausea hit her. She lay flat, her face against her arm. *Jesus, please help me.*

After a few moments, the queasiness passed.

And she knew she could keep going.

Indio's words pressed in upon her. *Jesus is there.* Claire didn't see anything now except that old root cellar and the angry faces of her parents. But from the depths of her being, a new understanding took hold.

In the mystery where time did not exist, Jesus was. He had been with her when she was a little girl. He had wept for her. He had died on the cross for her and for her parents and for the awful hurts they'd done and for the awful hurts that must have been done to them.

"Lord, help me forgive my mom and dad. Help me forgive Max."

In the pitch black, Claire felt the tunnel sides give way. She must have reached the first small opening. Slowly she shifted to a sitting position.

The night of the fire, tumbling from the confines of the tunnel, she had screamed. She had known gut-wrenching terror. She had seethed with hatred for Max. She had vomited, her body rejecting it all, but the ugliness and fears were not released. They remained inside of her, where they had resided since that day long ago when she was three years old.

Until now.

A quiet flowed over her like a soft desert wind. Its warmth seeped through into her very bones.

It was over.

She smiled. "Thank You."

"Max!" Claire called as she wiggled toward the sunlight. "Max!"

His face appeared at the end of the tunnel. "Are you okay, sweetheart?"

She laughed. "I am so okay."

At last she emerged from the tunnel. He helped her stand up and scooped her into an embrace. "I love you, Claire."

She kissed him soundly on the mouth. "And I love you, Max. Hey." She leaned back to look him in the eyes, seeing a flame light there that surely mirrored her own. "I was wondering. Do you want to spend the night at my place?"

His burst of laughter rolled through the hills.

Grinning, she leaned into him, her face against his chest. As the rumble of his laugh faded, his heartbeat resounded in her ear. She listened closely, as if it were a piece of unfamiliar music. She let its strong, steady cadence flow through her until her own heart pulsed with it.

And then . . . she felt safe. So . . . incredibly . . . safe.

In the cave, alone with God, she had reached at long last her true safe harbor. She understood that. Now, though, enfolded in Max's arms, it seemed God poured yet another gift into her soul: a husband whose love would be her home, her earthly safe harbor.

"Max." She looked up at him.

His half-masted eyes said they'd talked enough for one day.

When he kissed her, it felt like the very first time.

She began to imagine shoving her stuffed lion into the trash bin. She hoped it would fit, because it sure wasn't going to fit in her bed anymore.

Ninety-three

The next morning, Claire smiled at Max across the small dinette table that filled up half of her small living room. "That was nice."

His dark eyes twinkled. His lips curved into a sly grin. "Nice doesn't begin to describe it."

"I was talking about breakfast."

"Breakfast was great too."

She sighed. "Is this our future? Here it is a Friday. We spent yesterday with your parents. Today we ate breakfast together. We even cooked together. And you're not jumping up to go to the office. I could get used to this."

"Me too. Except the part about telling my parents I won't be home until morning."

She laughed. "Seriously, could you get used to this?"

He studied her face. "Hmm. Something is on your mind."

She grinned. "You're getting awfully good at reading me."

"I certainly hope so." He reached across the table and squeezed her hand. "What's up?"

A tingle sent shivers up and down her spine. The delicious sensation had been occurring frequently the past few weeks. She suspected it had to do with getting used to the idea that Max wanted to be with her.

"Sweetheart?"

The quiver melted into an ooey-gooey contentment. She knew

she could say anything to him. "Okay, here's what I'm wondering. Do you think consulting for Phil will be enough for you to do?"

"I'm sure it will."

"Come on. Give it a little thought."

"I admit it won't be easy. And I've told you that for a while I will be going into the office regularly."

"Mm-hmm." She tried not to wrinkle her nose. It seemed a setup for him to easily slide back into the old routine, but she refused to dwell on that thought. "Regularly. Not as in the old regular sixteen hours a day?"

"No. Some days I take the reins back from him and don't even realize I'm doing it. He's strong enough to talk straight, though. He tells me to back off. I'll get reprogrammed, and I will be fine."

"You might need a hobby. Or . . . something."

His brows rose.

"Remember when we first met? We both wanted to save the world. I jumped on your bandwagon because you had the greatest idea: a staffing firm. You could find jobs for people. What better way to save at least a corner of the world?"

He nodded.

"It was a good work you did, Max."

"Thanks."

"Maybe there's another corner of the world for us to work on." She paused. "This just came to me last night. You know what the world doesn't have enough of? Safe harbors. There used to be this perfect place up in the hills. It needs some work. A lot of work, actually. But the walls are there, solid as ever. The roof. And the reputation. The owners are aging. They need some help." She shrugged.

"Hmm."

"Hmm."

"Hmm." His tone went up.

"Mm-hmm."

Max leaned his head to one side. "It's something to consider."

"And pray about."

"Definitely. I don't want to leave God out of the equation any longer. I think it's time we started praying together too."

Claire smiled. "I think it's time I moved home."

She watched the tears well in his eyes and knew without a doubt it was time.

"Want to help me pack?"

He nodded, and his tears spilled over.

She went around the table, slid onto his lap, and pulled him close. "I'm your safe harbor, too, hon."

He nodded again and blubbered like a child in her arms.

Ninety-four

"It's a no-brainer." Max nuzzled the back of Claire's neck.

"What is?" She twisted around, planted a kiss on his cheek, and then turned again to the kitchen counter. "Stuffing this turkey?"

He watched her deft finger truss up the huge bird's legs. Claire's hands fascinated him. In years past, he'd never really noticed them. But for three weeks now, since she had moved home, they had intrigued him, most especially when she played her violin. He would sit with her, dazed, admiring their strength and dexterity.

There had been so much he never really noticed. Like stuffing turkeys.

He said, "No, I'm not talking about the turkey. I will never say again that anything related to homemaking is a no-brainer. Helping you prepare this morning—or is it night? It's still pitch-black out there." He glanced through the windows. "I had no idea the amount of work that goes into making Thanksgiving dinner."

"I appreciate the appreciation." She winked at him.

"It's a little overdue."

"I'm okay with 'Better late than never.'"

She kept forgiving him like that, quick as the blink of her eye. He smiled. "The no-brainer is figuring out what I'm grateful for this year."

"That is an easy one."

"I mean besides all the obvious things, like we're alive and we're together, blah, blah, blah." He nibbled on her earlobe and whispered,

"I'm grateful my folks are still asleep, and soon as we shove this bird in the oven, we have nothing else to do until the kids show up, hours and hours from now."

"Oh my. You do live on another planet."

"What?"

She moved to the sink and washed her hands. "There are potatoes to peel, crystal to wash, and a table to set. That's just for starters. All of which I would have done yesterday, but we were too busy."

"Like every day. What exactly did we do?"

"Exactly doesn't matter." She opened the oven door. "We're together."

He picked up the heavy roasting pan and slid it into the oven. "Like never before."

Claire shut the door and slid her arms around his waist. "Like never before."

He laid his hands on her shoulders. The day held more in store for them than a turkey dinner.

He took a deep breath. "Okay, here we go. Are you absolutely sure about this?"

"I am absolutely sure about this. Are you?"

"Yes, absolutely."

She smiled.

"Claire, I love you so much." He kissed her. And he kissed her. And he kissed her. Until time and space faded from his consciousness.

She sighed and looked up at him, her face rosy, her eyes unfocused. "That was nice, dear." Her voice was thick. "But you still have to peel potatoes."

Max stood in the living room, a crackling fire in the fireplace behind him, a white, shirt-sized gift box in his hands. Claire had tied a yellow ribbon around it and formed a simple bow on top. He never would have thought of doing that, but now, alone with his parents, he was grateful for her simple, feminine touch to soften the moment.

"Max," his dad said from the love seat. "Today is Thanksgiving, not Christmas."

"And besides," his mother added, "you've given us way too much in recent weeks, and I have to go help Claire in the kitchen."

"We need to do this now. It's not exactly a gift." He cleared his throat. Maybe he should have let Claire help him through this.

"Max?" His mother leaned forward.

"Okay. First of all, I apologize for not remembering sooner. Between the fire and the . . . uh . . ." *Divorce papers.* "Uh . . . and everything, I just did not remember. And you know, emotional kind of stuff just didn't register with me . . ." His voiced trailed off again. "Before."

Ben rolled his hand, telling him to get on with it.

"The thing is, I had a safe-deposit box in the bank. It's full of old things I haven't thought of in years. Things like my marriage license. Which I thought of recently. Which I wanted to see recently. So I went and, well, this was in the box too. It isn't much, but it's yours." He handed the box to his mother. "Happy Thanksgiving, Mom and Dad."

Indio laid a finger on the ribbon, as if in awe, as if she sensed what lay inside. Then, very slowly, she untied the bow and lifted the lid. "Ohh."

It was a long, low moan.

She and Ben gazed into the box and gently touched its contents.

Long ago, after his brother was declared MIA, Max had spent an angry afternoon at the hacienda, rummaging through BJ's room and his own childhood room. He'd grabbed things, shoved them into a shoe box, and stashed that in a trunk with his old books and other junk. Eventually the junk got tossed, the books given to a library, and BJ's things put in the bank.

"Mom, I'm sorry there's no baby stuff."

She wiped at her cheeks and shook her head softly.

There were photos, mostly of BJ from teen years with friends, one of him wearing the high school homecoming king crown and a grin as big as all outdoors. There were photos of him with his fiancée, Beth, a few of him and Max as little guys in the courtyard and on the backs of horses. There were newspaper clippings of BJ's school and athletic accomplishments. There were stones, comic books, Boy Scout patches, scraps of this and that, school reports, love notes from Beth, her class ring.

And there was a letter from BJ.

His dad found it. He turned damp, questioning eyes to Max, a faded blue envelope in his hand.

"It came after he was gone." *A letter from the dead,* Max had thought at the time. That was the day rage almost consumed him. He'd gone to the hacienda, torn apart their rooms, grasping for pieces of a brother he already could not remember having.

"He sent it to you?" Ben read the address—Max's apartment at the time.

"Yeah. Nothing profound. No premonition. Just totally BJ. Confident, happy, missing you two, pining away for Beth. His usual crap about me getting my act together."

Max's throat felt thick. No more words came. His mom and dad held their arms out to him. He knelt before them, their hands on his shoulders, the box between them all.

Never in a million years could he conjure up such a beautiful scene as the one before him. Of course, it was one of those perfect moments that would dissipate like a downy dandelion in a puff of wind. It would probably fly away before the night was over.

But Max wasn't going to miss it while it lasted.

He leaned back in his chair and quietly observed his noisy family gathered around the dining room table. Remains of the best Thanksgiving dinner he had ever eaten cluttered the tabletop and buffet, but no one moved to begin the cleanup.

At the far end, opposite him, sat Claire, the love of his life. He prayed that above all he would love her well, that she would never feel unsafe with him again.

Jenna glowed like a newlywed, her hand never far from Kevin's arm or shoulder. He, in turn, was especially attentive to her. Now and then the undercurrent surfaced, though. Her smile wobbled. His jaw tightened. Max knew in those moments they counted the days to his departure.

Erik's charm had returned stronger than ever. His gorgeous blonde coanchor, Felicia, sat beside him. Their personalities meshed in a sparkly way on and off the screen. There was no question why they were considered the darlings of local television.

Lexi reminded him of a butterfly, stretching her wings, moving in a new world and liking it. She wore the status of heroine as if it was made for her. Magazine articles about her revealed that his shy, skinny daughter had grown up. The whole family anticipated the arrival later that evening of her first-ever boyfriend, Zak the fireman.

Danny's change was subtler. While he joked as raucously as the others, a new reserve had taken hold of him. Claire said it was because his black-and-white world had been threatened. If his parents could go off the deep end, nobody was safe. Better he learn it from them than an enemy.

Max looked at his parents and felt a rush of gratitude. They were obviously older than they'd been before the fire, and not just by ten weeks. The experience had sapped their strength. But at least they recognized it. Their new willingness to receive help somehow made it easier for him to love them.

Which was one reason he and Claire could do what they wanted to do.

Max pushed back his chair, tapped his water goblet with a spoon, and stood.

Claire caught his eye and smiled. Eventually conversations stopped, and everyone turned toward him.

"My sweetheart and I have some news."

"Yow!" Erik shouted, cupping his hands over Felicia's ears. "Sorry. They're getting so embarrassingly sappy."

Lexi groaned. "Dad, please don't talk like that when Zak gets here."

Claire laughed.

"Moving right along." Max settled his expression into one of serious business. "I have an emergency meeting in Fresno tomorrow, and I hate that I have to leave tonight, but these things can't always be helped." Fierce glares bombarded him. "What? Did somebody just die?"

"Max." The sight of Claire's ashen face promptly ended his joke.

"Sorry, guys," he said. "Just kidding."

"Not funny, Dad." Erik frowned.

"Right. Got it." He gazed at his eldest, overwhelmed with a deep desire to make it all up to the little boy who must have felt abandoned by his dad. When had he nicknamed Max "The Putz"? Ages ago, and deservedly so. "Actually, Erik, somebody did die. The Putz died. At least I hope he did, anyway."

Erik glanced away.

"Okay, moving right along again." He turned to his parents. "Mom and Dad, Claire and I have something to propose. What do you think about us working with you and reopening the Hacienda Hideaway? We'd like to run it."

For a moment no one reacted.

Then his mother grinned. His dad coughed. The kids burst out with a dozen questions.

Max held up a hand. "We want this to be our full-time job. From remodeling to advertising it as a safe harbor to taking care of the guests. We want to sell this house and move into the hacienda."

His dad coughed again, harder. It sounded like a choke.

"Dad, you all right?"

Ben waved his hand, and Indio chuckled. "What a wonderful solution! That Realtor woman is coming over tomorrow. Was. Ben, we have to tell her not to bother. We have other plans."

Ben cleared his throat. "But, Max, you've never been the least bit interested in the place. You think you want to take care of guests instead of clients? These people can be downright weird. And, Claire, you'd wear yourself out driving into the city for all your activities."

Max felt an old familiar twist in his gut.

Claire, however, beamed. "The thing is, we want a brand-new start. We don't just want a project to do together. We want a life to live together, a life in service to other people. First of all to you, Ben and Indio, and then to as many weird guests that God sees fit to bring into our safe harbor. Will you help us do that? Will you teach us how to do that?"

Indio said, "Hallelujah."

Ben harrumphed. "Not to hurt anybody's feelings, but if I wanted to live in a nursing home, I'd check myself in. I'm old, and I like my quiet and my open space. I don't want to mess with a retreat center and grumpy guests anymore."

Suddenly Max intuited what his father was saying. "Okay, Dad. How about Claire and I mess with it? You answer our questions, give us advice. Now and then. We live in the hacienda; you and Mom live somewhere else if you like. I'll build you a bungalow way down the lane or out behind a new barn."

Ben squinted at him.

Time felt suspended. Max held his breath.

At last Ben spoke. "I'm not taking any greenhorns out horseback riding."

"Nope."

He gave a quick nod. "Deal."

"Okay, deal. How about the rest of you?"

"Wait!" his mother said. "I'd like a turn."

"Sorry, Mom."

"Ben," Indio said, "just because you're antisocial doesn't mean I am. Claire, can I help more than just now and then?"

She smiled. "Of course. You and Paquita can still have full rein in the kitchen if you want. You can definitely be in on everything. I will be a total fish out of water in this endeavor."

"All right." Indio grinned like a little girl. "The place really was getting to be a bit too much for us."

Max returned her wink. "Now how about you all? Erik, Lexi, Danny, Jenna, Kevin. Felicia, feel free to jump in too." He looked around the room, into their eyes one at a time. "Will you give us your support? Will you allow your mother and me to start over?"

They exchanged glances with each other.

Jenna said, "You mean we have to drive an extra thirty minutes if we want to see you?"

Danny added, "And call you on a land line? Man, oh man. That's asking a lot."

Jenna smiled.

Kevin gave a thumbs-up.

Even Felicia nodded.

Erik's expression remained frozen in neutral.

The kid was a hard nut to crack. Best to give him some time and just go with majority rule for now. Where was Lexi's vote?

Her mouth twisted.

Claire interpreted it faster than he could. "Hon," she said, "we need you to do the landscaping."

"You'd want to hire a firm. You need more than me and José and a few gardeners."

Max said, "No. We want you and whoever you want to hire."

"Really?"

"Really."

"Well. Um, I'm like Papa. I love my space. Sometimes I don't even care to talk while I work."

"Not a problem."

Lexi smiled.

Max returned the smile.

Claire sighed. "Thank you. Thank you all. We love you. Okay, who's ready for pie?"

"Sweetheart."

All four of his children groaned in unison.

"Deal with it," he said. "Sweetheart, dearest Claire, I'm not quite finished."

Max walked around the table to her, pulled a jeweler's ring box from his pocket, and knelt on one knee in front of her. His heart ka-booming like a huge kettledrum in his chest, he laid the black velvet box in her palm.

Ninety-five

As Max set the ring box in her hand, Claire fought back a nauseating wave of defeat. It pounded in her head, thundered down into her chest, and rumbled in her stomach.

Since their reconciliation had first begun on that rocky overlook at the ocean six weeks ago, Claire had felt similar reactions. Besides frustration, she battled fears, anger, distrust, and outright panic. At least twice she seriously considered throwing in the towel. Things were not going to work between them.

The assaults came in response to things he said, did, or didn't do. Sometimes she told him about her reactions, and together they pressed on, working out who or what was at fault, figuring out whether those reactions were groundless or not. Some things, she understood, would simply have to be accepted. Some things were based on old thought patterns that she should put to death.

They had discussed the expensive gift thing. He disagreed with her aversion to them. He said they were expressions of love; she said they were guilt offerings and brought to mind all those times he had hurt her and then given her a gift, as if that would erase the pain. He hadn't presented her with one again . . . until now. Why now? It had been a perfect Thanksgiving Day in every way.

They'd just announced they were starting over. She and Max had spent weeks analyzing what it meant. It meant selling their home. It meant living off of the proceeds. It meant sinking the money made from the sale of Beaumont Staffing into the Hacienda Hideaway, a break-even venture in a good month. And there wouldn't even be a chance at a good month until they opened for business, which at best might happen a year from now. It meant seeing each other every day. It meant a whole bunch of unknown. It meant—

"Claire." Max angled his head almost onto her lap to make eye contact. "Open it. You'll be surprised, I promise."

The soft expression in those brown-black eyes did a number on her. Her heart physically ached. Tandy said it was that part she'd closed off from Max years ago. She said it would hurt for a while whenever he got close enough to touch it.

"Trust me," he whispered.

That was her problem, of course. She didn't.

But she so wanted to.

She tilted back the lid.

Nothing sparkled up at her. "Hmm."

Stuck in the slot where a ring should have been was a tiny, folded piece of yellow paper. She pulled it out and carefully opened it.

Sweetheart . . . The slanted block print was Max's. *Will you marry me again?*

"Oh," she breathed.

He grinned at her. "Is that a yes or a no?"

"It's a definite . . . maybe."

"Huh?" The grin vanished.

"Well-l-l . . ." She rolled her eyes, true Jenna style.

"Mom," Erik said, "collective bated breath here."

Max whipped around, his eyes mere slits.

"The thing is . . ." she said.

He looked back at her.

She smoothed away the wrinkles on his forehead. "The thing is . . . the last time we did this, we went to Las Vegas. Our friends weren't there. Your parents weren't there. I wore blue jeans. Elvis stayed in the motel room next to ours. Two days later, we opened the office."

"You're right. Well, we can try, sweetheart, but I don't know if we'll be able to duplicate all of that."

Claire's giggle started somewhere deep inside. It tickled her from toes to head and burst out in an uncontrollable belly laugh. Her husband understood her. He loved her. He really and truly loved her!

Max kissed her hand. "Is that a yes?"

She wiped tears of joy from her eyes. "Yes, that is a yes. I will marry you again."

A cheer went up around the table. Then someone mentioned pie. Chairs scraped and dishes clattered and conversations ensued.

Amid the hubbub, Max and Claire didn't move.

"Do you want a church?" he asked.

"Mm-hmm. And Jenna and Lexi as bridesmaids. Your mom and dad to give me away. The boys to stand up with you. A big party afterward."

"It's all yours."

She smiled. "Let's invite that social columnist from the newspaper. It'll be our grand farewell. 'Old, Already-Married Beaumonts Host Their Own Do-over Wedding.'"

He chuckled. "What would Emily Post say?"

"I don't know. I don't care. But think of the free advertising for the Hideaway."

"Are you turning businesswoman on me?"

"Maybe." She paused. "Max, I want to be the perfect partner for you this time."

"All I want you to be is first fiddle in my heart and in real life."

"I think you just put me there."

"You always should have been there." He stroked her cheek. "I promise, from now on, you always will be."

She leaned over and kissed him. "Then I'll always be at home, safe and sound."

Acknowledgments

The real writing always happens behind the scenes. Without the help of family, friends, and business associates, my stories wouldn't even begin to happen. It is a privilege to give thanks to:

Gary Smalley, my wise and gracious coauthor. Long before I had words to portray a picture of emotional safety in marriage, he was teaching the concept in practical terms. His insight into relationships added a rich depth to these characters and continues to make an impact on my life.

Lee Hough, my agent who doesn't quit and doesn't let me quit. He coaches me far beyond my writing comfort zone.

Elizabeth John, my right-hand woman in this project—researcher, editor, proofreader, idea-bouncer, daughter, and friend.

Joey Paul, Ami McConnell, Natalie Hanemann, and Leslie Peterson, the professionals who made it all come together.

Tracy John, my reader of early drafts and advisor—quite a gift of a daughter-in-law.

Dave and Amy Wilhite, Peggy Hadacek, and Karlie Garcia, my technical consultants who were there at the drop of an e-mail.

Carrie Younce, my writer friend who knows how to read fiction, drink coffee, listen, and encourage beyond measure.

Tim, my husband, who faithfully sailed beside me into our safe harbor.

Reading Group Guide

1. The series title—Safe Harbors—refers to the overall series theme: people need relationships in which they feel completely safe, emotionally as well as physically. What do you think a safe harbor looks like? What doesn't one look like? Do you have one?

2. Why does Claire leave Max? Why now and not sooner? Is it a conscious decision? What's not right between them?

3. Discuss the consequences of her actions on herself and on others (Max, their children, his parents).

4. Claire has stepped into a season of "tearing." It precedes one of "mending" (Ecclesiastes 3:7). As her life falls apart, deep needs and deep wounds are revealed. She must address these issues before she can move forward in her relationship with Max. What are those needs and hurts? How are those needs filled and wounds healed?

5. Have you experienced seasons of "tearing" and "mending"?

6. How do you relate emotionally to the women? Claire, her marriage, her loss of self? Indio and her regrets as a mother? Jenna trying to define her role as wife? Mother, daughter, and in-law relationships?

7. Eventually Max's wounds are also revealed. Discuss the hurts that stem from situations with his parents and his brother. How has he coped with them in the past? Why is he able to "go there" at this point in his life?

8. In what ways have Max and Claire built walls between each other? How have these prevented them from creating emotional safety within their marriage?

9. Claire wants to be first in Max's life. When he finally "gets it" and sells the business, why can't she receive this, his supreme act of love? What happens that allows her to receive it?

10. In what ways have you been unable to receive love or forgiveness?

11. What role does faith play in the lives of Claire and Max? It is mentioned that they turned to God early in their marriage. Why did they? What do you imagine happened between then and the time the story opens? How does their faith take on new dimensions by the end of the story?

12. What signs do you see in Erik, Jenna, Danny, and Lexi that they have been impacted negatively by their parents?